some people's children

BRIDGET CANNING

All of the characters and events portrayed in this book are fictitious. Any resemblance to actual persons, living or deceased, is purely coincidental.

Breakwater Books
P.O. Box 2188, St. John's, NL, Canada, A1C 6E6
www.breakwaterbooks.com

Cover image: Mike Gough, *We Left at Night* (acrylic, acrylic transfer, pastel, and graphite on panel, 48" x 36"), 2012, © Mike Gough.

A CIP catalogue record for this book is available from Library and Archives Canada.

We acknowledge the support of the Canada Council for the Arts, which last year invested $153 million to bring the arts to Canadians throughout the country. We acknowledge the financial support of the Government of Canada and the Government of Newfoundland and Labrador through the Department of Tourism, Culture, Industry and Innovation for our publishing activities.

Printed and bound in Canada.

Breakwater Books is committed to choosing papers and materials for our books that help to protect our environment. To this end, this book is printed on a recycled paper that is certified by the Forest Stewardship Council®.

Canada Council   Conseil des Arts
for the Arts   du Canada

Canada

Newfoundland
Labrador

FSC
www.fsc.org   MIX
Paper from
responsible sources
FSC® C016245

For Mark

prologue
August, 1974

Maggie wakes on the bed. The bedspread is itchy on her bare skin. Smells like cigarettes. She is alone. It is not her bed.

She remembers standing outside the bathroom. Tony's voice was a hiss: "I thought you said you were seventeen." She tried to speak around the lump in her throat: "Please."

Someone walked by and laughed, sharp and small like a bee sting. Tony pulled her into the bedroom.

"But we care about each other." She kissed his neck. That's one of the things he likes. He shook her off. He slammed the bedroom door as he left.

She was crying on the bed when the voices started. The party banged on around the edges of the door, but these were new sounds. Mostly barked commands:

Get back in there, my son.

If you don't, I will.

Get it get it get it.

And then Tony was back. He shut the bedroom door to a rising cheer. She remembers reaching for him. They'd never been inside before—twice in the woods on a blanket, twice in the backseat. She remembers wishing hard for no one to come in. Please let the door be locked.

And now he's gone. She has to go home. She sits up.

Cecil Jesso stands by the bed. Her jeans and pullover are bunched in his hands. His pale eyes are bulging like marshmallows. His pants are undone to reveal a triangle of white cotton. Matted hair. She buckles into a ball.

"Cec! Get out of here!"

"This is my room." He points at her. "You're on my bed."

She pulls the bedspread up from under her, to cover herself. Cecil clutches her things to his chest with one hand. He reaches out with the other and grabs the bedspread from her hand. "Lemme see," he whispers. His bottom lip trembles.

"No!" Maggie swipes at his hand. Her naked breast brushes his forearm. She scrambles to the foot of the bed. It is hard to move away and keep herself covered. She hears Cec's breath suck in, wet and beastly. He moves closer. No no no no. Everything is no. Everything is help. Her guts fold in on themselves. They remember something sweet and sickly from earlier and don't want it anymore.

Now Cec is gasping mouthfuls of garbled fury. He drops her clothes and puts his hands to his wet face. Maggie wipes her mouth, panting. The smell of her own bile hits her and she's sick again, this time off the side of the bed. Cec backs out of the room. "Jesus fucking Christ."

Her hands move without thought, top on, legs in jeans, underwear and bra shoved in pockets. She stands. Her body sways. Get out, get out. The hallway outside the room reeks of cigarettes and rum. Everyone is gone. She half skates down the hallway, through the kitchen. She snatches her shoes from the porch. Cecil stands in the doorway to the living room, rubbing his face with a towel. "You're a little savage," he says.

"You're a piece of shit. You ever touch me again, you're dead."

"I never touched you, Maggie Tubbs," he says. His voice is sooky and slurry.

A half-empty Labatt 50 bottle sits in the porch, like someone left it when they were tying their shoes. Maggie grabs it around its stubby neck and flings it at him. He steps back, missing the splash of beer. It hits the floor and rolls away.

"When Tony finds out, he's gonna kill you," she says. "You're fucking dead, Cecil Jesso."

part one

one

Imogene wants out of this house before the store closes. She has enough change for a Charleston Chew bar and about five Dubble Bubble. The coins are lined up in the side pockets of the Kangaroo sneakers Maggie gave her. She was the first kid at school with zipper-pocket shoes, but now the fabric over her big toe is near transparent.

Nan and Great Aunt Bride are at the kitchen table for one of their big yak attacks. Their fingertips are ashy with tea-bun flour. When they laugh, it sounds like two crows trapped in a wooden box.

"Look, Bride," Nan says. "She got those shoes this spring and they're already wore through."

"Yer gettin' some big."

"Maggie was the same, grew up all of a sudden."

"She was an early bloomer. You'll be one too."

Imogene does not want to talk about blooming. Bad enough they have to notice how big her feet are. Cousin Rita likes to say Imogene's shoes are like pontoons.

"Nutrition is almost too good today," Great Aunt Bride says. "Everyone's taller and girls start developing younger all the time. Sure, Dina's daughter already wears a bra and she's only ten." Great Aunt Bride jiggles her head at the thought. She has puffy white curls and the tips are tinged with the last stains of blond. From a distance, her head is a fresh popcorn kernel.

"It's true," Nan says. "Even the Chinese that comes over and eats like us grow tall."

"And the early puberty. I didn't start *my* monthlies until I was sixteen."

Imogene is gone at that, doors banging. But it's colder than she thought. She needs her mitts. The door leading from the porch into the kitchen is open a crack. Nan and Great Aunt Bride now speak in regular, honest tones.

"She's sensible," Great Aunt Bride says. "You don't have to worry about her."

"I know. But it started so young with Maggie. Would have been different if Gus hadn't passed. Or if her brothers were home. That bastard would have been too scared to touch her."

"Gus was intimidating."

"Maggie minded her father. But I never knew what to do with her. As soon as she developed, it was men sizing her up. And she knew it too, the way she'd walk, her chest stuck out. Deep down, I knew she'd end up with a baby."

Imogene slips back outside. Her stomach shifts in confusion. She stuffs her bare hands in her pockets and makes her way up the path. The tops of the mud puddles are frozen, but hollow inside, and the ice shatters like glass when she steps on them. She does it to each one in her way. The tang in Nan's voice was the same sound she makes when she talks about the price of getting the transmission fixed on the car. Everything is urgency and high cost.

Last week on the ride to school, her cousin Rita used a saying Imogene hadn't heard before. "Anyone can get their skin off her," Rita whispered as Rosarie Coish climbed on the bus. Mrs. Coish brought back a crimping iron when she was last in Corner Brook. Rosarie's blond hair hung down her back in perfect crinkled strips, like fried bacon, her hips swaying in tight faded denim. Imogene thought Rosarie looked beautiful.

"She'll be gettin' her skin tonight," Rita said, corkscrewing her elbow into Imogene's side. Imogene nodded. She thought of Rosarie Coish with arms outstretched, receiving a neatly folded blanket made of some kind of skin, like cured leather. Rosarie passing on the skin to someone else. This can't be what it means.

Imogene starts down the road to the Kwik Stop. Maybe someone will offer her a ride. Although, really, she doesn't want to talk to anyone. Imogene would like to avoid the road altogether and walk along the beach all the way to the store, but there aren't many places to climb up the banks. They would be solid now, but they soften in the spring and you can sink into the mud. Aubrey Murphy has lost a sheep or two like that.

She feels the wind lift her hair and shake it, as if to see if it will come loose. One time, her hair was blowing all over the place and Rita said it looked like her head was on fire. When Rita makes comments like this about Imogene's red hair, it's never clear if she's joking. Imogene pulls up her hood. There's always some kind of wind in St. Felix's. Sometimes a cold wind off the water to spoil a warm summer day. Or a Wreckhouse blast that gouges the breath from your mouth and tries to suffocate you right out in the open.

A pickup truck passes. Rosarie Coish and her dad. His fingers rise briefly off the steering wheel. Imogene waves back. Rosarie is sixteen. A year older than Maggie when she had Imogene. Must have been A Scandal. Last year, everyone talked about that girl in grade twelve who had a baby—Susan Benoit—but everyone knew Dan Snow was the father. No one knew who Imogene's father was, so it must have been Big News.

Maggie will likely call tonight. She calls every week from Markham where she lives with a man named Robert Cronin. Robert Cronin is a real-estate agent, a nice man with thick ashy hair and crinkly eyes. Good for Maggie, Nan likes to say, just what she needs. Both Nan and Maggie agree on that; a good man is good for Maggie.

When Maggie and Imogene speak on the phone, Maggie talks about the real-estate projects she and Robert Cronin work on. Their focus is primarily in the GTA, but Maggie says they plan on buying at least one property in St. John's. "If you decide to go there for university," Maggie says, "you'll have a place to live." And later she'll say, "Robert says hello," and Imogene will hear him sing "Hello!" from some nearby room or the opposite side of the table. Then Imogene will hand the phone to Nan, who listens and sighs and clucks her tongue.

Imogene starts down the hill towards the Kwik Stop. The Sampson's van is parked in front. Good, they're home. Even though the Kwik Stop is supposed to be open until five, sometimes they close up early and you're shit out of luck, as Doug Sampson says. It's getting close to four thirty, which means Loretta Sampson leaves the door leading from the store to their house open so you can see they're getting ready for supper and won't waste time shopping.

Three figures bounce out of the store and yank bikes off the ground. Maybe it's Quincy and his cousins or Nick Cleary. No, by the way they move, it's definitely Liam and Randy Lundrigan and Donny Martin. Frig. She sweeps her hair back and composes her face: eyes cool, chin out.

The wind comes up from the bottom of the hill and makes water in her eyes. It gives the boys an extra push and they bounce towards her, jogging the pedals of their bikes. They pant and grin. Liam Lundrigan aims the front wheel of his bike at her and hunches forward, eyes slurred. She forces her legs to keep moving. Liam's pale hair blows forward around his face, like a bud of dandelion silk. He waits until he is about two feet away to squeeze the handbrakes. Randy and Donny squeak to a stop behind him. Donny plants both legs on the ground and plucks his jeans off his arse. Randy snorts and rumbles snot in his throat as if to hawk it, but doesn't. Too windy for that.

"Not chicken much," Liam says.

"Don't need to be."

"Where you going?"

"Store."

"Gettin' smokes for your nan."

"My nan don't smoke."

She tries to step around the front wheel of Liam's bike, but he pushes it forward. There is a crust of something reddish-brown near the edge of his mouth and he has dried sleep in the corners of his eyes. He wipes his hand on his shirt: red and black checkered flannel covered with about ten million flecks of lint and mystery stuff. He reaches out and runs a finger along her sleeve.

"Nice coat. Where you get it?"

It is a nice coat. Maggie sent it last Christmas from Toronto. It hangs past her hips, corduroy in a kind of deep fuchsia. No one else in St. Felix's has a coat like it.

"My mother got it for me."

"Your mom's good at getting all kinds of things, isn't she?"

"Frig off."

"She is good at getting things. She got you, didn't she?"

He grins at her. Tiny crack lines appear in the crust on his mouth. Imogene steps over the wheel of his bike and keeps on. The wind blows their laughter out of her ears. When she gets close to the bottom of the hill, she looks back. They are gone, pedaling fast with the wind's support.

two

In class, Sister Patricia gives an assignment which everyone fails. It is a list of directions:

1. Read all the instructions before doing anything.
2. Get out of your desk and stand on one foot.
3. Hop up and down on one foot.
4. Stop hopping and fold your arms.
5. Nod three times.
6. Spin around.
7. Whistle.
8. Clap your hands.
9. Sit down.
10. Wait for the teacher to say go before doing directions 2 to 9.

And so on. Everyone hops and bops and laughs. Afterwards, Sister Patricia announces they have all failed because they didn't read and pay attention to the first and last directions. She hopes this will teach everyone to pay closer attention. "You people would have learned what the activity was all about if you'd just paid attention," she says.

Imogene didn't read the list well. But in general, she has been paying more attention to everything since overhearing Nan and Great Aunt Bride. Like last week when she was with Nan in the post office. Marie Whalen looked her up and down.

"Which one are you?" she said. "Eli's girl?"

"This is Imogene," Nan said.

Marie's eyes met hers and there was a click of recognition. "Oh yes. Young Maggie's child." Nan's mouth made a sharp line. She nodded to Marie and collected the flyers in silence.

Imogene will have to listen hard because she only knows four things about her father and no one talks about him. Last Christmas, when Maggie was home, Imogene asked her about him and received another version of the four things. And then Maggie cried and said she was sorry.

These are the four things Imogene knows:

1. Her father's name is Anthony Green. His name is on her birth certificate.
2. He was a young fisherman who worked on the crab boats for a season. He and Maggie started going out. She told him she was older than what she was. When he found out she was underage, he disappeared.
3. Nan sent letters to his old employer looking for him. There was no response. The letters were sent to Marystown, where he moved after St. Felix's. The last letter was returned from the employer stating Anthony moved away. No forwarding address.
4. Anthony told Maggie he was from Port aux Basques, but according to Nan, no one there named Green knows anything about him.

Anthony Green is spoken of in blasphemous tones; he is Unmentionable like dirty underwear and the secret name of God. And Maggie went to work in St. John's when Imogene was about four, and then Ontario, and now she can only come down once or twice a year. When she's home, every day is an event and it never seems to be a good time to request more information.

Imogene's memories of Maggie are like a vine which grew straight at first and then sprouted branches, spreading in all directions. Her earliest recollections are lying next to Maggie, waking to the shape of her back and cloak of dark hair. Maggie's arms swinging hers as they danced on the carpet to ABBA songs.

And then came the calm explanations. "Mommy will only be gone a little while. See this square on the calendar? This is when Mommy comes home. She'll call all the time on the phone and tell you stories. She'll have presents for you."

Then Maggie's pink, streaming face. Maggie lifting her suitcase. Nan prying the damp hem of Maggie's red sweater out of Imogene's fists. Maggie's brown hair whipping straight up in the wind as she walks to Uncle Eli's truck. Her shoulders quaking.

And then, everything was busy. Legos with Rita on Aunt Trudy and Uncle Eli's rug, being pushed on the swing in their backyard, whispering with Rita over their sleeping dolls. Being scolded as a pair: Good girls share. Good girls don't fight. Nan lying on the couch with a damp facecloth on her eyes: "Imogene, go over to Eli's for a bit. It's their turn."

Uncle Kenneth got Maggie a job in St. John's. She stayed with him to save money, working at the Purity Factory all day and finishing her GED at night. Then it was secretarial courses and a new plan. When there was enough money, Imogene would join her.

Imogene recalls the house changing whenever Maggie was home, the way it smelled like Love's Baby Soft and watermelon-scented hair spray. Eli's truck rumbling down the driveway and Maggie bursting in to sweep her up, her long dark hair over her shoulders, her brightly coloured clothes. Maggie pulling gifts from bags, chocolates, new shoes, a copy of *The Velveteen Rabbit* with a brown toy bunny which Imogene named Teeny.

And then school and firmer, more concrete events. Maggie home for Christmas. Imogene had asked Santa for a puppy, a golden retriever, like the one on the long-distance telephone commercial: two blond children open a big box and the puppy bounds out. She remembers Maggie handing her a box. Inside, a stuffed toy dog. "Oh," Imogene said. "That's not the kind of puppy I wanted." Maggie shrugging. "Your letter to Santa said puppy. It didn't say what kind."

A summer visit, Maggie's legs long in jeans with patches and zippers, her hair down to her elbows. Giving Imogene a piggy-back ride down to French Brook. Pretending to throw Imogene into the water. "Mommy! No!" Imogene screeched. And Maggie's fingers stiff in her armpits as she was deposited on the grass. "I was only playing, Imogene."

And the boyfriend she brought home when Imogene was seven. Shane Hearn. He had eyebrows like caterpillars and black, curly hair that was long in the back. He wouldn't stop tickling Imogene's feet. He'd sweep her up on his lap as she walked past, then pin her arms to her sides with one arm and tickle her feet. Every time she squealed and kicked and said no and he said things like, "You like it, you're laughing." And twice he did it at night, when she was going to pee, ready for bedtime in her nightie. She wanted to kick out at him, but was too scared he would see she didn't wear underwear to bed.

He stopped the evening Imogene wouldn't kiss him good night. That was the routine; she'd kiss Nan good night and any other relatives in the house when she was going to bed. Nan, Maggie, and Shane sat in the living room. She kissed Nan and Maggie, then froze in front of Shane. He held open his arms to her. "Where's my good-night kiss?" And her legs wouldn't move. "Imogene," Maggie said, "don't be rude." But Nan spoke with a hollow darkness. "That's okay, Imogene my love. You go on to bed."

After Shane Hearn, there was Robert Cronin. She remembers a visit to St. John's, her and Nan on the bus. Robert taking them all to Ponderosa. The back of his giant head in front of her on the Trinity Train Loop. And afterwards, the change in plan: Robert would return to Ontario to start his own real-estate company. Maggie would help him organize it. Imogene would join them when they were set up.

That summer was a long visit with both Maggie and Robert. Imogene was going into grade four and it was the first time she heard the word *quaint*. The word Robert used to talk about everything in St. Felix's. The houses were quaint, the church was quaint, the school was quaint. But when Rita, Wish Benoit, and Natalie Sampson came over to play, they weren't quaint. "Don't go jumping on the furniture," he said. And this was a strange thing to say because it hadn't crossed their minds at all. Wish laughed. "We aren't monkeys," he said. Robert said it wasn't funny.

He talked about Ontario all the time, the way the houses are made of brick there and it's so strange there wouldn't be brick houses in a place called *the Rock*. He said things like, "Why don't people use garbage cans instead of wooden boxes? It's like everyone has a bread box for their trash." And, "It's too bad you can't sell beauty. It's the only way this place wouldn't be poor." When Robert talked, Maggie laughed a lot and Nan squeezed and released her fingers, over and over.

In the fall, Imogene's Ontario move kept changing time frames. It would happen once the house is sorted out. Once the office is organized. Once their client base is established. Finally, Nan said no. "It's too much to yank her out of school," she said. "She's got roots here. Sheldon Cleary says they hold youngsters from Newfoundland back a grade when you move up. It's not fair." And all talk of it ended. Now it's phone calls and maybe two visits a year. Now it's the name "Maggie" spoken more often than "your mother."

Imogene decides if she's to learn more about Anthony Green, it's a good idea to listen closely to Nan's conversations. This is easy, since Agnes Tubbs likes to know what's going on and St. Felix's one main road functions as a conveyor belt of information.

St. Felix's itself stretches down the coast with fields cut off into steep banks and rocky beaches. The main road exits the highway past the occasional house or cluster of homes, the school, the church, the post office, the Youth Centre, the Kwik Stop, trees, field, trees, field, until the pavement ends right after Joyce MacIssac's house. Then it becomes a dirt road leading Up Back, where people cut wood for Abitibi-Price and teenagers go parking.

If a police car or an ambulance passes Agnes Tubb's house, Joyce MacIssac is the strategic destination for the first phone call. If the cops or ambulance pass Joyce's, it means there might have been an accident or something happening Up Back. Nan frets over this—after all, that's how Pop died. "If a man like Gus cutting wood all of his life can get caught under a falling tree, it can happen to anyone," she says into the phone. Then sighs of agreement. Yes, girl, safety first.

If the cops or paramedics haven't gone Up Back, this means the commotion involves someone in one of the ten houses between here and there. The next house up is Bryce and Arlene Benoit. No news? A couple more phone calls narrows it down; if they passed Sheldon Cleary's place, but not Charlotte Whalen's, it's down to four households. If it's an ambulance, it might be poor Mrs. Collier, finally going, God bless her. If the cops, it's most likely the Lundrigans, with their "issues," or that Cecil Jesso. Nan's detective work is a thorough process of elimination.

On a Thursday, Imogene arrives home from school to find the phone cord stretched across the kitchen. Nan has the earpiece wedged between her cheek and shoulder as she stirs chicken stew. Her voice is crisp and peppery. "How long have they been there? Are they searching his place?" When she hangs up, she immediately dials someone else. "Can you see the cops from your house? I bet they could get him on all kinds of garbage." She eyes Imogene, standing in the doorway holding her bookbag. "Go bring in some wood," she says.

That night, Imogene goes to bed early so she can read *Harriet the Spy*. She likes how Ole Golly takes Harriet for egg creams. She doesn't know what egg creams are, but imagines it's what people in New York eat all the time, like vanilla cake batter you can drink.

Now Harriet's friends have read her notebook and no one likes her anymore. They do horrible things out of revenge. Imogene turns the page and hears Nan's voice in the kitchen. She's on the phone with Great Aunt Madonna in Moncton. Her voice is barely audible through the wall, but there's that fry, the sound she gets when she's feeling confessional.

Imogene creeps to her bedroom door. Through the dim light of the living room, she can see Nan's shadow in the kitchen. She sits at the table, holding a glass of something.

"The cops were at his place today. Oh yes, he's still at that. If it's three a.m. and you want liquor or drugs or smokes, go knock on his door. I wish the cops would throw him in jail. Maybe someone in prison can take care of that fucker."

Nan's swear makes Imogene curl her toes into the fibres of the carpet. She hears her take a long sip.

"Honestly, Madonna, I try my best not to think of it. But there's the hair and the height. And Maggie's state that night. All she could say when I asked where she got the alcohol was 'Cecil Jesso.' I remember thinking, Oh Christ, and I helped her to bed and goddamn if her sweater wasn't on inside out. And two months later, she's pregnant. And suddenly, there's this Tony Green. Tony Green's the father, she says. Who's that, I said. I never once laid eyes on any Tony Green."

Nan pauses and drinks again. The shadow of her hand runs through the shadow of her short hair. "No, she definitely wouldn't be buying booze. I would have noticed if she'd taken money and we never gave her any allowance. Because she never did any friggin' chores, Madonna! So you can't blame me for thinking what I'm thinking, can you? Anyway, the thought of it upsets me. When are *you* coming home?"

Imogene creeps back into bed. She hikes the bedspread over her ears. Nan's voice becomes a dim trill in the background. She closes her eyes and pictures Cecil Jesso's house. It's down the road, a one-storey bungalow with faded yellow siding, sitting in a graveyard of dead cars and trucks. She passes it twice a day on the route to school and back. Rita and some older kids on the bus say he's a bootlegger, good for a bit of hash or maybe something stronger. Always loaded. A wall of a man with a halo of frizzy red hair. Face like a boiled dinner with permanently sunburned skin,

SOME PEOPLE'S CHILDREN • 11

crimson and chapped from working outside. Sometimes he wears a ball cap with a Labatt logo, the blue mesh backing adjusted so it perches on the top of his head, practically jaunty. He lurches when he walks, like each step is a deliberate process to be planned and executed. He says very little, and when he does, his voice is slurping and muffled, like speaking through a mouthful of wool.

Imogene saw him up close once. She and Nan were in church, kneeling to pray after communion. Imogene peeked behind and there was his face hanging over the back of the pew, cheeks pink and flaky, like canned salmon. His eyes were oysters, their wrinkled lids scaled and grey, blinking slowly over milky masses of pale blue. A chip out of his nose above his left nostril, like he picked a pimple off and it didn't heal. If he noticed her looking, he didn't seem to know her. His lips quivered in what she assumed to be prayer, but forming the same syllable over and over, a goldfish's mantra. One hand gripped the pew with nicotine-yellowed fingers. When she sat back, his head was by her shoulder. She could smell the sweetness of rum and bile on his breath, the funk of his hair.

Kids on the bus make jokes about Cecil. Teenagers snicker about whose car or truck they recognize in front of his house. Children torment each other on the playground: "You smell like Cecil!" There are impersonations, catch phrases: *Washoo ooking ack? Shumbitch.*

The next day, Imogene tells Nan she's sick and stays home from school. She lies on the sofa while Nan watches her stories. She makes lists in her head to soothe herself. Maybe Cecil was different back then. She remembers seeing a picture of Wish Benoit's dad, Bryce, when he was young and she was startled at how handsome he was. And last week, when she read in the *Herald* that Harrison Ford is forty-six years old, the news dashed her Han Solo/Indiana Jones crush. Maggie was fourteen, Cecil was thirty, forty? Maybe Cecil was like that for Maggie.

Or, this could all be a concoction of Nan's mind. Nan also believes bats can lay eggs in your hair. She holds her breath when she passes cemeteries. Who can really believe Agnes Tubbs? A frazzled old lady, her knee-highs bunching around her ankles. Agnes Tubbs, calling up to interrupt your supper every time a ghost car passes the house.

And if it is true, it may only be Maggie and Cecil who know for certain.

three

Fall, 1988

Thanksgiving weekend is long and grey. Rita says she doesn't want to make Halloween costumes this year because she's in grade ten and too old for that stuff. Now she's mad because her brother Steve won't give her and Imogene a ride to the Youth Centre. She tells Imogene to stand guard while she searches for change in Steve's room for a trip to the store. "Cough if you see him coming," she says. She comes out with a handful of quarters and nickels from the jar by his bed. "If we don't get out of here, Mom will make us peel potatoes," she says.

Imogene knows Rita only wants to go to the Youth Centre to see who's there. They walk towards the store and meet Natalie Sampson along the way.

"Store's closed for Thanksgiving," Natalie says. She smells like Bazooka gum. Imogene imagines it's what happens when your folks own a store; you can grab a handful of something on your way out the door. Natalie's cheeks puff out with each chomp. She doesn't offer them any.

"Everyone is going down to play softball," Natalie says.

"Who's going?" Rita says.

"Everybody."

"Who's everybody?"

"Everybody. There's nothing else to do."

"Well, I'm not playing," Rita says. "But we can go watch."

Imogene knows Rita wants to know if Nick Cleary is included in every-body. Nick Cleary has shiny black hair and his bum looks good in a pair of gym pants. His name is often seen written on binders and bathroom walls. A lot of Rita and Imogene's time is spent watching groups of boys that include Nick Cleary play sports. There are other cute boys, like Wish Benoit, who has a sweet smile and built shoulders, but overall, watching the guys gets pretty boring.

And lately, it feels like Rita doesn't have much to discuss with Imogene. There are always many things to *tell* Imogene, but these are told without expectation of a response: "Let's walk past Nick's house. If we see him, we're on our way to the store. Cough if you see him. Don't stare at him, just cough."

Otherwise, they can walk together for an hour and only exchange a few words. They share a seat on the bus, but rarely chat on the journey. Imogene sometimes feels even though they are cousins and have always been friends, for Rita, it is more like a habit. There are things Rita wants to do, but won't do them alone—having Imogene present makes them safe. Also, Rita is in grade ten, a grade ahead of Imogene, and if more of Rita's classmates lived close by, she might prefer different company. Definitely not junior-high company.

But overall, it doesn't really bother Imogene because Rita has baker's chocolate-coloured hair, which flows past her shoulders, and she possesses the right level of funny, saucy, and sweet. Everyone likes her, but they aren't hungrily jealous of her. No one wants to get on Rita's bad side, so there's less chance of getting a hard time.

And hard times get given. Quincy MacIssac is a usual receiver, with his nervous ticks and mouthful of foamy braces, his ironed jeans from Zellers and clean cotton polo shirts. Quincy, who speaks like he's been practising his sentences all day. Quincy, who has trouble keeping eye contact and will focus on a spot just above or beside your head.

On listless days, roving packs of St. Felix's youngsters descend on the MacIssac household to politely knock on the door and ask Joyce MacIssac if Quincy will join them: "Can Quincy come out to play? What's Quincy doing, Mrs. MacIssac, we're all heading to the beach."

Quincy might be safe inside watching *The Edison Twins* or reading a comic book, but he will be bustled out by his mother. "Your friends are here, get outside, it's a beautiful day." And he will want to resist, but his mother is so happy other children want to see him. And he will look out and see their earnest faces and maybe they do want to see him. They are seeking out his company. He will haul on his coat and boots and they will scamper up his driveway and down MacCullen's Hill together, like adventurers, like pioneers. And as soon as they are over the hill and out of sight of the road, it's Free Smacks on Quincy and he will be pinned down on the damp grass while grubby hands smack and twist and pinch and rub glowing welts into his soft white belly. "Wince, Quince, wince! Free winces from Quince!" No one would ever play a trick like that on Rita.

Natalie and Rita walk in front of Imogene on the way to the softball game. Natalie has flaxen blond hair, and with Rita's brown hair and Imogene's red, they remind her of Neapolitan ice cream: three flavours together. She feels like saying this, but doesn't.

Bikes line the fence by Aubrey Murphy's field. A line of kids stand on the grass. Corey Mercer and Wish Benoit are picking teams. Rita leans against the fence. Nick Cleary stands in the line, back on to them; his grey sweatpants flutter against his legs.

"Good, you three are here," Corey says. "We're short."

"Rita's on my team," Wish says.

"We're just watching," Rita says.

"C'mon, Reet."

"I can't play," Natalie says. "I gotta hole in my heart."

"I don't want to play," Imogene says. "I'm not very good."

"It's just a game. Help us out."

"Yeah, no one gives a shit."

Imogene knows this is lies. People always say it's just a game and then they scream when you drop the ball. School claims it's all about teamwork and fun and new skills. But serve the volleyball too low and see how pissed off they get. When Great Aunt Bride goes on about how half the country is fat, Imogene knows it's because sports are such a miserable experience. Who wouldn't want to go home and sit on their hands after being bitched at for eight innings?

There aren't enough gloves to go around so they have to trade between innings. Donny is the only one with a left-handed glove, so Imogene has to use his. It's damp inside and she tries not to think about him wiping his nose. She goes into the outfield when Wish's team is up to bat and hopes no one hits it far. The grass has faded into dead yellow with dried cowpats here and there. No balls come her way until Nick Cleary is up to bat and he hits it right towards her. Everyone screams and she jumps in the air to catch it, but it sails over her, at least three feet above her head. Groans. "Git the ball!" She scrambles after it and throws it as hard as she can towards Randy on first base, but Nick is already on his way to second. The ball lands in a pile of dry cowshit about ten feet from Randy. He yells "Fuck" really loud.

The whole game is like this, like someone has collected all her physical weaknesses and created a performance. "Run faster, Immy! Eye on the ball! Throw it here, harder! Here, b'y, here." After seven innings of displaying her shortcomings, she feels they are the only things known about her.

In the last inning with two out, Imogene is up to bat. Her team grumbles. She picks up the bat as casually as she can, like she doesn't care, like an illiterate ripping pages out of a book. The outfielders move in with wide, resolved steps. What bullshit all this is. She swings and misses. Moans. She swings and misses. Cursing. She swings and misses. Natalie boos from her perch on the fence—the hole in her heart doesn't prevent her from eating Smarties and offering commentary.

Imogene's team yells and swears and the other team razzes them and she would like to go home. Rita is chatting with Nick Cleary. His head is low and leans into her hair. She catches Imogene's eye and gives a quick shake of her head. So, home then. Imogene strolls off, trying to be nonchalant.

She kicks loose gravel off the pavement. Why is softball something she is expected to be good at? Besides a couple of weeks in gym class, she's hardly played it. Who was supposed to play catch with her all these years? Maggie Tubbs? Nan? What an idea, Agnes Tubbs throwing loping underhand pitches in her paisley housedress. When she goes home, she'll go into her room and close the door. She has about thirty pages to go in *Many Waters* and then she will be finished the *Wrinkle in Time* books. She will tell Maggie this the next time they talk and Maggie can think of another series to pick up for her in Toronto.

When she first hears the voices, she thinks they are calling for her to stop.

"Seize."

Liam, Randy, and Donny are a couple of yards back, grinning like jack o' lanterns. They don't say anything when she looks back at them. She keeps walking. *Seize.* Liam's voice and an immediate hiss of laughter from Randy and Donny. Seize what? Her guts sink in bubbling trepidation. Maybe an in-joke she doesn't know. Maybe something stuck on the back of her pants. She concentrates on walking like a cool person.

"Seize, b'y."

She looks back again. Liam's face is a bright lively scowl. Randy and Donny walk crooked lines, doubled over in laughter. Liam makes sure to make eye contact. "Seas. Sheeeees-shoool."

Cecil. Cec and Cecil.

She wants to run, but can't run because if she runs they will *know* and they will *know* that she *knows*. She doesn't run, but succumbs to walking fast in a compulsive, jittery gait.

"Fire up Cec's hole today, b'ys."

Howls from Randy and Donny. The pavement's edge is riddled with cracks; the ditches choked with dark alder bushes. There is nowhere to go. She wishes she could step off the road and be gone, like Meg in the tesseract.

Eventually, they give it up—Cecil Jesso's house is on the way to hers and they're not that brazen. As soon as they turn back and are out of sight, Imogene runs. She runs to her driveway and through the door and into her room and lies in a ball on her bed. The light of the overcast sky glows around the curtains, clarifying their edges and imperfections. She tugs the covers up and lies there until supper. She shakes like a minnow out of the water, translucent and weakening.

four

Monday is the Thanksgiving holiday. One Tuesday, Imogene is re-baptized at Immaculate Mary Academy. It starts on the bus in whispers and cackles and stays all day. Cecil. Baby Cec. Cecil Jr. In first period, she raises her hand to answer a question and it hisses behind her: *Cec.* Teddy Campbell says "Cecil" in a sneeze while she is working out a problem on the board and Sister Patricia says, "Bless you," and the class collapses in giggles. After lunch, Sister Bernadette catches her with gum in her mouth and tells her to spit it out. A voice from the back of the room: "Yes, cease chewing gum." Raging titters of laughter.

Older girls in the washroom glare at her. When she stares back, they ask her what her problem is. Guys in the hallway lunge, then laugh when she jumps. When she passes the desks of certain pristine girls, like Crystal Seymour, noses are wrinkled, eyes are rolled, and gum is chomped in warning. If she passes a boy's desk it is "Fuck off" or something gets flicked, a piece of a pencil eraser, a spitball. "Washoo ooking ack?"

At first, Imogene feigns confusion. Then she thinks she should object; she should tell them they're wrong. But what evidence does she have to the contrary? Anthony Green's name on her birth certificate. Who's that then? A mystery man from Port aux Basques? She might as well say her dad is Joey Smallwood or Don Johnson. Instead, she stays mute and feels her face heat up, like she is transforming into Cec himself, red-faced and stunned, the Incredible Hulk of Cecil.

"Just ignore them," Rita tells Imogene in the girls' washroom. "They only do it to get a rise out of you. If you act like you don't care, they'll stop."

"But I don't say anything," Imogene says.

"Yeah, but it's real obvious it bothers you."

Rita teases her bangs in the mirror and Imogene tries not to glare at the back of her head. Sure, when Rita is around, people like Teddy Campbell and Donny Martin don't make comments. But the girls' volleyball team is doing well, and Rita loves hanging out with her teammates. When they are around, she doesn't mind Imogene's presence, but Shelly MacInnis pretends not to hear Imogene when she speaks. And Cherry MacIssac and Rita now have matching friendship bracelets. Cherry isn't mean, but would rather whisper in Rita's ear than include Imogene in the conversation.

Every day Imogene hopes it will fade. Randy writes *Imogene = Cecil* with his finger in the grimy condensation on the bus window. It stays there for a week until Malcolm Whalen, the bus driver, cleans it off. In math class, Sister Patricia makes her pass out homework sheets and Crystal Seymour accepts hers with the edges of her fingertips, then makes a big deal about shaking off the Cec germs. Imogene is picked last for dodgeball, which isn't a change, but when she throws the ball, everyone screams dramatically and dives out of the way, laughing.

And the worst is Liam Lundrigan. Which is no surprise. Liam has been in her class since he was held back in grade three. He is always in some kind of shit: detention, suspensions, penalty box. In grade four, the class had to bring a living thing into school for science—no pets, it had to be something found in nature. Most of the kids brought in plants or bugs in jars with holes in the lid, but Liam Lundrigan and Donny Martin arrived with a tall salt-beef bucket. Inside were rocks, weeds, bog water, and a large frog. A salt-beef bucket ecosystem. Sister Abigail was very impressed. They both got As.

The next morning, Crystal Seymour went straight to Sister with the information that after Liam and Donny received their As, they didn't return the frog back to its natural habitat. Instead, they tied it to the railroad tracks with bailing twine and waited for the train. Sister Abigail was horrified and from the look on Liam and Donny's faces, she knew it was true—not like Crystal would ever tell a lie, little holier-than-thou cow. Even though the class had never seen anyone get the strap and, apparently, it required parental permission and a witness, the rumour was that Sister Abigail went through the paperwork for Liam and Donny.

In winter, Liam never had mitts or a hat. Half the time, he didn't have a lunch. Kids said he had worms and scabies, don't get Liam Lice. But over the summer of grade five, he had a major growth spurt and perfected the art of Chinese sunburns and several Hulk Hogan wrestling moves. Suddenly, he had lots of friends.

Liam loves calling Imogene "Cec," like it's his first and only hit single. If Imogene has to pass by his desk, there is a slap with a ruler, a foot in the aisle, a jab with a pen, its top chewed into a spear. So Imogene avoids his desk altogether. He lays booby traps for her—Imogene catches the thumbtack taped point-up in the middle of her seat, but not the thick layer of liquid paper painted under the top of her desk. As she walks to the washroom to scrub the stain off her jeans, white where she crosses her legs, he bellows, "What's that white stuff? Too much time on your knees?" Imogene bites her tongue hard, as if to punish it.

She choreographs a series of movements for manoeuvring her way to her desk in the grade nine classroom. At the back of the room is a large open-ended closet for coats and shoes. She cuts through it and walks up behind rows of desks to avoid crossing in front of the class. She learns to do this almost silently. Before sitting, she runs her hand over the seat and under the top of the desk. If she leaves class for any reason, she takes her things, even to the washroom. Otherwise, Liam will dump out her binder on the floor or write *Cecil* on her exercise books.

Days are a routine of staying expressionless and waiting for the moment the bus returns her home after school. At recess and lunch, she retreats to the library where she reads or helps the librarian, Miss Coffey, lay out new magazines and return books. In the library, anyone who enters has to be quiet. On the bus, Imogene slumps against the window while Rita sits by the aisle, leaning out to chat with the grade ten girls and fellow members of the volleyball team. Imogene stares out the window, not turning, not looking, never investigating anyone else on the bus. At her stop, she walks to the front doors through a chorus of snake sounds: "Ceeecc." Rita says something like, "You guys are losers."

The bus door hinges open with a see-saw sigh. Sometimes there is one final blare: "Cecil!" And brays of laughter. Her feet down the steps and firm on the pavement. The door squeals closed and, finally, the wheezing groan of the bus trailing away. And then a silent walk up the overgrown driveway, worn car tracks in embedded gravel, a few patches of grass leading to Agnes Tubbs's clean and simple house with its white clapboard and burgundy trim around the windows and door. The kitchen window faces the road with Nan's outline framed inside, watching for any activity, who's that, what's that one doing now. Imogene's bedroom window beside it, small and curtained.

For the first week or so, coming home from school is a reprieve. But soon Imogene finds herself glaring at the house, the chimney puffing out the exhaust of Nan's day: cooking, baking, knitting, cleaning, talking, puttering. She enters through the dark pantry leading into the kitchen with its faded linoleum and Formica table. She grimaces as she is struck by the wave of warm, trapped air, sickly sweet with the smell of dryer sheets and baked bread.

And Nan's voice, like polished stones, asking questions, gossiping on the phone, talking back to the radio. And her endless stream of soap operas: *All My Children* at 2:30, *Another World* at 3:30, and finishing off with *General Hospital* before supper. Friday night reruns of *Dallas*. *Coronation Street* after Sunday Mass. Endless cheese and scandal with Nan's tongue clucking in fake disgust.

Imogene takes up the outdoor chores. She chops wood, rakes leaves, picks rocks from the vegetable garden. When the snow comes, she shovels the walkway. She stamps paths to the shed and the brook. After supper, she does her homework and reads in her room. On weekends, she sleeps in as long as she can and cleans the house while Nan is out running errands. Sunday dinner rotates between their house, Great Aunt Bride's, and Uncle Eli's. Imogene passes potatoes, peas pudding, cabbage, and turnip. She speaks as little as possible. Nan apologizes for her: *She's some quiet. She's in her moody years. Still waters run deep.* Otherwise, Nan doesn't ask questions. Teachers don't seem to notice anything different. No one seems to know except everyone.

When Maggie calls, Nan gets on the extension and interjects with scraps of information. "Immy got an A in English, but a B in French. I think she can do better. Immy, you tell your mother Charlotte Whalen is having twins? My God, she's some size."

On Maggie's end, Robert's mainland-deep baritone resonates in the background. Maggie says things like, "So, Imogene, how is everything with you?" Imogene answers, "Fine."

In her room, Imogene makes lists in columns, a whole table. What if she tells Maggie about what is going on at school? If she knows it's not true, it can stop. She starts a table in her notebook, but doesn't label it.

True	False
Horrible.	Good.
Means _____	Means it's all just gossip.

She stares at the blank on the True side. The idea that Maggie, at her age, would trade sex for booze or something. Could Imogene be the result of some kind of sex bargain? And people used to get married and have babies young, but there are laws against adults being with teens. That's why Maggie lied to Anthony in the first place. But if she lied to Anthony, would she have also lied to Cecil?

No. Cec is from here. He knew all along how old she was. Would they have had a thing, a fling, *an affair*? Maggie said she was *seeing* Anthony. If she had a thing with Cecil, why wouldn't she admit it? Imogene's stomach wrings and releases. Because she didn't. She didn't want to be with him.

Rape is one of those words like *skin* and *faggot* and *slut*. When the guys wrestle or try to take the ball from each other in basketball, sometimes one of them yells "Rape!" to make the others laugh. And during Sister Abigail's lessons on the saints, it came up with one of the St. Marias: "A man wanted to rape her. When she would not submit to him, he murdered her. She is honoured for her purity." "What about that man?" Liz Constantine said. "St. Maria died forgiving him," Sister Abigail said. Then Liz said she hoped he went to hell and Sister Abigail told her to watch her tongue.

In the library, Imogene puts books away. One is a text on Canadian Law. It's a nice day and everyone is outside playing sports or smoking. She scans the R section of the index. There are multiple listings under Rape.

Statutory Rape: *Sexual intercourse by an adult with a person below a statutorily designated age. The criminal offense of statutory rape is committed when an adult sexually penetrates a person who, under the law, is incapable of consenting to sex. Minors and physically and mentally incapacitated persons are deemed incapable of consenting to sex under rape statutes. These persons are considered deserving of special protection because they are especially vulnerable due to their youth or condition.*

The perpetrator's age is an important factor in statutory rape where the offense is based on the victim's age. Furthermore, a defendant may not argue that he was mistaken as to the minor's age or incapacity.

There is a list of ages and numbers. Fourteen is the limit and it depends on whether or not the relationship was "exploitive." The statute of limitations doesn't end for statutory rape. So, depending on the relationship, Anthony might be a rapist. And Cecil, definitely. Whoever her father is, he could go to jail, right now. Her existence is evidence.

She places the book on the shelf. Miss Coffey has piled books to be returned on a table and Imogene pretends to examine their labels while taking deep breaths. Imagine if Maggie pointed the finger at Cecil. What a scandal. Everyone would talk and talk and talk about it. Like the cases on the news about the priests and the altar boys. Nan turns the volume down when it pops up on *Here and Now*: "The details, my God. Don't they know this is when people eat their supper?"

What would people call her if Cecil or Anthony were accused, if it went to court? Rape Baby? But she is anyway. According to the law, this is what she is. It boils down to which guy is less of a piece of shit. And Cecil would have known, for sure. He's the biggest piece of shit.

When the bell rings, she makes her way back to class. Donny Martin almost bumps into her: "Watch it, Cec." She moves past him without acknowledgement.

That Sunday, Maggie calls to see if Imogene wants some new books. "Robert was saying the other day what a prodigious reader you are. You're much better than I was at your age. All I read was fluff. *Flowers in the Attic* kind of stuff."

"Good lord," Nan says. She stands in the kitchen, examining a bowl of dough. "Why isn't this yeast working?"

"What about my dad?" Imogene says. "Did he read much?"

Nan's back stiffens in her peripheral vision. There is a pause on the phone.

"Yes," Maggie says. "I remember being surprised that he read so much. But I guess there's not much to do when you have spare time on a boat."

"What did he like to read?"

Another pause. "He said his favourite book was *The Stranger*. By some French philosopher." Robert's voice mutters something beyond the phone. "Albert Camus," Maggie says.

"I'd like to read that," Imogene says.

"Hold on." Another pause. "Robert says it's pretty sinister. It gets studied in philosophy courses."

"That's what I want to read."

"Okay. I'll see if I can find a copy."

"Good. Here's Nan." Imogene passes the receiver to Nan and goes to her room. Anthony was a reader. That's something then. She doubts Cecil even knows how to read.

When the book arrives, she is disappointed with its small size and thinness. But the content is darkly satisfying. Mersault feels nothing as he goes through life. His mother dies—what odds. He helps out Raymond, who's a proper bastard. He kills a man. He doesn't care. How great would it be to not give a shit what anyone thinks? So what if her father's a rapist or everyone in this shithole gossips about her mother? If she was like Mersault, she could shrug it all off.

She tells Maggie she likes *The Stranger* and Maggie says, "Good," and then tells her about the raccoons fighting in her and Robert's backyard.

"Did my father ever say why he liked that book?" Imogene says.

"Well, he never had much time for religion, I know that. And the book is about a very unconventional character, yes?"

"Yes." Imogene wants to tell her about the line she likes, but Nan would freak. She wrote it down: *I had only a little time left and I didn't want to waste it on God.* Everything on the news with the priest and molestation, yet the nuns won't discuss it at school and it never comes up in church. Everyone in St. Felix's talking without talking.

"There you go," Maggie says. "Tony came off as pretty unrepentant himself."

"What do you mean?" But then Maggie says something over the mouthpiece to Robert in a high, sweetened voice and the subject is changed. So annoying. It shouldn't be this hard.

In her room, she lists questions. Things to ask her mother if they ever get a frigging moment of privacy together. And if she wants good answers, she can't upset Maggie. She must ask them calmly, show she is okay with everything. She jots down all the questions she can think of. Then she arranges them in an order with the less intense ones at the beginning.

Questions for Maggie (First Draft):

1. What was Anthony like?
2. Am I anything like Anthony?

3. Why doesn't Nan know anything about Anthony?
4. Why hasn't Anthony been found? Does he really know I exist?
5. Why do people talk about Cecil Jesso and you?
6. Did something happen between you and Cecil Jesso?
7. Is there any chance Cecil is my father?

She erases the last question. And then paints liquid paper over the pencil shadows of the words. What if someone takes her notebook and reads it? Cecil and *father*, written in her own handwriting. It gives her instant gut rot.

There was some plot line about proof of fatherhood in one of Nan's stories last week; a character got DNA testing to find out who was her real dad. A blood test, the results in a white envelope. This is something that could happen with Cecil and her. And if it was true, there's her and Cecil, tied together in a file forever. She'd have to get a new birth certificate. What would happen if Cecil knew she was his? Would he feel some kind of ownership? Would he see her as evidence of his crime? Imogene paints extra layers of whiteout on her penciled words. She tears out the page and rewrites the list in her journal again, but only questions one to six.

Questions for Maggie:
1. What was Anthony like?
2. Am I anything like Anthony?
3. Why doesn't Nan know anything about Anthony?
4. Why hasn't Anthony been found? Does he really know I exist?
5. Why do people talk about Cecil Jesso and you?
6. Did something happen between you and Cecil Jesso?

She tears the original list into the smallest pieces she can. Nan has a fire in the woodstove. She tosses the paper inside and watches them burn. If it ever comes out Cecil is her father, there would only be two things she'd want to do.

1. Move somewhere no one knows her.
2. Make him disappear.

Liam has no new tricks. She dodges his feet and hands; she shakes out her books before opening them. His pranks descend into insults and throwing things: balls of paper, paper airplanes which cling to her hair. Imogene thinks of Mersault and tries to stay composed. She hopes he will become bored and find a new victim—Crystal just got a spaghetti perm and it looks retarded. Quince got his ear pierced. Every day at recess, Teddy Campbell dumps the water from his tin of Vienna Sausages on top of the pencil shavings in the class garbage can—someone should pick up on how gross that is.

In the spring, the grade nines play floor hockey in gym class. Phys Ed. is Imogene's least favourite class, but floor hockey is better than volleyball and much, much better than the gymnastics unit they did this winter. At fourteen, Imogene's legs compose two-thirds of her body. For gymnastics, Mr. Percy, the Phys Ed teacher, stood by the vault to help students with hand flips. For Imogene, he had to give both her legs a shove so she could hurl them over her head. She hated feeling her body escaping her. Everyone else looked bouncy and graceful, but it's just tits over arse with her. Off an inch and crunch, she's paralyzed. And since Liam is the biggest guy in class, the nuns will make him carry her up the stairs for the parts of the school with no ramps. He'll pretend to trip, throw her down the stairs, and leave her there.

But it's been raining all week and Mr. Percy wants them to run around. So, floor hockey in the gym. Everyone scrambles for equipment: plastic hockey sticks in yellow or blue, edges curved and warped with use. Nets and balls are dragged out of the storage room. The air smarts with rubber and old sweat. Sticks clatter over the long hardwood floor, the slightest drop gives a satisfying bang that echoes throughout the auditorium. Everyone runs around, hogging the orange balls with the people they like until being ordered to stop.

They are divided into mixed teams. Mr. Percy makes Imogene's team wear the coloured bibs and they all groan because they probably haven't been washed in months, if ever. Liam is a forward on the opposite team and Imogene is on defense. This is a relief; she won't have to face off with him. But throughout the game he glares at her and mouths things like *bitch* and *Cec*. The other defense on her team is all ninety pounds of Gerald Constantine and he won't get in Liam's way. There will be no protection if Liam decides to hit her. And if he takes a shot and she does nothing, she'll get shit from her classmates for the rest of the day. She figures if Liam gets the ball, he'll charge forward as close as he can get to the net and she'll have to make an attempt to stop him. She'll try to do this without getting too close.

At the start of the second period, Imogene's team is losing by one goal. Mr. Percy waits for them to switch sides, his silver whistle jutting out under his thin, silky moustache. After the faceoff, Liam gets a breakaway. Gerald moves like his feet are in quicksand. Imogene's team screams at her: "Go, move, go!" Liam's face is all teeth and evil and he keeps himself wide open. Screw it. She rushes forward; she'll slap the ball away and run like fuck.

When she gets in front of him, he lets her take the ball for a second. Then he crashes into her, "Cec Cec Cec Cec," under his breath. The ball is right there by her foot, she can get it and then he is leaning over her, back on to Mr. Percy, his teammates speeding towards them. His breath hot on her cheek, stale cigarettes and ripe perspiration, stick in one hand, the other landing square on her breast. "Slut," he says. And he squeezes.

She means to push him away with both hands, but she is holding her floor hockey stick, so instead, she strikes him across the chest and collarbone with the broad edge. Liam gasps. His face is red and indignant. "You bitch," he says. Like he is this precious, fucking little prince. Like he is about to declare How Dare You.

Imogene brings the blade of her stick up and across Liam's hip as hard as she can. He screams. She does it again. He moves to the side and starts losing his balance. She makes sure to come forward and push him again. He falls. She kicks him in the ribs. And again. Now she is too close to keep hitting with the hockey stick. She drops it, sits on him and punches, his face, his neck, his head, his chest.

It is the first time Imogene has ever really hit anyone. Being one of the tallest means no one has ever seriously tried to fight her. She hits Liam over and over. She is impressed by how good she is at hitting— every time she strikes him something happens: a reaction, a brighter colour, a new sound. It isn't until Mr. Percy pulls her off him that she feels the pain in her hands, holy, do they ever hurt. Her knuckles bleed, her wrists ache.

"Let's go, Miss."

Imogene's feet move on invisible bicycle pedals. She can't look behind her to see what's going on. The gym rings in tight silence. "Help him," Mr. Percy says. The squeak of scrambling sneakers. Mr. Percy pushes open the door and deposits Imogene in the hallway.

"Go to the office. Now. I'll be there in a minute."

His voice terse, his eyes avoid hers. She yanks off the smelly bib and moves down the hall on spastic legs. Past the library, past rows of grey lockers. Her T-shirt peels itself from her cooling skin all the way to the open door of the office and the closed green door of Sister Bernadette, Principal. She sits in one of the chairs along the wall. Wendy Martin, the school secretary, stops typing and assesses her.

"Yes, Imogene?"

"Mr. Percy told me to wait here."

Her eyebrows rise, but she returns to typing. When Mr. Percy appears, he is flushed and out of breath. He raps on the green door. A murmur in reply. He steps inside and closes the door. More murmuring. The door swings open.

"Go on in, Miss Tubbs."

Sister Bernadette's office smells like rose-scented air freshener and instant coffee. Imogene expects her to look angry, but her expression is calm and blank. She sits behind a solid pine desk, bare except for a few pens, a phone and a few small ceramic figurines on the front edge—Jack and Jill, Little Bo Peep—the ones that come in the boxes of Red Rose tea. High above on the wall is a white crucifix with a gold plastic Jesus nailed to it. Mr. Percy leans on the wall beside the desk with folded arms.

"Hello, Imogene," Sister Bernadette says. "Take a seat. I've already contacted your grandmother to take you home. Would you like to tell me what happened now or wait for her and tell both of us?"

Imogene shrugs.

"You can tell me and I can tell your grandmother, if you like. I need your story regardless." Sister intertwines her fingers in front of her. "You're usually a quiet girl and a good student. There must be a reason for this outburst."

Imogene opens her mouth and closes it. Should she start with Liam's hand on her breast? Or the Cec and Cecil and pokes and prodding? Will it go in a file? Her name on a paper with Liam Lundrigan's and Cecil Jesso's, all their names together.

"I hit him because he was being a real asshole, Sister." She hears the quiver in her voice and clamps her mouth shut.

Sister Bernadette says things like temper and consequences. Mr. Percy says things like no excuse for this kind of behaviour and everyone needs self control and violence is not an answer. Imogene nods and picks her cuticles. When Nan shows up, Imogene is told to wait outside while Sister Bernadette and Mr. Percy speak with her.

Nan emerges from behind the green door. Her face is flat and unreadable. They leave. She says nothing in the car. Imogene doesn't do any outdoor chores. She sits on the sofa with bags of frozen peas on her wrists. During the first commercial break for *General Hospital*, Nan speaks without looking up from her tea.

"What did that boy say to you, my dear? What did he do?"

"He called me a slut. And he grabbed my t—breast."

She freezes waiting for Nan's repulsion. Nan stirs her tea and nods with her eyes downcast. She clanks her spoon against the top and lays it on the saucer, with the tiniest flare.

"Good for you, my dear. If he does it again, go for the pain places. Crotch, bridge of the nose, Adam's apple."

six

Imogene is suspended for the rest of the week. The Sunday night before she has to return to school, she lies in bed, unable to turn off her brain. She writes out a list of possibilities.

Things to Prepare For:
1. Liam's Revenge. He may not pick a fight with a girl, but he might get worse with the teasing. Or he will recruit others.
2. New challengers. Once you're known for getting in a scrap, people want to see if they can take you. Girls like Antonia Martin and Liz Constantine like a racket.
3. Reputation as a Crazy Person. Crazy, psycho, fucked up Imogene.

She imagines eyes on her, like insect legs on her neck. She imagines whispers that sizzle like bacon. She imagines delight sparkling in grinning jowls. Calling her Cecil obviously drives her crazy. Why would it bother her if it was a lie? They know she knows. They know they are right.

She reads for distraction to put herself to sleep. In *Ender's Game*, Ender worries about his brother Peter's anger, his mad mood. Maggie sent the book in a box for her birthday along with yellow slouch socks and a brightly coloured Swatch watch. Maggie, who can't talk about her dad or Cecil, but can select items just for her, a new novel, a pair of shoes.

On Monday morning, Imogene slips into class around the back as usual. She doesn't look around until she is safe in her desk. Liam is nowhere to be seen. Outside, it is grey with drizzle and the mood carries into the room; students sit in their desks like they're made of string.

Crystal Seymour whispers with Shelly MacInnis. She pauses to give Imogene a tiny wave. Her eyes glisten with a devilish light.

The bell rings. As Mr. Benoit moves to close the door, Liam darts in. Mr. Benoit opens his mouth to speak, but just shuts the door instead. Liam slouches down in the first available desk. He wears a ball cap clamped down over his face. When he reaches up to adjust it, Imogene sees red scabs along the knuckles of his fingers. Did she hurt his hand? Did she step on his fingers? Along his jaw, a yellowing bruise. The hockey stick connected there.

He says nothing all day and doesn't look at Imogene. No one says much of anything. Liz Constantine, always ferocious in her royal-blue eyeliner and stirrup pants, nods to her in the hallway. Imogene feels like she is wearing the Cone of Silence from that old show *Get Smart.* Everyone slides past her keeping a neat, invisible circumference.

In gym class, Mr. Percy makes Imogene apologize to Liam in front of everyone and for him to accept her apology. No one looks at her when she says, "I'm sorry." Liam folds his arms and stares at the floor. Then Mr. Percy claps his hands. "Warm up. Fifteen laps around the gym." A radius of about three metres is maintained around her as she runs. Later, she is the fourth person chosen when sides are picked for volleyball. There are no complaints when she messes up her serve.

At lunch, Rita smiles at her from her group of friends and invites her to sit with them. Cherry MacIssac offers her a cookie. During math class, Imogene leaves her binder on her desk and it remains untouched. In the bathroom, Antonia Martin stares at her hard, cracks her gum and says, "Imogene, I like your Swatch watch." Shelly MacInnis says, "Imogene, my sister pays a pile of money to dye her hair close to the colour of yours. You're some lucky."

Two weeks later, she walks into the library as Liam exits. She freezes. He angles himself around her and floats out the doorway. He keeps his head down as he walks up the hallway, his hand rubs the back of his neck. From a distance, he looks like a bird with its head tucked under its wing, avoiding the light in order to sleep.

seven

In June, Imogene gets a good report card. When she starts grade ten, she'll be in the academic stream and can take advanced math if she wants. Maggie's voice chirps with enthusiasm in the earpiece of the kitchen phone. She says she's sending a bus ticket in the mail, round-trip to St. John's. She and Robert will be there for a real-estate conference in the middle of August. Imogene can go up in July and stay with Uncle Kenneth—he's on board with it all. Imogene can stay with him and Beth, and later, Maggie will arrive to visit with her. She'll take Imogene shopping for school supplies at the Avalon Mall.

Nan gets on the extension and says that's ridiculous and it's too long a bus trip for a young girl all by herself. "Well, Mom," Maggie says, "You can come too if you want. We'll send two tickets and you can see your youngest son's new place."

"No thank you very much," Nan says. "I'm just fine here." And then she huffs and puffs for a few minutes and says, "Fine, 'cause I knows now Imogene will mope all summer if she doesn't go. As long as someone is there to meet her, she can go by herself."

The night before she leaves, Imogene takes out her list of questions. The last time she saw Maggie was two Christmases ago. Last summer, Imogene was supposed to go up to Ontario, but she broke her collarbone jumping off Uncle Eli's trike and spent most of the summer indoors, watching reruns, sooky and bored out of her wits. And then they thought Maggie would visit at Christmas, but it turned out Robert bought her a cruise and the two of them were off to the Caribbean. So, when Imogene and Maggie are together in St. John's, it will be the first time they've had a private, face-to-face conversation in over two years. It is time for a talk. And as far as Imogene knows, Maggie has no idea about all the Cecil shit. Her suspension has never come up in telephone conversations. If she's going to find out the truth, she should be prepared.

Questions for Maggie:
1. What was Anthony like?
2. Am I anything like Anthony?
3. Why doesn't Nan know anything about Anthony?
4. Why hasn't Anthony been found? Does he really know I exist?
5. Why do people talk about Cecil Jesso and you?
6. Did something happen between you and Cecil Jesso?

Imogene brings three books to read on the bus, but spends most of the ride staring out the window. If the drive was by car, they'd be there in eight hours, but the bus ride stretches it out to eleven. They stop at gas stations and intersections and the overpriced airport cafeteria in Gander: five friggin' bucks for a small fries and a fountain Coke. Sometimes someone just puts a box on the bus; sometimes passengers stagger on and drink out of hidden bottles. Imogene lets her eyes be dragged into a dance over tens of thousands of treetops and clusters of alders. She sees two moose, she sees kids on trikes. She sees one of the cutest guys she's ever seen in the parking lot at the Clarenville stop and when the bus pulls out, she opens her hand in a wave at him and he waves back and she smiles to herself for a long time afterwards.

It is dark when the bus arrives. Uncle Kenneth and his girlfriend Beth are there to meet her. Beth has kind, crinkly eyes and her hair hangs in a thick, blond braid stretching to her shoulder blades. Uncle Kenneth is the same as when he visited last Christmas: big dark mustache and gruff voice. He's lost a little more hair, his forehead is ridged with thin spokes. Beth says her daughter Violet is back at the house. Imogene will meet her when they get there.

Imogene is told there is a park across the street from the apartment, but it is too dark and shadowy to see when they get out of the car. Just rustling trees and a dark path. The apartment is on top of a medical-supply store. They climb a narrow staircase to an apartment with hardwood floors, burgundy walls, and Violet on the floral-print couch. Violet has spiky, sandy hair cut short in front and long in the back. Her earrings don't match, and her eyes don't match either, one blue, one hazel. She gives Imogene a big grin and shakes her hand. Imogene has never had a girl shake her hand before; it's always been Uncle Kenneth or Uncle Eli and they do it in a jokey way. Violet looks Imogene up and down. "Well, look at you," she says.

"Look at you too," Imogene says and Violet laughs. She asks Imogene how old she is and Imogene says fifteen. Violet is seventeen. "If you don't have plans tomorrow," Violet says, "I'll take you around." Imogene can't imagine any plans she would have.

That night, Imogene watches the headlights of passing cars reflect on the ceiling through the gap between the curtain rod and the window. Engines, footsteps, and the occasional snippet of conversation, a laugh, an exclamation. She thinks about how in St. Felix's she can recognize everyone's vehicles by their headlights and here, she won't see anyone she knows and she is glad.

When she gets up the next day, Uncle Kenneth has already left for work. Beth says, "Let's have our toast and tea in Bannerman Park." They wrap the buttered toast in paper towels and place it and a thermos of tea in a silver lunchbox. The three of them trot across the street to the park. Beth and Violet hardly pause at the crosswalk.

The trees of Bannerman Park are enticing to Imogene, which seems silly since all she sees in St. Felix's are trees. But St. Felix's trees grow sideways in the wind and these are tall manicured beings with beckoning paths beneath them, leading out to swings and a tube slide and a blue swimming pool. They sit at a picnic table and Violet kicks her red jelly shoes off and smooshes her toes in the grass. "Watch out for dog shit," Beth says. They drink tea and munch toast. They watch people wander around, babies in strollers, dogs on leashes and teenagers on bikes selling Dickie Dee ice-cream novelties: yellow Pac-Mans with a gumball eye, Rockets and Mr. Freezes. A couple lolls a blanket in front of the gazebo, making out like animals. Beth says, "Some people have no shame." Violet just laughs.

Violet is supposed to be looking for a summer job, but when she takes Imogene to the mall, she doesn't fill out any applications. They wander around to see who's there. They eat potato chips in the food court and Violet asks her questions. "What kind of music do you like? What do people do out your way for fun? Any hot guys in your school?" She shakes her head at Imogene's musical tastes except for when she says Depeche

Mode. "Me and my ex used to drive out to Outer Cove and listen to *Music for the Masses*. Best album to drive to," she says. She asks Imogene if she watches Much Music and declares Nan a tyrant for refusing to get cable.

Imogene is fidgety with want over so many things: ankle boots and bracelets and INXS tapes and a long black top that hangs over one shoulder. Nan gave her sixty-five bucks for the three weeks and expects money back. "That's over twenty dollars a week," Nan said. "Why would you need more than that?"

They take the bus back downtown. Walking down Water and Duckworth is fun, but the trudge up the steep hill to Military Road is a pain. "Downtown townies gotta have strong arses," Violet says, smacking her own bum.

Beth and Kenneth let Imogene and Violet sleep in most mornings, but expect chores to be done, like hitching up the tiny washing machine to the sink for small piles of laundry. The clothesline goes out the bathroom window and if anything falls off, they have to run down the stairs and rescue it from the backyard before it blows into the street. Violet complains about having to hang their nightclothes out for all of downtown to see. Drawers and bras are strung along the shower rail.

On the first weekend, Uncle Kenneth brings them out to a U-pick for strawberries and says he'll pay twenty bucks to whoever picks the most, as long as they do it without complaining. Imogene wins. They eat berries in the car and he drives them out to Cape Spear. It's very pretty, but Imogene can't get that excited about cliffs and water since St. Felix's is all cliffs and water. There is a sign that says Cape Spear is the most easterly point in North America. Uncle Kenneth takes a picture of them next to it, but Violet won't give him a big smile because she says she has strawberry in her teeth. Uncle Kenneth sighs loudly at her and when he gives Imogene the twenty bucks, he slips her another ten.

Violet takes her around downtown. They watch boys Violet knows play games in the arcade on Water Street. They watch boys Violet knows skateboard by the War Memorial. The boys complain about cops. Violet knows a lot of people and complains about having nothing to do.

The boy Violet talks to the most is named Chad. He is seventeen and parts his hair to one side so it hangs in a bleach-blond wing over his left eye. He tells them his older brother has left him his hatchback to drive all summer. Violet just nods at this, so Imogene does too. Chad's best friend is Anton, who is tall and dark. Chad announces it's because he's part Paki and Anton just shrugs. He asks Imogene if that's her real hair colour. She says, "Why would I dye my hair this colour?" Anton says, "Why not?

I would." And he runs his hand through his black, black hair and when he smiles, his teeth are white, even perfection and his eyelids make him look mysterious. Imogene would like to stare at him for a very long time.

The first day it rains, Violet tells Imogene to order a pizza for pick-up from Venice Pizzeria. Imogene has never ordered a pizza before. Beth and Violet get very excited about this and giggle so much when Imogene is trying to listen to the list of toppings that she just tells the guy to put on whatever. When she arrives in her poncho to pick it up, it's not ready because they thought it was a prank phone call.

August starts and the Regatta gets a lot of hype with ads on the radio and people gleeful with the possibility of a day off. Imogene looks forward to it, but on the day, it's like a large garden party with bigger teddy bears for prizes. The crowd moves slowly around the lake and junk-food stands and the urge to spend her money annoys her. They watch the boat races for a while, but she's not sure who to cheer for and Violet is more interested in looking at guys.

They meet Chad and Anton sitting on the pan of a pick-up by the boat house. Chad passes out cans of beer. "They're IDing at the beer tent," he says. Violet bums a smoke from Chad and he gives Imogene one as well. She swallows the smoke instead of breathing it in. It tastes like dried garbage. But Anton can French inhale and the smoke drifting up into his nostrils is sexy in a dirty kind of way.

The crowd wanes and fog starts to roll in. Chad wants to go for a drive. Anton gets a case of beer at an Irving station. "Let's go out to the fort," he says. They drive under the overpass and down a narrow street with worn-looking houses. They park by the warning sign for tourists and head towards the grey walls. At the top of the stairs, Chad holds up a hand to wait and as soon as the foghorn blast ends, they scamper down and past it. At the landing, there is light from the moon and her foot kicks a chunk of glass against the rocks. "Figured there would be others here," Anton says. "No one on the go tonight."

Violet and Chad move to the wall and are silhouetted against the glowing sky. Violet's nose is short and neat, like a young animal's. Imogene thinks it is a beautiful nose. And Violet is beautiful herself, they are all beautiful. Anton hands her a flask and she lets the smoky liquid make a path in her throat and Anton is beautiful and he makes her feel beautiful. His eyes are darkened, but she can feel them on her and when she passes back the flask, their fingers touch. "Your hand is cold," he says and he takes it and puts it in his jacket pocket with his own.

"So, you're only around for a few weeks?" he says. "That's too bad."

"Yeah, I don't want to go back."

"Stay here then."

"Easy for you to say."

"Why not? You could work it out here." His fingers stroke hers in his pocket. "If my mom can come here and get used to the cold, anyone can do it." He takes a sip from the flask and passes it to her. "I mean, it's why everyone came to Canada and the US anyway. If where you're from ruins your life, fuckin' leave."

"Yeah, but my nan would kill me."

"Well, you can't mess with Nan."

"I'm starved," Violet says. "Froze to death."

Back in the car, Anton brushes his lips against Imogene's and then down her neck, which creates a swarm of shivers. And Violet laughs at them for kissing and they stop. But he kisses her again when they pull up to his house and his tongue goes into her mouth and she can feel the bumpy ridge of his taste buds. She lets him probe her mouth, her eyes squeezed shut. And right before he gets out of the car, he says he'll see her at the show tomorrow.

But he doesn't show up at the all-ages show and she and Violet and a girl named Mireille dance in front of the stage. Imogene feels a secret relief that Anton didn't come and it makes her dance with increased freedom. She doesn't know the name of the band, but they are loud and energetic. Everyone does whatever they want when they dance. Back home, everyone only dances facing each other in matching lines, boy and girl or girl and girl.

Afterwards, they try to get into bars on George Street, but none will let them in except the Corner Stone. The guy at the door nods quickly, like he's pretending they aren't real. The downstairs is a pub with older guys watching sports. They go upstairs where there is a dance floor with staircases on either side. Violet has money from babysitting and Imogene has her berry-picking money. She tries a white Russian and a rum and coke and a beer and pukes them all up in one go in the bathroom, but doesn't make a big mess. Beth and Kenneth aren't home when they get back and the next day they don't notice how crappy she feels.

Then Maggie calls to say they're not going to come down. Robert thinks the conference in Niagara makes more sense right now. "I'm sorry,"

Maggie says. "This is what happens when you become your own boss. If Cronin Realty is going to succeed, we have to grab all the opportunities we can."

"Oh, that's too bad."

"It really is. I'm so sorry. We'll try for sometime this fall. Or Christmas."

Imogene's core tangles with the sink of disappointment and a pang of relief. Once again, another Maggie shag-up. Another stretch of time without the clarity of a face-to-face talk. But she's having fun. It's nice to be a *new* person. No history. No past impressions. And what if Maggie's answers aren't what she wants to hear? Maggie might treat Imogene differently if she suddenly has nothing to hide. If it's true, Imogene won't want to go back home. And how could she ask Maggie if she can live with her?

Maggie asks Kenneth to give Imogene money. She'll pay him back. Kenneth tells Imogene this and says all he has right now is seventy-five dollars. He places three twenties and a ten and a five in Imogene's hand and it immediately burns to be spent. She and Violet take the Route 3 to the mall.

Maggie says the money is for school supplies and new runners. "Is she going to check your bags?" Violet says.

"Nope."

"Then, what do you really want to buy?"

"These," Imogene says. The ankle boots are turquoise vinyl with a spiralling pattern of pin holes on the sides.

"Get 'em," Violet says.

And the jeans with the zippers on the bottom and the long flower-print T-shirt with the pocket over the heart. Imogene makes sure to pick out things no one has in St. Felix's and that Violet approves of. A long strand of turquoise beads to match the boots. A pair of earrings that are silver puffed hearts.

"Those are cute," Violet says.

"They're for Rita. I don't have my ears pierced."

"Well, I know what you're spending ten bucks on."

The girl at the salon uses a piercing gun to double-stab Imogene's earlobes so they look like tiny vampire bites in each. The piercings come with free studs, so she gets one gold and one rhinestone diamond for each ear. When they exit the salon, they see Chad and Anton in the arcade. Anton puts his arm around Imogene's shoulders and it feels cool to stand in the arcade looking like a couple. They go into a photo booth and take two strips of photos making faces together and then a third strip where they're kissing and they split those—two photos each. "When do you leave?" Anton asks. "Tomorrow," Imogene says. "Shit," he says. "Give me your address."

When they leave the mall, Imogene has the jeans, the ankle boots, two T-shirts, two strings of beads, an armful of bangles, the photos of her and Anton, Rita's earrings, and two studs in each earlobe. Violet pays for Imogene's second piercings as a gift and gets her own done way up on the top of her ear. No school supplies or sneakers. "Fuck that," Violet says. "I'll give you my stuff. Like anyone needs half that shit."

At the apartment, Violet hands Imogene a pair of dusty canvas sneakers, a plaid pencil case containing an array of pens with chewed tops, and a Pluto Pez dispenser.

"There," she says. "Supplies covered."

The next day, Imogene tries not to cry when she gets on the bus. "It doesn't matter anyway," Violet says. "Ken got me a job up at Mount Scio picking savory. I'd be busy all the time now."

"It's only for a couple of weeks," Kenneth says. "It will cover your back-to-school clothes, which seems to be the only thing that motivates you." Violet rolls her eyes.

On the bus home, Imogene lets her forehead rest on the window. It rains through most of Central. Drops of water congregate and chase each other down the glass. She puts Violet's taped-off Depeche Mode tape in her Walkman and listens to "Never Let Me Down Again" over and over, stop, rewind, play. When the bus arrives at the Petro-Can, it's dark and Nan is waiting. Imogene snoozes in the Beretta on the drive back.

The next morning, Nan asks how Maggie and Robert are. When Imogene explains they didn't come down from Ontario, Nan has a fit.

"The whole purpose of sending you across the province was so your mother could see you," Nan says. "Jesus Christ, two years since she's seen her own daughter." Nan gets on the phone. "Margaret Josephine Tubbs, I can't believe you. You couldn't even see her, you couldn't bring yourself to prioritize your own child. She's been running wild around St. John's all summer. No, I will not listen."

Imogene goes to her room. Where to go. She'll go over to Uncle Eli's. Even if Rita's not home, they'll let her hang out. She puts the heart-shaped earrings in her pocket and boots it out the door. In the kitchen, Nan's voice has climbed to a pitch that could shred tin.

On the way to Uncle Eli's, she sees three figures on the road. Her stomach flips for a second; maybe it's Liam and his friends. But the figures are definitely female: Rita with Natalie Sampson and Cherry MacIssac. When they get up close, Imogene can see they all have their hair in banana clips with their bangs curled.

"When'd you get back?" Rita says.

"Last night."

"Your hair's some long," Cherry says. "How was your trip?"

"It was great. I got my ears pierced." Imogene pulls back her hair to show her double-pierced earlobes.

"That kind of piercing can get infected easy," Natalie says.

"Sure, I did mine myself," Cherry says. "All you need is an ice cube and a needle."

"Ew, Imogene, one's turning pink."

"I got a bunch of new clothes too," Imogene says. "And Cousin Violet is friggin' wicked."

"Look at you, talkin' like a townie now."

"Uncle Ken doesn't have any kids," Rita says.

"Violet is his girlfriend Beth's kid."

"She's not really our cousin, though," Rita says. "I met her last Christmas. She was right stuck-up."

"I met a cute guy too," Imogene says. She takes out the strip of photos of her and Anton in the mall. Rita wrinkles her nose. "He's some dark."

"You got a funny definition of cute," Natalie says.

"Did you hear who Nick Cleary is going out with?" Rita says. Natalie and Cherry shake their heads in disapproval.

"Teresa Fucking Loder."

"He's only with her because she's a slut," Natalie says.

"Oh yeah, and a bunch of cabins were broke into last week," Cherry says. "Everyone thinks it was Liam and Randy."

"They might have to go to court."

"If they do, they'll probably send Liam off to Whitbourne. He's already on probation for taking money from the school canteen."

"B'ys, we gotta go," Cherry says.

"We're going to Stephenville with Cherry's sister," Rita says. "Going to get school stuff."

"And see a movie."

"Cool," Imogene says.

"Sorry, there's only room for four in the truck," Cherry says. Natalie smirks, her shiny cheeks pink and round. Imogene makes a fist around the earrings in her pocket. The bottom tips of the puffed hearts stab her palm.

Imogene goes to the beach. The waves scrape the pebbles forward and back, offering and retrieving. She takes out the earrings. She thinks about how they would look flying up and over and into the water. She returns them to her pocket. Violet is right; they are cute. They'll look good on the first day of school.

eight

In Biology class, Mr. Wall puts everyone in groups and has them fill out a survey. How many in their group have brown eyes? Blue eyes? How many have joined earlobes? A widow's peak? Does anyone have pinky fingers that bend towards the ring finger? Can everyone roll their tongues? Imogene is grouped with Crystal Seymour and Quincy MacIssac. They examine each other's foreheads and hands, and stick out their tongues at each other. Crystal points out she has green eyes and it's not on the form. "Write it in," Mr. Wall says.

The results are tabulated on the board. Most people have brown eyes; it's a dominant gene. Mr. Wall gives it a large letter B. Joined earlobes, straight pinkies, and the ability to roll your tongue are also all dominant. Blue eyes are recessive and represented by a small b. For blue eyes to happen, both parents have to have a recessive gene. They do calculations for blue-eyed offspring scenarios: Bb + Bb = 25% blue eyed. BB + bb = 0%. Bb + bb = 50%. Donny Martin says most people in this class have brown eyes 'cause they're a bunch of jackatars. Everyone laughs and Mr. Wall gives him a warning.

Imogene is in the blue-eyed column. Maggie has brown eyes, so she must carry a blue-eyed gene, which makes sense as Nan has blue eyes. And Imogene's father would have to have blue eyes or brown with a Bb gene. Imogene also has crooked pinkies. She doesn't remember what Maggie's hands are like. And red hair is recessive, Mr. Wall says. "So is blond hair and green eyes," Crystal says. Donny says, "Sure, you've only been blond since Miss Clairol came to town."

When Imogene goes home, she tells Nan she is working on biology homework and gets her to fill out the survey for Maggie. When it's done, she makes a list of traits that she does not share with her mother: red hair, blue eyes, pale skin, tallness, big feet, freckles, crooked pinkies. She and Maggie can roll their tongues and have attached earlobes. But big wow. Can Cecil roll his tongue? She tries to picture his ears, but can only think of cabbage leaves. And when she tries to picture his hands, she thinks about Maggie. Did he hold her shoulders down, did he push her? Was she passed out? She might have been passed out. Sister Bernadette gave a lecture in health class last year about alcohol and sex, about girls getting raped when they've had too much to drink. Maggie might not have been awake. Imagine, waking up pregnant. A few years ago, when everyone was talking about Susan Benoit being knocked up in grade twelve, Imogene had dreams of waking up with a big pregnant belly. In the dream, she stood in her bedroom, feeling the fringes of green shag rug between her toes and looking down, seeing the round orb of herself jutting out her nightie. Oh no, how did this happen. And then, hearing Nan's movement in the next room and wanting to hide, looking around her room, how could she get rid of it before Nan saw? And then she'd wake up and clasp her hands to her belly and think how ridiculous. She hasn't even had sex yet.

Biology class continues the next day with examples of brown and black cows. Rita looks at Imogene's book over her shoulder on the bus and rolls her eyes. "Genetics, we did that last year. So boring. Everyone in my family has brown eyes so I have brown eyes. Quelle surpreeze."

Imogene regards her cousin next to her on the vinyl bus seat. Rita, with her long brown hair, brown eyes, and skin which turns butterscotch in summer. Nan says Rita is true Tubbs, just like her dad who is just like Pop. Petite too, the Tubbs are short and wiry. Little dark Tubbs, full of athletic ability and good humour. No one would consider questioning Rita's DNA. And DNA tests cost a lot of money, according to Great Aunt Bride. "They do them all the time on the TV, but they cost an arm and a leg in real life."

When she's off the bus and into the house, Nan tells her to go to the store for butter and brown sugar. "I have to make date squares for the Women's Institute tonight," she says. So annoying. Imogene has money, she could have got off the bus at the store and walked back. Nan never knows what she needs until she needs it. The wind is like frozen sandpaper and she fumes for the whole walk. She doesn't notice whose truck is parked outside the Kwik Stop.

Inside the store, Cecil is at the counter. Imogene's chest gets all tangled and she forces the grimace off her face. His back is hunched in a camouflage hunting jacket, like a sack of potatoes trying to hide. She glances around the store. No other customers in sight. She could get a look at him and check his earlobes and pinky fingers. Loretta Samson is at the cash and she eyes Imogene walking to the cooler for butter. Frig off, Loretta. Imogene gets a bag of brown sugar and heads to the cash. She pretends to be interested in a display of plastic beads for making friendship bracelets and watches him from a distance.

Cecil buys a pack of smokes, a lotto ticket, and a dozen Black Horse. He takes his change with his left hand—maybe he is left-handed, like her. Is that genetic? It seems like it would be random. When he steps away from the counter, there is a ticking sound on the floor. The plastic tip of his bootlace is loose on the tile.

"Your shoe's untied," she says.

"Huh?"

"Your shoe...your boot's untied."

Cecil blinks at her, mouth parted. He bends and yanks the laces up. The pinky finger of his right hand turns in like a subtle comma. She stares at his dangling pinky. She coaxes her lip not to shrivel up in disgust. Fuck fuck fuck. She could kick him, right now, a boot to his stupid, orange head. Or, in the second he puts his hand down for balance, she could step forward. His fingernails crunching like snail shells under her foot. This is for my mother, she'd say. You. You fucking prick.

"Tanks," he says. He carries the box of beer by one handle. The door jangles shut behind him. His pack of Player's Light is forgotten on the floor. Imogene pockets it while Loretta rings her in.

On the walk home, she climbs under Butter Brook Bridge and stands in the culvert to be sheltered from the wind. She lights a cigarette with a match. A vehicle passes above. Maybe it's Cecil, returning to the Kwik Stop for his smokes. Well, fuck you, Cec, they're gone now. She takes a puff and swallows it, like she did with Violet, then lets one in with a shallow breath. Fuck that piece of garbage and his smokes and his ginger hair and his stupid mouth. Fuck that fucking guy.

nine

If the bishop wasn't such a bastard, Imogene wouldn't have to go to church. Confirmation was supposed to happen in junior high, but the bishop hasn't been able to make it all the way out to St. Felix's for over a year. "Once you're confirmed, you can decide whether or not you want to come to Mass," Nan says. "But if he can't get here, it could be a sign."

"He's probably too busy going to court, like the rest of them," Great Aunt Bride says.

"Jesus, Bride," Nan says. "Don't spread rumours like that."

Imogene waits out Mass in beats. Gifts brought up, transubstantiation, bells, shake hands with those around you as a sign of peace (if Wish Benoit is nearby, he tickles her palm with his index finger), lamb of God takes away sins of the world, not worthy to receive you, hymn, communion, kneel, sit, stand, another hymn, get up and get out. So much of life is sitting, pretending to listen, and making the right gestures. Sometimes Rita nudges her into silent giggles by staring at anything odd close by—like Malcolm Whalen's gap of bald head, visible through the mesh backing on his ball cap. He doesn't wear his hair piece when his hat's on. But tonight, there is a view of Nick Cleary, two pews ahead, and Rita's eyes are gelled to him. Imogene tries not to stare at Murray Wells's shoulders in the front pew with their impressive coating of dandruff.

Afterwards, Nan lingers in the porch to see and talk. This part isn't so bad—it's nice to be out of the pew where she feels overly aware of her sit-bones on the cold, hard wood. With everyone clustered together in the porch, the mix of perfume, cologne, and incense residue could make her high.

A blond woman in a green leather jacket with huge shoulder pads waves her hands in the air. "Agnes!"

"Oh my goodness, Kelly," Nan says. The blond woman flings her arms around Nan. From over Nan's shoulder, her eyes meet Imogene's and widen. They are bright, unnaturally blue. Maybe she has those tinted contacts. Imogene saw an ad for them in *Seventeen* magazine.

"Immy, this is Kelly Abbott. She and your mother were best of friends growing up," Nan says. Her eyes shine up. "My God. I still think of you as sixteen."

"Sure, you're sixteen yourself, Agnes."

Imogene waits while Nan and Kelly gush and ramble. Kelly is home from Labrador City for her new niece's baptism. She works as a medical secretary and her husband, Paul, is an engineer, doing some well, oh my, yes. Maggie will be home the summer and Kelly will be too, that will be wonderful.

Kelly moves to Imogene and stares into her face. "I held you when you were five days old," she says. Her blue eyes are doll-like and a little hard to look at. "You had this tiny sprout of orange hair. I told Maggie you looked like a fairy."

"I've seen pictures of you," Imogene says. "Maggie has them in an album."

"Your mom does, yes," Kelly says. She darts a look at Nan. "Look at the hair on her. Just lovely. I always wanted red hair."

Kelly's honey-blond curls pour over her shoulder pads. Like fuck she wants red hair. "Thank you," Imogene says.

"Bride is just outside," Nan says. "Kelly, you've got to come say hello."

"Oh my God. I'd love to see Bride," she says. She leans into Imogene's ear. Her perfume fills Imogene's senses, rose petals and baby powder. "Imogene, I'd love to have a chat with you," she says. "A one-on-one."

"Okay."

"Tell you what. You should come over and visit me."

"Oh. Okay. I can do that."

"You around tomorrow? I'll give you a call?" Kelly's eyes give cartoonish blinks.

"Sure. If you want to." What is she supposed to say? She feels herself flushing a bit. Some strange lady is going to call her. It's embarrassing and she's not sure why.

"You look so much like your mother," Kelly says. "It's been years since I've seen her. I feel like you've been hidden away from me."

"Okay, yeah, that would be nice. But I don't have my own line. Nan usually answers." She glances around, but Nan has gone outside to fetch Great Aunt Bride.

"I'll keep that in mind," Kelly says. She squeezes her hand and moves towards the door. Imogene catches the pitch of her voice rising to meet Great Aunt Bride's squeal.

Kelly calls early the next afternoon. "Why don't you come over for supper?" she says. "I know it's Sunday night, but I'm only home for two more days. And I loves your mother to pieces and you're a gorgeous piece of her. I want to get a bit of ya before I leave."

"Sure, I can do that."

"Oh my God, I'm right excited. I feel like I used to when Maggie and I would be getting into trouble," Kelly says. Her titter pings in the earpiece.

Kelly greets her at the door with a wide hug. Her hair is teased tall in a banana clip and her nails and lips are coral pink. The front door leads right into the kitchen, which is homey and decorated with checkered curtains and cutesy placards on the wall: *Bless this Mess* and *Welcome to my kitchen, many have eaten here, few have died.* Kelly wears a shiny turquoise blouse and faded jeans. She looks like a parrot in a log cabin.

Supper turns out to be chicken fingers and taters from the takeout. White Styrofoam containers line the table. "Gotta have a droppa grease when I'm home," Kelly says. She plucks ice cubes out of a tray with her pink nails and drops them in glasses.

"Fine with me," Imogene says. "Every Sunday, it's usually Jiggs' with Uncle Eli and Aunt Trudy. Or Great Aunt Bride."

"Your mother used to get sick of it too," Kelly says. "She'd spit the salt meat out in her napkin."

Kelly pries the lids off the macaroni salad and coleslaw. "Mom and Dad have a card game and took Paul with them," she says. "I said, you can all get lost and leave me to my girl time." She pours Lambs rum into her cup and tops it off with Pepsi. "Cheers, my love," she says and they clink their glasses together. Imogene hopes for a splash of rum herself, but her cup is straight mix.

They talk about the basic stuff: what Imogene likes doing in school, what she wants to do when she graduates. Kelly gets nostalgic on the third refill. "I loved your nan and mother growing up. And your pop. He was so funny. I don't think many people knew that about him, how funny he was. My brothers were scared of him. He was so strong and had one of those stern faces, you know? And he tanned right dark. My brothers called him Black Gus. 'Look out, here comes Black Gus.'" Kelly dips her tater in the Styrofoam gravy bowl. "Such a loss when he died. I was over with Maggie in her room after the funeral. I'd say a thousand people came through your house."

"Yeah, Uncle Eli said the same thing."

"Maggie was devastated. But Agnes, my God. She was crushed with grief."

One of the only things Imogene knows about Pop was that he was crushed by a tree. She chews a fry and contemplates what a terrible thing it would be to mention the coincidence at this point in their conversation.

"But we all deal with tragedy differently," Kelly says. "My sister, she drove herself a bit nuts when her husband died. Made herself busy, never stopped moving, went back to school, like she could work through her sadness. Agnes did the opposite. After the accident, she was a different person for a while."

"What kind of person?"

"Oh, you know. How do I say this?" Kelly's pink lips flex. "When I got married, I said to Paul, 'I'm not being one of those women who gives it all up to take care of a man.' And your nan, well, I loves her, but she's of that generation. So there's Agnes and she becomes Mrs. Gus Tubbs when she's nineteen. And she has three kids and puts supper on the table every day. And Gus goes to cut wood and a tree falls on him and he's gone. And where did that leave her? Who was she anymore? It was hard to watch."

Imogene tries to think of the saddest she's ever seen Nan. She's seen her frustrated many times. But as for sadness, she's seen her eyes well up here and there. Always gone with a swipe.

"I would come over to see Maggie, and Agnes would be in bed. Or in her housecoat. She moved like everything hurt. Like the air was water around her and she was wading through it. Maggie couldn't stand it. 'Let's go out,' she'd say. Up the road, in the woods, as long as it wasn't in that house. And your pop, well, like I said, he was strong and scary. Gus had rules. And they all died with him."

"The rules?"

"Yup. Maggie started doing whatever she wanted." Kelly slurps her rum and Pepsi. "And you know, it was fun for me too. Mom didn't know what it was like at Agnes's. No questions asked."

Imogene twists a chicken finger in the capsule of barbeque sauce. "Did you know my father?" The sauce plumps up around the meat like it will spill out.

"Oh yes, I knew Tony. I was there when they met."

Kelly hops to her feet and strides out of the kitchen. Did Imogene say the wrong thing? Will she get kicked out now?

Kelly reappears with a large photo album. A sailboat scene graces the cover. "I know it's in here somewhere," she says. She flips through pages. "Here it is." She removes a Polaroid photo and hands it to Imogene.

The picture shows teenaged Maggie, pink tank top and cutoffs, long brown hair over one shoulder. She stands next to a dark-haired man with his arm around her waist. The man stares at the camera with a firm expression. Squarish jaw, small eyes.

"I took that on Butter Brook Beach," Kelly says. "I think they'd been on the go for a few weeks then."

The man's hair is slicked back, showing a V-shaped hairline. A widow's peak. Another one of the genetic things they did in biology class. She and Quincy and Crystal held back their hair to check each other's foreheads. Widow's peaks are recessive. Imogene does not have a widow's peak.

"What was he like?"

"He was nice. Quiet though. Not the most social guy."

Imogene holds the Polaroid close to her face. Nose, mouth, eyes. She can't tell if they look like hers.

"You've never seen a picture of him before?"

"No."

"I took a few that day. Your mother should have at least one," Kelly says. She studies Imogene's face. "She's never shown you a photo of Tony?"

"No."

"Well. It was pretty hard for her. She was a mess when he left. Let alone when she found out she was pregnant. I wouldn't want to look at his face either."

"Do you think I look like him?"

"It's hard to say. It was so long ago. You look like Maggie to me, but taller, with different colouring."

Imogene lays the photo down by its edges. It wouldn't be good to get chicken grease on it. She takes a deep breath. Kelly is leaving in a day. Now or never. "Did Maggie...were you guys around Cecil Jesso much? Back then, I mean."

"Cecil Jesso? I mean, I didn't really. He had parties all the time, though."

"So, Maggie didn't go to them?"

"They were mostly Cecil and his friends, as I recall. They were hard tickets even back then."

"So not as far as you know?"

"I mean, she might have." Kelly frowns. "Why do you ask that?"

"I was just wondering." Imogene clasps her hands together to keep them from fidgeting. "Some people say things about him and Maggie. And me."

"Who says that?"

"Kids at school." She can't say Nan. If she says Nan, Kelly might say something. To Nan, to Maggie.

"Well, those kids at school are little shits." Kelly stands and moves to the counter. She tops up her drink. "This place is rotten for gossip. Nobody has anything better to do than make up stories."

"So, it's not true then?"

"Of course it's not true." She grabs her purse from the counter and removes a pack of Du Maurier. "I mean, it's true Cecil Jesso couldn't be fuckin' trusted with his own mother. That guy is garbage." She digs out a cigarette. "I suppose they have a big tale about it, do they? That she was left alone at his house? That I'm no kind of friend to let her go somewhere like that?"

"No. No story, I mean. They call me Cec Junior. Things like that."

"Jesus fucking Christ." Kelly lights her smoke. "Does your mother know about this?"

"I don't think so."

"Good." She inhales deeply and glares at the lit end like it's betrayed her. "You tell anyone who says that to you that they're a fucking liar."

"It's not really happening much anymore."

"I gotta get an ashtray." Kelly stomps out of the room. Her voice trails off into the living room. "People got no idea about what poison their mouths can do, do they?"

"I guess."

"Hold on, Mom's always hiding the goddamn ashtray. She thinks it will keep people from smoking."

A mirror hangs next to the front door. Imogene takes the Polaroid to it. She scrutinizes his face and holds it next to her reflection in the mirror. The man in the photo seems aggravated; there are other things he'd rather be doing than get his picture taken. Maybe he's annoyed at Kelly, taking the photo. Imogene makes a face like him. Tony has sharp edges she can't see in her face.

"But if it's not happening anymore, it's okay, right?" Kelly's voice pours in from another room. "I mean, you don't believe any of that, do you?"

"No," Imogene says. She takes the bottle of rum and pours some into her Pepsi. She stirs it around with her finger. "I don't listen to what people say."

ten

1990

Two years ago when they replaced the bridge over St. Felix's River, they said it would last a hundred years. But it's going to wash out with the spring thaw. Fluorescent warning signs and pylons pepper the pavement before it. Everyone who lives on the other side of the river has been instructed to get over, ASAP. But it's only Joyce MacIssac's family and a couple of Benoits and they have relatives on the other side to stay with.

The river is packed with ice slabs: thick, and marbled with filth. Uncle Eli says it's from all the rain this spring and the erosion from clear cutting. There is so much ice it brims over the edge of the pavement under the guardrail. Like there's no need for a bridge, one could step neatly across on the level mountain of ice and sludge.

The CBC is out to film the bridge washing out. People wait in parked cars and trucks to witness the disaster. Imogene and Rita ask Nan to take them down. "It's deplorable how people around here love misery," she says. "I wouldn't be surprised if they bring popcorn." And a few minutes later, "I suppose it's a good thing for you two to see what happens when you don't do something right the first time." The three of them head over in the Beretta.

From the back seat, Imogene can see Liam, Randy, and Nick standing close to the bridge's edge. Liam's hair is longer in the front these days, similar to Nick's. She realizes she hardly sees him now that he's been put in the Basic stream and she's in Academic. Even in a school of 130, it's possible to avoid people.

Every few minutes, the packed ice emits a loud, dry groan, and Liam, Randy, and Nick match the sound with whoops and yeahs. They're just trying to get on the news. Losers. "Nick should stand farther away," Rita says.

The cracks and moans quicken and multiply. "Sounds like it's giving birth," Nan says. A police car arrives. The three boys take begrudging steps away from the bridge. Liam pauses to flick his cigarette into the ice.

The cracks fill the air and then there is water. It overwhelms the paved surface of the bridge and the packed gravel on the edges sweeps away like fine dust. "Sweet Jesus," Nan says, her palms on the dashboard. The pavement disappears under a flood of brown muck and then a deeper grinding and groaning.

"I wonder how long the culvert will last," Rita says. Imogene has been in the culvert; she has hidden both there and under the Butter Brook one to smoke and listen to the echoes of passersby. Names and messages are spray painted inside: RC + DA for Rosarie Coish and Dwayne Abbott. FUCK YOU in block letters, probably a contribution from Liam.

The pavement strips off like leather. There is a metallic boom. Scraping sounds pierce the air. The culvert dislodges itself and the storming army of ice and water shove it out. Shouts and exclamations bellow from neighbouring vehicles. The CBC reporter moves the camera to follow the culvert, now fully free. It twists 180 degrees and begins rolling down the river, pushed by the flood of ice, out towards the bay. It's like watching a toilet paper tube crush an ant path. Imogene feels her eyes widen at the spectacle, the pure destruction of it. Go, dirty culvert, go.

Shrill stinging whoops fill the space around them. Nan sucks air through her teeth. "Moron," she says.

Cecil Jesso stands on top of the cab of his truck, toasting the escaping culvert with a bottle of Black Horse. "Giver, ya fuckin' bastard," he yells. Masculine cackles egg him on from below: Murray Wells and Bryce Benoit inside the cab. Cecil bounces on his heels, waving his beer, his orange hair electric around his head. He wears a blue and black plaid shirt and its tail flaps around his saggy denim arse. He turns to toast the CBC van. Imogene can see his fly is undone.

"Just what we need as a community," Nan says. "That drunken idiot on the provincial news."

Her irritation heats up the car. Rita wipes condensation off the window while hiding a giggle in her other hand. Imogene keeps her face straight. Who knows who is watching her reaction? She catches a glimpse of Liam, Randy, and Nick standing on the side of the road, all doubled over with laughter. What if other bridges wash out? French Brook or Butter Brook? They're already on a boil order. If other bridges wash out, it would take nothing to chip St. Felix's into smaller bits. And if Butter Brook Bridge washed out, they'd be stuck on the same bit as Cecil. They'd have to share resources. What if they'd all have to gather somewhere, ration fresh water and food? Cecil bringing them dirty potatoes, a brace of rabbits. Right proud and heroic. Kelly's voice comes back into her ears, tart with rage. *Cecil Jesso couldn't be fuckin' trusted with his own mother.*

The night Kelly and her ate chicken, she felt like asking to keep the Polaroid of Tony and Maggie. It sat on the table and Kelly kept glancing at it as she smoked. Like she wanted to give it to Imogene, but it might become an issue if Maggie found out about it. And it's probably for the best, because this way, Imogene doesn't have to look at it over and over. She tries to picture it sometimes, searching for resemblance. But it's already blurred in her mind. It's better not to have it. After all, it's just one photo. You can't tell much from one photo.

Murray coaxes Cecil down by showing him where to put his foot to lower himself. What if she could make him fall with the power of her mind? She imagines him toppling, full upside-down. Flat on his head, done with a snap. And he'd be gone. She thinks about when she hit Liam, so many times. How good it felt to let herself be mean. If Cecil was gone, she wouldn't have to worry about bumping into him. People would shut up about what might have happened between him and Maggie; no point in speaking ill of the dead. Or maybe people wouldn't be afraid to finally say what he is. Everyone would line up to spit on his grave.

There is a large bang. The culvert, going over something hard. It is in the distance, swaying on the beach.

"What will they do with it?" Imogene says.

"Drag it up on land somewhere," Nan says.

"It'll do some damage out there."

"Yeah, it might rearrange some beach rocks," Rita says. "Can't have that."

"I think we've seen enough," Nan says. "Let's beat the rush out of here."

"Yes, there must be at least fifteen cars," Rita says.

Nan shoots Rita a look to silence her. They pull out past the CBC van. Imogene looks back at the culvert, spinning on the shore. She imagines how it sounds inside it now. The drum of the waves, the wet static of rain. It could soothe you to sleep, if you weren't scared of rolling away.

eleven

Everyone is losing their minds over the wrestlers. The St. Felix Helixes took gold in the regionals and the school will host the provincial tournament. Mr. Percy has sent three notices home so far: Please support the visiting athletes by offering to billet one.

Nan says if the school really wanted people to allow a bunch of strange boys into their homes, they'd pay them. Who knows who these boys are, who knows how dirty. Someone could bring bedbugs into your house. Or rob you blind. But on Wednesday, she announces Imogene will be sleeping on the couch and the billet will take her room. No one's going to say Agnes Tubbs isn't charitable.

At first, Rita and her friends complain because volleyball practice is on hold due to preparations for the wrestling tournament. But when they realize there will be up to sixty guys ages 15 - 18 competing in singlets, they join the excitement. Wish Benoit brags about his training routine: before matches, he runs in layers of sweaters topped with garbage bags. "Sweating off a few pounds helps if you want to drop into the top of the weight class beneath you," he says. "I eat lots of garlic and onions before every match. When we start, I breathe right in my opponent's face. Right when we shake hands. Hhhhiiii."

Imogene is not looking forward to a weekend with some strange guy around. How embarrassing it will all be. Imogene's little house, like a large shoebox, no basement, no second floor. Hard to imagine at one point Nan, Pop, Uncle Kenneth, and Uncle Eli all lived here. The boys were almost grown when Maggie was born, so Nan never felt the push to expand. And when Pop died, there was less incentive and money. Imogene feels like her and Nan are always on top of each other. A stranger in the house will be two days of inescapable discomfort.

Corey Mercer says if Dwight Talbot is with the Gander wrestling team, he's getting a pounding. When Gander lost the finals last year, Dwight and a couple of others keyed up the buses of the rival schools. They wrote *faggots* and *fuck you* on the St. Felix bus. The other ones don't wrestle, but that fucker Dwight does. Corey's claims get equal amounts of steely approval and eye rolling. Natalie says Corey's all talk and when Nick threatened to jump in for Randy Lundrigan that time Corey and Randy got into it, Corey backed right off.

"There could be other reasons for that though," Crystal says. "Corey had no problems with Nick."

"Yeah, but the number one reason is Corey knew he'd get his ass kicked." And Natalie's cousin Georgette goes to school with Dwight Talbot and she says he is way bigger than Corey.

On Friday, Nan goes to pick up the billet. Imogene clears out the top drawer of her dresser where she keeps her underwear so it will be empty for the billet to use and he won't get a chance to peek at her panties. "Maybe he'll be cute," Rita said on the bus. "Call me after and tell me what he looks like."

Rita hopes to get Ashley King as a billet. He went out with Teresa Loder a couple of years ago and if she and him hang out, it might make Nick jealous. Nick and Teresa have been going out for over eight months now and it remains Rita's main disdain. "What does he see in her?" Rita says. "She's a little bitch. She has the worst home perm. She never closes her mouth when she chews her gum." "Like a cow and its cud," Imogene says. Rita delights in this image and whenever Teresa leaves a room or passes them in the hallway, she mimics her slack, churning mouth.

Nan returns a bit after four. She opens the door and a dark-haired boy with a duffle bag enters. He is tall, stick-thin, but sweet faced, big clear eyes and smiley. He looks around. "Cool," he says. He sees Imogene.

"I'm Jamie."

"I'm Imogene."

"I know. This house is wicked."

"Yeah, right."

"It's like a Christmas card."

"Here, you can put that in my room."

Imogene reaches for his duffle bag, but he takes it himself. She points to her bedroom door and he opens it.

"This your room?"

"Yeah."

"Cool, not what I expected."

Imogene glances around. The room still has the pastel forget-me-not wallpaper Maggie liked in junior high. Imogene has enough stuff up so the dainty flowers act like frames around images. The Depeche Mode poster Violet gave her, pictures of INXS and Billy Idol, movie posters from the Kwik Stop's video rentals: *The Return of the Jedi, Dirty Dancing.* A framed photo on her dresser of her and Rita dressed up as Bert and Ernie for Halloween. Her old bunny, Teeny, propped up on her pillow. An ancient bulletin board with song lyrics clipped from *The Newfoundland Herald.* Some of her lists hang there too. Shit, she should have put those things away.

"What did you expect?" she says.

"I dunno, girl's room. Unicorns and pink things. I don't have any sisters."

"Well, I didn't get the canopy bed I asked Santa for, so this is it."

"Ha. You're a hard case."

He pulls a Kodak Instamatic out of the top of his duffle bag. It looks like a slim black brick. He points it at her and clicks.

"Hey, let me know first," she says.

"That wouldn't be fun though."

"So, you're from St. John's?"

"Hardly. I'm from Mount Pearl."

"Sounds mountainous."

"It is. Lots of mountains. And the mountains are round, like pearls."

"You do much skiing?"

"Oh yeah, all the time. Is it just you and your grandmother here?"

"Yup."

"No brothers or sisters?"

"No." She almost says as far as I know, but doesn't.

"Nice. I got three older brothers. They're assholes. And they stink."

"At least it's not quiet all the time."

Nan calls them out to the kitchen. She's made tea and arranged jam-jams and lemon cream crackers on a plate, like when she has the Women's Institute crowd over. "Cool," Jamie says, "I love tea," and he eats a jam-jam in two bites. He asks Nan question after question: "How many children do you have? Grandchildren? How old is this house? Have you always lived out here? What was it like then?" Nan practically purrs at him. She refills his cup three times and asks if he wants anything in particular for breakfast or snacks, she can run out and get whatever, it's no bother.

Jamie says he'd like to take a walk around and take photos if it's okay and Nan says of course. "Go with him, Imogene," she says. "Imogene can show you some spots. She's always hiking around. Sometimes she comes back smelling like cigarettes though. You don't smoke, do you, Jamie?"

It's the first time Nan has acknowledged Imogene smokes. "No, I don't smoke," Jamie says. "That stuff will stunt your growth." He winks at Imogene behind Nan.

They tramp down the path to the brook. Jamie takes a second camera with him. He says it's a 35 millimetre Minolta, and Imogene nods even though she doesn't know what that means. He stops to take pictures of all kinds of things: a rusty tire by the path, droplets of water on tree buds, a dead bird. He has his own smokes and balances one in his mouth while he frigs around with his fancy camera. "This place is gorgeous," he says. "You can just walk down to the ocean, anytime? Wicked. Do you and your nan own all this land? Wicked. I bet some pile of magic mushrooms grow around here."

"Do you have an art project you're working on or something?" Imogene says. "It's too bad it's all spring muck and dirty grass right now."

"No, I just like taking photos," Jamie says. "If I lived around here, I'd watch the sun set all the time. And the sun rise. I'd have to balance that out. What deadly pictures I'd have. I bet I could sell them."

Imogene takes him to the shore and he uses up a roll of film on waves and clumps of seaweed and Aubrey Murphy's worn-out lobster pots. On the way back, they meet Rita and Cherry. Jamie tells them to pose and they strut around on the road, striking cheesy poses in their track jackets. Cherry tells Jamie he has a townie accent and he pretends to not understand her. Rita mouths, "He's cute," at Imogene and she shrugs back at her. But yes, Jamie is very cute.

Cherry says they have to get back to help her mom. "Immy, can I get a ride with you to the dance tonight?" Rita says. Which is surprising since she usually gets a ride with Steve. Imogene says sure.

She and Jamie walk the pavement and he takes pictures of patterns in pavement cracks. Quincy MacIssac and Teddy Campbell appear on their BMX bikes. They stop and Quincy asks Jamie a bunch of questions about wrestling and what weight class he's in and then runs through a list of who he'll probably be matched up against. He asks Jamie how long he's been wrestling and Jamie says he's been on the team for two years. But he's got three older brothers, so really, he's been wrestling his whole life. Teddy does pop-a-wheelies back and forth on the road and says, "Hey, you should wrestle Cec here for practice. She's a savage."

"Fuck off, Teddy."

"Why do you call her Cec?" Jamie says. Imogene's guts clatter down a flight of stairs.

"Everyone calls her that," Teddy says.

"Why?" Jamie says.

Teddy's lips buckle with consideration. "Cause her and Cec both have red hair, I guess," he says. "Watch this, I bet I can catwalk all the way to that tree."

Nan drops them off at 9:30 for the dance, even though Imogene tells her no one shows up until at least 10:30. Dwayne Abbott and Rosarie Coish are doing the music, and their heads are visible behind the speakers and stacks of tapes at the back of the Rec Centre. Tables and chairs are shoved against the walls. A few dark shapes sit at them. The visiting teams stand around in self-protective clusters. The gym floor is deserted. Dances never get going until the older students arrive and most of them drink in the woods behind the building until later. Mr. Percy tries to enforce staying in once your hand is stamped, but you can't really make anyone stay in one place if they don't want to.

Everyone has their coats on. "The place is an ice box," Rita says. "You'd think they'd turn the heat up a couple of hours before the dance starts so it isn't freezing. Let's go see who's outside."

Imogene and Jamie follow Rita along the path by the Rec Centre walls. There are a few empty parking spots at the back before the ball field and they head towards the trees behind the bleachers. Imogene recognizes the head and shoulders and neon yellow ball cap of Wish Benoit. Nick, Teresa, Cherry, and a couple of visiting wrestlers stand with them.

"Hi," Cherry says. Wish tips his beer bottle at them. When Teresa sees Rita, she turns to face Nick and coils her hands around his waist inside his jacket.

"Wish, you better watch out for Percy," Rita says.

"He's too busy babysitting inside," Wish says. "All this 'you people are ambassadors' shit is to make sure nobody fights. He's not going to care about a couple of beer."

"I'm froze," Rita says. She turns to Jamie and lays her fingers on his cheek. "Are you cold?"

"You're like ice," he says. "You want my coat? He shucks off his Mount Pearl school jacket and hangs it around her shoulders. Rita smiles at him in thanks and it bites Imogene somewhere deep under her lungs.

"What a gentleman," Cherry says.

"We should get coats like those," Wish says. "Percy says if we win, we'll get championship tracksuits. Coats would be more useful though."

"You can't believe anything out of that guy's mouth," Nick says. "He promised the softball team hats and T-shirts last year and nothing happened."

Headlights appear around the edge of the Rec Centre.

"Who's that now," Wish says. "Probably Mark."

A voice from the front of the building reaches them: "Cops cops cops."

Overhead lights flash on the car in a blue-red swirl. "Shit," Wish says. He lurches into the woods. Nick grabs the case of beer from the ground and follows. "Go a different way," Wish yells. Their backs retreat into swaying evergreen branches, Wish's neon ball cap like a bouncing signal. "Hat," Jamie calls. "Take off your hat." Wish yanks it off and they disappear into the dark.

"Should we run too?" Jamie says.

"We're not doing anything wrong," Imogene says.

The cop car pulls up side-on to them. "What are you doing out here in the dark?"

"Getting some fresh air," Rita says.

"This area is off limits after seven p.m."

"Oh, we didn't know."

"It says so on the sign."

"Sorry, we didn't see that."

"You didn't see that sign on the fence?"

"Sorry, officer," Jamie says. "I'm from Mount Pearl. We didn't know where to go."

"Go into the dance now."

"Okay. Thanks, officer."

The appearance of the cops makes people mill inside. Rosarie and Dwayne start playing faster stuff and favourites: AC/DC and "The Babylon Mall." Rita disappears into the bathroom with Natalie Sampson. Jamie takes Imogene by the hand and they're off. They fast dance to three songs in a row and his three teammates appear beside them. Jamie introduces all of them to Imogene and one of them, a tall guy with his head shaved on the sides, twirls Imogene around a bunch of times all corny old school, but funny. When the song ends, she catches Crystal Seymour staring at her with something like confusion.

Corey Mercer shows up after eleven. Sister Bernadette leans way in to stamp his hand and get a whiff of his breath. Mr. Percy has said if you show up at a dance with any sign of intoxication, you'll be expulsed from the building and face suspension. Imogene doesn't see the point of throwing someone out. What will they do then? Hang out in the parking lot? What if it's below zero outside and you get hypothermia? It's not like they can ever prove someone's been drinking. Rita once said Crystal Seymour will have a sip of beer, just to get the smell on her, then act drunk all night and none of the chaperones do anything. "That's 'cause she's a shitty actress," Imogene said.

Dwight Talbot stands by the canteen, surrounded by the Gander team. They all make a point of laughing loudly at each other's jokes. Corey and Donny pass them and they all exchange slinky-eyed glances.

"Corey's here," Imogene says. "I wonder if there will be a racket."

"Is there going to be a fight?" Jamie says. "Excellent. Big ol' tiff."

"What do people do in Mount Pearl when they fight?" Imogene says. "Have a ski-off?"

"We hurl pearls at each other."

"Sounds expensive."

"We can afford it."

When "We Will Rock You" comes on, the Gander team takes the dance floor and start headbanging in a circle. It causes a ricochet effect; the rest of the teams congregate, bouncing and screeching the lyrics. Jamie slides his slim Instamatic camera out of his pocket and aims it at the dance floor. One of them sees the camera and hauls down the edge of his track pants to expose a moment of butt cheek. Jamie laughs. Click-wind-click goes the camera.

Corey and Donny have collected recruits: Liam, Randy, and Quincy, of all people. They inch closer to the bopping bunch of Gander guys. When Dwight headbangs his way to the outer rim of the circle, Corey bolts forward and shoves him hard. Dwight staggers and Corey punches him in the stomach. The Gander guys rush in and then Donny, Liam, Randy, and Quincy. "Fight fight fight." The Rec Centre lights open all at once, screaming fluorescent on the wiggling heap of polyester and cotton, track jackets hiked up on grappling bodies, expanses of white cotton briefs against bare backs. Booing and jeers from students as they follow the boys being dragged to the main doors. Imogene catches a glimpse of Rita's brown hair and Nick's face separating behind a stack of chairs in the corner.

Mr. Percy drags Corey and Dwight by their collars. Sister Bernadette pops open the double door for more room. "Let 'em fight outside," Wish yells. "Let 'em work it out." Imogene hears a snuffling sound. Jamie stands beside her, shaking in laughter. He holds his camera at collarbone level and winds and presses, winds and presses. Click, wind, click.

The next morning, Mr. Percy and the Gander coach announce that all members of the St. Felix's and Gander teams involved in last night's fight are disqualified from participating in the tournament. They are deeply disappointed that a few people have to leave such a negative taint on an event like this, an event everyone has worked so hard to organize. Corey, Liam, Randy, Donny, and Quincy are not allowed in the Rec Centre to watch the tournament, but Imogene, Rita, and Jamie spy them in the distance. They perch on swings in the community playground, smoking and calling out obscure, warbled exclamations, the occasional swear word.

As they watch from the parking lot, a passing car slows. The window lowers, a can of 7UP flies out and hits Rita square in the back. "Ow!" The car pulls away with a hand out the window, middle finger extended.

"Who was that?"

"Teresa," Rita says. She straightens her coat. "Fucking soaked now."

"You crowd are all cracked," Jamie says. He crouches and takes a photo of the 7UP can, sputtering on the gravel.

Mr. Percy has arranged volunteers to carpool the wrestlers out to the bus station. Jamie gets Imogene and Nan to pose in the living room. They smile on the sofa with their lips and knees shut. "I'll mail you a copy," Jamie says. Nan insists on taking a photo of him wearing his silver medal. "You'll want to remember," she says. "It's good to be proud sometimes."

Nan says she's going to make Jamie a sandwich for the bus. Jamie props up his camera on Imogene's dresser with a couple of books. "Wish I had a tripod," he says. He sets the timer three times and after each one, he hops back to sit next to Imogene on her bed with his arm around her shoulders. She lets hers slip around his waist, the skin between the edge of his jeans and his T-shirt on the inside of her arm is right there. There is a blue spot on the side of his forehead, by his hairline. She presses her fingertip to it. "You have a pen mark right there," she says.

"It's a scar," he says. "That's what happens when you get stabbed in the head with a pencil."

"Who did that?"

"My brother Eric. He's an arsehole."

"Why'd he do that?"

"Like I said, big arsehole." Jamie's fingers brush her shoulder, inside the sleeve of her T-shirt. "I think it was for something I said, like the Habs are better than the Leafs. He looks for any reason to call you a homo and pound you."

"It looks like a blue freckle."

"I tell people it's a tattoo. I'm going to build onto it someday, make it into a third eye.

After the third photo, he turns his face to hers and they kiss soft, then with rhythm and tongues. "You're a good kisser," he says. "I could kiss you all day." Imogene wants to close the bedroom door, which is slightly ajar, but Nan would be over like an alarm. So they kiss and check for Nan and kiss and check. Nan calls from the kitchen about the sandwiches being all done. Imogene hops up. "You go on out," Jamie says. "I need a minute."

She waves when he gets in the car and calls Rita to tell her about the kissing. Rita is happy about it, but happier Nick and Teresa are broken up now. "He hasn't called me yet, though," she says.

Two weeks later, a thank-you note from Jamie Clark arrives in the mail with the photo of Imogene and Nan on the couch. There is a separate envelope for Imogene, which she snatches out of Nan's hand and takes to her bedroom. A photo of her and Jamie on her bed. Written on the back: *Some cute. Look me up if you're ever on the Avalon. xo.*

twelve

If you don't tell Clyde Campbell what you want on your fries, he adds everything: ketchup, vinegar, gravy, dressing, salt, pepper. Imogene doesn't mind, really. "How can you eat that?" Nan says. "That man is foolish. Looks like a chemical spill." Meanwhile, she douses hers with so much vinegar, her eyelids flicker while she eats. Imogene imagines Nan with a secret vinegar addiction. She's picked it up from years of using it as an all-purpose cleaner. It's gotten into her system and now she has to have it, she's a junkie, man.

They are waiting at the Petro-Can for the bus to arrive. Maggie arranged to fly into Deer Lake. On the phone, she said she wants to take the bus to St. Felix's so she can enjoy the scenery. "I can't imagine enjoying the scenery," Imogene said. "Once you leave, you realize how beautiful it is," Maggie said. Imogene rolled her eyes on the phone at that one.

Maggie will stay the summer with Nan and Imogene. She wants to help Nan with the house and work occasional shifts for Uncle Eli at the club. Miss Coffey suggested Imogene's name, and now Imogene has a summer job at the Youth Centre library. Her days will be spent repairing or replacing damaged books, reorganizing the card filing system, helping catalogue new additions and guaranteeing she gets no tan whatsoever. Which will get some comments. *Oh my, you're some white. You been sick?* But it will keep her out of the house and away from people she doesn't like.

"There's the bus," Nan says. "Come on, she probably has lots of stuff." A surge of anxiety wafts through Imogene, like she's about to walk on stage. Before she left the house, she went through her notebook and reviewed the questions:

1. What was my father like?
2. Am I anything like him?
3. Why doesn't Nan know anything about him?
4. Why hasn't Tony been found? Does he really know I exist?
5. Why do people talk about Cecil Jesso and you?

She drew a line through number six: *Did something happen between you and Cecil Jesso?* Staring at it made her shake and she slapped the notebook shut. What if the answer is yes? Maybe it's better not to ask. Maggie will be here until Labour Day. There will be time to ask these and other questions. Like, how did she and Tony meet and was he nice and what the fuck can we do to convince everyone in this dump that Cecil Jesso has nothing to do with them? She's not going through this shit again in grade eleven.

Maggie is the fifth person off the bus. She wears tight faded jeans, high-top sneakers with baby-blue slouch socks and a baby-blue baggy sweatshirt. Her bangs stretch up, reaching for the sky before arching back in sweet surrender to form a frozen wave of rich, dark hair. She smiles, exposing her deep-set Tubbs' dimples, like nickels in her cheeks. She is thirty-one years old.

Maggie hugs Imogene hard, and then regards her at arm's length. Imogene imagines she looks pretty unkempt (bit of a streel today, according to Nan). Ponytail, oversized T-shirt and jeans. They look each other up and down. Maggie's smile is huge, but her eyes are too shiny. Everything feels a little off. Which is to be expected. Who is Imogene to her anyway? Some foreign thing that invaded her body before she knew her body at all? The Creature from the Swamp of Past Mistakes in Judgement. The Secret Monster from the Dark Pit of Wrong Place, Wrong Time. Imogene averts her eyes from Maggie's. "I like your blue clothes," she says. Maggie hugs Imogene again, leaning into it so their shoulders touch, but no chest to chest contact. "My God," Maggie says. "You change so fast. We're going to have so much fun doing your hair."

On the drive home, Maggie sits in the front of the Beretta and spouts about Ontario and Robert. She makes comments about the potential real-estate value of random St. Felix's homes. "With the fishery in trouble, there won't be new families moving out here. But as retirement homes or upscale cabins, there could be some great spots." Nan says nothing, but a tiny spasm flutters through her closed jaw.

Over supper, Maggie asks Imogene questions. "How was your report card?"

"Good."

"Do you like school?"

"Sometimes."

"Who do you hang out with?"

"Rita."

"Gotta boyfriend?"

"No." (Although she has the photo of Jamie and her in her bedroom and the ones of Anton, so some proof something happened a couple of times.)

Maggie continues to grin in a way that doesn't touch her eyes. She makes a show of doing the dishes. "I'm not a guest," she says. "I'm going to be here all summer." She produces gifts: a new popcorn maker, a forest-green hooded Roots sweatshirt for Imogene. She says everyone wears them in Toronto. Dark green is a good colour for Imogene.

Before bed that night, Imogene tiptoes out into the living room to get her copy of *The Handmaid's Tale.* Nan is asleep on the couch, *The National* blaring on TV. Maggie is on the phone. She leans against the wall, eyes on the kitchen window. Each time she speaks, she makes sure to smile, but her face is wooden as she listens.

"I forgot how fresh the air is here," she says. "I love seeing the cliffs and the water. No, Robert, you can't compare it to Lake Ontario. Here, you can see where things end. I like that. The house needs a coat of paint though. Maybe that's something Imogene and I can do."

Jesus, more chores. Maggie lets out a sharp sigh. "No. No, I'm not getting into it. We've been over this." She passes a hand down her face as she listens. "Robert, I told you, that isn't why I came home. I'm focussing on making positive memories, okay? Just let me have a nice summer with my mother and Imogene."

She doesn't say my mother and my daughter. Imogene steals another look before turning back. Maggie's gaze centres on the window, the image of the trees silhouetted against the darkening sky and her own reflection in the glass.

thirteen

The Youth Centre library has racks for paperbacks and magazines. These are closest to the tables. Most of the paperbacks are romance and horror, lots of Danielle Steele and Stephen King. Mothers sit at the table and send their kids to pick out a quota of books from the children's section. They browse through the latest *Chatelaine* and *Good Housekeeping* while they wait. Some of them use the magazines to hide the steamier novels; Imogene regularly dislodges bodice rippers from *Women's World* magazines.

Her job entails a bit of everything. She stamps book cards when Miss Coffey is on break, she organizes the card catalogue, she helps people find what they're looking for. Charlotte Whalen needs information on the history of the Catholic School Board for a distance course with MUN, Aubrey Murphy is putting in a new septic tank. She re-glues and tapes binding back into books, she arranges things in ABC order. Everything has a place and a designated category and everything is out in the open. She likes being surrounded by answers and history. She likes finding out what people want to know about. She reads during her lunch breaks, mouthfuls of peanut butter and banana sandwiches over *Biloxi Blues, The Greenlanders, Less Than Zero, Skeleton Crew*.

When Imogene isn't working, she tends to take long walks. Maggie sleeps on the couch, so the whole living room feels like her space. Nan is always in the kitchen. With Maggie home, there are regular visitors: relatives and old friends from school. They sit around the kitchen table, gabbing and making comments on Imogene if she is present. "My, she's so tall, Maggie. And the red hair. Who's that actress, the redhead? Molly Ringwald. But she doesn't look like her." Or, "Why don't you smile for us, Immy? Give us a smile. Oh, you're right lovely." Great Aunt Bride comes by with a shoebox of old photos which Maggie and Nan gush over for hours. "Look at this one, Imogene," Great Aunt Bride says. "This is your mother before you were born. You can really see her in you." She holds up a picture of Maggie and Kelly Abbott. Kelly wears overalls and has fluffy blond hair. Maggie wears her hair parted in the middle. Her arms are slender in a tank-top—the same one she wears in Kelly's photo of her and Tony. A silver heart on a chain around her neck points to breasts which look newly large. Less than a year before she was born. Terrifying.

On walks, Imogene usually ends up by French Brook, where she sits and practices her smoking. She doesn't want to be a smoker, but figures she should know how to smoke and not gag, like she did with Violet. She now can inhale without choking and hold the cigarette casually. Smoking gives people an excuse to stand in a circle and talk. Imogene doesn't think the smokers at school are cooler than anyone else, but they do seem to be having better conversations.

Imogene walks along French Brook until she reaches The Best Rock, a large grey slab of granite sheltered by an overhanging tree. The rock juts out so she can perch on its edge and look straight down into the current. She sits and smokes and watches the water. The best times to do this are cooler, overcast days. The coldness of the water creeps up through the rock and into her legs and up her back and she lets herself get colder. And being cold is okay, because she can leave any time—be home in minutes, safe and warm. There's something delicious about it because she can walk away and nothing bad happens. Like letting a dog in a cage sniff your hand against the bars.

One day in early July, she is perched on the rock, trying to blow smoke rings. The trees across the brook rustle and part and there is Liam Lundrigan. They haven't spoken since the gym class after the infamous floor hockey game and Mr. Percy's enforced public apology. And now, he stares at her over the water. He is three stepping stones away.

"What are you doing here?" Liam says. His eyes narrow in the sunlight.

"I live here," Imogene says.

"What, under that rock?"

"No, this is my grandmother's land."

"Like fuck." Liam spits on the ground as some kind of emphasis. "Agnes Tubbs only owns half this brook. Murray Wells has the other half."

"Yeah, and I'm sitting on my half."

"Depends if you want to split it right down the middle. Maybe you actually own the top half and Murray owns the bottom half."

"Don't be retarded." This is the longest two-way conversation she has ever had with Liam Lundrigan. "Anyway, what do you care?" she says. "You're trespassing either way."

"Not true. I'm working for Murray," he says. His chest puffs out slightly. "I'm getting paid to be on his property."

"Well, I guess we're both in the clear then."

"Guess so. Give us a smoke."

She looks down at the pack of Player's Light beside her. "Here," she says. "I'll toss you one." She scrambles to get the pack open.

"Fuck that, Cecil, you can't throw for shit. I'll come over there."

Imogene takes a quick glance around for weapons: a stick or nice-sized rock. But it is too late, two giant strides and he arrives on the grass next to the tree. He could stretch out towards her. One push, she'd be in the water, hard slimy stones in her back. She jumps to her feet. Liam raises his eyebrows. Smelling fear, he can smell fear.

"If you're going to call me that I'm not giving you anything," she says.

She balances herself on the rock and gets ready to bolt. He takes a small step closer:

"Jesus, sorry, *Imogene*. What are you going to do, go up to your house and get your hockey stick?"

In one movement, he reaches out and plucks the pack of smokes from her hand. He rummages one out and lays the pack gently on top of the rock.

"I didn't know you smoked, *Imogene*." He opens his mouth wide to over-emphasize her name. She doesn't know what to say. She fishes out a cigarette as well. Smoking: something to fuck around with when you can't think of anything to say or do. The cool way of twiddling your thumbs—that could be a slogan. She tries to light one of her matches and hears a click. Liam stands with his lighter out. She hesitates for a second (what if he tries to set her on fire? He could light her hair or eyebrows) before leaning in. She keeps her eyes down. His T-shirt is splattered with white paint. He looks down at it.

"I'm painting Murray's fence," he says.

"Fun."

"Heard your mom was home."

"Yep."

"Must be nice. She's up on the mainland, right?"

She examines the tip of her cigarette. When the comments about Maggie come, she's out of here. Although, it would be interesting to douse her smoke on his arm first.

"I'm only asking," he says. "My aunt Kelly went to school with her. She said she was nice." Liam inhales and blows out a line of smoke. "My old man showed up last week. He says he's going to stick around this time. We'll see about that."

"Where was he?"

"All over. He drives rigs."

She tries to picture Liam's father. Bill Lundrigan. She has a memory of a blond man in a truck, passing by.

"Anyway. I better get back to work before you decide to pound me." He tips the cigarette at her and moves back to the stepping stones. Thank Jesus. She drops hers on the ground and starts towards the path.

"Thanks for the smoke."

She glances back. Liam stands on Murray's side of the brook. He waves. Seriously? She stares at him. He blinks at her in the sun, and walks off. She itches to give the finger to his back. No, don't do it. He doesn't need encouragement to be a fucker again. The fact he thinks he can strut over and be a smoking buddy goes to show he's a remorseless arsehole. She spits on the ground where he stood, but it comes out stringy. Gross. Good thing he didn't witness that. Cec Jr, can't even spit neat. She tramps back to the house, looking for something to kick. But the path is bare. Nothing feels satisfying.

fourteen

Maggie lets Imogene drive the car. It's much easier than driving with Nan in the passenger seat, who white-knuckles the armrest and pumps the ghost of the brake pedal. They drive down to the end of the pavement, turn around in the MacIssacs' driveway and then up to the church parking lot. Maggie keeps two orange pylons in the trunk so Imogene can practice parallel parking. "This will be the hardest part of your driving test," she says. Imogene parks the car, over and over. Sometimes there are people in the cemetery. Once, Bryce Benoit and Murray Wells leaned on the fence and watched Imogene park while their wives weeded graves. "Well isn't that charming," Maggie said.

Maggie also likes to take Imogene "out." She dresses up for it every time. She packed an array of planned outfits, belts that match tops, earrings that match bracelets, shorts that show off her hips and neat little legs. It's a bit much as there are only three places to be taken: Seymour's Pool Hall, the take-out, and the Petro-Can. Maggie likes Seymour's the best. It has one pool table, three pinball games, a Space Invaders tabletop console, Pac-Man, and a jukebox that hasn't been updated since 1986.

Seymour's is two large rooms: one for the arcade and canteen counter, the other a barren room for the occasional teen dance. Every year, Victor Seymour paints the walls a pastel shade of cheap, latex paint, and if picked at, it peels off like sunburned skin to reveal the previous colours. There is a sign that reads *Any vandals will be banned from Seymour's and have to deal with the* RCMP.

Maggie and Imogene go to Seymour's during quiet times, like early Monday evenings. They play pool badly, but can do so without shame. Bending over the long green table feels vulnerable when there are others present. Imogene expects a shove, a goose, a rude comment, farting noises. But her and Maggie bend, shoot, miss, and scratch in peace. Maggie punches Opus's "Life is Life" into the jukebox. She does most of the talking. "We should play pool all the time! You can go back to school a pool shark. I want a Space Invaders game like this! Robert and I could use it as an end table." Crystal works the canteen counter for her summer job. She offers an occasional baleful smile at Maggie's exuberance.

One night, the pool table is occupied, so Maggie buys two hotdogs and two cans of pop and they drive all over St. Felix's. "This is what we used to do once we got our licences," she says. "We just drove around all night. Nothing better to do. I guess not much has changed." She says this with a titter.

She's still on edge. Imogene forces a smile. Imogene the silent alien. Or the Tony Green Monster. Or the Creature from the Rapist Lagoon.

"Butter Brook Beach," Maggie says. "Ha, this is where everyone used to go parking." She aims the end of her straw into her mouth while she drives. "You know, Imogene, you don't say much. And Mom doesn't tell me anything. All you've done is work at the library and skulk around the house. Who do you spend time with?"

Very few, actually, since most people see her as half drunken mongoloid and half skank. Very few because Imogene has proven she's angry and violent. She chews her hotdog. "Me and Rita do stuff," she says.

"Well, I hope things are okay. If you ever want to talk, you can call me. I know my mother's resources are limited, so you can always ask if you need anything."

Imogene nods. This is it.

"You and Tony drive around much?"

Maggie places her can in the cup holder. "Yes, he and I drove around. He didn't have a vehicle, but he'd borrow one from one of the guys he was working with. I'd tell Mom I was going for a walk over to Kelly's and he'd pick me up." She crumples her napkin in her fist. "Jesus, if Dad had been alive, he would have killed me."

"For being with him?"

"Hell, yes."

"Whose vehicle?"

"I told you, he didn't have one."

"I know, but whose did he borrow?"

"Oh, one of his buddies. Bryce or Murray probably. Aubrey Murphy."

"You didn't know?"

"Well, he had different ones all the time."

"They'd give him their car?"

"Sure. Those guys were all buddies."

Imogene thinks of Bryce Benoit's truck. One time, he was parked outside the Kwik Stop and Rita leaned against it while she was fixing her shoe. He and Wish came out and he said, "Wish, tell your friends other people's vehicles aren't for them to touch." He wiped her fingerprints off the door. Would Bryce Benoit loan some guy from Port aux Basques his truck? To drive around with Maggie Tubbs?

"Never thought you were around those guys much," Imogene says.

"Well, through Tony. Funny to see them around now. They seem so much older."

"They're up at Cecil Jesso's a lot."

Maggie stares out the windshield. "Yeah, they did back then too."

"Did you?"

"Did I what?"

"Hang out at Cecil's." Imogene's voice turns to dregs, like water sucked down a drain.

Maggie doesn't say anything, but she flicks the indicator to pull over. She parks the car on the edge of the ditch.

"Okay," she says. "I was a little afraid of this."

"What?"

Maggie shakes her head. "People whispered a few things back then. Rumours and lies." She keeps her hands on the wheel, like the car might decide to take itself out of park. "Only a couple of people knew about Tony and me where I was young. Besides Kelly Abbott, we were around Cec and those guys because Tony wanted to party and they were partiers. So, people think they're putting two and two together. They're not."

"Okay."

Maggie flicks the indicator again to turn onto the road. Her eyes are too shiny. "And when people don't know anything, they should keep their mouths shut."

"It's okay."

"I've been away too long. It's not fair to you. I haven't been fair."

"Don't worry about it."

Imogene should do something. Hug her. Say something good. Maggie exhales hard and grips the wheel. "Let's go home. I feel like just sitting on the couch and watching some crap on TV. Sound good?"

"Sure."

Maggie puts the car in drive and pulls out. She sighs a little. "Like I was saying before, think of us when you're finishing school. Because you don't have to stay here."

"I know."

"Robert and I are waiting to hear on a house in St. John's, something to rent out. If you want to go there, there will be a place for you. Maybe Mom too."

"Really?"

"I worry about her health. I'd like to see her closer to hospitals."

"I can see that."

"I'm not saying you have to leave here or that you should. I mean, Ontario drives me nuts sometimes, but when I left, I liked that no one knew me."

Imogene nods. Yes. Being a stranger. A great release fills her chest. Maggie says it's not true. She can say that now: my mother said it's not true. She gazes out the window. Past the Whalens, past the Clearys. They're all full of shit. Everyone can take their ideas and opinions and beliefs and stick them in their individual wood stoves.

"I mean, there's lots of great things about St. Felix's," Maggie says. "But in a place as small as this, people think they know your story. They trap you with it. Feeling trapped is the worst. You'll never be trapped if we can help you, Imogene."

"Thank you."

She takes one hand off the wheel and presses the radio on. "Every Rose has its Thorn," by Poison fills the car. An insipid song. She's relieved. If one of her favourites was on, it might make her react. She and Maggie, staring out the windshield, choking on silence.

Maggie stuffs the napkin wad into the ashtray. It struggles to stretch out, sides un-sticking from each other, like a waking moth. They turn around in the MacIssacs' driveway and head back.

fifteen

No one comes to the library on nice days. Miss Coffey tells Imogene to stay, in case anyone shows up. She says she has a doctor's appointment, but Imogene suspects she's going to her cabin. She's probably not supposed to leave the summer student in charge, but what odds.

Imogene turns on OZ FM and opens the front windows. It's sunny, but the breeze is cool. Around here, a day without goosebumps requires some kind of magic weather equation. If she wasn't in clear sight of the road, she'd sit outside and practice smoking. But all she needs is some nosy passerby calling the house. *I saw young Imogene having a puff in front of the children's library. Tsk, tsk.*

At least she can sit outside on the bench and read. Who could complain about that? She takes a stack of magazines with her. This is her summer—complete solitude or total lack of privacy. Both are inescapable. She opens a *National Geographic* magazine. "New Orleans contains a unique blend of American, Spanish and French culture," it says. The music, the food, the creepy graveyards that inspire crime movies and novels about vampires. She could go there, go to Mardi Gras. She could walk around fanning herself.

Someone is coming up the road. The silhouette and the slight hop in the swagger announce Liam Lundrigan. She holds the *National Geographic* to her face. She should have picked something bigger.

Liam starts up the Youth Centre driveway. Is he coming all the way over to torment her? What a loser. But he slows when he notices her and confusion ruffles his forehead. She should have stayed inside.

He stops at the bottom of the steps. "You work here, do you?"

"Yep."

"Summer job?"

"For now."

He spits on the ground. "Must get some boring."

"Better than sloggin' around a farm all day."

"I guess. You here by yourself?"

"What do you want?"

"Gotta get a book." He nods at the door. "I heard there might be some in there."

She sighs and lays the magazine down. She walks in first without holding the door for him.

"I need a book on how to build a deck," Liam says. "Or woodworking or something."

"Okay."

"Dad's been sayin' he's going to put a deck on the house for years. I didn't think he was ever gonna do it, but he brought home the lumber yesterday."

"We've got some stuff over here." She walks to the home section. Liam follows.

"But he wants to build it straight off the back of the house," he says. "I don't see the point in having a deck if you can't see the water from it. Even if it is less windy that way."

Imogene yanks books off shelves: *Home Renovations. Basic Carpentry. Home Repairs.* "What about this?" She hands him a glossy book entitled *Outdoor Building.* The cover shows a man in coveralls standing proudly by a spacious cedar deck.

"Yeah, something to give him ideas."

"Great. That all?"

He stares at her. His face is browner than the last time she saw him. He's kind of buttered-toast colour. Compared to him, she must look paper-white, like a New Orleans vampire.

"I don't know," he says. "This the best you got?"

"B'y, it's not like you're paying for it." She gestures to the shelves. "Go ahead, find something else."

"No. This looks good. I trust you."

"Yeah, right."

"I do. I'll sign it out."

Imogene scribbles his name and the date on the card. He stares at the return date like he's trying to memorize it.

"Maybe when the deck's done," he says, "you can come over for a barbeque."

"Maybe when the deck's done, I'll come over and set it on fire."

"Sounds like something you'd do." He folds the book under his arm. "Thanks for helping me out with my dick. I mean, my deck." He grins. "Maybe I'll tell people Imogene was by herself in the library and she helped me out with my deck."

"Maybe I'll tell them it wasn't a big problem."

"Oh. Nice one." He gives her a wink. She doesn't smile. "See you around," he says.

When his back disappears up the driveway, she shuts the windows. Anything to get the place ready to look closed, if necessary.

The next day, it rains so hard the walk from the car to the Youth Centre drenches her. Miss Coffey sits at the desk pinching the bridge of her nose between her eyes. "This rain is killing my head," she says.

No one shows up. Miss Coffey makes Imogene reorganize the card catalogue. Before closing, a figure comes up the driveway. The rain blurs everything, but Liam moves the same when wet. Imogene braces herself, but he uses the outside depository and leaves. He stamps down the driveway, hands thrust in his pockets, shoulders tight into himself. She retrieves *Outside Building* from the depository. Completely soaked. It's about a mile from the Lundrigans' place to the Youth Centre. He must be feeling pretty spitey to walk the whole way in the rain.

According to Miss Coffey, when books are returned damaged, a form has to be filled out. The price of the original book has to be retrieved from the files and a bill is mailed to the person who returned it. Imogene takes the book to the kitchenette in the back and presses it between two dishtowels. Maybe Liam and his dad had a fight. Maybe he refused to do the deck. Before she leaves, she opens the book and hangs it upside down between two tables so the pages dangle and don't dry stuck together.

The next day, the book is dry, but the pages are warped and crispy. She returns it to the shelf. Liam wouldn't pay that bill anyway. If Miss Coffey asks, she'll feign ignorance. Better for everyone.

sixteen

Maggie wants to go to Ship Cove Beach for swimming and a picnic. She invites Rita. "Invite anyone else you want," she says. Imogene can't think of anyone else.

Rita invites Cherry MacIssac, who never has much to say to Imogene, but is at least nicer than Natalie Sampson. Maggie and Nan make chicken-salad sandwiches and pack cheese and crackers and a thermos of lemonade. "Take your sunscreen," Maggie says to Imogene. "You don't want to broil your lovely complexion." Which is a kind way of saying, pale as fuck.

Rita and Cherry both wear perfectly frayed jean cutoffs and Imogene realizes they made them together. The trail to Ship Cove Beach has been fixed up with a walkway of wooden boards. Rita and Cherry walk behind Maggie and ahead of Imogene, their flip-flops echo on the planks. They talk about who was at Corey Mercer's two nights ago and what a racket Wish and Donny got into. Imogene wants to ask about it, but Cherry might think she's interested in Wish, who Rita insists is too short for her. Or Imogene is too tall for him. But it's not cool to think Wish would get into a fight, especially with someone like Donny, who probably fights dirty.

"What a glorious spot," Maggie says. "You don't see anything in Ontario like this." From the top of the banks, they can see the stretch of grey sand lining the beach and the two towering sea stacks which mark Ship Cove as the closest thing to an exotic locale.

"My cousins went to Owen Sound last year," Cherry says. "They said the beach there was deadly."

"It's not the same," Maggie says. "Can't compare a lake to the ocean."

They descend the wooden stairs to the sand and lay out blankets. Rita and Cherry both have neon bathing suits from Sears, but Imogene's is new, a burgundy Speedo.

"Nice swimsuit," Cherry says.

"Thanks," Imogene says. "Maggie brought me three from Toronto. I like this one the best."

Cherry nods and Imogene catches a flicker of a shared glance with Rita. "Maybe if I have any money left from babysitting, I'll get a new one," Cherry says.

"End of the summer sales," Rita says.

Imogene fishes out her book. Let Rita and Cherry have their exclusive shit. A memory flits into her mind, she and Rita playing *Anne of Green Gables* on Butter Brook Beach. Maggie had sent the book and Aunt Trudy read them a chapter a day. Rita liked to braid Imogene's hair in pigtails and together, they'd search the beach for thin slabs of slate. She'd designate a rock for Gilbert Blythe's head and they'd act out the scene when Gilbert calls Anne "Carrots" and she loses her temper. They'd take turns screeching at Gilbert and cracking the slate over his rock head. This continued until the chapter when Matthew dies. Rita cried on the living-room floor. Then she didn't want to play Anne anymore. Or say the words "bosom friend."

Rita and Cherry stretch out, angled away from her. They pass a bottle of Hawaiian Tropic tanning oil back and forth. Both have good tans, Maggie too. In order for Imogene to tan, she'd have to work on it every day for short periods of time and even then, her skin would turn ruddy and harsh like she's been out picking turnips all day. Rita rubs oil into her calves and Imogene burns a little in jealously. Look at Rita with her cute legs, muscled from sports, her uniform colour and beauty. All she does is pine for Nick Cleary when she could get out with any guy she wants.

"I'm going for it," Maggie says. She dashes into the water. She shrieks with the initial cold, but sinks down. "It's great once you're in." She soaks her head and her tall bangs vanish. Suddenly, she is natural and young.

"So, what have you been up to all summer?" Cherry asks.

Imogene leaves her thumb in her book to hold her place. "Just working really. Pretty boring."

"It must be nice to have your mom home."

"Sure. I mean, the house is crowded."

"This is the first time she's been home in what?" Cherry asks. "A year?"

"Almost three."

"Almost three?" Cherry's mouth stays open. "That's a long time to go without seeing your mom."

"Maggie calls Imogene all the time," Rita says. "They're always in contact."

"Oh, but you'd have to call all the time," Cherry says. "I mean, to have any idea of how your child is doing." She flicks a bug off her knee.

"I was supposed to see her last summer," Imogene says. "When I was in St. John's. But it got cancelled."

"You must have been so upset," Cherry says.

"Shit happens."

"I know I'd be upset," Cherry says. "If I didn't get to see my mother in so long and then plans changed."

"Lots of people see their kids all the time and are still rotten parents," Rita says. "And it's hard when you're in two different provinces."

"Oh I know. Just look at Liam and Randy's parents," Cherry says. "Their father comes and goes. No wonder they're the way they are."

"I'm getting in," Imogene says.

"The water's freezing."

"Go for it," Rita says. "You're braver than us."

The water shocks Imogene's thighs and hips, but she propels herself forward. Maggie cheers her on. The waves cover her face and make her gasp and then the water is part of her. As long as she keeps moving, she won't freeze. Maggie splashes in the waves and claps her hands. "That's my girl," she says.

On the walk back, Maggie pauses to adjust the towel on her waist, to fix her shoe, to admire a purple iris. When they reach the dirt road at the end of the wooden walkway, she stops to read the sign indicating the continuation of the West Coast Trail. In the distance, an engine rumbles and stirs up dust. "We should hike to the Spout sometime," Maggie says. "Maybe in August so we can pick blueberries." She stoops to pull back grass at the edge of the road. "Wild strawberries. I miss stuff like this." Rita and Cherry wear patient faces as Maggie fills her palm.

The cloud of dust and engine gets closer. Someone on a quad. Maggie stands up straight, ready to wave. The quad bumbles over the rough rocks on the trail. Cecil Jesso, maneuvering along. His Labatt's cap is clamped on and he wears a yellowing undershirt over brown cords. Who wears cords in July? Imogene catches the shine of a beer bottle balanced between his thighs.

Maggie's face is stone. Cecil gives a nod without looking up, his eyes on the path. Maggie reaches out and clasps Imogene's arm, yanking her near.

"He looks loaded," Cherry says and laughs. Rita laughs too, but her eyes dart back and forth from Maggie to Imogene.

Maggie looks down at her hand. "Damn. I squished my berries," she says. Her hand opens, stained with red. "Better get back to the car," she says. "It's going to be an oven in there."

In the car, Imogene stares out the window. Cherry complains about potholes and how someone should rake the roads. Imogene considers her list of questions. Something must have happened, but she's not going to ask. The woman is trying to get whatever pleasure she can out of this summer. She glances at the rearview mirror. Maggie's eyes focus on the road. She wants to do something, touch her. Refer to her as Mom. She deserves something nice.

Rita turns to Imogene, "What are you doing tonight?"

"Nothing."

"We might go to Seymour's," Rita says. "I'll give you a call." Cherry's mouth curls slightly, but Rita offers her a blank look.

"Sounds like fun," Maggie says.

"Yeah, sure," Imogene says. "Give me a call."

seventeen

Joyce MacIssac comes into the library every week for a new book. "My summer reading," she says. "Between driving Quince and Cherry around, any time I can stop and enjoy a book is sacred." Joyce signs out Sidney Sheldon, Danielle Steele, and whatever romance novels have steamy covers. Imogene keeps the new Harlequins for her, but Joyce wrinkles her nose. "I like the old ones," she says. "It's nice to dive into a traditional romance."

One day, Joyce taps the cover of one of her returns. "This heroine in this one is named after you," she says. The cover picture shows a woman with long dark hair whipping in the wind. Behind her, a man nuzzles her neck, his arm tucked supportively under her breasts, which are ready to explode from her lavender gossamer dress. *Swept Away by Passion* in raised, golden letters.

Imogene has never seen her name in a book or movie or TV show. It's never on monogrammed key chains or mugs in gift shops. When she signs the novel back in, she checks the card. Maggie Tubbs was one of the first people to ever sign it out. December 4th, 1973. She would have been about five months pregnant.

Imogene's guts skip. She has never asked where Maggie came up with her name. It certainly isn't from their family tree; the Tubbses tend to favour fausty old names like Eli and Augustus and Pius and Mary. Names that would give a Catholic priest a chubby just from writing them on baptismal certificates.

Imogene reads the book on her breaks. At first, she's tempted to bring it home to show Maggie. But Miss Coffey is pretty stiff about making her sign out whatever she is reading and there's something about her name on the same book card as Maggie's. If Joyce MacIssac can pick up on it, so could anyone else. She hides the novel inside issues of *Seventeen* and *Sassy*, keeping note of what pages have been folded down. Which is foolish: anyone could have done that over the past sixteen years. Yet you never know.

But the book is trash. Heroine Imogene is a young, naive schoolteacher, orphaned when her parents die in a train accident. She is entrusted with the care of her sick, older sister, who has always been more beautiful and beloved. She feels there will never be room for love in her life as taking care of her sister and guiding her students absorb all her time. And then she meets an arrogant, but handsome, young doctor, who believes he can treat her sister's illness. Some seem to feel he will be a good match for her sister once she recovers. But no, it's Imogene he wants and he chases her along the beach in the moonlight after a misunderstanding and blah blah blah. Heroine Imogene is wide-eyed and doesn't know how beautiful she is. She's stunned as a boot.

Imogene finishes the novel, then skims through it for anything that stands out. Nothing. It's just the kind of thing Joyce MacIssac wants to read on her deck recliner while she drinks slush and yells at Quince to mow the lawn.

In December 1973, Maggie would have been fourteen years old. She turned fifteen in February, two months before Imogene was born. The book was probably a distraction. She thinks of Kelly and Maggie and their strong reactions. They're so angry. *No, nothing happened. But fuck that guy.* Maggie's face on the quad trail.

Maybe she just wanted something pretty. And Imogene is a pretty name—she hears it often. Imogene Lacey Tubbs, how pretty. How Teenage Mom obvious. It's like how Susan Benoit named her kid Fallon, everyone knew it was straight from *Dynasty*. But watching *Dynasty* was probably a treat for Susan Benoit at the time. A reprieve from everyone whispering on the school bus, a break from the tsking tongues of nuns.

Imogene gets a new book card for the novel and slips it in the back. She places it back on the shelf with the others. All the romances have dog-eared corners and forlorn girls in shifting clothes on their covers.

eighteen

Maggie doesn't have to work at the club tonight, but she and Kelly Abbott are going there anyway because Kelly and Paul are down from Labrador City and she wants to get on the go. Kelly sits at the kitchen table with her flask of Lambs and a two litre of Pepsi. Maggie talks about Toronto real estate and refers to her Ontario clients as "complainlanders." Kelly has to clamp her hand over her mouth to keep from spitting. "Don't mind us, Imogene," she says. "You must think we're cracked." Imogene wonders if Kelly thinks she's never seen people being silly before.

"Immy, let Kelly braid your hair," Maggie says. "She used to do mine all the time when we were your age." She sips white wine from one of Nan's crystal goblets. Maggie dropped Nan at bingo and went straight to the liquor store. "You should have a shed," Kelly says. "If I wasn't able to escape into Dad's shed, I don't think I'd come home."

Imogene straddles a kitchen chair so Kelly can access her hair. Kelly produces a brush from her purse. It has a spray nozzle in the handle for carting around a spritz. "Imogene, we didn't talk about boyfriends the last time I saw you," she says. "You seeing anyone? You must have all the boys gone mad."

"Not right now," Imogene says.

"I think she's being secretive," Maggie says. "She must have someone on her mind."

"There's no one decent around," Imogene says.

"I don't know. My nephew Liam is working with Murray Wells," Kelly says. "That boy has grown. He has Springsteen arms now." She makes some kind of smacking sound with her lips. Jesus. "But your mom liked to keep secrets too."

"She doesn't need to hear about that."

Kelly has a firm grip on Imogene's hair and she can't move her head to see Maggie. "Every other day, I'd get a call from Maggie. 'Kelly, if Mom calls, I'm going to your place, okay? Kelly, tell my mom if she asks, I was with you last night, okay?' All so she could go off with Tony, the mystery man." Kelly gathers up the strands along Imogene's neck. "My god, you got a lot of hair."

A sigh from Maggie. The sound of wine pouring. Kelly's fingers caress the nape of Imogene's neck. What a shit disturber. Imogene likes her more for it.

"I remember when they met," Kelly says. "My older sister Nancy was home from Ontario with her new car. She must have been twenty then. She took us driving and here are all these young guys, hanging around the club. Nancy knew a couple of them and they came over to the car. Tony thought Maggie was the same age as Nancy. And you didn't correct him, did you?" Kelly giggles. Imogene gets a whiff of rum. "What was he like?" she says.

"Handsome and intense," Kelly says. "There we go." She releases Imogene's hair and she can finally turn her head. Maggie twists the stem of her wineglass on the tablecloth.

"What else?" Imogene says.

"Your hair looks great," Maggie says. "Go check it out."

Imogene goes to the bathroom to inspect Kelly's French braid. Young Maggie in a car, with older girls, by a club. It wouldn't be too hard to assume they were all the same age. How did they get on the go from there? That's what she'll ask next. The braid is a slippery rope and she likes how it hangs down her back.

In the kitchen, Kelly shakes her purse to fit the brush back inside. Maggie has her shoes on. "We're going to head over to Eli's before the club," she says. "You haven't seen Eli yet since you've been home, have you, Kell?"

"Nope." Kelly doesn't look up. Something's shifted. Her Pepsi-rum giggles have evaporated.

"You're going already?" Imogene says.

"Yes, lots of visiting to do," Maggie says.

"Well. Thanks for doing my hair," Imogene says.

A dull glimmer of something in Kelly's eyes. Dismay or shame. Like she's been caught passing notes in class. "My pleasure, sweetheart," she says. "I'll be outside, Mags."

"Goodnight, love," Maggie says. She gives Imogene a brief, clutching hug. "I'll see you later. Nan's getting a ride home with Joyce."

And they're gone. Imogene watches them from the kitchen window. Maggie walks fast, a pace in front of Kelly, who's saying something. Imogene gives their backs the finger. They don't turn around. When they're gone from sight, she stomps to her bedroom and pulls out her notebook with the list of questions.

What was my father like?

Am I anything like him?

Why doesn't Nan know anything about him?

Why hasn't Tony been found? Does he really know I exist?

Why do people talk about Cecil Jesso and you?

Imogene presses the pen hard. She wishes the paper could bleed.

WHY AM I NOT ALLOWED TO KNOW ANYTHING?!!!!!

She throws the notebook Frisbee-style across the room. Fuck this place. Fuck this house, this stupid room where her young mother cried because she was going to have a baby by some fucking horrible man who used her up. Some horrible man who could be out there, anywhere, right now, doing more horrible things. Or maybe still, down the road, doing whatever he wants, content as a pig in shit. She roots her pack of cigarettes from its hiding place behind Teeny the toy rabbit.

It's warm enough outside she doesn't need a jacket, but she puts one on anyway because Kelly has forgotten her flask of Lambs and she can't just walk out with it in her hand. There's about a third left. Kelly won't be back for it. Or, Imogene could replace it with water and make a point of emptying it in front of Maggie and Nan tomorrow before it's in the trash. She shoves the flask inside her jean jacket and zips it up. An excited tingle flares in her stomach. Something else to practice before she gets out of this place and away from these people.

But the tingle vanishes when she gets to the brook. There is Liam Lundrigan, skipping rocks. On her side no less. If she's quiet, she can turn and head back to the house. But he senses her and looks over.

"Hey."

"Hello."

"You come down for a smoke?" He fishes out a white plastic case, one of the ones that hold rollies and look like travel soap dishes.

Fine. She leans on the rock and takes out her pack. The flask shifts in her jacket and she catches it before it falls out.

"Whatcha got there?"

"Nothing. Rum."

"Yes, b'y." Liam lights his cigarette. "You were just going to come down here and drink alone?"

"Yeah."

"That's a sign of alcoholism, you know. Drinking by yourself."

"Maybe I'm an alcoholic then." She unscrews the top and takes a swig. He holds out his hand.

"I only have enough for me," she says.

"Oh, come on. It's less sad if it's social." She hands it to him. He takes a swallow and passes it back to her.

"Who got that for you?"

"None of your business."

"What did you do, steal it from your mom?"

"No."

"Why not? I steal booze from my folks. Most of the time they don't remember how much they drink."

"Nan and Maggie mostly drink wine." She tucks the flask under her arm and takes out a smoke.

"Fancy." He leans forward to light her cigarette. His hair is long enough it hangs in his eyes. Its usual dirty blond colour is almost white from the sun. "You got that book back, right?"

"That wet book? Yeah, we got it back."

"Shit. I thought it would stay dry in my jacket. Do I gotta pay for that?"

"If Miss Coffey finds it." She takes a sip of rum. It's nice to have both hands busy.

"You had two weeks to bring it back."

"Yeah. I wasn't thinking at the time. I'm bad for that."

"No shit."

"You'd know about that, huh? Me not thinking." He scoops up a flat stone and skips it over the brook. "My father says I'm stunned as a box of rocks."

She watches the stone skip once, twice, three times before sinking. "Sure," she says, "everyone could use a box of rocks."

He laughs, short and shocked. "Yeah, keep them by your front door."

"No more buying Girl Guide cookies. Get off my lawn, kids."

Liam laughs again, harder. "The old man's right though." He flicks another stone across. "When I think about that now, all the tormenting

I did to you, I think, the fuck was I doing? Picking on a girl. Only real tools do that."

Imogene says nothing. She swallows more rum. She hands him the flask and he brings it to his lips. The summer evening light softens his features and, for a moment, with his pursed lips on the bottle and his head tilted back, he looks like an advertisement for something. Cigarettes or jeans or cologne. Imogene lowers her gaze. The hairs on his forearms are bleached golden. Springsteen arms indeed. A long-sleeved pale-blue sweatshirt is tied around his waist, and his sweaty grey T-shirt has the sleeves rolled up over his shoulders. He points his cigarette at his rolled-up sleeve.

"Trying to not get a farmer tan," he says. "Dad likes to walk around the house in just his drawers. His tan lines are like he's wearing a T-shirt with a picture of chest hair on the front." He makes a circular motion in front of his chest with his cigarette hand. Imogene nods and stares at his chest to avoid eye contact.

"Why don't you just take your shirt off then?" she says. "I mean, why don't you just work with your shirt off or something?"

Liam takes a deep puff from his cigarette and nods, considering. "I would," he says, "but you get so scratched up with the hay. Then you put on a long-sleeved shirt and sweat to death."

"Yeah," she says. "Probably not a good idea. You wouldn't want to chafe your nipples."

She flicks her ashes casually and takes another sip. What a thing to say, for fuck sakes. He raises his eyebrows at her and laughs. "How did you know I had such sensitive nipples?" he says. His fingers dance over his chest.

"I don't know," she says. "Guess I know what it feels like. I am a girl, you know."

Again. Holy stupid. He laughs even harder. She doesn't know what to do, so she blows out a stream of smoke as nonchalantly as possible, which makes him almost double over.

"Perhaps from now on your name will be Tender Nipples," he says. "Anyway, I gotta go home. Thanks for the rum, Tender Nipples." And then he's gone, two strides and back on the other side, stomping off through the bushes, still laughing.

She finishes the rum and throws the flask in the woods. She takes off, legs fast and wobbly. Will he have everyone calling her Tender Nipples now? He'll use this as new ammo to torture her. But now, he'll make her look slutty and sexual and in some gross way—she remembers over-hearing some of the guys on the bus talk about some girl one of the guys claimed to have met on vacation, how he stuck a carrot in her pussy and she liked it. And jokes about Rosarie Coish—Dwayne claims she's loud, loves the cock. And Liz Constantine, how she's twisted, likes to be tied up. That seems like the kind of story to be made up about her. She'll be Imogene Jesso, creeping around the woods, brooks, and streams by herself, rubbing her tender nipples. She stomps back to the house, all the way to her room.

nineteen

The Blueberry Festival Planning Committee encourages residents to decorate their houses with blue or purple outdoor Christmas lights. The field behind the St. Felix's Lions Club acquires a stage and makeshift dance floor. By day, it's a garden party for kids; by night, local bands play. "Three times a night is too many times to hear Boot Scootin' Boogie," Rita says.

"Three times is too many times to ever hear Boot Scootin' Boogie," Imogene says.

She and Rita sell raffle tickets and work the bake-sale table (Blueberry pie! Blueberry muffins! Blueberry jam!). The festival receives four spectacular days of warm weather. Rita sprays Touch of Sun in her hair and it transforms into radiant, brassy waves. People say she and Imogene look like sisters. Rita doesn't complain.

On the last night of the festival, Imogene and Rita finish early and are determined to obtain and cash in as many drink tickets as possible. Rita's brother Steve buys the tickets for them with no complaints and the bartenders accept them bemusedly. They get cans of Black Horse and Molson Canadian and stroll through the Lions Club parking lot. Clusters of people drink beers from coolers smuggled in their hatchbacks and pickups. Rita laughs and tosses her new auburn hair, Imogene smokes and sips beer, smiling as much as possible. Again, she appreciates how smoking gives her other hand something to do while she drinks.

Nick Cleary has set up his folks' camper close to the parking area. There is a Coleman stove, two coolers, and lots of foldout chairs. He's organized.

He offers them both beers and tells Rita her hair looks like a new penny. She punches him in the shoulder, "Shaddup."

The screen door of the camper squeaks open and Liam Lundrigan exits. He saunters over and pulls his plastic cigarette case from his jean jacket. He asks Imogene for a light. Rita raises her eyebrows behind him.

Imogene plans on passing him her lighter, but instead she lights it. He cups her fingers and leans in. His hair falls forward slightly, shanks of golden silk frame his face like a heart. His eyes glance up, startlingly blue in his tan face.

"Didn't get a farmer tan after?" Imogene says.

"No. I'm like this all over." He grins. Rita's eyes bulge at her, inflated with questions.

They end up on the foldout chairs. People come and go all night. Guitars appear, songs are sung, a discreet fire is lit. Faces glow around the flames and Imogene is struck by how the light enhances everyone's good features. What a photogenic bunch, as Jamie from Mount Pearl would say. The beer can is cold in her hand and Rita and Nick make jokes and flirt. Liam sits across the fire. At one point, they catch each other's eyes. He better not say any of that Tender Nipples stuff. But he says nothing and a half smile curls his mouth. She has to admit he looks good. For an idiot. Later, he approaches and squats next to her.

"Can I have another light?"

It seems a little silly with the fire in front of them, but she lights his cigarette for him.

"Those two," he says, tilting his head towards Rita and Nick, "they should get on with it already." He hoists himself up. "Be careful with the fire, b'ys, if the festival crowd see it, they'll throw you out."

And then he leaves, like he suddenly remembered somewhere else he has to be. Imogene watches him walk away, his back muscles obvious in his thin T-shirt, a little bounce in his step.

twenty

It rains on and off all Labour Day weekend. Nan is determined to cook all Maggie's favourite meals before she leaves on the holiday Monday. Crab legs. Fishcakes. Jiggs' dinner. Pots on the stove spit and complain.

When there is a break in the rain, Imogene ducks out for some peace. She goes straight to the rock by French Brook. She flips up the hood of her Roots sweatshirt and buries her chin between the tassels. It is full of house smells: peas pudding and laundry detergent.

Yesterday, Maggie took Imogene and Rita school shopping in Stephenville. When they came home with all the bags, Nan declared Maggie spent too much money. "You're spoiling your daughter rotten." Imogene is still pissed about it. If Maggie wants to get her three pairs of jeans, isn't that her prerogative? Does Imogene not deserve nice things? Nan sees anything a little bit extra as a Blessing. If you want nice things, to her, it's like saying you deserve extra blessings. Hell is full of greedy children who asked for more whipped cream on their sundaes.

And Rita kept screwing up her face at the things Imogene picked out. "My god, your shoe size is so much bigger than mine." "All the clothes you like are dark colours." "Where you gonna wear those earrings?" And bringing up Liam Lundrigan to get a reaction. "Liam's gotten in good shape this summer." "Liam said to Wish that he thinks you're a good laugh." Pathetic. And going on and on about Nick Cleary to Maggie on the way home, how after he and Teresa broke up, he said he was going to call her, but he never did.

"You have to play it cool with guys like that," Maggie said to Rita. Even though Maggie sounds nothing close to cool on the phone with Robert.

Last night, Imogene listened while Maggie's voice cracked on the extension in the kitchen. "I wish you'd let this go. Why do we always have to get into this?" What is he bringing up? Maybe it has nothing to do with her. Maybe it's about one of their investments. Not like anyone's going to tell her.

Which, really, is for the best. This is what she has decided. She sat down with her notebook and her list of questions last night. Maggie denies anything with Cecil. Which might be a lie. But if it was her, she'd lie too. In fact, pushing Maggie about it would make things more stressful. It's a horrible truth and if Maggie acknowledges it, then it's this shit reality they have to live with. And Maggie is already an occasional visitor in her life. Two more years. This time, in 1992, she'll be out of here. She can be someone else with a different history. She tore the sheet of questions into pieces small enough to flush down the toilet.

A speck of rain hits her cheek. She leaves it there. This time, in two days, she'll be in school. Tuesday will be a short day, meetings and notes home. Months ago, she expected to dread September, but now she feels almost excited. Grade eleven and she doesn't seem to be the local leper anymore. The Tender Nipples thing didn't happen. She knows she will never be *popular*, but that's always been out of reach. She just wants to move freely and fearlessly.

The trees across the brook sway in a sudden breeze and she glances up. Just the wind. Her chest deflates. Does she want to see Liam? She would like to bump into him, just to see what would happen. Since he admitted to being an idiot, she's been flush with relief about the okayness of everything. It feels more than a truce, it feels almost—respectful? Apologetic? Appreciative? A history exists now. They are in each other's stories. They are something they both overcame.

She wraps her arms around her bent knees and pulls herself in. She stares at the water and the reactions of the current, falling under its thrall: eddies and waves, bubbles and froth.

"You do live under that rock, don't you?"

And there he is, by her side, wearing hip waders and holding a fishing rod. How long has he been watching her be a lump on a stone? She unhooks her chin from her shirt.

"You scared the shit out of me," she says.

"You look like a little conch, all coiled up in yourself." He plants himself down next to her and pulls out his cigarettes. She does the same. What to say.

"You working today?" she says. Obviously not. Fuck sakes.

"No, we finished up Friday."

He lights both their cigarettes and leans back. He wears grey sweat-pants under the hip waders. They are damp and cling to him. His T-shirt is smeared with blood and fish guts and when he folds his hands behind his head, the pits of his T-shirt are stained yellow. He reaches out and rubs the hem of her sweatshirt between his fingers.

"Nice sweatshirt. Looks right soft and comfy."

"Leave it alone." She swats his hand away.

"What? I can't admire your top?"

"You'll get fish guts on it."

He looks down. "Oh, look at that," he says. "I look like the before part of a Tide commercial."

They smoke in silence. What to fucking say, fuck. "You looking forward to going back to school?" she says.

"Jesus, b'y. Whaddya gotta bring that up for?"

"Because it's that time."

"No. Too many people there I don't like."

"Like who?"

"Who do you not like?"

"I don't know. I try not to let people bother me."

"We both know that's not true." He blinks or winks at her. She can't tell.

"I don't know." She tries to think of a neutral person. "Corey Mercer."

"Really? Corey's not that bad, b'y."

"His mouth is always open. Like someone has to remind him to close it."

"True. Who else? Gimme another name."

"Ummm...Crystal Seymour?"

"I can't fucking stand her. She gives me the piles."

"She's a snot. And everyone thinks the sun shines out of her ass."

"I don't think she's hot. The mouth on her when she smiles. She's got more teeth than a louse comb."

"Every time my nan sees her, she says, that one's done up like a stick of gum."

"What does that even mean?"

"I have no idea."

"Extra flavour."

"Maybe it means she's ready to be chewed."

Liam laughs. Suddenly, he has one arm over the back of the rock and leans over her. Her mouth slaps shut. His eyes are half open, face smooth and serious.

"You," he says. "You hardly ever say anything and then, when you do, it's filthy."

"Does that make me a freak or something?"

"No. It makes you worth listening to."

He leans in and kisses her. His mouth is soft and tastes like cigarettes and Juicy Fruit. A stick of gum. She closes her eyes and tries to relax her face. Their lips part and his tongue darts in to meet hers. They kiss slowly, and then he pauses and plants a light kiss on her top lip, then another on her bottom lip. Holy fuck. He leans back, finished. She swallows hard and resists the urge to touch her mouth.

"I have to go," she says. "Maggie's leaving and Nan is cooking supper. It's all a big deal. I should be helping or something."

"Right on." Liam hops back off the rock. "Here. She might want some fresh fish before she goes."

He reaches down into the short white pail and pulls out a medium-sized river trout. His fingers hook into the gills.

"Hold out your hand."

He slides the trout from his fingertips onto her own, a slight sucking sound as the fish transfers hands.

"Um, thanks." She keeps her hand frozen in midair, fish dangling, her fingers inserted obscenely into the gills.

"See ya." He smirks and pinches her chin with his fishy hand. Imogene stares at his retreating back. Then she boots it back to the house, holding the fish out in front of her body like a live grenade.

twenty-one

On the first day of grade eleven, the hallways rattle with the unpracticed sounds of new combination locks and the squeak of fresh sneakers. Imogene fills out schedules and writes her name on the covers of clean notebooks. In the girls' washroom, Crystal asks her, in sugared tones, how her mother liked her summer, is she back on the mainland now? Everyone and everything looks like the freshness seal was just peeled off.

Imogene sits in the back of homeroom and answers when addressed: "Here." "Yes, my summer was good." Teachers take attendance and hand out notices. Liam is the last to stroll in before the bell. He descends on the first available seat closest to the door—the third in the first row, far away from Imogene. He wears faded jeans and a grey T-shirt. Neither look new. She sneaks peeks at him, but he faces forward. He stretches out his legs and chats with Corey Mercer. When homeroom period ends, he vanishes out the door. Did he even see her? And then no sign of him for the rest of the day.

The next day goes similarly. When the last bell rings, she walks out to get on the bus and he passes her in long strides. No acknowledgement. And he doesn't take the bus home.

The third day is the same. If he passes Imogene in the hallway, he finds something on the floor or in his hand which requires all his concentration: putting papers in a binder, wiping a smudge from his wristwatch. Twice she opens her mouth to say hello, but reins it in.

Friday morning in math class she needs her geometry set, but it's in her locker. Ms. Janes allows her to get it. "Make sure you're prepared for class next time."

While she is shutting her locker, Liam and four other boys bluster out of the gym doors. They saunter down the hall, but Liam pauses to tie his shoes. He goes down on one knee, rooting with the laces. As Imogene walks by, he grabs her hand.

"Three thirty," he says.

"What?" Her voice squawks. Liam's face glows with sweat and his eyes bore into her. He squeezes her hand.

"Meet me in the parking lot at three thirty."

"Why?"

"'Cause it's Friday. Don't you like to have fun on Fridays?"

"What do you want to do?" She looks down at the geometry set in her hands. The compass could be used as a weapon. He jumps up. The tips of his hair are dark with sweat.

"I don't know. Find something to be at. See you at three thirty." He steps around her and trots down the hall.

The remainder of the day is full of fluorescent lights and arduous subject matter. Passing bills into laws. The process of mitosis. Their meanings hang in the air while Imogene considers how she didn't really do anything with herself today—hair in a ponytail, sloppy jeans. If she could just go home and shower. But why? For a date? He might be planning to tie her to a tree. She could be tarred and feathered by suppertime. And if she doesn't show, what then? What kind of new resentments will he create?

When the bell rings at three o'clock, she goes to the bathroom and checks herself. An aura of frizz has surfaced around her ponytail like a radioactive sunrise. Eyes bleary and bewildered. She splashes water on her face and tries to tame the frizz. How can she be frazzled from sitting still all day?

She shouldn't be seen not getting on the bus and have to answer questions about how she's getting home. Once the last yellow bus groans onto the main road, she ventures into the parking lot. He didn't say where she should wait. Bastard. The place is empty except for the line of staff vehicles: teachers and administration. She thinks of them in the staffroom, loosened up from the last day of the first week of school, making jokes. Someone will notice her hovering outside. Maybe Mr. Percy or Sister Bernadette. *That's not like Imogene.* They will take note. They might call out to her from the window.

She strides away from the entrance of the school and heads to the side of the gymnasium where everyone smokes. No sign of Liam. There are a few cars and trucks in the parking lot by the public entrance to the gym. This is where students tend to park. Imogene can see shadowy outlines of people sitting in cars. Hanging out, invulnerable. *Luh, what's Immy doin'? Gettin' her skin tonight.* This is obviously a trick. Or he forgot. Best to get out of here. Get on the main road. Call Nan from Seymour's, ask for a ride home. Say she stayed for a sports event or something. She starts to walk away.

"Hey!"

A voice from one of the parked pickup trucks, a black one, covered in dust and scratches. She keeps walking.

"Hey, where are you going?"

The window rolls down and Liam sticks his head out. Nick Cleary is behind the wheel. Of course. Sheldon Cleary's truck. Rita said Nick's father bought a new Ford and gave the old truck to him. Imogene approaches. Does she seem too eager? What if the truck starts right now? They could pull out laughing just as she reaches Liam's door. Tear through a puddle, leave her dripping with shame. Liam leans out the window:

"Where you going?"

"Nowhere. I don't know. Going home." She stuffs her hands into her jacket pockets.

"What, you're going to leave? Sure, school just ended." He regards her with half-closed eyes, like opening them is too much effort.

"Why were you watching me stand around?"

"I was waiting for you to come over."

"How am I supposed to know you're in the truck?"

"Windows are see-through." He slowly passes his hand in front of the windshield like he's doing a magic show for the mentally challenged.

"So, I'm supposed to check all the vehicles on the chance you're in one? Work on your communication skills." She turns on her heel and walks away. The door creaks open.

"Come on."

Liam hops out. Nick says something like leave her. Liam half runs across the gravel and bounds in front of Imogene. "Just get in the truck," he says. "It's Friday. It's TGIF time."

His voice is soft. She hates him. She gets in the truck.

The cab of the truck has beige vinyl seats and is surprisingly clean. Nick has already added his own flavour to it: a cardboard air freshener with a photo of a topless blond lady, an AC/DC sticker over the radio. Liam moves over and makes a kissing sound in Nick's ear. "Take us away from all this." Nick grunts and puts the truck in drive.

Imogene can hardly concentrate on where they're going or collect thoughts to make comments. Liam stretches both his arms across the backs of the seats so one is behind her, but not around her. Her ponytail brushes against the crook of his elbow, his ribs press against her upper arm.

They drive to the Petro-Can. Nick's cousin is working and can get them beer. Imogene darts in to call Nan and makes up an excuse about going over to Cherry's house with Rita. When she hangs up, Nick asks her for money to pitch in for beer. She doesn't have any and this annoys him. She didn't even know she was going anywhere. Why would she have beer money? Liam and Nick get a case of Canadian and rest it on the floor of the cab.

They drive around. They turn down side roads that lead to dead ends: beaches, campgrounds, wood-clearing areas. Most are empty, but some have empty vehicles parked around—twice Nick and Liam recognize one and they turn around. "I'm not going anywhere that fucker is."

They take Thom's Lane all the way to the end and park the truck. Trees and alders, no houses. "C'mon," Liam says. He hooks his fingers into the case of beer. Nick leads the way down a narrow path peppered with cigarette butts. Imogene follows behind Liam with her hands in her pockets. Any second now, Liam and Nick will take off, double back on some path only they know about, leave her to walk all the way home. Cec ya later. Or worse things could happen. Her fingers consider her keychain. She grips it so the keys stick out between her knuckles.

The path widens and rises up into a tall mound. Faint voices behind it. From the top, she sees the shed, bare weathered-grey planks, a rusted chimney pipe. Corey Mercer dangles from the top of the doorway, hoisting himself to do a chin-up. Of course. This is his camp. She's heard it mentioned at school. *What a tear we went on at Corey's camp last weekend.*

Liz Constantine and Antonia Martin stand outside. They look back at Corey and laugh. Antonia turns as they approach. When she takes Imogene in, her cheeks puff out, pregnant with ideas. Liz sips her beer and raises her eyebrows.

Inside the shed is a small wood stove, a bunk, and scattered vinyl deck chairs. Donny Martin crouches by the stove, balling up old fliers and poking them inside. The far wall is covered in graffiti. So-and-so was here. This one lubs that one. Claims on certain teachers being assholes and/or cunts. A drawing of Mickey Mouse with a huge cock. There is a line of empties by the door and Liam plunks his case of Canadian next to them. He pulls out two bottles and passes Imogene one. She wishes she had brought her smokes. Donny lurches over to them, stooping to grab a bottle from a case of Black Horse.

"How ya gettin' on, faggot?" he says to Liam. He looks over at Imogene. "Oh, sorry. How ya gettin' on, faggots?"

"Pretty good, arsemuncher," Liam says.

"I never sees you out, Imogene," Donny says.

"I'm here now, aren't I?" Her voice is too high and defensive.

"I'm only sayin'," Donny says. "It's a rare sight."

"Well, you never extended an invitation before." She tries to say this light and easy, but it sounds accusatory.

"That's right, Donny," Liam says. "How she's supposed to be seen by you if you don't ask to see her?"

"Jesus, I'm only sayin'. I suppose if I spot Bigfoot on my way home, I'll blame myself for never *extending an invitation* to him before. Smoke?" He extends a pack of Export A. Thank fuck. She takes one and he sidles out the doorway.

When Antonia and Liz come in, Antonia walks up behind Liam and knees him in the back of his knees, so that they buckle. Liam tries to kick her in the ass. Liz stands next to Imogene. She cracks her gum. Her eyes narrow at her. "That your natural curl?" she says.

"Yeah."

"You don't use a perm?"

"Nope."

"Never had a perm before?"

"Never."

"You curl your hair in the morning?"

"Nope. It's just like this."

"All natural curl?"

"Yep."

Liz chews her gum hard. "Nice," she says.

They drink and smoke and talk. Shadows lengthen. Everyone moves inside, but Liam takes her hand and leads her behind the shed. He leans up against the wall. She can hear voices rattling inside, laughter like a spray of pebbles on thin wood.

"Having fun?"

His eyebrows rise up and disappear under the fringe of his yellow hair. He tilts his head back, Adam's apple fully exposed, like an offering. She shrugs, hands balled in her pockets. He pulls her to him by her forearms, like she's an urn.

"Are you glad you came?"

He kisses her before she answers. His lips are dry, his mouth warm and smoky. She lets him explore her tongue with his. The first time they kissed, she was shocked. This time, she tries to sink into it, hoping it will feel less alien. Liam Lundrigan is kissing her.

A sharp knock sounds from inside the shed, banging the wall next to their heads. Then husky cackles of laughter follow.

"They can probably see us through the cracks," she says.

"Let them. Anyone who peeks through cracks is a loser." He slides his hand into her back pocket and presses his face behind her ear. "You smell nice," he says. He kisses her neck. It does not feel alien at all.

twenty-two

Liam and Imogene meet again the next Friday. And the following Friday, same thing, right after school. Both times, it feels like a game of chance she assumes she will lose and end up walking home alone. But he is there in the truck, smoking out the window while Nick Cleary sits behind the wheel with an air of tolerance. On the third Friday, Liam asks to see her the next day, and in the afternoon, they walk up to Corey's camp. No one is there, but Liam knows where the key is. They spend over three hours rolling on the floor, her bra undone, their tops hoisted up to their armpits, but not off, not yet. She lets him put his hand down her pants, but not take them off, and afterwards, he complains he might have chafed his dick against his zipper with all the dry humping.

They're not a secret, but there's no advertising. And less of a reason for it as he really did get hot over the summer. In the bathroom, Imogene overhears Shelly MacInnis remark to Crystal about how cut Liam is now. "I'd like to get him unconscious and feel him up," she says. "Just for me. I wouldn't want him to know I did it." "Yeah, it would go to his head for sure," Crystal says.

In school, from Monday to Friday afternoon, they do not approach each other. Avoiding Liam during the week is easy as the only class they share is homeroom. They orbit the school in their own spheres. Imogene and Rita and her cluster of friends, Liam skipping off class to disappear behind the Rec Centre. They glide past each other from the opposite ends of rooms. Imogene glimpses the slope of his cheekbone, his hands pushing through his hair, the back of his denim-clad thighs where his track jacket ends. A sample of his voice reaches her: a jeer, a snippet of laughter. After school, she works in the Youth Centre or has to help Nan. It's easy to avoid whatever this is during the week.

On Fridays, when they drive around with Nick, they get someone to pick up flasks of Lambs or Golden Wedding, which they mix with Pepsi or 7UP. There is never a plan. They look for things to do. Nick is charming and Liam slightly feared, so they are always welcomed. One night they join a fire on the beach, one night a house party. One night, they smoke up in the Anglican cemetery with a bunch of last year's high-school graduates, the taste of the hash oil harsh in the cigarette and having zero effect on her. One night, they end up at a shed party with a bunch of fishermen, two of whom knew Imogene's grandfather and keep her in a corner, telling stories and drinking rum until Liam yanks her away.

Nick and Liam assign her to do small tasks like buy onesies (you're a girl, they'll just give them to you), watch out for cops, enter a party first. She loans them some kind of legitimacy. It is good to feel useful. Before Nick drops her home on Fridays, Liam sorts out somewhere they can meet on the Saturday. "Not having a vehicle sucks," he says.

In class, she tries to remember how his hands look, their tan shape on the leg of her jeans. She forgets if he is taller than her or not. She thinks about things she'd like to try. In a way, it's ideal; he's not her boyfriend, so she can practice for the real thing. By Thursday, she is counting the hours left in the day. She busies herself planning what to wear, what to bring to school for Friday—makeup, money, cigarettes, an extra sweater. By two o'clock on Fridays, her muscles tense and release, gearing up for the walk to the parking lot.

One day, Crystal interrogates her in the bathroom. "What's going on with you and Liam? Are you going out?" Imogene shrugs and smiles. And when Rita finds out, she is thrilled with it all. On the fifth Friday, she follows them out of a shed party. "Hi, guys, where you going? Immy, I have to tell you something." And she hops into the front next to Nick, making Imogene and Liam squeeze into the back seat of the cab. Nick drops Rita off last.

Within a week, Rita and Nick are Going Out. They are always touching, connected by any available joints and appendages, names written together on textbooks and locker doors. Rita sits on Nick's lap in the lunchroom, his head against her shoulder, the ends of her hair brushing his forehead. They walk with hands in each other's back pockets, they neck at school dances. Junior-high girls request slow songs for them: "Right Here Waiting," "Lost in Your Eyes."

Rita and Nick's new coupledom highlights Imogene and Liam's vagueness. Imogene isn't sure what's happening, but it's fun to have a bit of badness on the go. It reminds her of those first couple of weeks after she was suspended, the quiet respect around her. The acknowledgement of her potential.

But the thought of doing boyfriend and girlfriend things with Liam, like holding hands or making out in public seems ridiculous. Even when they are alone together, it feels otherworldly, like they are different versions of themselves. It's only outside of school she wants him next to her. She wants his voice in her ear. And when no one can see, she wants his hands on her, his tongue in her mouth, his skin on hers. Everything is something new she can take with her.

twenty-three

The last Friday night in October, all four of them end up in Aubrey Murphy's field. They play an idle game of Truth or Dare, which becomes Just Dares as no one wants to confess anything. Rita has to flash her tits at the cows, Imogene has to moon them. Liam has to put his tongue on the salt lick. Nick tries to approach a cow so he can write on it with a magic marker, but it keeps slowly walking away, no matter how nicely he speaks to it.

When it gets chilly, they pile into the truck, Liam and Imogene in the narrow back seat, Rita next to Nick in front.

"What now?" Nick says. "It's only early."

"I dare Immy to go see if Cec is home." Liam squeezes the bottom of her thigh.

"You're a funny fucker." She looks into his face so he knows how not funny it is.

"Have you ever looked in his house?"

"Why would I go to his house?"

"I don't know. Selling raffle tickets or something."

"I bet he lives in squalor," Rita says. "If he keeps that many old cars in front of his place, it's probably a state inside."

"People visit him though," Nick says. "Must be at least room to get fucked up."

"It didn't look like anyone was home when we drove past," Liam says. "Just go check. If he's there, make up some excuse like you need to use the phone. And if he's gone, get us a souvenir."

"I think you need a souvenir to remind you of what an asshole you are."

"Oh, for fuck sakes. That was a million years ago."

"That was a year and a half ago."

"Fine. I'll do it myself. You owe me though." He leans forward and kisses her on the mouth. "I can think of a couple of things I can get you to do."

Nick, Rita, and Liam chat excitedly about what they imagine he keeps in his house. Dope likely, contraband booze and smokes definitely. Imogene stares at the dark shapes of her feet under the seat. Her veins feel like they are sinking deeper into her flesh, leaving long wiry imprints.

Cecil Jesso's windows are dark and his old Dodge pickup is nowhere to be seen. "I think there's a vacancy at the old inn," Liam says. They pull over and turn off the lights. He is out and trotting down the street in seconds. "What a hard ticket," Rita says.

Imogene watches the back of Liam's untucked T-shirt flap down the street and hates every inch of him. He might have shown regret this summer, but obviously he hasn't really thought about it. Because if he thought about it for five fucking seconds, he would know what it meant and how shit it is to do this to her. Fucking stunned tool Liam Lundrigan.

Liam cuts through the trees rather than walk up the driveway. Wasn't the deal supposed to be knock on the door and make something up? He darts between trees and old cars and vanishes. Five minutes pass. Ten. Imogene tells Rita and Nick to shut up and they roll down the windows, straining their ears to hear something. Even if Cec isn't home, anyone could be over there. What if Liam is caught trying to take something? Imogene imagines his body on a floor, bludgeoned with something heavy. Or he and Cec sitting in front of a woodstove. Drinking a beer. Laughing like old friends.

There is a rustling. Liam scampers towards them. He hops in the cab with a whoop. Nick starts the truck and they take off.

"What did you get?" Nick says. "Did you go in?"

Liam pats the front pocket of his jeans. "Found me an Easter egg."

"We're your escape vehicle," Rita says. "Let's see."

She leans over and tries to put her hand in his pocket. Imogene slaps her hand away, surprising herself. Liam laughs and pulls it out—a thimble-sized lump of hash in his palm.

"Nice," Nick says.

"Where did you find it?" Imogene says. "What, he leaves them for decoration?"

"I took a quick look around. It wasn't hard to figure out."

"I see."

"Were you nervous?"

"No," she says. "But you're still an asshole."

Liam leans in over her. His sweat smells new and piquant. "I think I can change your mind." He kisses her and moves his hand up her shirt. His fingers slip under her bra and she feels something pressing against her breast. A note? She looks into his face. Liam retrieves his hand and presses one finger to her lips. "I wouldn't go in there without finding something just for you," he whispers.

When Nick and Rita aren't looking, she fishes it out of her bra. A folded square. Carefully, she flattens it out in her lap and stares at it in the dim light through the window. A fifty-dollar bill. She slides it into her back pocket. In the front seat, Nick and Rita discuss where they should go to smoke up. Liam stares at her across the darkness of the cab. She gives him a smile. Her skin shines a galaxy of goosebumps.

twenty-four

Even with a sweater and jacket, the cold from the stone seeps into Imogene's back. The overcast sky is a dead, milky eye above her and Liam and French Brook. The cuffs of his sweatshirt are tugged up over his knuckles, making his hands into cat paws. Imogene regards the fifty-dollar bill in her palm.

"So, you got in through the window?"

"It's better if Nick and Rita think I did." He grins at her. Like it's all fucking cute.

"I doubt they believe you either."

"Fine. I know where the key is. Well, I had an idea and now I know."

"How did you know?"

"Something Murray said." Liam examines the ground with a concentrated face. Or he's concentrating on not looking at her. "He took me over there a couple of times when I first started working for him."

"Yeah?" She wonders what would happen if Cec had any idea of how Liam used to get on, using his name as an insult. Liam skims a flat rock over the smooth centre of the brook where the water is calm.

"So, what did you do at Cecil's place?"

"Drank. Smoked up. It was only a couple of times. Me and Murray and Bryce Benoit. Not the most fun."

"Why not?" Imogene collects a handful of damp pebbles at the bottom of the Best Rock. They look vibrant when they're wet, but dry, they're just dull and chalky like the rest.

"Those guys—fuck. Get a few draws in Bryce and he never shuts up. Goes on with some gross stuff."

"Like what?"

"You really want to know?"

"Yep." She fires one of the pebbles into the brook's centre. It vanishes with hardly a splash.

"Okay, well, don't say anything to anyone."

"Who am I going to tell?"

"If Wish knew his dad said this kind of shit, he'd lose it. Or if Arlene found out."

"I won't say anything."

"Okay, so Bryce went on about this girl Murray brought over one time. He had met her in Codroy and she was out camping in Fischels. Bryce kept going on about how much fun they had with her, especially after Cec gave her some skin juice."

"Skin juice?"

"Yeah. Cec said it's his recipe. Moonshine and Crystal Light mix, with lots of sugar and ice. He said 'Sometimes I puts a little Spanish Fly in it too.'" Liam says it like Cec would: *Spa-nick fly*. "Murray and Bryce kept laughing and going on about this girl. Bryce is like, 'Remember, Murray, you were in her ass and I was in her mouth and Cec walked in? The look on her face. I thought she was going to bite my pecker off.'"

Imogene throws the biggest pebble into the brook. It makes a deep guttural clunk. "What did Cec say when Bryce said that?" she says.

"He laughed. 'Skin juice is magic.'"

"Fucking repulsive."

"Cec kept asking me if I had a girlfriend. 'No one brings no girls here anymore,' he said. 'Be nice to have a girl around.' Then later on, he asked me if I wanted to buy some perks, five bucks each and I said no thanks, and he got all ticked and said, 'You can't just come around here drinking other people's beer and smoking their draws and not spend your money.'"

"Friendly."

"When we were leaving, Cec had passed out. We got in the truck and Murray said he forgot his smokes. Bryce goes, 'The door's locked, you know where the key is?' And Murray goes, 'Four by four.'"

"Four by four? Like under some wood?"

"Nope. Bryce had his eye on me, but I thought I saw Murray stooping by the door. And I remembered the patio tiles he had on the ground. They're laid out in rows. Four across or four down I figured. And I was right."

"Good job."

"I went straight for his bed. That's where my old man hides things he thinks we won't find. Pulled that fifty right out from between his mattresses. I bet he has money stashed all over the house."

"In nooks and crannies." She flattens the bill against her leg. How would she feel if Liam spent fifty dollars on a gift for her? What kind of present could she ever give Liam? A carton of cigarettes? A dozen beer? She watches him pace on the grass by the rock. He pauses to bounce on his heels. Look at him, right excited.

"The place looked like he just had a party. Empties everywhere. People are always over. He won't know what happened to this and if he thought someone took it, he wouldn't know who." He peers over at Imogene. She keeps her eyes away from his, but nods.

"I wonder where he was Friday night," he says.

"No idea. I doubt he has many social engagements."

"Everybody has to go out sometime. Does he have any family?"

"Is that a dig?"

"Jesus, girl, you know what I mean. He must have a mom, he wasn't hatched from an egg."

"Maybe he was. He crawled out of the ocean all by himself."

"Do you think you can find out?" He lights a cigarette. The wind flutters his hair, the edges of his ears are turning pink. When ears get cold, they look like they're hot. They take what they hear and cook it up.

"If I start asking questions about Cecil Jesso it will look weird."

"Okay, fine. He lives down the road from you. Try to find out when he's not home."

"I don't like that fucking guy. I don't like looking at him or his house."

"I know." He leans forward and grasps her knees. "You think I don't know how angry it makes you? I still got the scars."

"Don't try to make me feel guilty."

"I'm not. Just keep an eye out. Take note of when he's out, days and times." The tips of Liam's fingers coil around her kneecaps. His nails are short, but uneven. Clean and rough. "What's your plan?" she says.

"I don't have one." He circles her knee with his right hand. "Don't get stressed out. It's just a thought. Not making any plans to do anything. Just wonderin'."

Imogene says nothing. Halloween in a day and the brook is dark and cold. She thinks about the fish Liam caught a few months ago and how he just gave it to her, an automatic gesture. Others might have kept all of them for bragging rights or to show off to his folks. But people think Liam's a liar anyway. Hard to brag when no one believes you.

"Don't say anything now," she says.

"Me? Who am I going to tell?"

"Rita and Nick already know. It doesn't take long for people to figure out you're up to something. All they have to do is see your vehicle nearby or overhear you asking a nosey question or see you going down the road at a certain time. People know my family hates him. And they think you're a case."

"I'm a case now, am I?"

"Don't act offended."

"I'm not."

"I've already heard my nan go on about how you broke into those cabins last summer."

"Oh, your nan doesn't like me, huh? Must be hard for you."

"I don't care what she thinks. She doesn't know the war's over." Imogene swings her legs to the back of the rock and stands on the grass next to him. Even though Liam's cold, his jacket is undone. She coils one hand inside it and brings it up to caress his back, but pokes her fingers into his armpit instead.

"Fuck! Your hands are freezing. That's me danger spot."

"I need to warm up my fingers. Armpits are a source of body heat."

"You're gross."

"I don't care what you think either."

She shoves her hand deeper into his armpit. He squirms and curses. She leans forward and kisses his mouth.

In November, Imogene tries to be observant. She takes meandering bike rides and runs errands. She and Rita go for walks. Rita rambles about Nick, the schools he's applying to, if they're still together at Valentine's, she'll ask him to grad. Every time they pass Cecil's house, Imogene takes note. He tends to be around his house in the day, puttering around the junk in his yard. Otherwise, he's out in his field, picking what remains of his potatoes, resembling a potato himself, bulbous and humped over. Every second day, he goes to the post office. Visitors don't appear until after dark. Most people stop in quickly. Some, like Murray Wells and Bryce Benoit, stay for hours, stay all night maybe.

On Remembrance Day, Nan wants to go to the Legion to watch the parade and the wreath ceremony. The wind is extra bitter. The local cadet corps stands at attention, all rosy cheeks and misery. The ancient Legion members and veterans lay wreaths, their berets squat on their white heads like mushroom caps. A thin bugle cry and a moment of silence, except for sounds of sniffling and instant crystallization of freezing snot in everyone's tolerant, sombre faces.

Nan volunteers Imogene to help pass out the cold-plate suppers for the cadets and Legion members. The Styrofoam plates contain scoops of potato salad, beet salad, a piece of iceberg lettuce, mustard pickles, and a slice of processed ham rolled up like a diploma. From a distance, the scoops of potato and beet salad look like vanilla and strawberry ice cream, then you get close and disappointed. Imogene brings them out to the tables and hands out matching Styrofoam cups for fruit punch and Tang.

Joyce MacIssac and Charlotte Whalen put together the cold plates themselves. Now they lean against the kitchen counter drinking Nescafé and talking and talking and talking. Their words waft in and out of Imogene's awareness as she fetches new meals.

"I don't know what to get the grandchildren for Christmas. They got half the Wish Book underlined and circled."

"My God, it's right around the corner. Comes faster every year."

"Is your oldest coming home?"

"Yes he is. Jerry wishes he was home now though, his father's going moose hunting next weekend."

"Oh my, he must miss that."

"Yes, Gerard goes every year, him and Walter and Murray and Cecil. Jerry hasn't been able to make it for years."

"Well at least he's home for Christmas."

So Cecil will be gone next weekend. Imogene keeps her face stone serious as she collects the pearly white plates. Once everyone is eating, she slips into the ladies' washroom and locks herself in a stall. She takes the fifty-dollar bill out of her pocket. The bill is almost new; it's not like fifties get handed around that much. Probably very few acquire that worn denim texture one sees with five-dollar bills.

If she tells Liam, it's happening. So. Is this what she wants? Pros. Cons. Cons are obvious:

Caught by the cops. Likely consequences:
- Go to court. End up in the Juvenile Detention Centre in Whitbourne.

- Do shitty public service. She'll have to face Cecil, probably apologize. Entire community knows. She becomes the focus of feverish, delicious gossip for years.
- Lifetime of enduring shame from Nan.
- Maggie's reaction. So horrible.

Caught by Cecil. He shoots her and Liam. He buries them in his backyard.
- The cops dig up their remains. Cecil is thrown in jail. Her and Liam are immortalized as St. Felix's legend. Some kind of warning about bad boys and girls with bad dads.

Pros.
- With Cecil's undeclared money and whatever else, it would be unlikely a break-in would be reported to the cops.
- Cash
- Weed
- Booze.
- Revenge(?)
- Collecting long overdue child support(?)
- He deserves it(?)

Liam won't admit to the rumours he and a few others (Donny Martin, possibly Nick) broke into several cabins by St. Felix's River two summers ago. Beer and liquor stolen, nothing else. No acts of vandalism. He probably did it to see what he could get away with. She could see his delight when he returned from Cecil's. "Hash and cash," he said. "That place is full of hash and cash." Maybe it's a game for him. If he knows it's there, he has to try and take it. Like knowing Imogene would be bothered by the whole Cec thing meant he had to torment her senseless. Maybe Cec is a good target because Liam knows she makes an easy accomplice. Maybe the skin juice stuff is bullshit.

When the cadets are finished, Imogene moves between the long wooden tables, picking up discarded plates and white plastic forks. Charlotte gestures to a lump of bright pink beet salad:

"Looks like something out of the special effects department. I think they used it in that *Star Wars* movie, with the big Jabba creature."

"Cold-plate special effects."

"That's all it is if no one eats it."

In level one, Imogene was corrected on an English paper for using the word *effect* when she should have used *affect*. One is a verb and the other a noun. Someone affects you, they don't effect you. She has potential to affect Cecil. His hand with its bent pinky on the floor, right by her foot. Imogene the Ineffectual did not step on his hand. She places an armload of plates on top of a bulging garbage can and presses them in. The pile hardly budges. She pushes the plates harder. There is a squeaking crunch and a shift as they compress and descend. Done.

She waits until she can leave, standing in silence until Nan finishes talking. She gets thanked and told she's a good girl. She smiles and says you're welcome.

Later that night, she and Liam meet at Corey's camp and the information empties out of her mouth, like the first loose rock of a landslide. She tells him all she heard from Joyce and Charlotte. All day she couldn't decide and then she tells him. Liam pulls her close. She lets herself be held and waits to feel nervous and scared and regretful. But she feels nothing. Except effectual.

twenty-five

Cecil's driveway is hardened dirt and they pad along through the dark, careful not to trip in the sloped hollows of evaporated puddles. She is relieved the ground is dry; they won't leave obvious footprints. Several dead cars lie scattered around: a wood-paneled station wagon, a rusted-out Chev Suburban, a large beige van missing the side door. She follows the shape of Liam's back and tries not to imagine shapes and figures in vehicles and trees.

It's dark, but the sky is clear and luminescent. She wears a bulky dark-blue jacket with her hair tucked into a ball cap. A glimpse of her orange hair would be all it takes to be recognized. Liam wears his regular track jacket, grey and black swatches with silver reflective lining, and it makes a synthetic swish-shish as they walk. She wants to swat him. "Sure, you're the one who looks like you're up to something," he says. "I'd rather be recognized and say I was minding my own business. You'd have to explain why you're dressed like a ninja."

They borrow Liam's mother's car and park it out of sight in a nearby field. They tuck small flashlights into their pockets. They walk as fast as they can with the intention of switching to a casual pace if headlights appear. But no vehicles pass.

Imogene starts towards the front door. "No," Liam says. "This way." He leads her behind the house. The back door hovers about two feet off the ground with just a metal lip at the bottom, no step. Nan once said it was one of those tax things, if your house is unfinished, you can claim something. Liam shines his flashlight under the metal lip. There are about two dozen beige patio bricks laid out on the ground, like stepping stones. He lifts up the fourth one in the fourth row.

"Four by four," he says.

"Yes, fine, shut up."

The key lies on the flattened rectangle of dirt, its eye points towards the top-right corner.

"Don't forget to put it back the same way."

"Yes, yes."

Liam fiddles the key in the lock and pushes the door open. They stand listening in the doorway. A refrigerator hums. Stillness. The porch is narrow, a scratchy-looking burlap doormat, a few nails for hooks on the wall. Liam shines his flashlight around. "Careful," Imogene says. "Don't shine it at the windows." The porch leads into the kitchen. There is an ancient Formica table in 70s avocado green with four mismatched vinyl chairs: orange, mustard yellow, brown. Three empty beer bottles on the table. A large ashtray acts as a centerpiece. Imogene moves closer.

"Don't bother," Liam says. "Anything out in the open is too obvious."

The state of the house is not what she imagined. She expected pungent odors, years of neglect, filth, obvious debauchery. She expected fruit flies and mouse shit and a thick layer of slime. But overall, Cecil's home is neat and sparse. The walls are mostly bare. Cheap wood paneling, dusty shelves, and faded furniture. The faint smell of cigarettes and Lysol.

Liam jerks his thumb down the hallway. Bedroom. She shines her flashlight down and sees three closed doors.

"We'll check his mattress first." He walks to the last door on the left and pushes it open with one finger. Cecil's bedroom is as unassuming as the rest of the house. A bed covered in a quilt with patches of blue and purple, a cheap plywood dresser, a framed picture of a boat. Liam lifts the lower end of the mattress. A scattering of bills in the centre of the bed, some flattened, some in wads. "He must just shove money in here," he says. They stare at the haphazard collection.

"What do you think, a few hundred?"

"Maybe."

He lowers the mattress and gets down to the floor. He shines his flashlight under the bed. "Dust bunnies and a rifle. He's ready for the bad guys." He shoves his arm under, stretching. He looks up at Imogene and smirks. He hauls out a shoe box. "This might be something."

"Remember where it was," she says. She imagines Cecil spying the trail in the dust, the marks of their fingers, his furious hands on the rifle.

"He's not going to notice we were even here. And if he does, it won't be for a while."

He opens the box. Four sandwich baggies of weed. A collection of greasy-looking brown vials, some full, some empty. "He won't miss a bitta hash oil," Liam says. He shoves one baggie and two vials into his pocket. He closes the shoebox and pushes it back under the bed. He bounces to his feet, eyes flashing. "Let's see how much cash he has around and decide what to take. I'm checking the dresser."

Imogene looks around the room. The picture of the boat hangs slightly askew. It's lower than eye level. She slides the frame aside. Behind it is a little shelf in the wall, like a medicine cabinet behind a mirror. It holds an assortment of zip-loc bags and pill containers. The labels are made out in Cecil's name. Percocet. Diazepam. Familiar names, even if she doesn't know what they do. Their labels fill her with a cold quease.

She moves the zip-loc bags gingerly, trying not to change their shape. One holds several tin-foil lumps. Hash, probably. One contains money— tens and five-dollar bills. She pulls it out carefully. Underneath the bag, something small and metal rests on the shelf.

Liam shifts through Cec's top drawer. "Ugh, this guy's underwear could crack in two. Five bucks for a pack of tighty-whities, b'y. Make an investment."

Imogene peers closely at the metal object. A silver chain and pendant. She pulls it out carefully. She tells herself to remember how it lay on the shelf, pendant first, the chain on top. The pendant is heart-shaped with a word engraved. She holds it in front of her flashlight. In italics: *Maggie.*

"Holy shit," Liam says. "This guy has a lot of nudie mags. And this sock has money in it." He sits on the bed, working the contents out of a long, grey wool sock. She keeps her breathing straight and regular. She lays the pendant back in its spot, coiling the chain on top of it. Her ears feel hot and glowing like cooking elements on the stove.

"So, there's about two hundred in this sock," Liam says. "Four something in the bed. Let's take around two hundred. He won't notice. We might even be able to come back some other time. Any cash in there?"

"No," she says. "Just this."

She tosses him the hash. While Liam fishes out a few lumps, she slips the zip-loc bag of bills into her coat pocket. As she replaces the bag of hash, her fingers touch the locket. She clasps it and thrusts it into the front right pocket of her jeans.

They put everything back and leave. Liam locks the back door and carefully replaces the key. They run down the driveway, their feet now sure of themselves in the dark. At the edge of the pavement, they pause and strain their ears for approaching cars and movement in the night. They take long, urgent strides, legs never stretching enough with each step, each pace striving to outdo the former, distance, more distance needed between here and there.

Back in the car, Liam empties his pockets and counts it out. Two and a half vials of oil, three grams of hash, two hundred and five dollars. "He might notice," he says. "But there's a good chance he won't right away. And if he does, he'll probably blame his friends or whoever he lets come over. It's not like he can call the cops. I figure we feel it out and maybe in a few months, if he's gone again, we can get a little more."

Imogene nods. He pulls her close. She tucks her arms around his waist and keeps her elbow close to her coat pocket so the plastic bag won't rustle. The heart pendant nudges into her upper thigh.

When she is home and in her bedroom, she removes the bag and spreads the bills on her bed. Only the few bills on top and bottom are tens and fives. The rest are mostly fifties and hundreds. As she counts them into matching piles, her stomach wads itself tighter and tighter, like a drowning man's fist on a line.

She finishes counting and makes it to the bathroom in three leaping strides, somehow landing soft enough to not wake Nan. Her mouth dangles open, but nothing comes out. Her empty stomach convulses. She squeezes her eyes shut against the number but it remains like a neon sign on the back of her eyelids. $2,160.

She shuts the toilet lid softly and tiptoes back to bed. She stares at the bag on her bedspread. $2,160, still there when she blinks. The number blares in bright white letters underlined with a ragged silver streak, shaped like the reflective lining on Liam's jacket collar, zipped to his chin as he steered down the dirt road, headlights off. The streak illuminated briefly in the oncoming headlights of a passing truck, the briefest lightning flash in the night, disappearing just as they turned onto the pavement.

twenty-six

November lumbers on. Imogene is twitchy. Shorter days mean more dark shadows to avoid. Her mind works itself into a lather every other day. She could be walking to the store and suddenly Cec's truck could appear, a quick swerve and she's in the ditch. What if she comes home from school and finds Nan destroyed somehow, lying on the floor, her forehead a bloody welt, the house in tatters? Or Cec himself, spread over Nan's crumpled body, his freckled back in a hungry hunch, Nan's thin calves under him, like crushed reeds. Imogene scrambles up the walk and barges into the house. "Nan!" And there she is, staring at her from her sofa perch in front of *All My Children*. And Imogene blurts something like "I'm home."

Every day she checks Teeny to make sure he hasn't been disturbed. Even if he hasn't, she still takes the bills out of the hole in his foot and counts them. $2,160. All there.

Liam calls her paranoid. He tickles her and squeezes her hips. He jumps out from behind her locker door, making her shriek and sending her binder skittering across the hallway. He laughs his head off. "You're a tool" she says. "Aw," Rita says. "Young love."

But overall, things stay quiet. The air is tight with cold, but no snow yet. Boys talk excitedly about the importance of frost before snow—ideal for a long stretch of skidoo season. Christmas decorations appear. No rumours. The windows in Cecil's house hold their warm light beyond the stretch of trees and vehicles.

Most nights, right before she tries to sleep, she takes out the pendant. Nan doesn't go in her room, but Imogene hides it in the back of her jewelry box anyway, under some old prayer cards Sister Patricia gave her. She holds it so it dangles above her face, like she's about to be hypnotized. She lets it swing back and forth between possibilities. Maggie was in his house, yes, but doesn't mean anything happened between them. Or it does. Or it only feels that way because of all the gossip. From how Imogene looks. From the denial and behaviour of Maggie. What if she'd left the pendant there and told someone about it? It could be evidence. No, it's not evidence.

When she gets angry enough, she takes the money out of Teeny. Its presence in her room scares her when she's not home, but when the bills are in her hands, she wishes she'd robbed him blind. She should have doused the place in gasoline, sparked flames in his gallery of old cars. All that dead grass and old wood. It would spread to the house in no time.

Distraction finally arrives in the form of a ticket to Toronto to spend the holidays with Maggie and Robert. Nan says she doesn't want to go, but Maggie and Imogene should spend time together—which actually means Nan's afraid of flying and cities the size of Toronto. Which is fine, because Imogene needs a break from Nan, who claims that since Imogene is no longer a child and since she chooses to ride in trucks with boys, she needs a work ethic. "You're a sensible girl," she says. "But you're not immune from being foolish. You just have to look at your mother for that." All fall it has been, "We're running low on firewood," or "They need someone to read at Mass" or "You should try to get babysitting work like your cousin Rita." Orders doled out in Nan's asphalt tone, no pleases or thank yous, as if to say this is what Imogene is good for, like a stray dog that wouldn't go away so you might as well train it. Imogene packs her suitcase a week early. She relishes the idea of briskly walking up the drive, vanishing into a vehicle and speeding away.

In the days leading up to her flight, she leaves the pendent on her suitcase so she'll remember to pack it. But it's always a bad idea by the morning. What is she going to do, give it to Maggie for Christmas? Imogene should focus on having a nice time. The pendant will stay home, hidden away. The money, though, that's another thing. Teeny's coming with her.

Liam jokes she's abandoning him for Christmas break. "Get me something in Toronto," he says.

"Like what?"

"Something you can't get around here. Something cool."

Imogene can't think of anything to get him. Unlike Rita, who has already bought a number of presents for Nick, including a royal-blue sweater. She is excited about this sweater. "It will look great with his hair and eyes," she says. Imogene tries to picture giving Liam a piece of clothing. The reaction on his face, pink and grateful. Watching him strut around, marked with some shared symbol of *them*, puffed up like a rooster.

And these days, things have shifted into the open. In school, Liam walks beside her in the hallway and holds her hand. He approaches her during recess and hugs her from behind. Each time, she freezes and focuses on being politely affectionate in return, patting his hand, letting him hang there. Their initials now appear on desks and bathroom stalls: LL + IT. She is the IT. Liam's IT.

As for their money, so far Liam has spent fifteen of his share of the two hundred and five dollars getting his ear pierced with a little gold stud. He has started spiking the front of his hair with gel that makes his fleecy blond fringe dark and geometrical. This new hair irritates Imogene and she feels guilty for her irritation which is also irritating. Liam can do whatever he wants with his appearance. But it annoys her that he didn't ask her opinion on his spiky hair, like she will just go along with whatever stupid decision he makes.

And his swagger is more pronounced since Cec's. He takes longer, exaggerated strides, his white, high-top sneakers flapping open like the mouths of slobbering dogs. Around school, he slides down banisters, he swings off the tops of doors. He sits in class, breaking up erasers and flicking tiny pieces of pink rubber at people. One day, Crystal calls him a drooling idiot and Imogene finds herself in silent agreement.

But there is a new acceptance she's never experienced. Having a boyfriend makes her more "okay" in her day-to-day life. Look, someone chose you. You must be some level of okay. When she is with Rita and the grade twelve girls, they ask her questions, they smile and say hello. Liz and Antonia regularly inquire into what she's doing on the weekends. On the bus, she catches Wish Benoit staring at her. It's all so new, and Liam is the first guy anyone can really connect her to, even though she tried to mention Jamie from Mount Pearl as much as she could last year. Which was only some kissing and one letter. But when she imagined having a boyfriend, he was the kind of guy she wished for: cute, funny, clever.

She tells herself she can get back into it, that deep down, she misses liking Liam. She insists they meet up more. If she invests more, maybe the feelings will return and this irritation will fizzle. Maybe she should make a big investment. After all, they've come close to having sex a bunch of times now. They'll be halfway naked and mouths everywhere and they'll make themselves cool off, slow down. For a while, she's assumed they'd end up doing it, but she put off the discussion out of fear. Pregnancy, reputation, AIDS. And the idea of Liam Lundrigan as her first. Fucking surreal. But getting it out of the way makes sense, especially now that they are comfortable with each other's bodies and they know what the other one likes. And being able to practice having sex makes sense. She can get good at it now so later on, with someone else, the discomfort and fear will be out of the way.

She tells him they can do it as long as he uses a condom. She predicts an argument about this. But not at all. "No problem," he says. When they meet up at Corey's camp on a Saturday afternoon, he has a strip of Trojans in purple and blue wrappers. He pulls an orange camping mat from his backpack. "For the floor," he says. "The bunk is pretty small." But the bunk is against the wall and not directly in view of the door or the window. "What if someone comes and finds us in the middle of the floor?" Liam grins and pulls a thin wool blanket from his backpack, the grey army kind. "I got your modesty covered, my dear."

The blanket is narrow and once her top is up and their pants are off, there's no way they won't be seen if someone walks in. How fast can she get her jeans back on if they hear someone coming? Liam's hands squeeze her bare ass, her thighs. She looks down at her white legs under Liam's skinny tan ones, covered in golden hair. She fights the urge to say stop. His breathing and the blood thundering in her ears makes it hard to listen. Are those footsteps outside? Voices? "Do you hear anything?" she says. "No one is coming," Liam says. "The door is locked. No one can see in." He moves his mouth to her nipple. "Relax."

The first time it's uncomfortable and pinches. She has to take deep breaths to calm herself and Liam finishes quickly. They do it again, each time no more than a couple of minutes, and after four times, she's too sore to keep going. "I can get more condoms," Liam says.

They meet up again on Monday and then every other day. It starts becoming more and more enjoyable, but as the pleasure increases, she has to squeeze her eyes shut in concentration, wishing for someone else to think about. But Liam's face and smell and sounds are her only reference. It is like trying to imagine what an egg cream tastes like when you've never seen one before.

Maybe when she returns from Toronto, her feelings will reemerge, the absence and the fondness thing. She tells herself to make sure to think about him, good thoughts, sexy things. She makes a list of fun stuff they've done together and reads it before going to sleep. She dreams she is under a blanket with Liam. They are naked. He holds up a fifty-dollar bill, folded, and presses it into her breast. It slides in, his fingers entering her skin like sand. "Stop," she says. He smiles at her. His fingers keep pushing.

Imogene leaves on the last day of school. Great Aunt Bride drives her to the Deer Lake Airport and Maggie and Robert pick her up at Pearson. They dress like they planned their outfits: both in wool peacoats and store-bought scarves. Robert's thick hair is neatly brushed back and his moustache is a tuft of hay. The unfamiliarity of him and the airport, with its crowds of every kind of person in the catalogue, is refreshing.

Maggie and Robert's house is a brown-brick, two-storey townhouse surrounded by streets of identical brown-brick, two-storey townhouses. Imogene wonders how often drunk neighbours walk into the wrong house. She asks Robert this and he laughs in a hard, coughing bark, like he is pushing something out of him. Maggie says people lock their doors around here; it's unlikely someone would walk into your house. Well, duh. Poor ol' Imogene, just in from the sticks, didn't even know people lock their doors. Perhaps Ontario keeps a bug up Maggie's ass.

Maggie and Robert's kitchen looks expensive and safe, with dark wood cabinets reaching to the ceiling and grey granite countertops, gleaming and cold. The floor tiles are beige with rocky flecks to pull it all together. Imogene is in the spare bedroom where everything is new and a step up in her comforts: a double bed instead of a twin and white paint instead of peeling wallpaper. The walls are bare except for a poster-sized print of Klimt's *The Kiss*. The space rings with a new-room smell. Lemons and drying glue.

Robert's mother and two sisters come over for supper. They are all petite and buttery-looking with chunky blond hair and round cheeks buffed to a shine. When Imogene meets Grace, Robert's mother, she squeezes Imogene's shoulders and assesses her with hungry, darting eyes. "Imogene, you're gorgeous. Have you been to Toronto before?" She pronounces the "ont" in Toronto somewhere deep in her face, like she is clearing her sinuses. When Imogene answers that she's been here before, but only for a couple of days, Grace bellows, "You don't have much of a Newfie accent." She says this in her Ontario accent: *Noo-fee ack-sant.*

Robert laughs. "Maggie's comes out strong after she's had a few," he says. "I always tell her that her roots are showing."

"They sure do mess up the Queen's English out there," Grace says.

Later that night, Maggie and Robert argue in low whispers. Imogene can tell they aren't used to that, to having someone around who can hear them, because at times their voices shoot up like boiling water.

"It's always the same with you," Robert says. "Can't say a word about anything out East, can't say a word about women's behaviour, any woman's, even a stranger."

"If you know it upsets me, why do it? Unless you want to upset me."

"Let it go. You get offended because you want to be offended."

"Or you're being completely insensitive."

"Well, Maggie, we both know that's wrong. We both know there are things I believe should be done. And aren't being done because of your sensitivity."

Maggie stomps off to bed. Robert stays up with the news on.

During the days, Maggie and Imogene go on excursions, to the Royal Ontario Museum, the zoo, the Art Gallery of Ontario. She learns acronyms: the ROM, the AGO, the TTC. They eat in a Greek restaurant on the Danforth that douses cheese in liquor and sets it on fire. They go to the top of the CN Tower and gaze at the sprawl, like someone unrolled a giant sheet of graph paper and piled buildings on it. Maggie complains about smog and traffic, how it's too cold in the winter, too hot in the summer. But Imogene loves it. A big friggin' city, vast and abundant. Lots of people who don't know you. Whatever you want to do, you can do it. She thinks of things she's wanted to try but can't in St. Felix's. Take dance lessons. A pottery class. See a rock concert. Things which don't exist at home and so nobody mentions wanting them.

At night, the Markham dark is full of movement and industry. When cars pass the house, their tires pause before mounting speed bumps. She likes the sounds of activity and strangers. People doing their own thing. One night she watches out the window as a patrol car lazily lumbers down the street and realizes she does not miss Nan at all. She has not missed anyone. She remembers Aunt Trudy and Uncle Eli sending Rita off to church camp when she was in grade five and bringing her home early because she was homesick. Couldn't do a week at summer camp. What is it like, to pine for home like that?

She and Maggie walk around the Eaton Centre and poke through stores. Oversized garish Christmas decorations dangle from the ceiling, choral music blares. Maggie makes her try on clothes, consistently picking out shiny or tight things for her, but Imogene can't imagine where she would wear any of it. They walk into a store with leather everything: skirts, dresses, pants. While Maggie idles through a rack of leather skirts, Imogene sees the jacket. Black leather, blazer style—no major details, just a slick shape. She slips it off the hanger and tries it on, the zipper sighs up her chest. It rests at her hips and gently hugs her waist, making her taller, slimmer. The leather like velvet. Maybe this is what new cars smell like.

"That looks great on you," Maggie says. "Really smart. You have decent posture—all Mom's nagging must have worked on you. Oh, $200 of course. You're like me, whenever I really like something, it turns out being the most expensive thing in the store."

"I'm...I have money for it, actually," Imogene says. The words feel like they came from the reflection in the mirror, the slender girl in the sharp coat.

"Oh, honey, no. Save your money for school."

"It's okay. I—" Imogene's mind flits through possibilities—"I actually won a bit of money through a raffle. Nan doesn't know about it."

"She'll know about it when you come home with that coat."

"I—we can tell her it was on sale."

"Oh, can we now?"

"Please? I'm still working at the library. It won't use up my money."

"Well. If you feel really strongly about it. You know, you—everybody deserves to get something nice sometimes. I'll chip in."

"No, it's okay. Seriously."

This one's on Cecil, see. He needs to pay up. She makes sure to open her wallet away from Maggie so she won't see the thick stack of bills.

She wears the jacket out of the store. They exit from Bay and Queen and walk west, past boutiques and Indian restaurants, past Much Music and tourists queued for Speaker's Corner. Maggie giggles at a sex shop and asks if Imogene wants to do any Christmas shopping there. Imogene rolls her eyes. They go into a Vietnamese restaurant and Maggie orders raw spring rolls with delicate leaves of fresh mint inside. They dip the rolls in a sauce that's hot and peanutty and sweet. Further down the street, Maggie takes her into a sushi place and shows her how to mix the alien green wasabi in the little trough of soy sauce with the tip of her chopsticks. Imogene is skeptical at first, but enjoys it; each little firm roll with its pop of caviar and warmth of cured salmon. They pop into an Italian ice-cream shop and get small cups of raspberry gelato, pink silk on a flat wooden stick. "You like all kinds of food," Maggie says. "That's great. Kenneth told me Mom wouldn't even try curry when she was last in St. John's."

They wait to take the red and white streetcar eastbound back to the subway station. As they stand in the glass box, Imogene notices graffiti sprayed across the concrete wall in an alley. *Derrick Tough is a Drug Rapist.* Maggie sees her looking.

"Huh," Maggie says. "Surprised no one's covered that up."

"Maybe everyone knows it's true."

"Good point. A warning to us all."

Maggie leans out searching for signs of the streetcar. Her long brown hair falls like a cape over her shoulders and Imogene wants to touch her, stroke her hair, say something. Mom, don't feel bad. Mom, it's okay if you feel bad. Something sensible and kind, something to show she understands there are walls of awful, just awful shit around them. But they've had a good day and they are both full and feeling pretty in the crisp December air. The College streetcar arrives, collects them, and skates off in the grooved pavement, like long scars stretching east.

twenty-seven

Liam's place is a small one-storey house with white clapboard and brown trim and rests at the end of the longest driveway in St. Felix's. From the pavement, it has a cookie-cutter look about it, like a tiny chalet. But that's from a distance. Imogene has never been inside or up close to it.

She trudges up the driveway with her hands in her pockets. The plastic bag around her wrist slaps at her hip. She feels like she's making an entrance. *Luh, here she comes, Imogene Tubbs. Not very lively, is she? Face on her like frozen bread.* The third of January and there was little snow over Christmas, but now the sky is silvery and pregnant with weather. The ground is hard and gusts of wind stir up brief dustings of snow across rocks and dirt.

The driveway ends at the lawn. Overgrown tufts of frozen grass crunch underfoot. The white paint on the clapboard is chipped and flaking in patches. The door to the front porch is a flat wooden slab, the latch a piece of hairy twine over a nail. Imogene lifts it and steps inside, submerged in dim light and woodstove heat. She knocks on the inside door.

Liam's mother answers. A tiny woman with twiggy arms, a blond with dark roots. She has tight acid-wash jeans, a long yellow T-shirt and a mouthful of gum.

"Come in," she says. "I'm tryin' to get this hole cleaned up. It never ends."

She seems to know Imogene, but doesn't say her name. She slaps across the checkered linoleum in pink flip-flops and leans out into the hallway. "Liam! You gotta visitor." She watches Imogene blandly while she steps out of her boots. "He's in his room," she says. "Go on in."

Liam's room is down the narrow hall from the kitchen. Imogene's feet sink into thick, yellow carpet. She catches a glimpse of the bathroom: pink furry toilet seat cover with matching mat, seashell wallpaper. The Lundrigan Bathroom.

She raps on Liam's door and it slides open. His room is a narrow rectangle with a window over the bed. There are more posters than she predicted: AC/DC, Iron Maiden, *Nightmare on Elm Street*. Liam lies propped up with his shoulders on pillows. His face is a sunset of colour. The right eye is purple and sealed shut, lip cut at the corner, jaw swollen and peppered with a line of yellowing blotches. The four fingers on his right hand are trapped in a bandage. When she sits on the edge of the bed, he shifts away.

"How are you doing?" She places the bag on his bed.

"This is it."

"I brought you some stuff."

Liam blinks. He stares straight ahead without looking at her.

"Magazines." She pulls items from the bag. "Roast Chicken chips. Twizzlers. I know they're your favourite. And the tapes you loaned me."

"Why did you bring them?"

"I figured you'd want to listen to them."

"I see."

"Nan made some date squares too. I brought some of those."

"I hates dates squares."

"Oh. Sorry."

"I told you that before." It comes out of his mouth like slush. He has missing teeth. "How was your Christmas after?"

"It was good, you know." She stares at her hands. There is a ridge of something dark under her thumbnail.

"Not really. How would I know?"

"It was the same old stuff. Have you had many visitors?"

"Nope." He tries to sit up and winces. She moves to straighten his pillow, but he jerks his head in warning. "I can do it," he says.

"Are you going to tell me who did this?"

"Like you don't know."

Her eyes travel to his posters. She stares at Angus Young's bare knees. "I find it hard to believe Cec did it by himself."

"He did my eye. And this." He waves his bandaged hand. The edges of the gauze tinged yellow. "His work boots are steel-toed," he says. "Murray lent a hand. Guess I'm not working for him next summer. And Bryce

Benoit. He still thinks I broke into his cabin that time."

How loud are they talking? She glances at the door. "Are you going to press charges?" she asks.

"She never hears anything," he says. "There's no sense pressing charges. It would mean more trouble."

"How do they know it was you?"

"Bryce saw me in Mom's car. They put two and two together."

Liam picks up one of the tapes. Meatloaf's *Bat Out of Hell*. He stares at the cover for a second and drops it. "Good thing you brought these back. Now you can make sure you don't owe me nothing."

"What do you mean?"

"You leave for two weeks. I get the shit kicked out of me. Still takes you four days to come over."

"I didn't mean to take so long. I was nervous. Do you want me to put your tapes away?"

"Don't worry about it."

"Did they say—"

"They didn't mention you."

"Oh. Okay."

"I mean, I'll probably get the shit kicked out of me semi-regularly, but hopefully I'll bite my tongue."

"What does that mean?"

Liam leans forward. He keeps his good eye on her. "They think I took a lot more than we did. Over two thousand dollars, Cec says. Missing from behind a picture."

Imogene forces her face not to reveal itself. Liam reaches out with his good left hand and rubs the cuff of her new jacket between his fingers. "Nice coat," he says. "Looks expensive."

The back of her neck heats up. She should have hung up her coat when she came in. "Maggie's boyfriend bought it for me."

"Look at Imogene, getting whatever her heart desires."

"Knock it off."

"I knew it. I know that had to be a reason you were acting so cagey."

"Yeah, I was fucking nervous. Don't you think it makes sense to be nervous?"

"Because you did it. You took the money."

"No, I didn't."

"You did. And you didn't say anything."

"You have no proof of that."

"Is this why we started having sex? So I wouldn't tell anyone?"

"Oh my God. You're ridiculous." She starts to move away, but he sinks his nails into the soft leather of her jacket sleeve. Everything in the room is too warm and sickly, her weight on the overly soft mattress, the quicksand plush of the carpet. Liam's breath in her face is bitter, nicotine and fermentation.

"You never called me once while you were gone," he says. "You don't even want to be here now."

"That's not true."

"All this time. Not saying anything." He lets go of her sleeve like it's contagious. "I've had nothing to do but lie here and go over it all in my head. How you never seemed that into me. How you don't like holding my hand."

"I just don't like holding hands."

"The way you squeeze your eyes closed."

"You're being an idiot."

"Because I am one," Liam says. He rolls his eyes up to the ceiling. "I must be. Fuck. I can't believe I didn't know better."

"That's a shitty thing to say." She swallows. Don't act guilty. "But you are being an idiot right now, though, going on with this."

"Oh, but being an idiot is all I know, see? All you gotta do is look at Mom and Dad for that."

"I don't know anything about your mom and dad."

"Like fuck you don't. Everyone in this place knows everything about everybody."

"They just think they do."

"Well, Imogene, I thought I knew you pretty good. But now, when I think about it, screwing someone to get what you want might come naturally to you. Seeing what you come from and all."

"Fuck you, Liam."

"'Fuck you,' she says. 'You're an idiot,' she says. Yeah, you really sound like a girl who likes me."

She stands up. "Tell you what, Liam. Call me when you heal up and stop being an asshole." The nervous sweat on her back bubbles in anger. The room swarms around her, the posters and their sharp-edged lettering, black and red and orange like old wounds. She could rip them down. Anything to make him shut up.

"I can't believe I actually thought you were alright," he says. His voice dips to a low hiss. "But I should have known."

"Oh, Christ. Listen to you. You're delirious."

"You're just like him, Immy. You're a fucking creep."

Her hand floats out and grips his left wrist. He brings up his right hand and she snatches his bandaged fingers. He yelps. There is something so satisfying about his yelp, like a puppy. She leans over the bed like she is going to kiss him.

"Why would I not take it?" she says. "What did you expect me to do? You thought I would be cool going into that bastard rapist's house for two hundred dollars? Just follow you around like your dog?"

His leg twitches. She brings her knee up and lets it hover over his crotch. He glares up at her, his chin trembling slightly.

"Fuck Cec. That money is mine," she says. "If he comes near me, my whole family will charge him with what he did to my mother. And you can tell him that. And if he doesn't think it will happen, I'm fucking evidence. And Liam, if you're too goddamn stunned to understand that, you deserve to have some sense beaten into you."

She releases his fingers with a flick and steps back from the bed. He buckles over his hand, cursing and moaning. She walks out of the room, her socks swishing through the shag. Liam's mother is rolling cigarettes on the kitchen table. "Take care," she mutters. Imogene doesn't look up as she shoves on her boots. The thin plank of the porch door clatters closed behind her.

Outside, the wind has picked up. It shoves into Imogene's back and half carries her up the stretch of driveway. It gathers up other items along the way: cigarette butts, a paper bag, dead leaves. It rushes her and all of it up the length from Liam's house, cheering them on, like they're competing in a hundred-meter dash of trash.

twenty-eight

School starts back up the following Monday. Imogene sits in the back of homeroom with slick palms, peeking up from under her hair at the entrance of every classmate. Teddy Campbell in a new Habs jersey. Antonia Martin with a new haircut. But Liam doesn't show. No sign of him the next day either. During attendance on Wednesday morning, Crystal wonders where he is. Donny says he's gone to Alberta. Imogene dulls her face to hide any flicker of surprise as Crystal spins around to look at her.

The month of January drags itself along. Teachers make jokes to each other. "Wow, is it January 75th already?" Then February bringing piles of snow and three days off school when the furnace dies. Valentine's Day gets postponed for blizzards and freezing rain. Parents complain about how the grade twelves might fall behind, especially since in two months all they'll care about is grad. What do they pay taxes for anyway? Every morning Imogene starts the woodstove to the distant oily whine of ski-doos. She tries not to think about how quickly someone could get to the house, just zip right over the brook and across the field, pull up right by her window. No evidence besides the trail of the track, dark figures in full-body skidoo suits and helmets. "Look at them flying around, it's a wonder they don't kill themselves," Nan says. "Bandits in the snow."

Imogene passes her midterms with an eighty average. Maggie phones to say how proud she is. They'll do something this summer, which feels forever away. Each time the wind whips the breath from her mouth, she feels like she deserves it. When she's inside with the woodstove on bust, she thinks of Liam's words and fresh sweat flashes on the back of her neck. If that's what he thinks, she's better off. Like she was ever better with him. What a fucker.

No one at school mentions Liam around her, but Nick finds reasons to leave rooms Imogene enters. She and Rita are often interrupted by Nick honking the truck horn or standing in a doorway. "Rita. You coming?" Rita flushing and shuffling off.

When Nick isn't around, Rita talks about grad and going to Grenfell in Corner Brook next year. She's found a picture of a dress she likes in *Seventeen*: strapless with an A-line skirt, Cherry's nan is going to make something like it for her. She's been accepted to residence at Grenfell and Nick will be starting at Fisher Tech, so they'll be close to each other. And in different schools, so they'll make lots of friends. She's not sure where she'll focus her studies, but she's narrowed it down to nursing or primary/elementary education. Occasionally, she leaves Liam's name in the middle of a sentence. "I think Liam wanted to get a skidoo like that. Liam said something like that once." Imogene doesn't bite.

With Rita wrapped up in Nick, Imogene sometimes goes out with Liz or Antonia, a friendship evolved from recess smoke breaks. She likes how laid-back they both are, but on weekends they usually want to hitchhike somewhere and the thought of Cecil or Bryce or Murray picking them up makes her nervous. Or a car full of Liam's friends, Randy, Donny, and Corey, out on the beer, vehemently silent at the sight of her. Or Liam himself, home for a visit, his face sliding into the same scowl he wore in grade nine when he'd see her and throw whatever was closest at her face.

She finds ways to stay busy. The Youth Centre takes her on part time in the library to help organize and set up for groups of kids. She creates displays of books. By size: big books for little hands; by colour: red for Valentine's Day, green for St. Patrick's Day; by topic: issues with the cod fishery; and by writer: Dr. Seuss favourites for the author's birthday. After her seventeenth birthday, Aunt Trudy brings her to Stephenville to do her driver's test. Maggie's parallel-parking practice pays off and she passes on the first try.

In late spring, a letter arrives announcing her preliminary acceptance to Memorial University. Next year, she just has to pass everything with a decent average and keep squirreling away money. When Nan tells Maggie, she and Robert order Imogene an electric typewriter through Sears. Maggie says you can save your documents on it and print them off at once. Robert says it will give her an edge. Imogene uses it for her final English assignments in June. When summer comes, she works at the library full time. She deposits her paycheques in her savings account. But when she counts the amount in her head, she adds her hidden Cec dollars. The total makes her warm inside.

In August, Maggie and Robert are in St. John's for ten days and they fly Imogene in via student standby. In St. John's, Imogene hopes to see Violet and Jamie, the billet. Jamie didn't respond to her second letter and when she looks up his last name in the phone book, there are twenty-seven entries for Clark in Mount Pearl. As for Violet, Uncle Kenneth and Beth broke up and he doesn't have her address. The last he heard, she was working at a record store in Halifax. Imogene's questions make his eyes fill with grey clouds.

They stay at Kenneth's new place off Torbay Road. "Everything around is strip malls and rundown apartments," Maggie says. "Don't worry, we're not buying around here."

"Why not?" Robert says. "It's dirt cheap."

Maggie and Robert bring her along on their various tasks, which mostly involve looking at houses they're considering purchasing and meeting guys Robert knows, all other Come From Aways, he calls them. The CFA they see the most is a tall man named Bruce. He has sideburns that emphasize his jowly face and he calls everything Newfie. Newfie food, Newfie music, Newfie beer. Four construction workers watching one guy dig a hole is typical Newfie work. Someone turning without using their signal is typical Newfie driving. When Imogene accepts the beer he buys her at supper, he says, "Oh, she's a Newfie all right." Maggie doesn't laugh when Robert does and Bruce says, "I thought Newfies love a joke."

"Sure," Maggie says. "I always laugh when I hear a joke."

That night, Maggie and Robert argue in their bedroom. "Why do you have to be like that?" Robert says. "He's an investor."

"Then he should invest in some manners."

"I can't talk to you when you're like this."

"Of course, because everything has to be on your terms."

The next morning, Robert is asleep on the couch under a comforter. Breakfast is a quiet meal and when Robert finishes his toast, he opens his wallet and peels out six twenty-dollar bills. "You ladies go shopping today," he says. "Get stuff for back to school." After he leaves, Maggie stirs her coffee for a long time. Imogene tries to think of something to say. "Probably lots of sales at the mall," she says. Maggie nods.

At the mall, Imogene gets new jeans and three new tops. Maggie is quiet, but busies herself with picking out clothes for Imogene, things in shades of green and purple, colours she says suit her. "But be careful wearing them together," she says. "Might make you look like an eggplant."

On their way to the food court, Maggie stops in front of the display window for Travel Cuts. A cutout of a palm tree and sandy beach takes up most of the window. *Come to Jamaica, mon* in hot pink letters.

"Imogene, if you were going to live anywhere, where would you go?"

"Most places look good. But being somewhere with no English is a little scary."

"Where then?"

Imogene thinks of when she saw that movie, *Manhattan*, on CBC late one night. Nan complained about Woody Allen throughout it. "What a creep he seems to be, always paired with a woman you know would have nothing to do with him if he wasn't famous. And we're supposed to believe him and that young girl are some kind of match. Pfft." But Imogene was transfixed by the black-and-white shots of New York. The movie wasn't available with the rentals at the Kwik Stop, so she got in the habit of scanning the TV guide for it. Most of the time, she just watched the opening scene, the crowds and taxis and sprawl and the sweeping Gershwin musical backdrop.

"New York maybe," she says.

"I always wanted to go to Greece," Maggie says. "Somewhere warm and distinct. It always looks so clean and gorgeous in pictures. Those white houses on the Cycladic Islands. Do you like Robert?" She asks this without looking at Imogene.

"Sure," Imogene says. "He's okay."

"Maybe someday I'll go wherever I want," Maggie says.

The next day, Maggie brings her to the airport herself. "I wish we had the house picked out already," Maggie says. "It will be sorted soon." She hugs Imogene and leaves without waiting for her to get through security.

twenty-nine

Imogene was expecting a different dynamic in grade twelve, but besides getting to sit at the back of the bus and teachers instilling the fear of public exams, things feel the same. In homeroom, Crystal Seymour nags everyone to join the grad committee, to meet after school and make decisions on songs and decoration colours. "Ten more months of this shit," Liz Constantine says and Imogene nods in agreement.

Even though Rita and Nick are going to school in Corner Brook, they come home most weekends throughout the fall. It's common to see Nick at all the same stuff from high school: at the Rec Centre for a floor hockey game, drinking in the woods behind the pool hall. Nan complains about the two of them on the phone with Great Aunt Madonna. "You'd think Rita would have more sense with her study habits."

On some Saturday nights, they pick Imogene up for a drive. Rita says Corner Brook is a laugh, but she doesn't like living in residence. "Too many snotty people," she says. She has to share a unit with three others and two of them complain about Nick coming over so much. The proctor threatened to call her parents, claiming they're paying for her to study, not for her boyfriend to live there.

"What a bunch of losers," Rita says. She sits squished between Imogene and Nick in the truck. "I know it was that Cheryl who complained and she's just jealous 'cause she doesn't have a boyfriend. There's so much screwing in residence. If they don't all get AIDS, I'll be shocked." She squeezes Imogene's arm. "Next year, when you start at Grenfell, we can get a place together. It will be cheaper than res and we can take turns cooking. If I pick up shifts at the club over Christmas and the summer, I can make enough for tuition and some furniture."

"I'm applying for MUN in St. John's," Imogene says.

"Why?" Nick says. "Cheaper to get home from Corner Brook."

The idea of living with Rita and Nick makes her want to open the door of the truck and dash into the woods, like a feral cat. But neither of them seems to want to hear no, so she says nothing for now.

"Christmas is going to be great," Rita says. "Natalie will be home from Dalhousie and Cherry will be back from Toronto. Gonna be a laugh." Imogene nods. The thought of Christmas makes her feel tired deep inside. Rita and Nick don't say anything about Liam coming home, and on the bus, Randy tells Corey that he's going to Edmonton for the holidays. "I might move up there too. Fuck this place."

Maggie didn't send a ticket to Ontario this year because Grace, Robert's mother, is sick. Uncle Kenneth has started seeing someone new, a woman named Susan. He says he's spending Christmas with her and her kids in Bay Roberts. Nan complains her children never visit.

The day before Christmas break, Imogene returns home to a high-pitched tooting, blaring out of the house. Someone playing the tin whistle in the kitchen. The Christmas visitors have already started. The sound grows stronger as she approaches the house. When she opens the front door, she realizes the sound doesn't change, it is just one high note. The kettle on the stove. She turns off the element and moves the kettle.

Nan is in the living room. She sits on the couch, eyes on the TV. *Video Hits* is on. The Whitesnake video with the redhead in the tight, white, short dress plays. Nan hates music videos. Whenever Imogene watches *Video Hits*, Nan complains. "Can they make one of these things without the camera trained on someone's arse?" But now she sits and stares at the screen. The hair on one side of her head is pushed forward and stuck to her cheek in thin wisps, like watercolour waves. Her mouth is a narrow line with trembling edges.

"What are you watching, Nan?"

"I don't know. I'm not well. I think I ate something that was off."

"You're sick?"

"I...I have to go over to Eli's. But I ate something. I think it made me stupid. I can't remember how to turn off the TV."

The remote rests by Nan's knee. There is a drop of something yellowish on the edge of it, something spilled. The spill continues along the bottom edge of the couch and across the floor. She's looking at Nan's puke.

"Nan, do you want to go to the hospital?"

Nan blinks in a deliberate way. Like blinking is a decision. "Yes," she says. "I think that would be a good idea."

Three transient ischemic attacks or mini-strokes are the doctor's words, occurring in her vision centre. Mini-strokes. The words make Imogene think of fingertips on something small: the back of a kitten, a puppy's ear. "She'll need help," the doctor says. "She won't be able to drive right now, but eventually her eyesight will improve." Nan sits up in bed, her hair limp and pushed into place. The bed is surrounded by flowers and cards with pictures of flowers on them. "It's a blur in here," Nan says. "A perfumed colourful blur. Like that French artist who paints the lilies."

"Monet," Imogene says.

Nan's eyes roam the room, but don't set on anything. "I can't wait to get out of here," she says. "Dying to shampoo my hair. You could fry an egg on my head right now."

Uncle Eli and Aunt Trudy bring over food, meals that can be warmed up, macaroni, beef stew. Aunt Trudy vacuums. Uncle Eli sticks rubber grips on the bottom of the tub. He puts neon stickers on doorknobs. He gets them a touch-tone phone with big numbers. Rita and Nick come by on the weekend and they take Imogene on drives while Eli and Trudy visit. Rita says, "I might know a couple of places for September."

"I don't think I'm going to Corner Brook," Imogene says.

"You have a lot on your plate right now," Rita says. "We'll sort it out."

Every second night, Maggie calls, sometimes calm, sometimes weepy. Grace is going through chemo and is in worse shape than Nan. "They say bad things happen in threes," Maggie says. "I cross my fingers every day. Two is enough."

"That saying is bull," Imogene says. But for days after the phone call, she finds herself looking for a third bad thing to check off the superstition list. Maybe it will be something small, like the car breaking down. She could handle that over another illness or accident.

One morning, she stands in the bathroom, lining up Nan's pills. The doctor has given her little plastic containers with dates and times on them. Nan can't see the labels well enough, so Imogene loads them up. And after she refills the pills, she'll line up Nan's soap and face cream and toothpaste, for easy access. And after she does that, she'll clean the bathroom. Nan insists on the tub and toilet scrubbed down every other day. "I can't see the dirt myself and I don't want anyone thinking we live in filth." Imogene catches a glimpse of her own face in the bathroom mirror. Her clenched teeth set her jaw like a fist. The light in her eyes seems both dull and rabid, like something caged for too long. Maybe she is the bad thing. That's the secret consensus, isn't it? Bad ol' Rape Baby Imogene. *You're just like him, Immy. You're a fucking creep.* "You need to get out of here," she says to the mirror. She nods to her reflection in agreement.

February is the due date for applications to MUN, Carleton, and Ryerson. Imogene isn't sure about journalism—she rarely reads the newspaper, does she really want to write for one? On the MUN application, she checks the box for St. John's campus. There can be no living with Rita. Her voice, her furniture, her Randy Travis tapes. Nick skulking on the couch, the hockey game on. Always, always on. She fills out an application for residence in St. John's and leaves all the Grenfell boxes blank. When they come home for March break, Rita says, "Did you fill out your applications?"

"Yes,"

"Next year is going to be a laugh."

"Sure is."

For months, Imogene drives, picks up groceries, reads out the mail, puts away the dishes, and drops heaping spoonfuls of sugar into steaming teacups. She sits next to Nan on the couch and narrates what happens on the soap operas: when the dialogue ends and the music intensifies. It is tedious, but she feels relieved for an excuse to avoid being out and about. If karma exists, maybe she'll make it lean her way. Dutiful Imogene. She keeps the door locked. Every day, she checks on the money in Teeny's leg. If she has to, she can run away. She can drive her and Nan to the ferry. She can pay the fare herself.

In the spring, Nan's eyesight has mostly returned, but driving makes her nervous. And the mini-strokes have loosened her tongue. Or nerves. Or patience. Maybe it's just being laid up for so long. Either way, Imogene wouldn't mind doing the errands so much if Nan would let her go alone. "I never get out of this house," she says. "Going friggin' stir crazy." Nan sits in the passenger seat and complains if Imogene plays anything that isn't VOCM or CBC. Uncle Eli and Aunt Trudy take her when they can.

"Next year, you'll be free of all that," Rita says. "Well, maybe not when you come home on the weekends."

At Easter, Nan wants a trip to the store. Chocolate eggs for Trudy's Girl Guide group. She stands in the aisle, lifting cheap chocolate rabbits to her face. Mr. Solid. Mr. Nutty. She notices someone at the end of the row. "Is that Malcolm Whalen?" she says.

She takes a squinting step towards the person. "Who is that, Immy?" she says, pointing straight at Cecil Jesso. He stands before a display of Vienna sausages, counting tins into his red grocery basket. He turns toward Nan's pointing finger, his bottom lip a slack ledge for his mouth, eyes bulging. "Who is that, Imogene?" Nan says.

Imogene swallows. "Cecil Jesso."

"Hullo, Missus Tubbs," Cecil says. His voice is clotted and damp. "Hope yer feelin' better."

"Don't give me any of your concern," Nan says. Her pointed hand rises to his face.

"What's yeh problem?"

"Don't act like you care about problems. I know what kind of problems you cause."

Nan's eyes are slits.

Cecil gapes at her. "Now, Missus Tubbs, I knows yer not well. But there's no need of that."

"I'll say what I want. Everyone's aware of what kind of dirt happens in that house of yours."

"You talk too much, Agnes."

"Maybe. Maybe I'll talk too much to the police sometime."

His mouth twists into an indignant coil. "I never did *nuttin*," he says. "I never *touched* her." His nostrils suck hard at the air and his eyes meet Imogene's. Watery blue and stormy. He looks back at Nan. "And you might wanna watch that girl of yours."

"My girls are not your concern," Nan says.

"Jesus Christ," Cecil says. His hand opens and the red grocery basket falls to the floor, sausage tins clattering. He stomps past the cash and pushes hard on the door, bell jangling on his exit.

"Bastard." Nan passes the Mr. Solid to Imogene. "If I could see and I was prepared, I'd shoot him."

thirty

1992

When it comes time to make decisions, there are options. Robert's mother passes away in a hospital in Brantford. With the money she left him, they can buy a bigger house in St. John's, buy it outright. Imogene won't need roommates; there's an apartment in the basement they can rent out to help pay the bills. And Nan, still too nervous to drive. And Trudy, busy with grandchildren and the business. So Nan can go to town with Imogene. Closer to Uncle Kenneth, close to major medical centers. Easier for Maggie to fly in and out.

"No way," Nan says. "I'm fine here. I have my house, I have Eli and Trudy."

"But Trudy and Eli have so much on the go with Rita in school. She doesn't qualify for student aid," Maggie says. "And Steve just got engaged. And the club is always high or low. Eli says the building needs a new roof and he might go out to Alberta for a bit."

"Never mind any of that, I'm staying."

And then in June the doctor says Nan has gout and type-two diabetes.

"Now your eyesight is in even bigger danger," Maggie says.

"Half of St. Felix's got the diabetes," Nan says. "It's like it's in the water."

Maggie and Robert buy the house and Nan keeps refusing until July when the fishery closes. The TV is footage of fishermen with defeated faces and symbolic empty boats. She's gone, b'ys, she's gone, the new catchphrase of the economically betrayed. It all makes Imogene want to be gone even more and it's just a matter of time now. Trudy and Eli talk about working in Alberta. The Sampsons might have to give up the store. The Coishes have family in Ontario who can help them get set up. Liam and Randy Lundrigan's mother boards up the house and takes the bus to somewhere, all at once, without telling anyone.

Trudy and Eli have Nan and Imogene over for supper. "It won't be so bad, Agnes," Trudy says. "You'll have Kenneth and Imogene to help you in St. John's."

"What do you mean?" Rita says. "You're going to St. John's?"

"Sure, that was decided ages ago," Nan says. Rita gets up from the table and goes into her room.

"You could excuse yourself," Uncle Eli says. "This isn't a cafeteria."

The next day, Rita shows up at Imogene's, stomping full force up the driveway with the wind at her back. Imogene is making piles: stuff for St. John's, stuff for the dump. Rita's bottom lip points at Imogene like an indignant slug. "So. When were you going to tell me?"

"I thought you knew."

"You said you were going to Grenfell."

"I never said that." Imogene selects sheets of newspaper for wrapping up glasses. "We're getting rid of some of the dishes," she says. "Take the ones in this box if you want."

"We've been talking about it since before Christmas."

"All you said was that you wanted to move out of residence and get a place where Nick could come over."

"Yeah, for the three of us."

"But I like the school in St. John's."

"Since when?"

"I've mentioned it before. And Maggie and Robert have gone to a lot of trouble. Why don't you just live with Nick?"

"Mom and Dad'd have a hernia."

"So, find another roommate who doesn't care if your boyfriend is over all the time."

"Who am I going to find? It's August now."

"Can you get someone off a bulletin board or something?"

"Immy, this is real fuckery."

"Why did you think this was going to happen? With Nan sick? Maggie got us a house in St. John's."

"So? You don't have to do the same as them."

"I want to. Honestly, I don't like Corner Brook anyway. I'd rather get farther away."

"What's the point if you're still living with your grandmother?"

"What's the point if you and Nick are just going to go home every weekend?"

"You're fucked in the head. You act like you're miserable and then you make sure your living situation doesn't change. You're going to be in St. John's surrounded by snot-nosed townies who think they're better than you."

"Right. Much better to stay as close as possible to this hole."

"Oh, because you're better than us? God, Nick was right about you."

"Right how?"

"The way you never go out. Or talk to anyone. You and your clothes and your trips. You think you're better than everyone, even though Maggie gets you all that shit out of guilt."

"That's what Nick says, does he? Well, guess you better believe him."

"Well, I didn't, but now I'm thinking he's right."

"And I guess it's never occurred to you that some people have more ambition than to stay in their mommy and daddy's village and suck Nick Cleary's dick at every opportunity."

"Fuck you."

"You're ridiculous."

The rage is high in Imogene's temples now. She feels like she could levitate on her own steam, high above Rita's blow-dried head. "Like I would want to be around you two tools any longer than I already have."

"Whatever. Good luck with Nan's shitty diapers." Rita grabs her jacket from the chair and thrusts her arm into it. There is a high ripping sound. "And now you made me tear my new Nike coat."

"You're welcome. It's ugly anyway."

"Liam was right. You got a real mean streak in you."

When Rita stomps out, the wind catches the door. It slams extra hard.

thirty-one

The house is the third one in from Merrymeeting Road, on Cook Street. All white, concrete steps, some grass. "It's a good neighbourhood," Maggie says. "If you're walking, it's less than ten minutes to MUN, less than ten minutes downtown, less than ten minutes to Churchill Square. Quiet street, but close to a main road. You can just dart over to the mall, the grocery store. Coleman's is just down the street and there's a Dominion in Churchill Square. Close to schools, lots of families around." Maggie talks with her hands, gesturing in the direction of the destinations she names. Nan picks at her hands in her lap. Uncle Kenneth drives.

Maggie opens the screen door and unlocks the main one. "Look at the woodwork on this door, Mom," she says. "Great details." She hangs the keys on a small hook in the porch. A hall runs through the centre of the house. The living room is to the right, hardwood floors, a large window facing the street. The kitchen is on the left, white tile, pine cabinets. The air smells like lemon Pledge and mothballs.

"This is a much bigger place than back home," Maggie says. "A full basement apartment and everything."

"There's people in it," Nan says.

"That's a good thing. Extra money." Maggie swings open the bedroom doors. "Lots of light in this room," she says. "And a deck outside where you can have your tea."

"I never ate outside when I didn't have neighbours right there to gawk at me. Not going to start now."

"Ma," Uncle Kenneth says. "Have you seen the size of your closet?" He opens the door to reveal a deep square closet with a shelf running along the top. "Look, you can walk right in."

"S'pose we can keep the Christmas decorations in there," Nan says. "I don't have that much clothes."

"We'll take you to Leon's now the once. Get you a new bed."

"My old one is coming."

"The springs are coming up on that bed, Mom," Maggie says. "I don't know how you can sleep on it. They're like tree roots in your back."

"It was fine for your father and me."

"After thirty years, you should have a new bed."

"C'mon, let's go get you one," Uncle Kenneth says. "You could fit a king-size in there."

"What would I need a king-size bed for? You think I'm going to be entertaining?"

"Whatever you want then. Imogene, are you coming?"

"No, I'll stay."

The car pulls away. Imogene sits on her step. The walk is a straight concrete path to the street. Lines of houses. White with colourful accents. They have a square yard and back space, like everyone else. They have sheers on the windows and a short iron fence. She will start classes in four days. When they drove around earlier, she could see the beige buildings of the university from the top of the hill by the graveyard. She takes a deep breath. The air smells like fried fish and marijuana. The nervous energy tingles the back of her thighs on the step and crawls up through her core. It is new and it is good. She can't wait.

part two

one

May 1993

Overall, Sherrie Duffy has Imogene quite a bit drove.

Sherrie purses her mouth around the straw in her White Russian so to not smudge her lipstick. She has sculpted her hair around her face so the sides fan out like stiff butterfly wings. The symmetry is impressive, even to Imogene.

"Guess who I saw the other day at Sobeys?" Sherrie says. "Mr. Rowe. He had, like, ten packs of Hungry Man dinner in his cart. My guts hurt at the sight of him."

"He looks like a Hungry Man dinner," Maureen says.

"So gross, bleh."

Imogene sips her beer. It dribbles down the side of her face. Someone at the bar laughs hard. She wipes it and rests her chin on her hand, like she meant to do it all along.

"Remember the time he called Jeremy an asshole?" Sherrie says.

"Oh my God, yes. What a racket."

"Jeremy went to the principal and Rowe denied it. Said he told him he was a 'hassle.'" When Sherrie tosses her head for emphasis, her hair wings flap.

"I guess they can kind of sound the same," Imogene says.

"Imogene, did you meet Jeremy at Christmas?" Maureen says. "He was home from Montreal then."

"No, I don't know him."

"He's such a laugh." Sherrie sips her drink. The last time they were out, she told Imogene if you drink White Russians before anything else, you won't get sick because the milk coats the stomach. Then she threw up in the cab on the way home.

"Remember that time Rowe was trying to remind us to draw a name for Secret Santa and said 'Don't forget about the Christmas draw,' and Jeremy was like, 'Yes, let's all get together for a Christmas draw?' Kicked him out of class. What an arsehole."

"Rowe was our homeroom teacher in grade twelve," Maureen says.

"Oh, sorry, Imogene," Sherrie says. "Maureen and I get on our memory lane kicks all the time."

"It's okay."

Memory lane can't be that long if the memories are less than a year and a half old. Imogene picks at the label on her beer. Two men with bellies and ball caps sit at the bar. One makes eye contact with her. He drinks and licks his lips. She looks away. There's a bulletin board in the porch of the pub, a natural focus point. She can just read the notices and wait for Sherrie's guts to be sufficiently coated.

Back in September, Imogene would have never had predicted how much time she would spend doing this very thing—reading bulletin-board notices. Large bulletin boards grace almost every landing of every building on campus. They beckoned to her: look at all our options. Here are other people's lists for you.

Party at the Dining Hall.

German Society Mixer.

Books for Sale.

Participants needed for Psychology Experiment.

Tutoring service available.

Toastmasters' Course.

Looking for Carpool.

Looking for Babysitter.

Looking for Love.

Imogene stood before them, her new MUN backpack firm on her spine, craning her neck to absorb the plethora of goings-on. She tore off tiny tongues of phone numbers for later. She shoved them in the change pocket of her wallet, like doing so would transform them into something monetary.

During those first weeks, she invested in high-quality bond paper and delivered her résumé to every business from the square to the mall.

Maggie and Robert agreed to pay for tuition, but stressed that Imogene and Nan had to cover textbooks. She scoured lists of used ones for sale like Uncle Kenneth instructed. She did the math and realized it was cheaper to photocopy anything slim and return it: Othello, Folklore 1000 readings. "Now there's a way to save money for the weekend," the guy behind her said when she hauled out the crinkled packet in English 1080.

But by Thanksgiving weekend, there was still not a single phone call or interview. "Now that the cod is gone, everyone's just hiring their cousins," Rita said. "Especially in town." Which Rita can say easily as Uncle Eli gives her whatever shifts she wants at the club, whatever matches her schedule when she's not in school. "I bet some people back home are crying nepotism behind your back," Imogene said and Rita didn't know what nepotism meant and Imogene made sure to roll her eyes.

By Halloween, bulletin boards just pointed out the range of experiences Imogene lacks—she's never written a review for a school paper, she's never participated in a French conversation language exchange, she's never sung in a choir. Volunteering at the radio station meant she would have to learn about actual good music, things she might know if Nan hadn't refused to get cable. She remembers Violet's disdain at her musical taste. She is crippled when it comes to trying to access and play what is acceptably cool. There are audition calls for small plays. Theatre arts was never offered out home. Meanwhile, it seems every townie got that shit done in some Christmas concert. Maureen says the drama clubs cast the same bunch all the time anyway, most aren't even students, just local actors who don't want to move to Corner Brook to study theatre.

Then there are the society mixers, all with hand-drawn photocopied signs: Labatt's products, NABs available. She imagines having to talk with interest about the mandatory history requirement with classmates who expect passion and in-depth knowledge. Then getting too drunk in the spirit of overcompensation and being patrolled out by MUN security. She refuses to be in any situation where there is a possibility she can be humiliated or branded. This is not what her life is now.

But the Alumni Association call centre didn't need experience. For almost a month, she spent evenings phoning former graduates for donations. There was a script on how to begin with a one-hundred-dollar request and work in how just twenty dollars gets the donor's name published in the alumni magazine.

She hated it—with every call, she fought the impulse to say goodbye and escape. But Maureen's name was high on the list of top callers.

Imogene recognized her from English class where she'd admired her hair from afar, her dark, slick bob with one frontal stripe dyed blond running along the edge of her face like a strategic checkmark of approval. At the call centre, Imogene watched Maureen smile into the phone to change the contour of her voice. Off the phone, her natural expression is set on sullen, but that's just her face. Witnessing it turn from flat to fake sincere entertained Imogene.

And then, the MUN library saved Christmas. A student assistant dropped out, could she start right away? It's mostly putting things back where they belong. Potential to carry on into the winter and spring. Yes, no problem, Imogene said on the phone. Thank heavenly fuck.

On her last day at the call centre, Maureen said they should celebrate. At the Breezeway, Maureen knew the bouncer and he looked the other way. She ordered tequila shots and retrieved two take-out packets of salt from her purse. "You'd be surprised how many bars don't have salt," she said. "How do you do tequila with no salt?" Later, they went to an after-hours party. And the following Friday, after their last class, they met up at the Breezeway again. Draft was on for seventy-five cents a glass. They carried on regularly for the rest of fall and over Christmas break. They both liked evenings with loosely made plans. They appreciated the element of not knowing what the night had in store. And then, in February, Maureen's friend Sherrie Duffy ended it with some guy named Rex and decided she wanted to go out with girlfriends again.

The light flashes off the Plexiglas box over the pub's bulletin board. Thursdays, 2 Molson Special Dry for $5.00. A flyer for a local band, Joyful Noise. These days, live music stirs her curiosity. She and Maureen went to a show in late January, a fundraiser for a local artist whose house burned down. The floor was slick with melted snow and salt muck from a crowd of stomping winter boots. Maureen gyrated her hips in her boy-cut jeans, christening Imogene's head with a pour from her Blue Star. Imogene woke up the next morning with sticky hair, her stomach muscles sore from laughter.

"My father has the VIP booth at the stadium tonight," Sherrie says. "There'll be a crowd downtown once the game lets out."

"Better get over to Benders quick"

"That place is gross, bleh. I say there won't be much of a lineup at The Sundance in a half hour."

Maureen stirs the lime around in her vodka and soda. "We'll see," she says. "My cousin might pop in."

Imogene has not known Sherrie long, but she's noticed how many of her sentences start with "My father" and onto whatever he has or says or gets. *My father has a new stereo picked out for our Mazda Miata. It's going to sound great with the top down. My father says he has a friend who can get me a work term at Scotiabank.* Guaranteed, she's never had to question what a great guy Daddy is. Or if her mother might prefer she didn't exist. Or have to clean up her grandmother's vomit.

She's also noticed that when Sherrie doesn't like something, she makes sure it's known. *You're doing folklore and English? Too much reading, bleh. You like this song? Too dark and depressing, bleh.* And always that little "bleh" sound at the end, a guttural punctuation made by jutting out her tongue. Doesn't matter if it's something you happen to like very much. If you're eating cheese and she doesn't like cheese, you're going to hear all about how cheese is gross. *Everything in restaurants gotta have cheese on it now. I had chicken tetrazzini last week, sure I would have never ordered that if I'd known there was a bucket of cheese roasted over the top of it, bleh.*

"Rowe once told me I was doing sweet fanny Adams in class," Sherrie says. "I didn't know what he meant at first."

"What does it mean?" Imogene says.

"Doing sweet fuck-all."

"Sweet fanny Adams sounds dirtier."

"It really does," Maureen says.

When the three of them go out, Sherrie likes to sing "Hey Everybody, Get Laid, Get Fucked," at the top of her lungs when dancing to Billy Idol's version of "Mony Mony." Twice, Imogene has mentioned a particular place to see a band and Sherrie has complained about the way people dress there. Two weeks ago, on Sherrie's suggestion, they attended a "Free 'til You Pee" special where all drinks were free until someone went to the bathroom and Imogene believes she might have permanent bladder damage as a result. All this is fun to Sherrie, who likes to point out Imogene's West Coast dialect and how she drags out the Os in words like *road* and *coat*. And calls Imogene Crunchy Granola because she wears fake Doc Martens from Aldo and likes The Clash. Drove. Sherrie's got Imogene drove.

The door swings open to a blast of outside air and a peal of laughter. It is as if someone is singing a belly-laugh and Imogene smiles on impulse without knowing the joke. The laugh enters like a cool breeze slicing through the room's drunken muddiness. In the Plexiglas box she can see part of the laugher's reflection: dark hair, big smile. He places a cigarette pack in the breast pocket of his jean jacket, still laughing at whatever was said or happened. Well now. He is a Joyful Noise indeed.

He looks over at their table and his face shows recognition. He waves. Maureen waves back. "My cousin's here," Maureen says. "He's best kind." She removes her purse from the chair next to her.

The Joyful Noise hugs Maureen before flopping down neatly in the seat. He exudes cool air and something cozy and radiant, like he contains an inner furnace that churns out charm.

"Hi, Sherrie," he says. "I guess they let any old riff raff in here."

"Har-de-har."

"You sound like your dad," Maureen says. "Riff raff and sleeveens."

"That's the name of my band, actually."

Sherrie snorts. "Should call it the Village Mall People."

"Either that or Jigs and Streels." The Joyful Noise leans back in his seat. He looks at Imogene and his smile is immediate, like a springboard. She grins back so big and automatic she can feel her top lip peel back from her gums.

"Hello, red-haired girl."

"Hi."

"I'm Jamie."

"I'm Imogene."

"Sorry," Maureen says. "This is my cousin Jamie."

"So rude, Maureen. Who raised you?"

"Your father's sister."

Sherrie stands up. "I'm getting another drink."

"I'd love a rum and coke," he says.

"That's nice." Sherrie's hair fans out as she makes her way to the bar.

"My god," Jamie says. "The attitude." He turns back to Imogene. His eyes are dark mischief. "I feel like we've met before."

"Yeah, you look familiar too." It's gotta be him.

"Where are you from?"

"St. Felix's."

"Oh my Jesus. I was out there before. I think I stayed at your house, sure."

"You did! You're Jamie. From the wrestling tournament."

"Holy crap, what a small world," Maureen says. "And Imogene's a laugh too."

"She is. I remember."

Imogene flushes. She knows the exact location of the photo he sent her, in the shoebox under her bed. It's in there with Maggie's locket. And her money, of course. She and Jamie, posing right before a brief make-out session. Does he remember that too? She thinks it would be great if he remembers.

Sherrie returns with her White Russian. "What's on the go?"

"Turns out Imogene and I go way back. I was out her way once."

"And she remembers? Must be a small place."

"Don't mind Sherrie," Jamie says. "She gets lost in Mount Pearl. If you blindfolded her and dropped her off on Commonwealth Avenue, she'd ask what currency to use."

Sherrie smacks him in the arm. He doesn't look at her. "Imogene, you live in St. John's now?" he says.

"Yes, we moved here last summer. Me and my nan that is. My mother is in real estate and she bought a house as an investment property, so we take care of it and rent out the basement. Mag—my mom lives in Ontario." Imogene is an overturned file cabinet, information spilling out on to the floor.

"You going to MUN?"

"Yeah, just General Studies this year."

"You like it? What are you going to do?"

"Folklore, I think. It's what I've liked the most so far. You in school?"

"Working at West Side Charlie's to save money. My folks won't help me out unless I decide to do science or engineering."

"Really?"

"Really," Maureen says. "I told them I was doing political science. They said I'd end up with a McJob."

"So, where's your new house?" Jamie asks. His face is flawless except for that blue freckle near his hairline and a tiny scar, an indentation on his bottom lip. Imogene wonders if she could feel the scar if she ran her finger along the edge of his mouth. Or if the edge of his mouth ran along her.

"Cook Street. Rabbittown," she says. "Is that Rabbittown? I'm not sure."

"Rabbittown ends at Merrymeeting Road," Sherrie says.

"No, Cook Street is part of Rabbittown," Jamie says.

"There should be a kiosk in the mall where you can find out," Maureen says.

"Ask a townie."

"That's a good idea," Jamie says. "Sherrie, you could work there as long as no one asks about anything beyond the Avalon Mall." Sherrie gives him the finger.

"So what are yous at tonight?" he says. "There's a show at The Loft."

Sherrie rolls her eyes. "The Loft, bleh," she says. "We want to dance tonight, not stomp around."

Jamie places his hand on top of Sherrie's. "Oh Sherrie," he says. "I'm sure someone will ask you for a stomp."

"Pack off, Jamie. You're just going to smoke up and sit on your arse all night. Some people like to do fun things. We're going to The Sundance."

"Forty minutes in a line-up to pay five dollars for dance music," Jamie says. "What a fun thing. I'm leaving now the once anyway. My buddy Darrin wants to meet up for a draw."

He glances at Maureen, then raises his eyebrows formally and gestures to all of them with a sweep of his arm. "Do we all enjoy cannabis?"

"Look out, Imogene," Sherrie says. "Jamie's a pothead, you know."

She takes a smug sip on her straw. Why does Sherrie assume Imogene shares her views? She's worse than Rita. At least Rita didn't get uptight about a draw.

"Who cares, Sherrie?" Maureen says. Sherrie's lip starts to protrude, but she sucks it in.

"I'm only joking," she says. "Do what you want. I just don't want to be taking care of anyone tonight."

They finish their drinks and walk to the steps connecting Duckworth to George Street. Jamie's friend Darrin is there, a lanky guy with a soft face and a combat jacket. They discreetly smoke a joint, which Sherrie refuses. Darrin and Maureen give each other sidelong smiles. Jamie arriving at the pub was a maneuver to get them together. Imogene thinks this is good of him. It's the kind of thing a friend does.

They end up going to Darrin's place on Queen's Road for drinks. They sit around the kitchen table while Darrin fixes them all rum and cokes with one of three two-litres of Pepsi in his fridge shared by him and his roommates. Imogene watches Maureen try not to smile as he sits next to her.

But then Sherrie starts in on how she wants to go dancing. Darrin and Jamie want to go to The Loft to see Dread Heavy. Maureen will want to go with Darrin. "Imogene," Sherrie says. "C'mon. You and I can go to The Sundance."

Darrin's kitchen has a back deck with a sliding door. Imogene ducks out for a smoke and a brood. Why does she have to be the one who helps out Sherrie? Jamie appears behind her. She offers him her lighter.

"Sherrie Duffy, hair big and fluffy," he says. "She's always got to yuck your yum."

"Yuck your yum?"

"Like, judge your tastes."

"Oh. Good one."

"Her whole family's like it, really." He flicks ashes off the deck.

"I don't know any of them."

"You aren't missing much. Are you going to The Sundance?"

"Honestly? I'd rather be kicked."

"Well, come with us then." Jamie smiles. Right at her, right for her.

"I want to, but it might turn into a thing. She really wants to go. We haven't known each other very long."

"Hold on." Jamie sticks his head into the house. "Sherrie. We're all going to The Loft. You coming?"

Imogene can't hear what Sherrie says, but it is shrill and ends with a "bleh."

"Well my dear, we all want to go and majority rules," Jamie says. "You'll have to get used to living in a democracy." The sliding door makes a satisfied sigh when he shuts it.

two

Nan stamps around so her slip-on slippers apply punishing slaps to the kitchen tile. She smacks the tub of margarine on the counter and jerks open the cutlery drawer so it rattles. The pots on the stove emit indignant puffs of steam in allegiance with her.

"I ask you to do one thing," she says. "You couldn't be bothered."

"I'll do it now."

"They'll be here any minute."

"Coleman's is two minutes away. They never get here before six o'clock. Pie crust. What else?"

"Get some squares. Not the snowballs. Rita's boyfriend doesn't like coconut." Nan shoves her hand in an oven mitt like a boxing glove.

The outside air welcomes her from Nan's low boil. Second week of May and green grass emerges around winter litter. Walking away from the house makes her skip a little. Last week, when Uncle Kenneth gave her a ride down to MUN, he said it was an upward swipe Nan had, back of the neck, base of the skull. "She'd tap me and Eli upside the back of the head," he said. When he saw the surprise on Imogene's face, he shrugged it off. "She was younger then. Less patient."

"I think she might be regressing," she said.

Imogene wonders if she'd prefer the threats and swats of Nan's younger parenting style to her present scowling prissiness. Nowadays, everything Imogene does is wrong. She gets a job at the university library, Nan says, "So you come all the way to St. John's and what do you do? Work in a library. You think you'd want to try something new." Imogene needs a language for a Bachelor of Arts and takes French. Nan: "All you had was French since grade three. What about German or Italian or Chinese? Something different?" Imogene points out how she has tried lots of stuff in this year of General Studies: linguistics, psychology, philosophy. Nan: "Yes, and those grades show how hard you tried too." Imogene has tried to explain how there can be a range of "good" depending on the course—she was consistently getting 75 percent in philosophy and had been frustrated with how she couldn't seem to edge it up until a classmate gaped at her mark. "That's wicked. Monroe never gives anything over eighty." But Nan will have none of it.

And Robert didn't help anything this winter getting spitey about Imogene dropping political science past the refund date. "You need to be able to manage your time and assignments, have a sense of your abilities. At least go over the syllabus and find out what they're demanding of you. You should be mature enough to do that by now." Maggie sighing in agreement, Nan's tongue clucking. Grow up grow up grow up outta it.

And it rots her because they are so fucking right. This term, she and Maureen took the second history course together because they heard the prof was cool and they could share a textbook and class notes. But Dr. Bridger applies a 15 percent participation mark and expects attendance and discussion. And, as they learned in class, she makes a point of pushing the women harder. Anytime a female spoke up it was, "Explain, elaborate, what's your point, how do you back that up?" while men got "Nicely said, Brian," or whatever the fuck. "I get what she's trying to do," Maureen said, "but Jesus Christ, why recreate a microcosm of society just because you can? I shouldn't have to be 30 percent smarter than every guy in the room just because that's how much more money they'll make than me."

And when Imogene watches Dr. Bridger in all her expensive elegance and toned arms and ready references to everything that has ever happened in the world, she would rather be kicked than reveal the depth of her ignorance. What Imogene doesn't know could fill a stadium, could coat the moon. There are so many ways she knows nothing, like how she can rattle off the titles of her favourite novels, but struggles remembering the authors' names. How she mispronounced "self-deprecating" in front of Sherrie ("Ha! It doesn't rhyme with appreciate, Imogene") and all Imogene could do was shrug and say she had never heard it spoken out loud before, which made Sherrie laugh harder. In Bridger's class and all her other classes, she does not want to open her mouth and expose the dirt road of her dialect, like the residence crowd does, arriving to class in January wearing shorts and Paton College jerseys, blaring their baymen-ness to all. No one needs to know where she's from. No one needs to know anything about her.

Inside Coleman's, it always feels like the fluorescent lights filter butter and sugar into the air. She gets pie crust and a pack of Nanaimo bars. The cashier is one she sees regularly, but they do not greet each other. It gives her a stirring of melancholy relief. It's a pleasure to be anonymous but a reminder that she is new and rootless and plain, like dandelion fluff.

She feels happy to be new enough in St. John's to not be dragging around her childhood friends like so many townies she meets. There's a difference between being friendly and welcoming, Nan says, and St. John's could learn a thing or two thousand about that. Imogene has conversations in class and in bars and in line-ups, but it rarely carries over into an actual connection. Even the ones from Carbonear are like that, everyone from the Avalon really.

She knows things are better now, but not what she's craved them to be, the selection, the abundance, what should she do this weekend, who should she give her time to. There is still this limit of one or two things. She's grown up on one or two things. Sitting alongside Maureen and Sherrie's conversations about high school: music class and theatre arts and cheerleading and dance recital and proper soccer fields. Swimming in pools. Swimming lessons. French immersion. She is already far behind and nothing she knows has any importance. How to bake bread. How to chop wood on a windy day. How to beat the shit out of someone.

She was ridiculous to think her presence would inspire curiosity. No one is like Violet, ready to take her under their wing. She and Maureen are friends, but Imogene is aware of being on the fringe of her life. Sherrie brings up birthday parties and bowling nights, things playing on in a background Imogene can't see. Names are mentioned with the suggestive air that Imogene should know who these people are already. All she can do is shrug and listen.

Back at the house, the pick-up is in the driveway. Aunt Trudy, Uncle Eli, Rita and Nick. Uncle Kenneth has arrived too; his girlfriend's red Honda Civic is parked on the street. Everybody's here. Away we go.

Inside, the kitchen is a peas pudding sauna. Aunt Trudy and Uncle Eli hug her hello. Nan has the dishes laid out on the counter awaiting their categories: cabbage, carrots, turnip, chicken with gravy, potatoes, salt beef, bag of peas pudding. Everything is cooking itself pale and soft with the colourful exception of pink chunks of salt beef. Oh, they'll sleep tonight.

"What a feed, Agnes," Aunt Trudy says. "This looks great."

Imogene doubts Aunt Trudy and Uncle Eli were excited about having a Sunday staple when they arrived in St. John's. She has never been able to get excited about Jiggs'. Boil out all the nutrients and salt it like it might come back to life and haunt you. Last week, she offered to make something. "Maureen showed me how to stuff a chicken with chestnut dressing," she said. But Nan refused. "*I'm* making *family* dinner."

Rita sips a glass of white wine. She still wears her hair long, but she's started putting blond highlights in it. They look okay when they're fresh, but then fade into greenish streaks. She's starting to thicken in the hips. Imogene feels a pang of sadness. Rita was always so active and lithe. Always catching and throwing.

Nick drinks a beer. He and Rita give Imogene hellos in low voices. He wears a hockey jersey and camouflage pants, work boots at the door. All his clothes are different types of gear.

"How long for supper, Nan?" says Rita.

"Probably twenty minutes."

Rita makes the smoking a cigarette gesture. Imogene nods.

On the front step, Rita busies herself with her pack of Matinees. "I want to quit," she says. "But it's so hard at the Petro-Can. Everyone smokes and takes their breaks together. I'm thinking we should all quit collectively. Maybe get sponsors, like for a local charity."

Imogene scans her mind for conversation samples. Something safe, but relevant and interesting. Rita blows her cigarette's cherry so it glows.

These days, she and Rita's conversations are parched with a new, persistent pettiness. Rita will call to catch up, ask Imogene how things are going. But as soon as she gets on a roll about school, Rita will interrupt with some tidbit about home or work or Nick. These are delivered with firmness, like if Imogene wasn't such an ingrate, she'd ask first without having to be told. And then Imogene's temples start heating up and in all the pauses where she knows Rita expects her to "uh huh" or "oh really" she delivers nothing but disinterest.

"How was the drive?"

"Alright. We almost ran out of gas between Deer Lake and Gander again. Dad loves to push it."

"Living on the edge. You still doing that correspondence course?"

"Finished. B+."

"Good for you."

Rita spits and flicks her ashes. "Last Nick heard, Liam Lundrigan is up in Edmonton."

"Yeah?"

"Yeah. He was working as a security guard in the West Edmonton Mall. But he got really fucked up on acid during a shift and jumped in one of the pools."

Imogene laughs. Rita tight-smiles. "Crystal Seymour and Quincy MacIssac are having a baby," she says.

"They're together?" Imogene says. "How did that happen?"

"When the pickin's are slim."

"I'm surprised she's still out there."

"Why?"

"Dunno. Just figured she'd leave. Didn't she want to become a beautician or something?"

"She did. It's a six-month program. She's got a set-up in her basement."

"Wow, sounds glamorous."

"A lot of people go to her." Rita's lip is up. Imogene has made her defensive. Now she has to watch what she says about Crystal Seymour? Fuck sakes.

"They say Cecil Jesso has lost his mind," Rita says.

Imogene smokes. Rita continues. "Loretta Sampson said he was in the store the other day. He had his money out and stared at it like he didn't know what it was. She had to take it from his hand and count his change for him."

"Maybe he was on something."

"That's what I said. But he's been wandering around. Sheldon found him on the side of the road once. He said he didn't know which way to go to find his house."

"Yep. Sounds high." Imogene flicks her smoke on the ground and turns back into the house. What's she supposed to do now? Talk with her doctor about future dementia risks?

Supper is ready. Imogene doesn't look at Rita when they're at the table, but she senses her exchange a look with Nick.

"This is so nice," Nan says. "I was saying to Imogene, we need to spend a Christmas out home."

Imogene scoops mashed turnip onto her plate. Yep. She didn't agree to it, but it was said.

"Look at you two," Nan says to Nick and Rita. "You will have gorgeous children. When are you going to marry Rita?" She gestures at Nick. She never remembers his name.

"Oh, Mrs. Tubbs, what are you tryin' to do?" Nick says.

"You should get one of your friends for Immy," Nan says.

"Nan, knock it off."

"Sure, she already broke one of my friend's hearts," Nick says.

"Really? What friend?"

"Her and Liam were on the go for a while."

"A while?" Imogene says. "It was like, three months or something."

"The Lundrigan boy?" Nan pokes her chin at Imogene. "I remember someone saying they saw you in a truck with him. You never had him over to the house."

"We weren't serious."

"Never took him to your grad. Sure, you never took no one to your grad."

"I didn't care about going to grad. And you were sick then." Imogene wills herself not to get embarrassed, but her face and neck heat up.

"I'm only saying," Nan says, "you're nineteen and I haven't met any boys yet."

"Well, just because you don't see something happen, doesn't mean it never happens."

Imogene stabs a piece of cabbage with her fork. "You always say to have faith when there's nothing clear to believe in. Maybe you should follow suit."

"What's the matter? What have I done?"

"Mom," Uncle Kenneth says. "We're just talking. No reason to get upset."

"All I said was that I never met any of Immy's boyfriends and she brings up the Church. I don't see what one has to do with the other." Nan plucks a tissue from the wad in her sleeve and dabs her nose. "You can't show any concern at all."

"So Susan, where is it you work again?" Aunt Trudy says.

The evening passes with stories told before, but with fresh embellishments. Old pieces of gossip are passed around; things hidden from Rita and Imogene as children. Mr. Percy and the way he gets on with other men. Murray Wells passing out and almost burning his cabin down.

Fat fire? Probably the hardest fire to put out. Wish Benoit got into the forces and the day after he left, his mother, Arlene, walked out on Bryce. No mention of Cecil losing his mind. Rita sliding it in like that just cements Imogene's conviction to avoid going back to St. Felix's for as long as she can.

Susan compliments Nan on the banana cream pie and she goes through the recipe, even though no one asked her the process. Imogene stares at the table doilies under their clear plastic cover, flat and frilly. One has a corner edge folded up and now it is trapped, creased forever under thick plastic and plates and casserole dishes. These people don't know who she is. They have always expected her to maintain the same interests and indifferences as them. Uncle Eli with his Christmas gifts of Boston Bruins paraphernalia because, one time, Imogene sat with him during a game and asked questions. In truth, she was bored waiting for Rita to choose an outfit so they could go out. And Uncle Kenneth and how he won't tell her anything about Violet, like Imogene asks just to pester him. And Aunt Trudy and the crucifixes and St. Christopher medals on birthdays and Easter even though Imogene stopped going to church after Confirmation. If someone was to ask her what she believed in, she'd probably say karma, although there definitely isn't any proof of that either. For sure, it isn't an organization where women run all the charities and bake sales and bingo games, but can't pick up a host and say, "This is the body of Christ." Or where women are canonized because they preferred to be murdered than raped. Or a thousand priests do things to children and everyone closes their eyes.

Her own family don't even think twice about comparing her single-dom to Rita and Nick. Rita going on about how she'll do nursing once Nick is finished school because, this way, they can support each other. "That's wonderful," Nan said. "Lovely to see young people from home being so committed and wise." Imogene felt like saying they won't be "from home" for long. When they're ready, Rita and Nick will get steady work somewhere like Alberta and buy snowmobiles and ATVs, boats, campers, dirt bikes. They'll have the same kind of yard Nick had growing up with a big shed and a gravel driveway. They'll have kids. They'll get fat and live in redneck opulence. Compared to them, Imogene is a different category, someone for whom sacrifices were made. Really, they don't expect her to have a boyfriend. They're just relieved she hasn't turned into some kind of lunatic.

"Get that, will you Imogene? It's probably for you."

The phone is ringing. She goes to her room to answer it. What a nice reason to walk away from the table.

"Hello?"

"Is Imogene there?"

"Speaking."

"Hey, it's Jamie."

"Hey."

"Whaddya at?"

"Sunday dinner."

"Oh, I can call back."

"No. I need a break. If I eat any more, I'm going to turn into salt meat."

He laughs. Like spring water on pebbles. Jesus Christ, her flakey heart.

"I was going through my photos and I found the ones I took in your hometown."

Town, what an odd way to think about St. Felix's. Should she mention she has the photo he took of the two of them together? No, wait on it.

"Really? That's cool."

"Yeah. Me and Darrin and Maureen are going for a game of pool tomorrow. You want to come? I'll bring the pictures."

"Okay. I suck at pool though."

"My dear, I couldn't hit the side of a barn if I was nailed to it. And I work in a pool hall. We'll be at The Brass Rack at eight o'clock."

"Sounds good."

"Okay. Enjoy your salt meat."

"I'll try."

"Bye."

"Bye."

She does a little jiggy dance on the rug. Yes yes yes. Outside the door, the supper voices creak and exclaim. She takes deep breaths to compose herself. Gotta avoid being question bait.

When she touches the doorknob, a feeling rushes over her, like deja-vu with epiphany. In spite of everything with school and Nan and Maggie and Rita, she actually has been happy for a long time. She has maintained some level of happy every day for over a year. Has she ever been happy like this, for an extended time? She must not, because this is the first time it's occurred to her. She turns the knob and steps out into the hallway.

three

Imogene knows she's done for when she visits Jamie's house, although she was already on her way there. When they were playing pool, she asked him if he still took pictures. "You had those two cameras on the go," she said. "You were pretty serious."

He looked at her all beamy. "I can't believe you remember that." He told her about the darkroom in his basement. He's sold a couple this year. If Imogene wants, he'll show her. Imogene wants. At home, she dug out the photo of the two of them and, over the evening, repeatedly went into her bedroom for indulgent stares until Nan said, "What are you doing? Preparing to smuggle smiles over the border?"

But there are already issues. He is Maureen's cousin and she has complained about other messes, like how Sherrie dated one of her brother's friends in high school and it ended badly. "He still won't come out if he knows Sherrie's around," Maureen said. "They're like a couple of fucking youngsters." She says Jamie is fresh out of a long-term relationship. Him and some girl named Jan broke up over Christmas break. They were together since grade eleven. "She did it on Boxing Day," Maureen said. "Like she was waiting to see what he'd get her for Christmas. He's on the rebound something fierce." According to Maureen, this is the reason she hasn't seen much of him this year. "He's on the go all the time, always at a party with new friends. I hope he's not going to turn into some kind of pussy hound." Imogene nodded and tried to project mild concern instead of the gagging flood of disappointment wrenching her insides.

Then, one night, Jamie and Imogene talk about movies. He bounces on his heels when she says she's never seen *The Shining*. "I own it. You're coming over."

The next day, she is in his house in Mount Pearl. They sit on an old green sectional couch, like a giant L in his basement, and watch blood slosh out of an elevator in the Overlook Hotel and Jack Torrence hack his way through the bathroom door.

Jamie's family's house is spacious and modern. "Parents did some renovations last year," Jamie says. "They picked what they wanted from catalogues." Most of the decorations are family photos and Newfoundland scenery except for a framed black-and-white photo of a girl, standing back on, staring through a window with long, lacy sheers. The light silhouettes her frame, her blond hair in mid-movement. "That's Jan," he says. "I got an Arts and Letters award for the photo. Junior Division."

"It's beautiful," she says. She tries not to scrutinize Jan.

Jamie's mother insists Imogene stay for supper. All of his three older brothers are there: Eric, the oldest, and Joseph and Thomas, the twins. Eric has his wife and family in tow. Joseph has his girlfriend next to him. The other, Thomas, helps set up the kids' plates. Imogene is taken with how attractive everyone is. The Clark men are the tall, dark, and handsome kind with big smiling personalities. The wives and girlfriends are dainty blonds. Imogene is seated next to Jamie.

"So, Imogene, Jamie says you're in school," Jamie's father says. "What are you studying?"

"I think I'm going to major in folklore."

"Oh yes. What would you do with that now?"

"Lots of interesting things can come out of that," Eric says. "We can't sell fish anymore, might as well get into tourism. Piles of people coming for the culture."

"It's hardly tourists," Joseph says. "Homesick Newfoundlanders on summer visits."

"Yeah," Thomas says, "cause they're the only Newfoundlanders with money."

"Well, they come and consume the arts," Jamie says. "They want to bring pieces of home back with them."

"How sweet," Joseph says. "The fruity-tooty artists can make a few bucks." His girlfriend swats him. "Stop."

"Imogene works at the MUN library too," Jamie says.

"Yeah?" Jamie's father says. "Well, that's good. Avid readers figure things out fast. Jamie's cousin did an English degree and piled up the huge student loan. But then he got a job as an auditor up in Toronto. 'If you can edit, you can audit,' they said to him."

"No flies on Imogene," Jamie says. He nudges her. She can't turn off the blush.

"Good to have a day job at your age," Jamie's father says. "None of these late hours, gallivanting around."

"Spending your tips 'til four in the morning."

"Doing who knows what with whoever."

"Mom," Jamie says. "You need a hand?"

Jamie goes to the kitchen. Imogene watches him leave. When she turns back, everyone seems to be smiling at her. She grins.

"Thanks for inviting me for supper," she says.

"We're very happy to have you, Imogene."

And then it happens. Like slow motion. Jamie's niece Emily pulls herself up into a chair. Her blond hair is tied back in a ponytail. As Jamie returns from the kitchen, he reaches out and smoothes Emily's ponytail from top to end. A little touch, natural, unthinking affection and suddenly Imogene is aware of everything, the time, the date, the position of her legs, the ribbed upholstery on her chair. She imagines him touching her own hair with soundless, instinctual action and the joints in her body vibrate and the muscles in her legs ache and cringe. She is bananas in love with Jamie Clark.

The evening goes well; his family likes her. She basks in their dynamic, the high expectations they have for each other, the way they can pick and razz without seeming afraid of emotional eruption. And each time Jamie meets her eyes, her bones fluctuate in response. Love, she's in love, it's everything, it's all of her, it's like when French Brook washed out with such force the entire landscape was changed. Everything is wonder and terror. Everything in the world is on fucking fire.

She knows it won't be enough if they got together for a brief encounter. The last year has been a scattering of insignificant flings. There was Andrew in September, who she met at a pub crawl. He said he planned to do engineering, but hadn't decided what kind yet. She hated how he wore a ball cap all the time, but he was a good kisser. They talked about sex before they did it, how many partners they'd had (just the one for her, three for him), how scary to be sexually active at university with AIDS and everything else. But then, after the second time they slept together, he said he'd been talking to his ex in Labrador City and they wanted to give the long distance thing a try.

"Good luck with that," she said. "You don't have to be sarcastic," he said.

And there was the flirtation with the bartender at Big Ben's who let her and Maureen stay after hours. They did shots of tequila and smoked pot. But after she woke up at his place, he rushed her out. And when she showed up at the bar the following Thursday, he had an oh-no shudder in his eyes. "A lesson learned," Maureen said. "Don't get dragged off from places you actually like going to. Now we have to find somewhere else that doesn't I.D."

And there was Vince, who smelled really good and was fun to dance with. But right after they did it on his bed in his room in residence, he got up, took off the condom, got dressed, and left her alone. She could hear him down the hall, talking about hockey with his buddies like nothing had happened.

And then David for a couple of months. They would drive up to Signal Hill and fuck in his parents' station wagon. But his friends were horrid and when they ordered Chinese, they called it Slant Food and they asked her if everyone in St. Felix's was inbred. He took off with them to White Hills over March break and didn't invite her, so she stopped calling him and he faded away.

For all of them, she got a bit sad. She cried over David for a day. But for some reason, the bartender stung the most: his blanket disdain and impatience when she walked into Big Ben's. For months, she got a flicker of panic when she went out, the idea she might meet his cold gaze again. One day he was in the cash line-up in Sobeys and she lurked in the frozen-food aisle until he paid and left. If only the sex hadn't been so hot. It's still up there as better than anyone else so far. She felt so denied.

If it's fleeting with Jamie, there will be Major Pain. She already fizzles with jealousy when he's around other girls. He'll be teasing the girl who bartends at Christian's, the waitress at Ches's and her feelings of misery are so strong, she has to hide her face somehow, sip her drink, stick a smoke in her mouth. Little else she can do since he likes to joke about how he will never get tied down again. "I'm going to sow so many oats, I'll have shares in Kellogg's," he said last week, and they all laughed and her heart fell down a flight of stairs. If she tells him how she feels, will he want to hang out with her? She thinks of Rita and her years of never-fading love for Nick Cleary. There was one time, back when Nick was dating Teresa Loder and Rita was fuming and Cherry MacIssac blew up about the whole thing. "For fucks sakes, Rita, will you just forget about him! Jesus, everybody knows you can do better!"

"How can I?" Rita had said. "How can I get over him when I see him every day? He's in my class, he's on my bus. It's like trying not to pick a scab."

Imogene would wait out the rebound if she knew he could see her as other than a friend. She could take a chance and tell him how she feels. But if he's not ready, he might make himself scarce. She sees three choices: all of him, some of him, none of him. Right now she's at some. Telling him becomes all or none. Damn it to fuck.

four

By the end of June, a Friday night routine has established itself. Maureen comes over first, sometimes with Darrin, sometimes without. Those two are on and off. Sherrie starts seeing a new guy and mostly vanishes. Smell ya later, Sherrie. Jamie shows up when he finishes work. He sometimes brings one of his buddies, like his friend Winston, who has long black curly hair and dark, sleepy eyes and speaks with a dreamy, half-stoned intonation. He and Jamie were coworkers at Sherlock's. Now Jamie bartends at West Side Charlie's and Winston is back at school with a radio show on the campus station. Everyone comes over and drinks in the kitchen while Nan watches TV in the living room. They sit on the front step if they want to smoke. They wait until they're gone out to smoke anything else.

Then one night, Nan changes the game. The house is walking distance to downtown bars, but Jamie lives in Mount Pearl. For him to cab it home costs at least fifteen dollars. Nan won't hear of it. "Stay here, my love," she says. "Any friend of Immy's can stay here. Drive down, park your car out front and go home after breakfast. Anytime." She flings open the hall linen closet and produces two folded afghans and a pillow for the sofa. "Here, Jamie," she says. "Take the couch."

The couch sits in the living room, right next to Imogene's bedroom. She nods in agreement. Rivers of possibilities trickle through her. Late night conversations could turn intimate, gratitude could turn to affection, drunken horniness could take over. A random storm. The power goes off. They need to use body heat to stave off hypothermia.

But on the first sleepover, Nan interrupts their whispering, puttering by on one of her nightly trips to pee, her purple terrycloth robe pinched together under her chin. Jamie feels guilty about waking her. "What a sin, poor Agnes." The next time, he crashes as soon as they come home. Imogene does the same, waving good night to his beauteous frame standing in loosened clothes and sock feet.

The third weekend, they go dancing. Jamie lifts her off her feet, spins her around. No guy has ever attempted to pick her up before. Liam tried once and said she was too tall. Jamie grabs her around the waist, he lifts and dips her. She throws her head back and laughs, she presses her breasts into him. She lets her face slide in front of his and their lips meet. They kiss quick and soft. But on the taxi ride, Winston ends up sitting between them in the back and he comes back to the house for another beer. He's high as fuck at the kitchen table, talking about his dead grandfather until almost four a.m. When he leaves, Jamie is ready to pass out. She doesn't even get a goodnight hug.

"Sorry about Winston," Jamie says. "Sometimes he doesn't know when to stop talking."

"No problem," she says, and goes to bed. But an hour later, she wakes, twitching herself conscious with an electric awareness that pervades everything. He is here, asleep and touchable in the next room. She closes her eyes and sees the living room, the early morning light hinting at the edges of the drapes, outlining all Nan's crap. The green ceramic cats in their stretching poses, the collection of tiny souvenir spoons mounted on a wooden cut-out of the map of Newfoundland, the silver-plated picture frames with Pop and Nan on their wedding day, Maggie holding her real-estate licence, baby Imogene in the jolly jumper. And Jamie on the couch, bundled in one of Nan's multicolour crocheted afghans like a Klimt painting, all angelic face and rumpled dark hair. Ridiculously lovely. Most people are all snores, drools and farts when they sleep, just releasing their day's worth of penned biology. Yet somehow Jamie Clark, balled up, reeking of booze and cigarettes, manages to look like the Christ child.

Once, she got up early and sat in the recliner by the couch with a book on her lap, pretending to read. Just to feed her eyes on him, like a sex offender in an elementary school parking lot. She rationalized it as a way of purging herself; if she could stare at him non-stop for a good solid stretch, her system would be cleansed somehow. He woke up and she pretended to be absorbed in her book. "Oh, you're awake. I couldn't sleep, came out to read for awhile, heh-heh." So, so stupid. Days later, the memory popped up at work and she physically cringed, shuddering over the cart of books.

Now it's Saturday morning, 5:34 a.m. on the clock radio. Jeans on the floor. Crystal ashtray by the bed overflowing with ashes like grey pot-pourri. Soon, Nan will get up. She moves slowly, but makes sure to bang the plates on the table and stir her tea like she's playing a gong. "Oooh, Jamie, did I wake you? How was last night? Tea?" All to get him up so she can talk about the way the downstairs tenants get on or the criminals in the neighbourhood or the lax attitude of city council. Jamie will chat with her in his politely teasing manner. Imogene will join them. He will smile at her.

But maybe he knows. After all, he plants himself here in her territory and everyone already thinks they're screwing. His brothers grin and wink when she's around. A man goes downtown with the same woman every weekend and he doesn't come home—what else could possibly be going on but cheap, fun, drunken intercourse?

Maybe he wants them to think that. Maybe he wants them to think that because he wants it to happen. She could make it happen. She could get up and go out in the living room and do something, touch him, kiss him. No explanation necessary, no planning, no words even. Maybe all she has to do is say, *Jamie, you can crash in here if you want*. Maybe she is wasting precious opportunity in this timid heap of herself.

She sits up and her brain groans. Her hair in her face reeks of cigarettes and she pushes it away and her fingers smell like cigarettes and she is an idiot who knows nothing and never learns. She still wears the ribby shirt from last night, the kind of tight one, black—she hoped it was slimming and made her tits look rounder. At least she made sure to sleep on her stomach. One time that fall, she threw up in her sleep. She could have been dead on her back, like Jimi Hendrix or Bon Scott. She imagined Nan finding her pale, greenish corpse. Nan, screaming her face off. Imogene scraped the puke into a grocery bag and hid it at the bottom of the garbage.

She retreats under the covers and closes her eyes. They kissed last night. For a second. This is good. But he was dancing with everyone. He swung Maureen around too, swung her so her legs flared out. And other girls too. He does what he wants. If he wanted her, she'd know. She may be a drunken twit, but she's not delusional. Her hangover wiggles itself deep into her guts.

But it feels right, says her head, in its thick, polluted state. When Jamie and she are together, they fit. They turn to each other at the same time. They hug hello, they sit close. The other day, he squeezed her hand. "You're the best, Genie," he said. "I never feel pressure when I'm with you. You're a sanctuary."

The digital clock says 5:51 a.m. She closes her eyes. Next week, if he stays here next week, she's going for it. She pictures herself floating, beyond her bedroom walls with their nicotine-tinged eggshell tones and chipped gyprock, up along the stucco ceiling of the living room, where she can hover and regard her friend for the work of art he is. If she stays still, the pain fades and she can detect all available sounds. A car passes outside, something rattling in its guts. If she stays still, the pain fades and she might hear the gentle cadence of his breath. In the distance, she hears the foghorn, sighing to itself.

five

Jamie and Imogene are in the food court of the Avalon Mall with fries and tall cups of fountain pop. The tables around them are barren except for occasional golden fried crumbs. A scowling teenager in the Dairy Queen wipes down his work area. She's procrastinating finishing her paper on shellshock and WWI veterans in Newfoundland and Labrador; he's procrastinating going home. They smoked a joint in the parking lot and now all they can do is eat and talk.

"So you have no idea who your dad is?" Jamie says.

"His name was Anthony Green and he was a fisherman. Not from St. Felix's, he was just around for a season. And he took off on Maggie."

"Do you know what he looks like?"

"Not really."

"So, he could be anybody," he says. "He could be...that guy." Jamie gestures with his elbow towards a rotund man walking away from Tim Horton's. "Or that guy." He nods at a suited man standing at the A&W cash register. "Or Rex Murphy. You're both redheads who know lots of big words."

"I don't think Rex Murphy spent much time fishing."

"You don't know that."

"Anyway. I don't think about it. I don't even know if it's true."

The gravy for Jamie's fries has grown a layer of skin, but he doesn't seem to notice. "Why wouldn't it be true?" he says.

She shakes the ice in her cup in an attempt at nonchalance. Two days ago, Joyce MacIssac called with a new Cecil story. Imogene was alone in the house and pressured to "oh yes," and "really" her way through Joyce's tales of Quincy's baby on the way and Cherry's job in Toronto. "And I come home the other day and who's sitting in my kitchen? Cecil Jesso. 'Hello, there,' he says. Like I'm a visitor in his house."

"Really?" Imogene said.

"Oh yes. Nobody knows what's going on, but he's losing it quickly. You feel sorry for him."

No, *you* feel sorry for him. Poor ol' Cecil, losing his mind. Let's forgive all his indiscretions in the name of Christian community. After she hung up, she sat on the couch and took several deep breaths. She doesn't live there anymore. She doesn't have to think about it.

But she loves Jamie. He should know. Fuck it.

"There were stories about this sketchy guy down the road," she says. "He sold booze and drugs and contraband smokes. He wasn't someone you wanted to be seen associating with. But apparently Mag—my mother used to go to his house. Or she was that summer, right after her dad died. People out home like to say something happened between them. Like a trade. He gave her booze and drugs and she gave him what he wanted."

"And she was how old?"

"She would have been fourteen."

"Well. That's scandalous. And fucking horrible."

"Yep."

Jamie folds his arms on the table. "Is that...do you believe that?"

"People out home love their stories."

"I'm not asking about them." He takes a sip from his drink and the straw echoes at the bottom of the cup. Imogene's stomach alternates between release and recoil.

"The man is a fucking pig," she says. "Trade, bullshit. She was fourteen years old."

"So if he is your dad... Shit. Okay, I'll just say it. He raped her."

"Yes."

"I mean, if a fourteen-year-old girl gets pregnant, that's always what it is, isn't it? Unless the dad's the same age? Fuck, I don't know. I'm sorry."

"Don't be sorry."

"I don't know how else to say it."

"Well. That's how to say it."

The Dairy Queen teen rattles out a mop and bucket from the back, like he's trying to punish it. "It's why it's never discussed," she says. "It's why Maggie gets upset whenever I ask about my dad."

Jamie chews thoughtfully on his straw. "I got an idea"

"What's that?"

"Let's kill him."

Imogene laughs. Jamie's face is serious. "Your poor mom," he says. "Only fourteen. What a bastard. Is he still out there? Did you have to see him all the time?"

"Somewhat. He lived less than ten minutes away."

"Jesus. Your family ever consider revenge?"

"Oh, I think so. I mean, I had pretty big ideas myself."

"Like what?"

She shrugs and pops a fry in her mouth.

"Being a bit cryptic there, Genie Tubbs."

"It's nothing. Nothing happened ever."

"I bet Agnes plotted a few things. I don't know how you didn't. Especially in a place that small. I mean, this place feels too small to me most of the time."

"But you can avoid people here much easier."

"You'd think. I guess it seems that way if you didn't grow up here." Jamie dips a fry in the gravy. "Jesus. So gross."

"I think it's molting."

"Friggin' gravy growing legs."

She laughs. It's too nice to be happily stoned and staring at Jamie's eyes and mouth. She wants to reveal everything: the Cecil taunting, the box under her bed. Still over sixteen-hundred dollars left. She could have pissed it away by now, but it's too important, too *hers*. It would feel so good to offer him all her secrets. If she knew he loved her back for sure, she would tell him.

"I'm sorry you had to deal with that," Jamie says.

"Thank you. Shit exists for most people though, I guess."

"It does. Do you find Maggie treats you funny?"

"Funny how?"

"I don't know. Like, it sounds like you both won't acknowledge what you both know? Never mind. I'm not making sense."

"She's never been *present* really. She's always been good to me. I know she loves me." Imogene's never thought too much about Maggie loving her. "When Maggie's around, I feel like she wants to run away. And I don't blame her."

"Run away from you?"

"Yes. And Nan. And home. I mean, she did run away, really. We rarely see her."

"I think everyone wants to run away sometimes."

"Oh, I know."

"For some people, it's the best option. What can you do when everyone thinks they know what you're like or what's the best for you? And they'll never change their mind? You just want to bang your head off a wall."

"I feel the same. I mean, imagine, you're a kid, some monster does that to you, and then you have to look at the half monster he put in your body? Walking and talking evidence that looks and sounds like him? I'm surprised she's been part of my life at all." The hand holding her drink trembles and the ice cubes poke each other. "I would never do it," she says.

"Oh, please." He reaches across the table and touches the rim of her cup with one finger. "Who wouldn't want to see more of you? You're pretty great, you know."

"A mistake is one thing," she says. "A crime is another. I think I remind her, all the time. I'm a thing she regrets."

"Regrets. Bullshit. If you tripped over a turd and found a diamond, would you regret getting your shoe dirty?"

"Wow. That's the best metaphor for statutory rape resulting in pregnancy ever."

"Well, you know. I'm deeply Christian."

"You should make billboards for pro-lifers."

They cackle like conspirators. "I'm serious though," he says. "Guy did that to my mother? I'd need some revenge. And fuck what other people say. If they won't change, they lose you."

Jamie drives her home. A small tear in his jeans above the knee exposes a strip of skin. It makes her think of trying to fall asleep in her old bedroom when Nan left the hallway light on, creating a sliver of light under the door. She'd close her eyes and still see its outline, like it was burned into her retinas.

"If it makes you feel better," he says, "and I know this is a completely different situation, but I wasn't planned either." He drives with his left hand, the other rests on his thigh. His nails are rounded and short, clean and smooth. They would feel like firm pressure points on the small of her back. He shifts his leg on the gas pedal. The tear in his jeans closes.

"Mom and Dad already had three kids and Dad was going for a vasectomy. I was conceived a week before the doctor's appointment. I asked Mom if I was an accident and she goes, 'Oh no, you were...a surprise.'

She was almost four months along with me when she finally went to see the doctor. She'd been on and off the pill, apparently that can make ladies irregular. Dad kept saying, Shirley, you're pregnant. Oh no, I'm just irregular, any day now. Shirley, you're pregnant. So she goes to the doctor to prove him wrong and the doctor says, Shirley, you're pregnant! Ta-da."

Imogene wishes she knew how to flirt. A flirty girl would reach over and poke her finger into that hole in his jeans, give a little giggle. It wouldn't be weird or uncomfortable. Girls like that blow her mind, girls like Rita and Sherrie Duffy, girls who can approach a guy and just sit on his lap: "Hi!" All in a way where the guy is thrilled and doesn't find it slutty or desperate.

"I'm sure they were real happy it was another boy," Jamie says. "First Eric, then the twins, then, surprise! Another boy! Thomas says that's why I like stuff like photography. Mom was hoping I'd be a girl and didn't force me to be a man."

The traffic light turns from yellow to red. Jamie presses the brake and they sway forward. "Whoops. My shoes are some heavy today."

Imogene laughs. He complains about his three older brothers all the time. When he was a kid, they would dangle him out the second storey windows by his ankles. They passed him back and forth, from one bedroom window to another. The game was called "Pass the Shitbag." And along with the blue freckle on his forehead from being stabbed with a pencil, the small scar on his lips happened when Eric chased him around the house, threatening to pound him for not writing down a phone message from some girl. Jamie wiped out on the grass and smacked his mouth on the edge of the step. "And he still gave me a boot in the ass while I was on the ground," Jamie said. "What a prick."

But she loves going to his house and he says he loves it when she's over because his family get on their best behaviour when she's present. Sometimes, she feels like she's in a kind of rapture there. She likes peering at their hutch full of photos and trophies—mostly for sports or academics (we're the clever jocky fuckers, Jamie says). Her eyes return to the picture of all the boys when they were in high school, Eric, the twins Joseph and Thomas, and Jamie, looking baby-faced at the end of the line.

And they like her. They lean in with interest when she speaks and refill her glass when it gets low. But with each other, they interrupt and torment. The last time she was there, Eric went on about how Information Technology is where it's at if you want to make money and Thomas pointed his fork at him and said, "Don't kid yourself. It's another TAGS-like trend. Make-work project bullshit." Eric threw his hands in the air.

"Why you gotta respond like that? Jesus, can't even put a little gas on your fire." "The less gas at this table the better," Joseph said and they all laughed. Later, when Jamie was driving her home, he said, "I swear, they all have the ego of a dog that chases cars."

If Imogene ever carried on like that with Maggie, there'd be tears. Or with Nan, there'd be a gasp and glare and then the story stored up to repeat at any opportunity. Might be ten years later during supper, someone will say "Pass the sauce," and Nan would reply, "Sauce? You should ask Immy about sauce. She once told me I didn't know what I was effin' talking about. That's sauce."

"Give us a smoke, please?" Jamie says.

Imogene takes one from the pack, lights it for him and passes it over. His lips puff at the spot where hers just touched, brown circle in white filter, like the yolk of an egg.

"Wanna get a coffee?" he says. "Get on the scene. With the caffeine machine." He rests his cigarette-holding-hand on the steering wheel and turns onto Freshwater Road. This can't go on forever. She has to tell him or give it up already. Piss or get off the pot.

He catches her staring. "I know what you're thinking, Genie. It's not reckless driving, it's multitasking."

She laughs. The car speeds up and the tear in his jeans opens and closes, like a wink.

Later, when he drops her off, they hug and her lips brush the space where his neck meets his collarbone. He squeezes her to him and their bodies are puzzle pieces clicking into place.

In the house, she goes to her room and grabs her notebook. She's stoned enough to really focus. A list isn't enough. This calls for a table.

The Possible Pros and Cons of Confessing True Feelings to Jamie Clark

Pros	Cons
• He might feel the same way.	• NO. Nothing like the same.
• He will be flattered.	• He will be embarrassed. It will
• Confession will be freeing and let me get on with my life.	all be embarrassing and horrible.
	• Confession will cause me to lose him. Pain. So much pain.

Looking at the table makes her tired. Christ, she's so exhausted of thinking about him and acting normal. Especially this jealous internal fretting over his interactions with girls who are not her. And looking for an excuse to touch him when they're together. *Oh, Jamie, you have an eyelash on your cheek. Oh, Jamie, there's a fluffy in your hair.* Her hands float towards him with the subtlety of falling trees.

Time to do something. If she's going to tell him, she must think of what to say, where to do it, how to say it. She has to be prepared to lose him. Probably not forever. He won't do that. But maybe for a little while.

Responses to Love Confession Organized Chronologically and by Likelihood

Immediate Responses	Short Term Responses	Long Term Responses
• Jamie is surprised. He says "holy fuck" a lot. Hugs me.	• Jamie continues to invite me out, but I don't accept as often, for a few weeks. He acts sweet and gingerly polite.	• The awkwardness wears off with time. We stay close and eventually get to a place where we can discuss this time in our lives with an air of nostalgia. It hurts, but he understands that it hurts and is good about it.
• Jamie needs space to think about everything.	• We hang out sporadically over the next few weeks, usually in groups.	• We remain close friends— no more sleepovers. It takes a while, but I get over it.
• Jamie already has an idea that I feel this way, but doesn't know what to say.	• We don't contact each other for a few weeks. We gradually return to normal.	• We remain close friends, but no more sleepovers. We stop confiding in each other. It takes years for it to stop physically hurting.

• Jamie already has had an idea that I feel this way and has a prepared response.	• We don't contact each other for a few weeks. When we get together, it's awkward.	• When we bump into each other, it's friendly, but we keep each other at a distance. It takes years for it to stop physically hurting when I see him.
• Both Jamie's unprepared and prepared responses go something like "I love you, but just as a friend. I'm so sorry. I've never wanted to hurt you."	• We don't contact each other for a few weeks. Jamie meets someone else and they start dating.	• Jamie and his new girlfriend fall deeply in love. I occasionally see them from a distance. It takes years for it to stop physically hurting when I see him.
• Jamie feels the same way/wants to go for it.	• We don't contact each other for a few weeks. Jamie misses me.	• Jamie realizes he loves me too. We fuck like minks blissed out on shrooms.

Horrible. She could never be a statistician. Who would want to tabulate the data of lost causes and hopeless cases? Either way, she should try. Next time he stays over, she'll try.

six

The old couch is gone. In its place is a green velvet hide-a-bed sofa. Nan has adorned it with a crocheted doily. Maureen nods with approval. "New couch, Mrs. Tubbs?"

"Yes," Nan says. "I traded the other one with our neighbour across the street. Figured it would be handy now with Maggie's coming home." She runs a hand across the back of it.

"Since when?" Imogene says.

"She called last night. It seems things have ended with Robert," Nan says. She purses her lips and clucks her tongue softly. Why that reaction? Relating bad news means making a sound like beckoning to a horse.

"Oh, that's too bad," says Maureen.

"They broke up a couple of days ago. She's coming home tomorrow. My God, she's some distraught."

"So Maggie will take the couch?" Imogene says.

"Well, I thought you'd offer her your room," Nan says. "I imagine she'd like a bit of space. She'll take over the basement apartment once the lease is up down there."

"So, I'm in school *and* working and I don't warrant a bit of space?"

"Well, this is her house, Immy. It's only right she has a room here. Don't forget, she gave us this place so that you could go to school."

"I'm sure I'll be getting lots of sleep with you watching reruns of *Dallas* every night."

"I can put the TV in my room if it bothers you."

"So, you get the TV and Maggie gets my room."

"It's temporary. Good lord, girl, you get so angry these days."

"I'm only saying, if I'm the only person working in this house, why am I the one that has to sacrifice the room?"

"Oh, I should go out and get a job so I'm equal to you? I get my own cheques, you know. I've worked hard all my life to raise all my children and you, but obviously you don't see that as any kind of work."

Nan's voice is the rattle of pebbles in a steel bucket. Imogene's jaw clenches. Where will Jamie sleep now? She was going to tell him this weekend.

"I'm not talking about you, Nan. I'm just saying, it doesn't seem fair that I work and go to school and help you and I have to give up my room for Maggie."

"Well, I just thought it would be nice, but if you feel this strongly about it, we'll talk about it when she gets here."

"Fine."

"And as you can imagine, she'll be in a sensitive place. I'm sure she'll appreciate any gesture of kindness from you." Nan brushes imaginary crumbs off the top of the "new" sofa and totters off.

"See that?" Imogene says to Maureen. "*Gesture of kindness*. She thinks she can use guilt to get me to do whatever she wants."

"That's families for you. Passive-aggressive weaponry," Maureen says.

"It's like I'm nothing." On Friday, can she wrangle it so it seems normal if she and Jamie both sleep on the couch? Maggie coming home. Maggie and Nan here. Fuck. Shit.

"But, is it really such a big deal? Let her have the room for a while. She is going through a divorce."

"They're not married. Well, I guess they might as well be. It's just... knowing certain things have to change."

Maureen leans over. She speaks in a voice too low for Nan's ears. "If it's about Jamie, you should know you're very special to him."

"Why do you say that?"

"Well, you get pretty happy when he stays over."

"You can tell?"

"Oh yes."

"God. I'm so transparent."

"Listen, Jamie is one of those people everybody loves. But he doesn't love everybody. He flits around. Especially lately. Ever since him and Jan and all this shit with his parents and school, he's all over the place. So, if you've become a routine part of his life, if he goes out of his way to see you, you're important. Winston said it after he met you. He said, good to meet the magic Genie in Jamie's life."

Imogene flushes. Maureen squeezes her hand. Jamie does get along with everyone. They'll be lined up at a cash register and he and the person in front will start talking about their purchases: "Is that on sale? What a deal." He gets cab drivers to reveal their life stories. People want to tell him things. He makes great tips at West Side Charlie's.

But later, when Maureen has gone home, she's still pissed with Maggie. Now everything has to change. It's her problem; why does it have to affect so many other lives?

She says this to Jamie when he comes to pick her up to play pool with him and Winston. She hopes to see disappointment in his eyes, about how it will be harder to stay over. Instead, he gives her a hard look.

"That's pretty harsh, Genie. The woman goes through a break-up and you have no pity for her?"

"How can you say that? You know the shit with me and Maggie."

"Yeah, but I feel sorry for her. She feels like garbage right now and she's coming home to a house devoid of empathy."

"Please don't think I'm mean. It's difficult enough with Nan bitching me out all the time. Everything's going to be so confined in this house." She can feel her voice rattle. It's so gross.

"Mean? Not at all." And then he's warm again and hugs her, quickly, his flat, firm chest against hers. She rests her cheek against his hair and takes in his sweet-smelling shampoo, his warm skin. "I have no right to tell you how to feel about your family," he says. His lips brush the edge of her earlobe.

"Yes, yes, you do. You can tell me anything about myself. Or yourself."

"It's hypocritical of me to tell you how to interact with them. I'd love to get away from my family for a while. I'd feel rotten if I had to come back to them and things were tense."

"Why would it be hard for you to come back? Your folks adore you."

"Yes, and I love them and I can't wait to leave." His arms loosen and he steps away. "I haven't told anyone this yet, but I applied to the photography program at the Ottawa School of Art."

"When will you find out?"

"Not for a while. I was up there last summer to visit my cousin. I liked it. You can ride a bike everywhere. It's a quick dart over to Montreal. I've been putting a portfolio together for a while, so I decided to apply. And now that it's done, I really want it. It feels right, you know? You ever have that? Make a decision and you know it's the best thing you could have done?"

Has Imogene ever felt that over a decision? University? She really only applied to MUN. Work? She's been working in libraries since she was fifteen. Everything else is impulse. The only concrete decision she can imagine making is sitting on Jamie to keep him from leaving.

"So, if they take me, I'm gone."

"Well, I hope all your photos are crap and you stay here," she says. They both laugh. Ha ha. Fail. Please, please, let him fail.

In bed, Maureen's words come back to her. "Very special to him." She retrieves Maggie's locket from under her bed and lets it sway between possibilities before her eyes. Special to him. But he's leaving. He'll miss her. He'll make lots of new friends. He cares for her. He knows she's available for him. But he must know, somehow, how she feels. Sure, and he isn't doing anything about it.

She puts the locket down and closes her eyes. Gregarious Jamie. She wonders if this way he has, this engaging with random people, is actually sincere for him. Does he actually embrace humanity or, like Liam, is he trying to see what he can get away with? Nan says most men are simple; they only want what's in front of them—that's why they cheat. She never says no to Jamie.

But he chooses to plant himself by her side every weekend. It's a sign that what they have is more than comfort and simplicity.

seven

Maggie's flight arrives at St. John's International Airport in soupy fall fog. Imogene and Nan wait for her at the bottom of the escalator. They wear their most accepting and optimistic faces. Maggie wears her most calm and grateful face. She doesn't walk down the escalator to meet them; she stands still and lets the machinery lower her down, her carry-on bag clutched to her side like it might spring away from her. Her hair is long and cinched at the back of her neck. It probably looked elegant when she brushed it back this morning, before three hours in an airplane seat.

Imogene busies herself fetching a luggage cart. Look, she's helping. Nan and Maggie talk about the fog and how the plane will probably not take off again now that it's here, it's a good thing she got in when she did, these foggy days, the air is like a milkshake, good thing she's not trying to get out cause she'd be stuck here. The pilots can land okay, but have trouble taking off. Or is it vice-versa?

At the house, they have prepared Imogene's room for Maggie, fresh sheets on the bed, dresser cleaned out. Imogene's clothes hang in the hall closet, but most of her things remain in the room, her books, her CDs. The shoebox under the bed. Would Maggie look inside? She'd know better than to take the money, but she'd see the pendant. And it is hers, after all. Imogene pictures the pendant in Maggie's hand. Would there be a confrontation? Or would she just put it back? Probably better to put it back. Why make things messy now.

Maggie says when she gets a job and the lease is up for the downstairs tenants, she will take over the basement apartment. She says this with her palms out like a peace offering. The first night, they rent movies—comedies, light and fluffy. They eat Chinese take-out.

Rita calls to see how Aunt Maggie is. Such a good niece. When the phone is passed to Imogene, Rita's voice is low in the earpiece. "Did you hear? Crystal Seymour found Cecil Jesso in her hair studio, sitting in a beauty chair. He didn't know where he was. She screeched her head off."

In the following days, Maggie, the guest/owner, moves gingerly around her house, touching things like she doesn't want to leave fingerprints. Nan talks like it's her divine duty to fill the air with sound. They are told news from home. Trudy says Nick wants to take the millwright course in Stephenville. Great Aunt Bride lost fifteen pounds with the Weight Watchers. Quincy and Crystal had a baby girl. Imogene is overcome with urges to step out of windows or into cupboards and closets. She wishes the house contained trapdoors or secret passageways—she could pull back a book from the shelf and unlock an exit. Be transported to Jamie's house in Mount Pearl.

Instead, she takes up running. Maureen talked about getting into it and showed her an outline for a program which claims to build a running habit in just five weeks. Start off running one minute, walking for four, for thirty minutes. Every week, add one minute from the walking side to the running. Maureen didn't enjoy it, but it works for Imogene so well she ends up pushing it so she's able to run for five minutes straight after two weeks.

Running is something she would never have considered doing in St. Felix's although she often thought about it, running across fields, along cliffs, in the waves. In reality, it would have been running down the road, gathering stares and comments ranging from curiosity to bouncy boob jokes. But here, people run all the time and no one cares. Nan's mouth will be in midsentence about the cost of Harvey's Oil while Maggie floats in and out of rooms, pale-faced with shattered eyes and Imogene throws on her sneakers and runs out of the gloom and into the fog. "Good," Nan says. "You're finally trying something new."

In the university library, she pushes the cart through the stacks, replaces books left scattered on tables and in study rooms. She keeps a list of articles she needs for her folklore courses and puts them aside—looking for them outside her shifts seems backwards. She reads when the Help Desk is slow. She can skim through paragraphs to find a summarizing quote to make it look like she read the whole thing. Author's name, title, publisher, date, page number, address. She stays in the stacks as long as she can stand it.

When she's with Jamie, he doesn't mention Ottawa. But he's waiting. Who else has he told? Does his family know? She's heard his brothers and his father grumble over their supper plates about arts funding and "hoity-toity tooty-fruity artsy-fartsies." So she doesn't ask him. And she runs in the fog, hoping everything will lift and blow away.

After two weeks of grey, the fog breaks and she and Jamie go to Bannerman Park. They lean against the gazebo and smoke up. It feels like the last nice day before full-on fall chill and the park is busy with stoned townies trying to get one more wear out of their summer clothes. Jamie tells stories:

"It was terrible. The whole time, Eric kept saying, 'Wow, you are really, really stoned.' And the twins pretended to hear noises, just to make me more paranoid."

"Who goes out of their way to ruin someone's first drug experience? What a shit thing to do."

She passes him a cigarette and takes the joint. They exchange them so from a distance it looks like they're just smoking together. He licks his finger and holds it to the base of the ember of the joint to stop it from canoeing.

"They're bastards. They really are. Just because someone is related to you, doesn't mean you have to like them. And Eric is a dirty fucker. He's the kind of guy who would show up at your house when you're having a party and steal your CDs."

"That's fucking vile."

"Nasty behaviour. That stuff's an investment, especially if you had to buy the bands you already have on tape over again."

"I just rip off Columbia House."

Imogene reaches out and pulls Jamie's wrist to her face to look at his watch. Like she cares what time it is. She is so obvious.

A couple walks towards them with a golden retriever puppy on a leash. The woman has long dark hair in a glossy French braid. She talks with flamboyant hand gestures. The guy with her has shaggy blond hair and smooth angular cheekbones. He nods at the woman while focusing on the puppy.

"Suffering fuck," Jamie says. "Look who it is."

"Who?"

"Sherrie Jesus Duffy."

Jamie calls out to them before Imogene can respond. Sherrie waves back with enthusiasm. She and the puppy are very excited to see them.

"Oh my Gawd," she says. "I haven't seen you in ages. B'ys, this is Casey Cahill."

She doesn't introduce him as her boyfriend, but she's puffed up with gleeful pride. Casey shakes their hands. Jamie offers him the joint and he takes it. Sherrie doesn't even flinch.

"Sherrie, I didn't recognize you without your mall hair." Jamie grins and Sherrie calls him a saucy fucker. She wears a flowing linen blouse that laces up peasant style and although the French braid is painstakingly neat, her hair doesn't have its previous height and power. Her whole demeanor is lighter and slightly derailed. She talks and talks. "If I make the dean's list this term, my father says he'll get us an all-inclusive week down in Cuba. And Casey's in a band and they're working on an album and when it's done, my father's going to send copies to all his connections. He knows the Sterlings. What are you guys doing for Halloween? Casey and I are dressing up as Batman and Catwoman."

She reaches out and musses Jamie's hair. Imogene looks away. Christ, it's so depressing. He and Imogene are so obviously platonic that girls can maul him in front of her. Does it even cross Sherrie's mind something might be going on? Is it so ridiculous a notion? When she looks up, the Casey guy is staring at her and she realizes she's been glaring at the ground. She composes herself and passes him the joint. He gives her a half smile. His lips are plump and pink. Sexy. She can see why Sherrie's smitten.

Casey and Sherrie make polite goodbyes and stroll off. "I've seen that guy in a bunch of bands," Jamie says. "He's the lead singer in Case and the Tickets. He's a deadly musician. When did she start giving a shit about music?" He shakes his head. "Maybe it's an opposites attract thing."

"Maybe he's used to girls who want to fuck musicians."

"Well, yeah."

"If that's the case, maybe someone like Sherrie would be...refreshing."

"Ah yes, a challenge. Don't we all love a challenge? It's like food tastes better if we can catch it ourselves."

Jamie leans back and closes his eyes in the sun. A warm breeze ruffles his hair. Imogene is the opposite of a delicious challenge. She is an open-faced sandwich, forgotten on the table.

"I told you about her and me hooking up, right?" he says.

"Sherrie?"

"Yeah. Back in January, right after me and Jan broke up. We went home together a handful of times."

"You slept with her?"

"Well, the first couple of times were more 'just the tip' situations."

He laughs. She takes a drag. She could pitch her guts on his boots.

"Hey, I didn't say I was proud of it," he says. "We all have past connections we're not fond of, don't we?"

He peers into her face. She stubs out the cigarette, digging her toe into the ground. A handful of times. She thinks about filling her hands with gravel and dirt and squeezing it into her palms to break the skin. "Did you like her?" she asks.

"Sure. I mean, she's attractive. At the time, I thought of her as more saucy and lively than annoying."

"She's so vapid. And vacuous. And vacant. All the V words."

"I know. But she's Maureen's friend and I've known her most of my life. These things happen."

They have history. Sherrie not only got to have him, but co-owns a wealth of memories with him. Sherrie Duffy in her rich family home, all brick walls and backyard barbeques, and her voluminous hair and knowledge of Jamie's skin against hers. Maybe that puppy will bite her.

Jamie looks at his watch. "I have to work in about an hour. You want a ride home?"

She feels like saying no and stomping off under the trees, but she nods. They cross the grass to where his car is parked on Bannerman Road. Litter peppers the edge of the sidewalk. Nobody cares about keeping things nice.

eight

The days get shorter and darker and Maggie follows suit. She folds herself up on the couch with her knees against her chest. Her dark hair shrouds her face like limp vines. She sifts into rooms and fills them with her mood. She sleeps until almost eleven and hangs around in her red plaid L.L. Bean housecoat. In the afternoon, she gets dressed and leaves for a few hours to put out résumés. Or so she says. In the evenings, she returns to eat supper in silence and watch episodes of *America's Funniest Home Videos* and *Days of Our Lives*. Late at night, Imogene can hear her in her bedroom as she listens to CBC Radio and smokes out the window.

Imogene has never seen her like this. But what does she know? Maggie's only been around for summers and Christmases. If Imogene had to return home at the age of thirty-something to her fussy mother and her rape-product offspring, she'd be pretty bummed too. And, for all Imogene knows, it's Maggie's nature to spend eight months of the year as the personification of a Smiths' song. Her depression seems part of her, like an organ or a vertebra. Imogene has moments when she wants to take Maggie into her lap, cradle her like a baby. Or go on a quest to bring her some symbolic trophy: handwritten apologies, the fresh heads of her enemies. Present something to her on a satin pillow. *Here is the head of Cecil Jesso. Let's move on.*

At supper, Nan puts out chili and toast and riddles off a ticker-tape of ideas over the dining table. "What about the real-estate places in the back of the *Buy and Sell*? They might be looking for salespeople. You have lots of experience."

Maggie nods without looking up from her plate.

"And what about temping?" Nan says. "Have you put your résumé into Manpower? You could always look in to writing the civil-service exam. You could get a job up in the Confederation Building."

"I've looked into those things, Mom. If people aren't hiring, they aren't hiring. All I can do is wait."

"You could look into doing a course."

"Maybe." Her voice is flat and airy like an overcast day. "Something will come up, here or somewhere else. St. John's is a nest of favouritism anyway. Townies overlook your qualifications and hire whatever losers they went to high school with."

Maggie scrapes her butter knife across dry toast like a warning. This be yer throat, ol' woman. But Nan wants something solid. She is a conveyor belt of nag. "Joyce MacIssac's sister-in-law works in town, she might be able to help you out. Anyway, you just got here. You don't have to run off right away."

She will, if you keep it up, Imogene wants to say. You'll prod her out the door. But Maggie nods and butters toast. She focuses on immediate items: a mug of tea cupped in both her hands. The pattern of the table-cloth. The sky above the rooftops. The television set. She moves to the couch with her toast. Her toes fold over the edge of the coffee table to anchor her down.

Imogene goes for a run along Duckworth Street. The courthouse is covered with chalk marks. She slows down for a closer look; they are messages from the Take Back the Night March. Maureen went last year and said they stop here and pass out chalk. Participants are asked to make a mark for every woman they know that has been raped or assaulted. Someone has written *And I have to see him ALL THE TIME* in yellow chalk, bright against the grey stone walls. They pressed hard with the chalk and the anger in their effort squeezes Imogene's core. Like Maggie's voice in the car that time, choked with tension. *I've been away too long. It's not fair to you. I haven't been fair.* But nothing was fair in the first place, so how could it ever be? Imogene keeps on running, but has to slow by the Anglican Cathedral to wipe her eyes.

On campus, Imogene stays in the library to work on a Newfoundland folklore assignment. She likes folklore more and more these days, its blend of history and imagination and how it shows the stories behind things they see and do every day. She interviewed Nan for an assignment on ghost stories from the Southwest Coast. Nan riddled off tales, one coiling off another like peeling a potato in one long strip. Then she cried while washing the dishes. "The only time you show interest in those stories is for grades," she said. "As long as you get an A, I guess." Christ almighty, there is never any friggin' pleasing her.

This one requires research on the influence of oral traditions on written literature. Wouldn't be so much oral tradition if people just kept their mouths shut. She lists all the crappy things she has ever heard Jamie say about Sherrie. When she sees him, she talks herself out of asking him direct questions, but little things slip out so she can analyze his reaction. *Hey, that puppy looks like Sherrie's. That cactus reminds me of how Sherrie used to wear her hair.* He agrees or shrugs.

But Maureen is more forthcoming. "Sherrie has no couth," she says. "First, she makes it clear to me that she and Jamie were just getting their rocks off. Then she says she thinks he's gay because he seemed distracted when they were together. Like he had to think about someone else," she says. "Jesus, you know? He's my cousin." Imogene nods and rolls her eyes. Leave it to Sherrie to base someone's entire sexuality on their rejection of her. She resists prodding Maureen for specifics Sherrie might have disclosed. More details might make her punch a wall. Must be nice when you're so used to getting your way that you think you can label a person like that. What a bitch.

At least Jamie's not interested in talking about Sherrie. Mostly, he complains about his family. His brother Thomas's ex-girlfriend got a restraining order against him and every time he gets drunk, he goes on about what a cunt she is. Joseph brags about how he and his buddies saw a queer coming out of Solomon's and chased him down Water Street, you know, for a laugh. His parents nag him to disassemble the darkroom so they can use the space for a pool table. Eric is always on his parents to babysit his kids. When Imogene and Jamie are in the basement, the children's little footsteps echo on the ceiling like the start of an avalanche.

Together, they occupy themselves with finding places to go. Jamie picks up Winston and the three of them take long drives, out to Cape Spear, out to Petty Harbour. They smoke up and Jamie takes photos of Imogene, posing by the lighthouse, of Winston, playing dead on the rocks. They poke around downtown, they order pints of Guinness at Erin's Pub and leave them at the bar while they smoke outside. When they return, the liquid has settled nicely to room temperature. They drink and watch the session players create frantic, meandering music. They drive around testing the skeeziness of bars outside the George Street/

Water Street radius: The Top Hat, the Grumpy Stump, Barkley's. Jamie brings his camera and pretends he's working for *The Telegram*, he convinces drunken regulars to pose for him. They drive out to Pouch Cove and try the VLTs at the Lions Club. Winston wins $120 and buys the bar a round. They stomp around trails at Long Pond, Mount Scio, Logy Bay. After every adventure, Imogene returns home and falls asleep grinning and exhausted, just to wake at 4:00 a.m. to stare at shapes in the living room. Framed pictures of family members, the smug green ceramic cats, Nan's rocking chair. This companionship has an expiry date. What the fuck is she going to do?

nine

"There's nothing on the go this weekend. St.Yawn's," Jamie says. He drums his fingers on the steering wheel. They dropped off Winston, but Jamie doesn't want to go home yet. "Let's get coffees and drive around." The traffic light is a long red at Logy Bay Road and Newfoundland Drive. "Everything in the East End looks the same," he says.

"Have you ever gotten lost driving?" Imogene asks.

"Around here? No. Winston and I drove out to St. Jones Within last year and we didn't leave until after dark. We couldn't find the road out to the Trans-Canada. Drove around for forty-five minutes. There were hardly any streetlights and we couldn't see a sign saying where to go. Kept slowing down thinkin' we'd found it and it would be someone's driveway. We finally stopped somebody and asked. Buddy had to come out to the road and point to where it was. He's probably still laughing at us."

"Same thing happened to me in Flat Bay once. We couldn't remember where the access road was and we'd been driving all over the place at night. My cousin Rita and I had to stop at some guy's house to ask directions. He was just hanging out doing bottle tokes. Turns out, he knew a whole bunch of people from our high school. Rita was mortified to think people would find out we got lost in Flat Bay." She doesn't mention that Nick and Liam were there too.

A dark green mini-van charges out of a driveway. Jamie has to slam on the brakes. Imogene lurches forward, the seatbelt bites her collarbone. Hot coffee douses her lap. Jamie is red-faced and spouting curses.

"Fuck! You okay?"

"Yeah. You have any napkins or something?"

"Fucking prick." He guns the car.

"What are you doing?"

"Goddamn piece of shit." Jamie glares ahead, reaching back with his right hand for something under his seat. He pulls out a wooden baseball bat.

"Jamie, what the fuck?"

"Relax." He doesn't look at her. They approach the van. The van speeds up. "No you don't, motherfucker."

"What are you going to do?" she says. "This is retarded."

The van turns with no warning and vanishes down Robin Hood Bay Road. Jamie starts slowing down.

"Fucking cunt." Jamie returns the bat to the floor behind him with a plunk. She could swat him.

"Jamie. Jesus," she says. "That was fucked. What were you going to do?"

"Fuckers want to drive and almost kill people, they deserve to lose a window or a headlight."

"If someone's stupid enough to drive like that, they won't hesitate to kick the shit out of you."

"Like I should care about that. Wouldn't be the first time I've had the shit kicked out of me."

She opens the glove compartment and locates some napkins. Her hands tremble as she unfolds them.

"You want another coffee?" he says. She nods. She just wants the car to stop. Jamie pulls into an Irving station. "Did I scare you?" he asks. "I scared you. I'm sorry. It's cause I'm right tough, see."

"Why do you keep a bat in your car?"

"It's good to have something just in case. I keep one under my bed too. Anyone breaks in—*pok*." Jamie makes a swinging gesture. She pushes a smile into her cheeks.

"We can get a coffee in here or go to the Tim's on Torbay Road," he says.

"I'm okay," she says. "I wasn't really enjoying the last one. There's nowhere open to get a good one now."

"There's nowhere to get a good nothing, ever." He puts the car in drive. "I need to get out of here." He pulls out onto the road gingerly, like testing the thickness of ice. "I told you I got into Ottawa, right?"

"No." No you didn't, for fucksakes.

"Yeah, I got in. But I postponed starting until next September. Don't have the money now. But I'm thinking I'm going to move to Ottawa after

Christmas anyway. My buddy Jeanette runs a restaurant up there. The minimum wage is higher in Ontario and she'll give me good hours. Tips are good there, too."

Who the fuck is Jeanette? How can he say all this to her so calmly? "How come you never told me this before?"

"I thought I did."

"You told me you were applying, you never said you got in."

"Well, you should know I'd get in. I'm the best, missus." He grins and squeezes her knee. The heater in the car is overpowering. All this warmth makes her want to gag.

"So, you'll be gone after Christmas?"

He nods without looking away from the road. "Tickets are cheap after the holidays."

"Ottawa's expensive. You'll make more money here. And you don't pay rent or have far to drive to work."

"Up there, I won't have to drive at all. And Dad wants to start charging me rent. And I already spend a fortune on gas and food and booze so that I'm home as little as possible. So fuck home. Home is where your stuff is. I want my own place where I can do my own thing and not be questioned like a degenerate over all my decisions."

"I wish you'd told me." She rubs the napkin across the coffee stain on her lap. It leaves white flakes, like peeling skin.

"I'm sorry. But c'mon. You knew I wasn't going to be here forever."

"Yeah, I just wish you'd told me when you found out.' She starts wadding the napkin into the lip of the coffee cup. "I should go home."

"Okay." Jamie signals to turn up New Cove Road. Imogene says nothing. He pushes play on the Smashing Pumpkins CD.

The house is asleep when she gets in. She arranges the blankets on the couch without pulling out the bed. The sobs churn out in dry whispers. Why did she want him to tell her right away? So she'd move? Dig out the rest of Cec's money from the box under her bed, slap it down for a plane ticket? Follow him to Ontario like a forgotten dog? Would she apply to the University of Ottawa herself and rack up $30,000 in loans? She is not a priority. She is a convenience. She gets under the blankets and covers herself completely except for a little breathing window out into the stillness of the living room.

ten

Imogene's CDs still live in her bedroom. She needs music, something, a distraction. Maggie says "Come in," when she knocks. The room looks surprisingly bare. Her few decorations are still up: *The Shining* poster she bought when Jamie and she went to Imaginus and a few photos. She cleared off the cork bulletin board and it hangs naked on the wall. She doesn't know why it surprises her to see it bare, that she imagined Maggie would use it somehow.

Maggie stands at the window. The sheer billows out softly around the shadow of her profile. Her hair is pulled up in a messy bun with loose strands snaking around her neck. She blows a thin stream of smoke out the window. She resembles the photo Jamie took of Jan. Imogene can see why he was taken with the image. She turns to Imogene and waves her over.

"There he is." She points to a man making his way down the street in wide, determined steps. The man's eyes are deep pits in his face. His grey hair flaps with each pace. He wears a long, stone-washed jean jacket that hangs open and floats out behind him like a cape.

"Who is he?"

"The Ambler. All day, he makes trips to Tim Hortons. He'll be back in about ten minutes with a cup. Then, in an hour or so, he ambles back." Maggie taps ash out the window, ignoring the ashtray. Nan would be ticked if she saw.

"And him there, he's the Gargoyle."

She gestures with her smoke to a figure, all in black, crouched on the stairs of a house across the street. His hood obscures his face, but what looks like black dreadlocks peek out. He squats outside the door, a smoke in one hand, a bottle of beer in the other. The front window next to him looks like a pink wall from here, but Imogene knows it's salmon-pink drapes with ruffled edges. Ceramic dolls line the sill inside, staring wide-eyed out into the street.

"The Gargoyle leaves once a day," Maggie says. "He brings a case of empties—always Molson Canadian—to the store and comes back with a full one. He never puts his hood down." She wiggles her eyebrows at Imogene.

"Do you think they have a name for you?" Imogene says. Rude. She shouldn't have said that, she's letting her mood overtake her. But Maggie considers it.

"Hmmm," Maggie says. "What do you think it would be? Window Gawker? Nosey Parker? Housecoat Helen?"

"Lady in Plaid."

"Lay-dee in plaaaad," Maggie sings, Chris De Burgh style, "is dri-ving me mad."

"Week after week."

Maggie stops singing and stares out the window. "I have an interview tomorrow."

"Where?"

"Some flooring company. Office relief. I'm pretty sure that's his grand-mother he lives with. The Gargoyle, I mean. He doesn't seem happy."

"I thought you never saw his face."

"Doesn't matter. I can tell." She flicks the butt out the window. Nan will definitely be ticked if the downstairs tenants complain. But it is Maggie's house. She can do what she wants.

"The Gargoyle moves like he's miserable," she says. "But who knows."

"Do you want help picking out clothes for the interview?" Maybe they could talk a bit. Although just saying Jamie's name out loud might be all it takes to break down.

"Oh, I think I know what to wear. I have an outfit just for interviews. Thanks, though."

"Okay, well, I came in for some CDs."

Imogene goes to the standing rack by the dresser. For a moment, she thinks about what else is in the room. The shoebox is just there, under the bed. She could take it out right now, pull out the pendant. *Look at this,* she could say. *I know about this. He's losing his mind now. He's almost gone. I understand that it's hard to be around me. It's okay. It's all okay.*

She pulls two CDs from the rack, Beastie Boys and Sinead O'Connor. "You have good taste in music," Maggie says. "I love that you have that Kate Bush album, it's one of my favourites."

"I hope you do well on your interview tomorrow," Imogene says. She opens the door, creating a wind tunnel that puffs out the window sheer. Maggie already stands back on, staring out the glass. The edges of her robe billow with the breeze.

Maureen comes over. She's had a wretched day. They smoke outside while she rants. "I can't believe I have a job where the main role is just talking to dickheads on the phone all day," she says. "I can't believe I've been seeing a dickhead like Darrin for this long. I feel like getting really drunk. And getting in a fight. And fucking somebody."

Imogene nods. Her week has involved waiting for her next scrap of privacy so she can succumb to another crying jag. And Jamie still hasn't told his folks about Ottawa. When he complains about his family, she wonders if she is supposed to cheer him up with the reminder that he'll be free of them soon. She'd like to tie him to a fence, she'd like to jump on his back and hang on. He's not even coming out tonight because he's picking up extra shifts at West Side's. "I need to save money for moving," he says. She needs to not think about him for a few hours. She walks with Maureen downtown. They take shots from Maureen's hip flask, little sips that burn holes in their moods.

There are a bunch of bands playing a benefit at The Ship. Imogene and Maureen sit on the window sill by the bar and compare random strangers for each other. "Which one would you fuck, the old guy in the windbreaker or the white guy with dreadlocks? The guy with the plumber crack or that underage kid?" This goes on and on. It isn't until the music starts that they notice Case and the Tickets are playing and Sherrie Duffy is there.

Sherrie dances before her boyfriend. Now that she's given up the bangs, her hair is full and luscious. It fans out as she spins and arches her back. "Look at her go," says Maureen. "She's so happy lately. Let's say hi." Imogene shrugs and follows her.

Sherrie dances up to them. She leans into Imogene and points at Casey. "Look at him," she says. Casey strums and sings, his hair tucked back behind each ear so that it parts in the middle and frames his face, Kurt Cobainesque. He and the rest of the band wear combat jackets. Imogene wonders if they coordinated their outfits or if it was just a sale.

"He's the best thing that's ever happened to me," Sherrie says. "He's a genius and he fucks me all night like a jet engine. Case and the Tickets! Whoooo!" She jumps and claps. "Where's Jamie?" she says. "I thought you guys were Siamese twins."

"He's working."

"A little bird told me he was moving away."

"You shouldn't worry about what little birds say."

"I don't have to worry about a little bird with Case, I tell you. Whooo-hooo!"

The band plays a fast one and Imogene is grateful for the distraction. Every time Sherrie turns to say something, she closes her eyes and pretends to be into the music. Sherrie tries to dance with her, wadding the back of Imogene's shirt in her hand and bouncing up and down, but Imogene refuses to jump. Finally, Sherrie moves up and writhes in front of Casey until she sees someone she knows by the bar. She throws both hands up in exclamation and dances over.

A slower song starts. Imogene's eyes dart to the entrance. Stop looking at the door, Jamie is not showing up. She's too used to looking for him, it's like some kind of nervous tic. When she turns to the stage, Casey is staring at her while he sings. His voice is pretty good, but forced at times, like he's trying to sound older, like Tom Waits or something. Which is okay, but does it work? She watches and wonders this.

And Casey does not look away. He is so bold and obvious. What a cocky fucker. But shit, it feels good to be seen. It's been a while since she felt noticed and Casey has a look like he wants to fill his face with her. She realizes that she is standing still, gawking back at him. Jesus. She does an about turn. Go to the bar, get a drink. She fights the urge to glance back to see if he's watching her leave.

After the show, Maureen wants to go to a party. "Darrin might be there," she says. They say goodbye to Sherrie, who dangles off Casey's frame. She makes a fuss over Maureen and Imogene by pulling them into her and kissing their cheeks. When she pulls Imogene in for a kiss, Casey sneaks a peck as well. "Isn't he the freshest thing," Sherrie says. "Yeah, he's pretty ripe," Imogene says. "Watch out for her, Case, she's a saucy one," Sherrie says and Casey says, "I can see that."

Maureen and Imogene trudge up Bates Hill to a house with people smoking pot on the steps. Darrin is there. He and Maureen give each other shrugging hellos and speak in aloof tones. Well now. Maybe Imogene will find someone she knows inside.

At the top of the staircase is a small kitchen where beer is being sold out of garbage buckets of ice. The Tragically Hip blares from the stereo and she sees Winston standing with a couple of guys. He calls her over and says he wants to talk to her about whether redheads have hotter tempers than non-redheads. Imogene picks up a frying pan and pretends to hit him with it, which makes the guys laugh.

In twenty minutes, Maureen still hasn't come inside, but Casey and his band show up. Casey's face juices up slightly when he sees her and he lifts his bottle in greeting. "Jesus," Winston says in her ear. "I can smell that guy's cock stand up from here."

"Shut up, Winston," she says. Casey's gaze is unnerving, but everyone here is happy to have his cool cred at their party. So that's kind of flattering.

Ten more minutes and Maureen still doesn't appear. Fucking Maureen and Darrin. Imogene doesn't know anyone else besides Winston and he's getting loud and sloppy. She looks for the bathroom to take a break. It's tucked away in a hallway by the bedrooms and it's quiet and makes her want to go home where she can think and not feel like an arsehole at a party because Jamie isn't with her. She fixes her lipstick and hair. She'll make an exit, say goodbye to Winston. Maybe a cool farewell to Casey as well. She'll go home out of it.

She opens the door and there is Casey Cahill.

"It's all yours," she says.

He steps towards her. He brushes his lips against hers. "I wanted to give you a real kiss before," he says. And he really is very hot and he takes up the whole doorway. She tips her face up. He kisses her soft and then hard, his tongue slides into her mouth and explores and Jesus, it's so good to be kissed. She runs her palms over his shoulders and they are molded slabs. He stops and looks down at her from under his eyelids. "If you leave, I'll follow you," he says.

"Where's Sherrie?"

"She went home."

"I can't be seen leaving with you."

"Meet me at the corner of George and Water in five minutes. We'll go to your place."

"I can't take you home."

"Why not?"

"No privacy."

"Shit. I can't take you home, either."

"Why not?"

"That's where Sherrie is."

"Lovely. I'm leaving."

"Come on. I really want to be with you. I've wanted you since I saw you in the park that day. You're like a strawberry dessert."

"I really gotta go."

He takes her hand and presses it to the front of his pants. "See how much I want you," he says. He kisses her again and she wants to move her hand up and down. He cups her breast over her shirt. "Damn, your tits are nice."

"We're going to get caught."

He straightens up. "Okay. You go out first. Fucking hell."

She walks a straight line out and towards the exit. No eye contact with anyone.

"See ya, Genie."

Winston. She waves back at him as she clops down the stairs.

Outside, Maureen and Darrin are gone. Maybe she could go back up. There are bedrooms. They must have locks. No, half of St. John's would know. And Winston would tell Jamie and Maureen. Jesus Christ. Dodge a bullet, go home, rub one out, go to sleep. She walks home, making sure to take the well-lit streets. If Jamie saw her, he'd bawl her out for not getting a cab.

eleven

Four twenty-three a.m. and Maggie is at the kitchen table. Scares the crap out of Imogene when she walks in.

"Jesus."

"Sorry."

"Just need some water."

Imogene focuses on walking straight to the sink. Chugging a glass of water is pretty tell-tale. She's slurry and needs to go to bed out of it.

"Joyce MacIssac called," Maggie says. "Bad news out home."

"Everything okay?"

"The house is gone. There was a fire."

"What?"

"And Cecil Jesso is dead."

Imogene stares at the tap. The reflection of Maggie's brown hair is squished in the faucet. "How?" she says.

"It seems he's been going into people's houses lately and not realizing it. He developed some kind of dementia. He went into our house. It looks like he passed out with a lit cigarette."

She turns. Maggie's hands are clasped calmly.

"Holy fuck."

"Yes."

"And the house is gone? Completely?"

"Yes."

"From a lit cigarette?"

"He was drinking moonshine too. And the place was old. It was past midnight. Malcolm Whalen was driving by and spotted the flames. He ran into the Abbotts' and called the fire department. But it was too late."

Imogene fills her glass of water and drinks half of it. Fills it again. Maggie's reflection in the tap is a smushed blur. She flicks on the kettle. The water's been boiled recently and it starts right up.

"And what's really disturbing is that they didn't know anyone was inside until they started putting out the fire. They saw his body through the window."

"Jesus Christ."

"He was dead when they got him out. Smoke inhalation it looks like."

"He was probably too loaded to be aware."

"Maybe."

"But not too loaded to break in?"

"Couldn't have been hard to get in the house," Maggie says. "Eli hasn't boarded the place up since it's been on the market. Trudy said there was nothing of value inside, so they hadn't bothered to put on a lock. Said it would be better if someone went in and poked around rather than break a window. I guess Cecil managed to kick or push in the door."

"So he's gone."

"Yes."

Imogene gets the teabags. She drops one in her mug. Does she feel a drop? Does she feel anything? "How's Nan taking it?" she says.

"Not good. I gave her an Ambien. She fell asleep about an hour ago. She kept repeating, 'We've lost our home. We've all lost our home.'"

The water is boiled. Imogene fills her mug. This will be good for her hangover. She fills up Maggie's mug too, and passes it to her. Maggie's face is posed and neutral. She stirs the bag in the water, making brown swirls. "Frankly," she says, her voice low, "and I don't mean to sound dark, but she'll get more in insurance than the house was worth. With the repairs it needed, she's better off selling the land."

"So he did us a favour," Imogene says.

"Shhh now."

"Probably the first time he's done anybody any favours."

"Dementia does strange things. From what Joyce says, he was very ill."

Maggie sugars her tea. Imogene imagines shaking her. First soft, by the shoulders, building into a hard rattle. C'mon, Maggie, get angry. Curse him at least. Or pop the cork on the champagne. Ding, dong, Cec is dead. Fucking talk about it already.

Maggie stands up, taking her mug. Their eyes meet and Imogene realizes her face is set on skewed, lips pursed and ready to swear. She lowers her eyes and blows ripples across her hot tea.

"You should get some sleep," Maggie says. "Mom's going to need our help tomorrow. We have to plan a trip home."

Imogene nods. Maggie pats her shoulder. "I'm sure you feel pretty numb about all this," she says. "It's difficult to process."

"Yeah."

Imogene sets up the sofa bed and gets in. Going home. A ten-hour car ride in a depression sauna with Nan and Maggie. Sleeping on the floor at Trudy and Eli's. Or sharing Rita's bed with her, their feet accidently touching under the covers. Nick's sour stares. And all the "Oh, my what a tragedy" from the same arseholes who laughed when she was called Cec and Cecil and Baby Cec. The ones who whispered about Maggie and rolled their eyes. She balls her pillow in her fists and squeezes. That prick. She thinks of Cecil's slurpy voice. Did he swear and search the house? He didn't find his money or the little trophy heart. He didn't find anyone to hurt. He is gone now. She never has to think about him again. She closes her eyes and falls asleep.

twelve

Nan won't get up. She lies back on to the door, all blankets and head. The bedroom is ripe and wet, wadded tissues flower around the bed. Maggie and Imogene bring in cups of tea, flat bowls of soup. Imogene conducts small busying tasks. Making raisin buns, slicing strips of mild cheddar, folding towels. Maggie makes phone calls, talks to insurance people, police contacts and St. Felix's neighbours. Uncle Kenneth and Susan come by with lasagna. They stay with Nan while Imogene is in class or at work.

Nan only rises for bedraggled trips to the bathroom. She crumbles back into bed, curling under the comforter. Attempts to get her to talk result in her eyes squeezed shut and shuddering sighs.

On the third day of Nan's hibernation, Jamie and Winston show up after midnight. "We saw your lights on when we drove by," Jamie says to Imogene. "Come with us. We're taking you out." She practically rips her jacket putting it on.

The car reeks of weed. Winston has the passenger seat. "I'm sorry about your house," he says. His eyes are pink with pot and emotion. "My parents sold my childhood home a few years ago and I took that pretty hard. But I can't imagine how it feels, to have it just gone like that."

"I haven't been feeling very much about it, honestly," Imogene says.

"Yeah, you're still numb," Winston says.

Jamie catches her eye in the rearview mirror and winks. "We're going out for dinner," he says. "Comfort food all around."

"I can't wait to have some fucking fries," Winston says.

Classic Café is one of the only downtown places open twenty-four hours. It's late enough to be busy and they get the last table. Jamie sits between Imogene and Winston and lets his knee slack against hers. She could hold up his knee forever. They order club sandwiches and perogies to share.

"So this is it, man," Winston says. "Won't have too many more nights like this when you're off on the mainland." He checks the top of the salt shaker to see if it's sealed. "Right loose. People are assholes."

"It's only Ottawa," Jamie says. "Not like I'm going to war."

"Whaddaya think, Genie? I say we start a campaign to keep him here."

"I agree. What should we do?"

"I'll pin him down and you sit on him."

Yeah, she'd be down for that. "Yes. Strong rope and chloroform."

"See? She's prepared." Winston tightens the salt shaker top. "But seriously, I don't see why you have to go to Ontario to be a photographer. We're living in a photographer's paradise."

"Good point, Wince," Imogene says.

"It's a lot more than that," Jamie says. "I need a change."

"What, 'cause of your folks? Fuck 'em. Move out."

"Yeah, fuck 'em," Imogene says.

"There's only so much I can pick up on my own," Jamie says. "And it's not just moving out of the house. They don't get me at all."

"Maybe they just need to get used to the idea," Imogene says. "I mean, you've been taking photos for years. They know it's what you love."

"They've always seen it as my little hobby. I remember a few years ago, I showed some of my photos to Joseph and Thomas, ones I took of some skaters out in the Goulds. They got all excited. 'Come take pictures of us playin' hockey,' they said. So I went to the arena with them, got some really good shots. Their teammates started posing and stuff for me. It was a laugh. But then I got a bunch of ideas. Like, I wanted to come back the next week and get candid shots of the game. I wanted to photograph the guys looking pissed off in the penalty box. But the twins didn't like that. 'What are ya, *National Geographic* or something?'"

"That's just them being macho cunts," Winston says.

"There's that, but it's more about how they want to see me. They don't want to see me as an artist, even though that's what I am." Jamie plucks the straw out of his drink so he can sip from the glass. "They have all these stupid ideas and can't admit to themselves that I'm something they know nothing about and don't want to know anything about."

"But still," Imogene says. "Fuck 'em. Go live on your own and do what you want."

"Yeah, listen to her," Winston says. "Be yourself. They'll get used to it."

"And be completely unsupported? Sunday supper with stupid comments? No, man, I wanna go to art school. I want to do what I want and be around people who accept that. And I want to go back to school already."

Winston sighs and nods. "Understandable," he says. "Gettin' pigeon-holed is bullshit. I know that feeling well."

Imogene stares at her hands on the table. The fucking Clarks. Why do they have to be such small-minded tools? If her and Jamie were together, she'd tell them all off. *Stop driving away your son and brother. Stop driving away the person I love.*

"Check out the customer base," Winston says. "Everyone here is drunk or high."

"I wouldn't want to work here," Jamie says. "Night shifts with loaded customers? No thanks."

"Tips would be good though," Imogene says.

"I have a tip for you," Jamie says.

"Crime Stoppers?"

He leans into her ear. "You're being sized up."

"Yeah? That's a surprise."

"Someone's always sizing you up, missus. But this guy looks sketchy. Want me to be your boyfriend? I'll protect you."

Fuck yes. "Where is he?" she asks.

"Ten o'clock."

Imogene sips her drink and draws a casual survey of the other tables. There is a booth of three meaty-looking guys, all in tight shirts with athletic logos. Two wear ball caps and the hatless one has blond hair buzzed short, military style. He stares at her. She holds his gaze. A rush of confused recognition passes through her until she realizes it is Liam Lundrigan. A harder, solid Liam Lundrigan with a harder, solid stare.

"Oh," she says. "I know him."

"Looks like a dick." Winston says.

Good eye, she wants to say. But she should go over to say hello. Otherwise, he might come over here.

"I'll be back in a sec."

Liam continues to stare as she walks over. His closed mouth works in a twitch between a smile and a glare, like a loose wire in the wind. What to do with her hands. She shoves her fingers in the tops of her jeans pockets. Nice, like a cowboy. Fuck sakes.

"Hey, Liam."

"Immy Tubbs," he says. "How are you?"

"Alright." Her hand in her jeans pocket is half in a fist. She flattens it against her hip. "You?"

"Decent. Yeah, Rita told me you were living here."

"Yeah, since last year."

"Right on."

"Where are you to now?" Her voice cracks and her face heats up. He stares at her mildly, in that infuriating way before they were going out when she would imagine he could smell her fear. She should have changed before she went out, put on jeans that fit better.

"Living in Edmonton. Working with my buddy's roofing company." His eyes drop down to her legs and back up again. The other two guys assess her as well. One has a yellowing bruise on his jaw and his eyes are steady on her chest. Liam does not introduce them.

"So, you're in town for a visit?"

"Yep. Not moving here, that's for sure."

"Only way I'd live in St. John's is if they put me in the Pen," Bruised Face says. His eyes don't move.

"I'm here for my buddy's stag party," Liam says.

"Oh, that sounds like fun." Jesus. Like it's church camp.

"Gonna be three days of whisky and peelers," Bruised Face says. Still staring. Liam looks over at him. Something happens under the table, a nudge or kick. Bruised Face's eyes jerk down to his placemat.

"Right on." She glances back at her table. If the food was there, she'd have a reason to return. Winston is saying something in Jamie's ear, but Jamie keeps his face turned to her.

"Was home for a visit, too," Liam says. "Too bad about your house."

"Yeah, Nan's kind of in shock."

"Ol' Cec was in hard shape. If I ever start losing it like that, I hope someone throws me over a bridge or something."

She nods. C'mon, food. The guy next to Bruised Face swigs his beer and belches.

"He was like a child," Liam says. "I was at his place with Murray and Bryce. He did everything they told him to do. 'Cec, get me a beer. Cec, sing a song.' Like a trained monkey."

Liam's eyes glitter with an old mischief. He looks rough. Rita said he lost a job for doing acid. How many other drugs does he do? "You were with Murray and Bryce?" she says.

"Bygones," he says. He shrugs and holds up his hands.

"Must be nice."

What a prick. Why do Rita and Nick continue to be friends with him? Liam Lundrigan is their ol' buddy, but Imogene is some kind of pariah because she didn't move to Corner Brook? She realizes her lip is curling at him.

"Thing is," he says, "he got sick at a real convenient time."

"Yeah?"

"Yeah. Some people were saying that he was being investigated."

"For what?"

"A bunch of stuff. Drugs. Things that happened years ago. He had a lot of enemies. Especially out in Codroy."

"Well, who liked him, really?"

"Exactly. And if he went down for something, he'd bring others with him."

Liam's eyes are the same blue with a few creases on their edges. What kind of cryptic bullshit is he on with? She holds his gaze with the best *you can't be fucking serious* stare she can muster. Fuck you and your bluff, Liam Lundrigan.

A waitress appears behind her. "S'cuse me." She lays three orders of fish and chips on the table. Bruised Face points to his beer. "Three more." His eyes follow her as she walks away.

"You been out home lately?" Liam asks.

"Not since we left. We're supposed to head out in a couple of days, to deal with what's left of the house."

"It's too bad. I guess you have nothing to go home to now." Liam shakes vinegar on his fries. "Must be hard, feeling like you can't go home. I've felt like that before." He lays the bottle on the table and pops a fry in his mouth. The look he gives her is satisfied and defiant.

Imogene leans over and takes a fry. "Mmm, these look good," she says. Gusto, she should eat the fry with gusto. She chews it, considering, before she speaks. "Could be worse," she says. "I like it here. If you're happy, anywhere can feel like a home, you know?"

"Depends, I guess."

"What does it depend on?"

Liam looks over at her table. "Your food's ready. Better go back to whichever one's your man."

"They look like they're each other's man," Bruised Face says. The other guy laughs. His mouth open, mashed with cod.

"I better go before it gets cold." She decides to put her hand on his shoulder. If he's going to be a jackass, she'll take the smug road. "Have fun with your party," she says. His shoulder is warm, like it contains sunlight. Molded and fit under her palm. Surprising, since he seems stockier than before. She glances down and he looks to his plate. "Take care," he says. He shifts the fries around with his fork.

"Where's the goddamn tartar sauce?" Bruised Face says.

Imogene adjusts her chair so she faces away from their table when she sits down. She removes the toothpick from a club sandwich section.

"Old friend?"

"Guy from home," she says. "We were talking about the fire."

Jamie strokes her shoulder. "Hard to get away from it, huh?"

"Yeah, you could say that."

She takes a big bite. Jamie and Winston tell stories. She pretends not to notice when Liam and his friends pay their tab and leave. When the door opens, she gets a short cold blast of outside air.

thirteen

On the fourth day, Nan gets up and showers. She puts on slacks and a blouse. She says she wants to see the wreckage. Uncle Kenneth offers to drive. Maggie's going too.

"I have assignments," Imogene says.

"That's fine," Nan says. "I have Maggie and Kenneth to help me. You should concentrate on school."

Thank the holy Jesus fuck. Imogene nods and feels the heavy waiting within her evaporate. The idea of being out home, the shows of sympathy, the awkward mentions of Cecil, witnessing grief for him and its sincerity or lack of sincerity, has hindered her sleep for four days. That and a memory of a summer from years ago, one of the last times Uncle Kenneth came out to St. Felix's to visit. He was walking across the lawn and Nan teared up at the sight of him: "I thought it was Gus, just then, coming back from the woods. I forget how much Ken looks and moves like him. Oh, my heart." What if someone sees more Cecil than usual in her now? Would she trigger memories like that now that he's freshly dead? It will be something that might happen whenever she's home. She'll move like him. She'll sound like him. So, she'll never, ever go home. Fuck it.

It's exactly what Liam wants. Him and his bullshit. But he's too stupid to realize he's done her a favour. Or maybe this is his way of doing her a favour.

Nan packs her suitcase, her old hard plastic one in '60s baby blue. She stands with her coat on, staring out the living room window for Kenneth to arrive. The way she pulls her shoulders into herself pangs Imogene in the guts. When they leave, she separates the laundry and wipes her leaking eyes and nose on the dirty towels.

In the library, she holes up in the Newfoundland archives, searching through sources for her paper on fairies in Newfoundland and Labrador folklore. A thesis on fairy stories around the Bell Island mine tells of miners leaving for lunch and returning two days later. They'd swear they were only gone for an hour. Maybe this is how Cecil's mind worked in his last days, wandering into houses, seeing himself as belonging there. Taking what he wants, but being confused as to what he wants. Or, it was all his way of staying out of trouble. Maybe those miners just wanted a couple of days off.

She finds stories of changelings, the substitute fairy children swapped for humans. Wouldn't it be better if that's how she was seen? Tony Green was actually a fairy, a little green man, popping around, knocking up young girls. Watch out, or the Green Man will get ya. He'll curse you with motherhood and whispers.

She writes down page numbers and authors' last names. Maybe she should have gone, for Maggie. This has got to be wretched for her. Or maybe it's better that she stayed here. Easier to pretend things will be okay without Imogene.

Her eyes skip through an index of articles, titles organized by their place of origin: Clattice Harbour, Cobb's Arm, Codroy Valley. The crowd from Codroy. What was it Liam said, years ago by the brook? *Bryce went on about this girl that Murray had brought over one time. He had met her in Codroy and she was out camping in Fischels. Bryce kept going on about how much fun they had with her, especially after Cec gave her some skin juice.*

Her hands shake as she gathers her things. She has enough to finish her notes at home. Outside the library, the cold air waters her eyes and speeds up her pace.

That night, Jamie and Maureen come over. It is a relief to have voices in the house. They make hot wings and french fries for supper. They drink beer and smoke joints out the window in Imogene/Maggie's room. Imogene points out the Ambler and the Gargoyle.

"I love people-watching," Jamie says. "It's like trying to figure out their secrets. Why do you think that guy walks back and forth to Tim's all day?"

"He's doing coffee runs for someone," Maureen says.

"But he only carries one coffee at a time," Imogene says. "I think they're for him."

"Maybe he has a crush on someone who works at Tim's," Jamie says. "He comes in to gaze upon them."

"If he lines up in front of them every day, maybe they'll notice him eventually," Imogene says.

"When are Maggie and Agnes back?" Maureen asks.

"Two more days."

"I took photos of your place when I was out there," Jamie says. "If I printed them for Agnes, maybe blew them up, do you think she would like that?"

"I think she'd love it."

"Do you have any pictures of the house? We could make a collage or something."

"Maggie might have some," Imogene says. "She has an old photo album."

"Let's look."

"That's nosey."

"I know."

They sit on the bed to flip through the pages. Maggie holding Imogene as a toddler, both of them skinny and wide-eyed. Nan with chin-length dark hair and a dress with a cinched waist. Pop holding up a huge cod on a line.

They find a photo of the house in summer, the view from the road. Nan and Pop standing arm in arm by the front door. "Oh my God," Maureen says. "Your house was so cute." That stings Imogene a little. Small and decrepit isn't cute.

"That picture's perfect," Jamie says. "I might be able to get it blown up."

He removes it from the album pouch. A Polaroid falls out from behind it. She knows what it is before she turns it over.

The photo is similar to the one Kelly showed her, maybe taken a moment before or after. Maggie's head rests on Tony's shoulder and he looks into the camera with a half smile. Imogene pulls it towards her face and stares. She has tried to remember how he looks so many times. Maybe now she can see something. His chin, his eyes. But she can't see it. He looks like some guy.

"Who's that?" Maureen says.

"My mother and Tony."

"Is that your dad?" Jamie peers at the photo. "Damn, it's too bad it's not better quality."

"Oh wow, he's handsome," Maureen says.

"I guess," Imogene says. "I've never seen him in real life."

Maureen squints at it. "I see a resemblance."

"How so?"

"I dunno. He looks tall. And the shape of your faces."

Imogene tucks the Polaroid back in the album and replaces the house picture. "When Maggie comes back, I'll mention to her that we want to borrow the house photo," she says.

"You okay?" Jamie says.

"Sure," she says. "It's just a shitty situation."

He puts his arm around her and she rests her head on his shoulder, like they're doing a reenactment of the Polaroid. Maybe if Maureen wasn't here, she'd give him a kiss.

"Let's put on some music."

The next day, Imogene looks at the Polaroid three times. This is the man whose name is on her birth certificate. She holds it next to her reflection in the mirror, like she did at Kelly's. Yes, he's tall and they have oval faces. It's not enough.

That night she dreams of Cecil. He stands in the middle of their living room in St. John's. He wears his blue Labatt cap and hunting gear, a fluorescent orange vest over a camouflage suit. The sounds of Nan washing the dishes are behind her. She and Jamie sit before him on the couch. "Your shoe's untied," Jamie says.

"Tanks," Cecil says. He bends and sets his shoelaces on fire. The flames engulf him. She and Jamie sit and watch as he calmly stands and burns.

Nan and Maggie return on Tuesday morning. Nan kisses Imogene's cheek with dry lips and plunges into her bedroom. Maggie carries their suitcases.

"How was it?"

"That was utterly exhausting," Maggie says. She flops onto the couch. Imogene puts the kettle on.

"There are leftover chicken wings," Imogene says.

"Ugh, I've been eating brown food for four days," Maggie says. "All everyone offered us was cakey or boiled. If people are still getting scurvy in mass numbers in this province, I wouldn't be surprised."

"What would you like then?"

"Juice?"

"Okay."

Imogene brings a glass of orange juice with ice cubes. Maggie half chugs it. "Parched," she says. She rests the glass on her forehead.

"How is the house?"

"Gone. Cinders. Mom sat on the step and cried. It was really hard."

"Jesus."

"It's rough. It feels haunted out there." She empties the glass. "And technically, it is now, I guess."

"That's what people will say." Imogene takes the glass. Maggie nods without looking at her. Maybe they'll be part of folklore now. A ghost story about Mad Cecil. "Refill?" she asks.

"Yes please." Maggie rubs the back of her neck. "It's heartbreaking. But, I think it would be better for all of us if we just sell the land. Financially and emotionally."

"I agree."

"Murray Wells is interested in buying it. He wants to plant trees. Maybe start a Christmas tree farm."

Murray Wells. *Bryce went on about this girl that Murray had brought over one time.* "Well, that's good then," she says.

"Mom doesn't like to think of it."

"Sounds good to me."

"Really?"

"Fresh trees and birds where our house used to be? I like that."

"Rather than your home?"

Imogene shrugs. "Home is where your stuff is."

Maggie stares at her. "That's a pretty frivolous concept of home," she says.

"I think it's a pretty practical concept of home. Makes things easier."

"Seems pretty cold."

"Why?"

"Well, I'm surprised. I mean, when I first told you, you didn't say much. But I figured it was the shock. And you'd been drinking. I guess I figured once you had a few days to process it, you'd be more emotional. The whole drive back, I was dreading talking to you about it all."

"Sorry to disappoint you."

"I'm not disappointed. Concerned, yes."

"Don't start concerning yourself, please." Shit. She shouldn't have dropped that *start* in.

"What does that mean?"

"It means don't worry about my feelings or lack of feelings about home. Sorry they weren't what you expected." She is full of hot steam. Maybe she hasn't talked enough this weekend. Too much time by herself. "I'm a bit surprised myself about your own expectations," she says.

"How so?"

"Why do you expect me to be so attached?"

"Because it's your home."

"And yours. And you left. And Kenneth's. And Kenneth left. See a pattern?"

"Kenneth is pretty upset."

"You don't know about my feelings because you don't know what it was like for me."

"Okay." Maggie stares at her glass. "I tried to know."

"It's a little too late to be surprised about something you didn't know about in the first place. It's like being surprised that unicorns have blue eyes at the same time you discover unicorns are real."

"Huh?"

"You want more juice?"

"Sure."

Imogene refills her glass with extra ice cubes this time. "Here you go," she says. "I'm going for a run." Maggie turns the TV on.

Imogene's sneakers swat the sidewalk and she focuses on the rhythm to soothe her. She shoves her headphones on and presses play on the Depeche Mode tape. How much nerve does that woman have? And not once does she bring up the fact that it's Cecil Elephant in the Room Jesso's fault. We're all supposed to ignore his existence forever, even when he sets your house on fire. Even when he's dead. She sucks cold air through her teeth.

She circles the soccer field three times. It's getting dark fast. Every third or fourth car has their headlights on. When she gets back, Maggie will be watching *Blind Date* and will be dull and pacified. Less than two months until the basement tenants move out and Maggie can hide out below. And Jamie will be gone. This will be a long, cold winter. She shivers and forces herself to keep running.

When she turns down Cook Street, the lights are on in Nan's room and the living room. Nan's up and probably wants supper. Maybe Imogene should have put something on. That would have been a nice thing to do, cook without being asked. They must think she's an ingrate. From the path, she can see the cigarette butts from the weekend under her/Maggie's bedroom window. They're bright white and Maureen and Jamie threw them in a scattered arc, unlike Maggie's little pile. She could at least pick up her friends' cigarette butts and not be a complete jerk.

She collects the butts in her palm. A blaring sound comes from the living room, like a spray of rocks on wooden planks. Nan's voice. "You don't know. You have no idea!" she yells. Maggie's voice in response is low and indecipherable. "You weren't around and you have no clue," Nan barks. "Do you even know what the other kids used to call her? They called her by his name. They taunted her until she fought them off."

Maggie's response is something small, the pop of a pebble in water. "So there you go," Nan says. "Don't you dare give her a hard time. She had to tolerate that. I'm surprised she didn't burn the place down herself."

Imogene scrambles back to the road, crouching low, dodging bullets. Maybe they won't see her retreating from the house. She shoves her hand with its wad of cigarette butts into her jacket pocket. She'll go for a walk, listen to side A again. Let them cool off. She meets the Ambler on his way up the sidewalk. He takes wide steps and sways a little in the middle, like he's gauging how long he can stretch his legs when he walks, how far away he can get without running. They each give a jerky nod as they pass each other. They walk away as fast as they can.

fourteen

On the last day of November, Maggie drags out the Christmas decorations. She knew Jamie would be over today. She's so transparent. "Christmas lights," she says. "Who's going to put them up?"

Imogene looks at Nan with raised eyebrows. Nan sips her tea in response. Sitting in her housecoat, her own pity-pot perch. Wonder where Maggie gets it from. Mortifying, the both of them.

"Maggie," Imogene says. "Leave him be."

"I haven't said a thing. It's not necessarily a blue job." Maggie titters at this. What the shit, blue jobs and pink jobs. Where'd she come up with that?

"Sure, Maggie," Jamie says. "I'll help you out."

Maggie's mood has brightened since she got the job at the Carpet Factory. Administrative Assistant. She's up and out of the house every morning, but still spends most of her weekends sitting still. She needs some friends. The days are now short and dark and Imogene tries to avoid thinking about two months until February when the sidewalks will be blocked with snow, the three of them rattling around in this house, and Jamie gone. Jamie up in Ottawa, being regularly felated by Jeanette or Janine or someone else with a similarly alliterative name. Jamie and Jeanette are having a get-together. Jamie and Jeanette are having a house-warming party. Jamie and Jeanette are having a fucking theme party where all guests must dress like their favourite literary characters or in black and white or as their sexy, perfect selves.

"I can't believe you're going to leave me with Tweedledum and Tweedledepression," she says. She wants to sound funny, but it comes out acidic.

"Move out, sure," Jamie says.

The snarl of Christmas lights rests in her lap. She tugs a loose coil out of the nest and plugs it in. The Christmas lights silhouette Jamie's profile. He's so pretty. He catches her and winks. "What are you looking at?"

"Your eyelashes are some long."

"Finally, they are. Mom used to trim them when we were kids. She'd cut our hair and my eyelashes. She said boys shouldn't have long eyelashes. Makes them look girlish."

"What? How? Did she use those little eyebrow scissors?"

"No, the shears. The first time she did it, she had finished cutting my hair and she snipped them off my right eye. One swipe. Then I had to sit still while she did the left."

"That's mental."

"Yeah. I started getting my own haircuts as soon as I got an allowance." Jamie attaches another string of bulbs and they light up. "Did I ever tell you about when Maureen dyed my hair?" he says. "Mom was pissed, but Dad really flipped out."

"How old were you?"

"Grade ten. Maureen bleached her hair and dyed it blue. There was some left over, so we did streaks in the sides and back of mine. When I came home, Mom started screechin'. Dad tossed a bag at me and told me to get out. "Don't come back 'til that shit's gone off your head," he said.

"Where did you go?"

"Stayed at Maureen's. Her mom got in a big racket with Dad and they let me come home after two days. But Dad made me shave it off."

"Your whole head?"

"Yep. There's about five bulbs blown here on the bottom." He holds up the end of a string with dead bulbs. "So I've been thinking," he says. "I want a good party before I leave. What do you want to do for New Year's Eve?"

"Dunno. It's such a racket. Bit early to think about that."

"We should go to the Radisson party."

"Really? Those tickets are pricey."

"They are. It's a swanky event. But Winston's aunt works there. She can get us tickets."

"Will Winston be there?"

"Dunno." Jamie plugs in his string of lights and they all light up. "See," he says. "All these bulbs agree. They know a good idea when they hear one."

"They're pretty bright."

"We can get a room so we don't have to worry about cabs at three a.m."

"Huh. That's a good idea."

"We can get cleaned up nice and swill champagne. We can pick fights with rich people."

"Can we trash a hotel room?"

"Fuck yes. Sex Pistols style. Or Mötley Crüe. Making memories, baby. Memories and carpet stains."

A hotel room with Jamie. In one month. Dear Jesus. She plugs in a string of lights and every bulb lights up like all the bad ideas in her mind.

That Friday, Rita calls to say she's in town and will come over Saturday afternoon. Maggie is working but can meet them for supper. "Cherry and I are staying at Uncle Kenneth's," Rita says. "We went to the Bon Jovi concert last night. It was wicked."

She arrives at the house with armloads of plastic bags. "Some Christmas shopping. Plus, gifts from people out home," she says. "They had a fundraiser at the Legion for you." She hands Nan an envelope with a bit of a flourish. Nan opens it and her eyes flood up. "My god," she says. "I don't know what to say." Rita hugs her and Nan makes small sobs. Imogene stares at her hands on the kitchen table. How lovely of Rita to bring all of these offerings and, of course, not bother to invite her along to the concert. Not that she's even a Bon Jovi fan. Whatever.

"They played 'Livin' on a Prayer' as an encore. Everyone went mad," Rita says. She opens bags and pulls out cookie tins. "These are from Joyce. Snowballs. And these are date squares from the nuns. Hopefully not too dry."

"Everyone is so kind," Nan says. "I wish we were home for Christmas."

"Well, now a bit of it has been brought to you," Rita says.

Imogene gets up to put on the kettle. Although a drink would be nice. And she'd rather not go through the formal ritual for Rita. "Tea or beer?" she asks. "I have a few in the fridge from last night."

"Oh, tea would be nice."

"I'm going to have a beer."

"Let's see what you bought," Nan says. A stuffed bunny for Steve's daughter. New jeans and a sweater for Nick. Ceramic figurines for Aunt Trudy. Hockey themed clothes for Uncle Eli. Imogene sips a beer and when Nan announces she has to make phone calls to thank everyone, she cracks open another. Rita continues organizing her shopping.

"I bumped into Liam the other day," Imogene says.

"Yeah?" Rita stuffs plastic bags into each other.

"Yeah. He's a real creep now, huh?"

"How so?"

"He was acting all dark and ominous."

"What does that mean?"

"Ominous means sinister, like something bad is going on."

"I know what ominous means. What did he say?"

"He went on that Cecil Jesso died in a weird way. Like that he was susceptible to suggestion in the end. That he had a lot of enemies."

"Well, he did. A lot of people really hated him."

"He hinted that Cecil was getting investigated."

"There's been talk about that, yeah."

"Like what?"

Rita glances at Nan's room. She's still on the phone. "I thought you knew about that."

"I don't talk to many people from home."

"Right. I forgot."

"Anyway."

"Okay, so you heard Wish Benoit's folks broke up?"

"Yeah."

"Well, word is that this woman from Codroy called Arlene last year. She said that when she was underage, she met Bryce and he took her to Cecil's. She never said anything afterwards because, at the time, she went there with the intention of getting drugs and thought she would have to explain herself in court. But when she was there, Cecil got her fucked up. And Bryce did stuff to her. Murray Wells too."

"Did stuff?"

"You know. *Rape.*" Rita whispers the word. "The woman tells Arlene Benoit this. And Arlene says, 'Go ahead and charge him. Just please wait until my son has gone to the army. I'm leaving Bryce then anyway.'"

"Yes, b'y."

"Yeah, it's fucked up." Rita sticks a thick ball of bags into a large Sears bag. "And then, apparently, this woman was planning on pressing charges and two other women popped up, one from Flat Bay and one from Stephenville Crossing and they said they'd press charges as well. Like dominos."

"So, three women had rape charges against Cecil?"

"No, against Bryce and Murray. Cecil was charged with being an accessory."

"Holy fuck."

"I feel so bad for Wish," Rita says. "He was trying to get into the Forces for months after school ended. And then he finally gets what he wants and all this horrible shit happens to his family."

"Yeah. I feel bad for Arlene too."

"Yeah, that's some scary shit to believe about your husband."

Nan's laughter echoes in from the bedroom. Imogene stares at Rita's piles. So glad she's not spending Christmas in St. Felix's this year. "Liam seemed to suggest someone took care of Cec. Or something."

"Yeah, well, Liam likes to be a case."

Imogene looks up at Rita's face. Her lips are pursed as she folds a Bruins T-shirt. "You know what else he said? 'Must be hard, feeling like you can't go home. I've felt like that before.' And then he acted smug, like he got one over on me."

"Well, he does know what it's like to not be able to go home."

"Jesus, Rita, why do you side with him?"

"I'm not taking sides, I'm just saying he's had a hard life. And he's kind of fucked up in general, so it's not surprising he's still mad at you."

"Mad enough to joke about my house burning down? That's more than kind of fucked up."

"Well, I wasn't there, so I can't really say. And I know it was a long time ago, but you did dump him out of the blue right after he got in that fight." Rita snips the price tag from a teddy bear. "I'm not saying you should have stayed with him. But you could have let him down better."

"Wow. Now, is that your opinion or Nick's?"

"Liam's been a good friend to Nick and me. He hasn't had the best home life, so he values his friendships. He's the kind of friend who stays a good friend."

Rita's mouth is as firm as a leather belt. She straightens out Nick's new jeans and folds them in two even halves.

"Well, if he thinks he was getting under my skin, he's confused," Imogene says. "I have no desire to go back to St. Felix's. So really, the house being gone gives me a great excuse to stay away." She takes a long sip of her beer.

"You're just upset."

"Don't tell me how I feel, Rita."

"Well, it's a shitty thing to say." She bunches the sweater into a bag. "I guess you think you're hurting my feelings by saying you don't want to come home to see me or any of us."

"See, I didn't say anything about you. I said I didn't consider St. Felix's my home. Don't you see the difference?"

"No, because it's my home and our family's home."

"Yes. And Cecil's home. And Liam's home. And everyone who called me shitty names and gossiped about Maggie and glossed over the fact that she was raped." Imogene finishes her beer and opens the fridge to get a third. She ducks her head behind the fridge door and blinks hard. Don't let Rita see her wet eyes.

"Has Aunt Maggie ever said that's what happened to her?"

"No, but something did."

"Do you have proof of this?"

"I think I'm proof enough."

"Oh, come on," Rita says. "It's gossip. It's gross and it's dirty, but come on. You don't know if anything like that happened to Aunt Maggie. No one really thinks Cecil is your father. It was teasing for the sake of teasing."

"How can you say that? You just finished telling me he was being investigated."

"Not for rape. And I believe people are innocent until proven guilty."

"Nan believes it. Great Aunt Bride believes it. Great Aunt Madonna believes it. Maggie has refused to talk about it my whole life because she doesn't want me to feel unwanted. Do you actually think everyone started calling me Cec randomly?" She flicks the beer cap towards the sink. It ricochets off the metal insides. "You can't say you don't believe it either."

"Of course I don't believe it."

"You sound like all those people who thought the Christian brothers at Mount Cashel couldn't have done those things."

"Look, I'm sorry you didn't know your father. Cecil and those guys are dirty pieces of shit. Aunt Maggie hung around them for a while because she was young and messed up because Pop had just died and she didn't know better. People said stupid things because people are stupid. It boils down to gossip from people with boring lives."

"I think you're not thinking about this enough."

"Maybe."

"Well, there you go. I think if you thought about if more, you'd have a little more empathy."

"Well, I think if you thought about the good things you've had, you'd be a lot happier."

"Oh wow. Are you serious?"

"Listen, all growing up, I had to hear from Mom and Dad about how great you were. 'Look at Immy, she works so hard. She helps Nan. She has a real job. She gets good marks even though she has it tough.' They have such a high opinion of you. And you had all the clothes and gifts and free trips. It was hard to take sometimes."

"So, I should be happy that Maggie wasn't around, but sent me lots of stuff?"

"No, that isn't what I mean."

"Tell me then, how is thinking about 'all the good things I've had' supposed to make me happy?"

"Because you're obviously smart enough not to let shit get you down. God, I was so happy when you started seeing Liam 'cause it meant you had weaknesses like the rest of us." Rita stops and sips her tea.

She's never really thought about me, Imogene thinks. She has the urge to go for a run, but with three beers in, she'll puke on the sidewalk. Nan's laughter echoes from her bedroom. "Let me see if I can find you some wrapping paper," she says. She takes her beer with her out of the kitchen.

fifteen

Now that Maggie is getting paid, she wants to make a big deal out of Christmas. She makes Nanaimo bars and shortbread. She says she'll take Nan to the Basilica Mass on Christmas Eve after they have supper with Kenneth and Susan. She rents *A Christmas Carol* and *It's a Wonderful Life* and *Scrooged*. She aims to keep Nan distracted through festivity. The house is full-on decorated with wreaths, pine cones, and Santa statues. The air hums a cacophony of holiday scents: gingerbread, pine, cranberry, all the flavoured candles she picked up in Churchill Square.

And overall, she is new and chipper. She goes to work fresh-faced, with extra mascara. She gets a haircut and a tight sweater. She eats rice cakes on the couch while watching *The Simpsons*, laughing in a high musical jangle, like she's practicing for later. Imogene overhears her on the phone with one of her Ontario friends and she mentions a Max, one of the managers at the Carpet Factory. Of course. Why else would she be in a good mood? Everything is about havin' a man. But then, what determines the state of Imogene's mood? Jamie. She is a wretched hypocrite.

Nan is more chipped than chipper. "Not the same here," she says. "No home to go home to. No visitors. No mummers. Just traffic and locked doors. I'd love to look out the window and see a familiar face comin' up the walk."

"Maybe next year we can spend Christmas in St. Felix's," Maggie says. "We'll stay at the hotel or something. I'm making money now, we can do it."

Well, go right ahead, Imogene thinks. Christmas at the Petro-Can cabins. She'll find an excuse to stay behind. Or go somewhere else. She has been listless and contrary since finals ended. She leaves the house whenever she's able, she holes up in coffee shops to read and make lists.

Reasons for Telling Jamie True Feelings on New Year's Eve
Rationale:
- Blame the booze if it ends up completely awful.
- Slightly diminished fear of destroying our friendship as he's leaving.
- Not telling him = regret. Last chance to do it, really.
- If he knows feelings, he may keep a romantic image of us in his mind. This wonderful friend who deeply loves him. He'll go to Ottawa and be lonely. Possibility of working out in the long run. Definitely still enough money to buy a plane ticket if he wanted me to visit.

Plan:
- Kiss him at midnight. Say *I love you*. Go to hotel room. Press the issue.

That's it then. She's going full-on, disrobing, dry-humping seduction if necessary. She's going to take advantage of the clearance sale.

sixteen

It's Tipp's Eve. Eight days until New Year's Eve. Ten days until Jamie moves away. He still works extra shifts, making deadly tips from home-sick Newfoundlanders back for Christmas vacation.

The photography book is over the twenty-dollar limit she and Jamie agreed on for Christmas gifts. Both were her ideas ("just twenty bucks, no pressure"). Perhaps she shouldn't have brought up gifts at all and just given it to him. But some selfish seed in her wants something from Jamie, something with wrapping paper and his writing on a card. When he's gone, she can say he gave her something.

And the photography book was too nice not to get. The bookstore where she found it smelled expensive, like cloves and patchouli, set up with overstuffed chairs and selections of crystals. She played with it a little, opening to a random page, looking at three different photos and asking herself why certain ones stand out to her. Jamie has shown her this practice, he calls it an exercise in looking. She wants to get him other things like a watch, some CDs, a black crew-neck sweater that is extra soft under her fingers in the men's department in Sears. But a box of treasures will reek of desperation. And if his gift to her is small, it might be embarrassing. She wraps the book in red and green striped paper and attaches a mini-flask of Captain Morgan rum to the top with red ribbon.

They exchange gifts in his car parked outside her house. They don't plan this, but the idea of Nan sitting in prim expectation, watching them unwrap their gifts is unacceptable. Jamie probably feels the same about his house and whatever joking commentary his brothers come up with. And Winston isn't around. Privacy is sacred.

Jamie flips through the book. "This is excellent," he says. "Inspiration." Imogene wants to keep the wrapping paper on his gift to her, but he says, "Rip that shit already." The box is a thin rectangle, inside is a chunky silver bracelet with square chain links and a framed picture. Jewelry is so much better than she expected. And when she turns over the frame, it is a photo of the two of them, curled up in a tipsy hug. Butter Pot Beach that summer. "It's wonderful," she says. "It's exactly what I wanted."

seventeen

New Year's Eve preparation — list of things to bring
- the black purse with lots of pockets
- wallet, money, ID, keys.
- compact
- lipstick
- lip balm
- dental floss in case something gets stuck in teeth, one of those little mini sample deodorants from the drug store
- hair elastic
- breath mints—no gum! No chomping in evening gown allowed.
- Sheik Thin condoms with spermicidal lubricant to be hidden in secret pocket of purse
- lambskin condoms if it turns out Jamie is by some chance allergic to latex.
- smokes
- silver engraved Zippo lighter (birthday present from Jamie last year)
- pack of matches—sharing a hotel room means sharing a bathroom. No need of Jamie having to endure the aftermath of nervous belly.
- prepared joints
- tissues
- safety pins

The Radisson ballroom is full of people twice their age in cheap-look-ing expensive clothes. Lots of black dresses with sparkly details and black suits with white socks. Jamie points out that there are thirteen different types of hors d'oeuvres.

"I should have brought a bigger purse."

"I like it," Jamie says. "We're getting our free tickets' worth. And we get complimentary party hats and noisemakers. And champagne at midnight. And you look hot."

"Thanks."

She wears a long black velvet dress with a slit up the right leg to the thigh. Jamie raised his eyebrows and smiled when she met him at the bar of the Radisson Ballroom. Yes, yes, yes.

"Look," Jamie says. "Case and the Tickets is the opening band."

"Did you know they were playing?"

"Winston said the original openers cancelled. Sherrie's probably here somewhere."

"Let's avoid her."

"Let's."

Imogene spots Sherrie standing by the stage while the band sets up. She holds a stemmed glass in one hand and points at things with mana-gerial grace. The musicians wear black suit jackets, dress shirts, and ties. Some are in full suits, but a few wear jeans on the bottom. Imogene can see Casey's head of marcelled hair, crouched down, plugging in cords. Maybe if she and Jamie dance a good distance from the stage, he won't see her. She doesn't need another layer of hyperawareness. Sherrie struts across the dance floor to the bar; she's a neat little package in a red velvet mini dress with spaghetti straps and tall black heels. Her hair hangs in long loose curls that bounce with her movements.

Case and the Tickets play some of their own stuff and some Neil Young and David Bowie. The main band plays covers all night and the crowd dies for it. "Imagine paying full price for this," Jamie says. "I wonder how many other people are here because their tickets were free." Imogene forces a laugh and drinks quickly. Her stomach churns. Such an important evening and the band plays "Achy Breaky Heart," as if to mock her. And then "You Look Wonderful Tonight," such a cheesy song, but Jamie holds her close. Maybe she should tell him right now. His ear is centimetres from her mouth, a little shell for secrets. "Jamie," she says.

"Yes, love."

"Hey, you guys!" Sherrie's hands on their backs. "Happy New Year!" Jamie gives her a one-armed hug and she kisses his cheek. Fuck off, Sherrie.

"Jamie, when are you leaving us?" Sherrie says.

"Three more days, baby."

"Maureen said your folks just about shit when you told them."

Jamie shrugs. He didn't tell Imogene this. She tests the resistance of her cheeks' insides against her back molars.

"That's all you can do," he says. "I gotta hotel room here, so at least I don't have to hear it."

"You're keeping it?" Imogene says.

"For one more day. It's free tonight, so it's not too pricey. And it's worth it. The fucking drama."

"Whatever," Sherrie hoots. "You love it."

"Gotta do what I can."

His shoulders tense up under Imogene's palms. Sherrie purses her lips in sympathy. "Oh no, I forgot to get Case's drink. Happy New Year, lovelies."

"What happened with your folks?" Imogene says.

"Nothing I didn't expect to happen. Mom got shrill and weepy. Dad said don't come asking for money. Eric said I was a dick for upsetting Mom. The twins just laughed at me. You can't make any of them happy." His head tilts away and his neck pinks up.

"I'm sorry."

"Fuck them. I'm having fun tonight. Let's do some shooters."

"Let's."

Countdown.

10. 10 Molson Canadian products consumed so far.

9. 9 smokes left in her pack of Du Mauriers.

8. She ate too many hors d'oeuvres and the top of her control-top panty hose is curling downwards.

7. In 7 seconds she will tell him. He's standing beside her, his arm is around her shoulder.

6. Sick. No, she's just sweaty.

5. Maybe she should wait until they have a few more drinks.

4. No, they're going to hug and kiss in three seconds. This is the time. If she waits there will be champagne and more drinking and dancing and the possibility of one of them passing out or meeting up with friends, getting kissed by strange girls, thin and exotic and oblivious to her presence.

3. He is not going to be any closer to her than he is now and in

2. 2 seconds she will be in his arms and her mouth will be right there by his ear, too close for anyone else to hear, everyone else will be screaming and singing, this couldn't get any more ready than it is right fucking now, holy Jesus, "HAPPY NEW YEAR!" and they turn and their lips meet, his are soft but firm and he takes her face in his hands, holy mother of Christ, the kiss ends, no tongue and another one, firm, soft, no tongue but so fucking beautiful, her bones churn with want in their cartilage, and she lets her fingers touch his hair, run through the back around the neck, warm and smooth and then they're hugging. She's out of breath, her hair's in her mouth, where's his ear? She leans in towards it with lips parted but suddenly his face is pressed against hers, cheek to cheek. "I LOVE YOU, GENIE!" "I LOVE YOU TOO, JAMIE!" oh my God oh my god oh my god oh "I NEED TO TALK TO YOU ABOUT SOMETHING" HOLYFUCKHOLY. "OK ME TOO!!" fuck.

And they're walking, his arm around her shoulders, hers around his waist, to the nearest corner. People around them hug and kiss and say happy New Year to them but Jamie and Imogene just say it back and keep walking. They're in the corner, there's a window sill to lean on, and they don't have to yell to be heard. Jamie takes out his cigarettes and gives her one, they light up. Inhale, exhale. And begin.

"Genie, I want to talk to you about something. Well, I have to tell you something, there's something you should know."

"Okay."

"First of all, I'm really going to miss you when I go."

"I'm going to miss you too, Jamie. Like you wouldn't believe."

"Oh yeah, oh fuck, me too, I've been trying not to think about it."

"I don't know what I'm going to do with myself when you're gone."

"Shit, I know. I love you, Genie, you know that."

"I love you too, Jamie. I'll always love you."

"I just want to tell you, you are the closest person to me. You are probably the only person I truly trust in the world. I trust you more than I trust anyone and I feel like you'd never hurt me. I don't even feel like that about my parents or anyone in my family."

"I'm the same, I mean I feel the same. I love you."

"Which is why I have to tell you this. Okay. When I go to Ottawa, I'm thinking about making some changes. Fuck, I'm drunk. Your dress is hot. You're some beautiful, Imogene. You look like Julia Roberts tonight. You're the only one I can tell. This is going to be the first time in my life that I'm not around anyone I know. I mean here, it's like everyone knows what you're doing and where you're going and who you're with. Jesus, my whole family thinks me and you are screwing because we spend so much time together so I've always been so afraid to even try, you know, to do what I want. It's my first chance to truly be myself, or find out who I think I am, anyway. And I've been thinking about…experimenting, maybe. With guys, I mean. I mean, I've kind of always felt like that in a way, you know, deep down. I mean, there's been stuff with Winston, but nothing big. Wow, I've never said that out loud before. Oh, fuck, you're crying, oh my god, Genie, oh god. Oh fuck. Tell me what you're thinking. Oh shit. Please, please tell me what you're thinking. Oh fuck. Fucking say something please. Fucking say something. Please, please don't hate me, you hate me don't you, oh Christ. Don't you see I don't know what else to do? Please tell me what you think. Please. Will you just give me a hug or something?"

"I'm just, I'm just surprised and I'm really glad you told me, that's all. I'm sorry."

"Oh fuck, I was so scared to tell you. Genie. If I lost you as my friend I don't know what I would do. You've always been there for me. Christ, you've let me practically live at your house. I knew I had to tell you."

"Okay, don't worry, don't worry about it."

"Thank you. I love you so much."

"I love you too."

"Happy New Year."

Another glass of champagne. They bop around to the band's version of "1999." She lets the champagne slide down her throat. And then there is another glass somehow and she takes that one too and swallows it down.

"I'm tired," she says. "I think I might go." Jamie's mouth an oh of concern. "And I might get sick. So I'm just going to go on home."

"Okay. Are you sure?"

"Yeah, you stay. Have fun. "

She turns and walks stone-faced, straight out the door. Keep it together. The air bites all the warmth off. Fuck. No cabs, nothing. But she can't go home without her coat. What is she thinking. What kind of idiot is she. Oblivious.

Elevator upstairs, go to room, get coat, go home. When she's home, she can cry. Key in door, coat on chair, leave room. Please let there be a cab out there. Can she get outside the hotel and not have to pass through the lobby again? She heads toward the exit sign at the end of the hall.

"Hey."

The voice is at the open door. Fuck off, drunk guest.

"Imogene."

She looks back. Casey leans out the door. His tie and jacket are gone and he holds a beer bottle. "Where you going?" he asks.

"Home."

"Sure, it's only early."

"I don't care."

"You okay?" He takes a step into the hallway. "You want a beer?"

"No, I gotta go home."

"C'mon. Have a New Year beer with me."

He steps back inside. Why not. She's just going to go home and cry. She might as well try to maintain her buzz.

The room has two double beds. Bottles and clothes are strewn on the edges of the dresser and end tables. She recognizes what must be Sherrie's shiny black winter boots by the bar fridge, with their little trimming of black fake fur. Sherrie. Even she knows better than Imogene, with her snotty appraisal of Jamie's sexual preferences. Sherrie, who knows everything and gets everything. The bathroom door is open and she can see make-up bottles on the sink.

She sits on the edge of the bed. Case opens a bottle of beer and passes it to her. She lets it pour right down her throat. "Your band staying here too?" she says. "It's a huge room."

"It's for me and Sher and whoever else needs to crash."

He plops down on the bed next to her. The hair at the back of his neck is dark with sweat, but the rest of it is soft and casually coiffed. The beer box is within reach and she's going to take another after this one. Too bad, buddy.

"I figured there'd be big parties going on up here," she says.

"Never is. New Year's Eve is Amateur Night. Forty year olds puking in parking lots. It's a shit show."

"Where's Sherrie?"

"Last I saw her, she was dancing with your date."

"He's not my date."

"Who is he then?"

"A friend." Her voice cramps from sob control.

"You don't seem very happy." He strokes her shoulder and his touch cracks her into jerky, shameful tears. "Hey, hey, hey," Case says. He folds her up to him and goes shhhh.

"It is so fucking embarrassing," she says. "I thought something was going to happen. But nothing's ever going to happen."

"You don't need to be embarrassed."

"Even if he wasn't...I'm so stupid to think he cared."

"Who wouldn't care about you? You're so beautiful."

His kisses start on her cheek and travel down her neck. She should stop him. But it feels good. And distracting. It means she doesn't have to think about Jamie. His hand moves from her back to her stomach and his thumb presses her nipple—how'd he find it so fast—and pulses there.

He gets up to lock and latch the door before he undoes his pants. It's too dangerous for them to get completely undressed, so she pulls her dress up and gets the top part down so that it's a wringed velvet belt around her waist. He stands over her, his shirt still buttoned, but loose while she lies back on the bed. He yanks her tights and panties off together. He pauses when she says, "Condom," and obeys.

The bed springs have reached soprano heights when the knocks arrive on the door. Case presses one finger to his lips and keeps going. Knock knock knock. Knock knock knock. "Who's in there?" Unmistakably Sherrie's brassy treble. The key clicks in the lock, but the door won't open past the bolt.

"Who's in there? This is me and Casey's room. You guys are dogs."

"It's okay," Case whisper-pants in Imogene's ear. "She'll leave in a sec. She'll think it's someone else. All the guys have keys." He pumps faster and the light in his eyes does something to Imogene. Sherrie, just outside, not knowing. Everyone, just outside, not knowing.

They actually finish at the same time. She's shocked she got off at all. She scrabbles for her tights, her shoes. Case in the bathroom wiping himself off with a towel.

"How am I going to get out of here?" Imogene asks.

"She's gone downstairs."

"How do you know?"

"She thinks it's one of the guys in here and she's gone looking for me. Or she heard a song she likes and went back to the party." Case splashes water on his hands and runs them over his face.

"She might be out in the hallway."

"I'll look first."

Case unlatches the door and looks both ways. "All clear."

And Imogene is gone, shoes, purse and coat in hand. When she reaches the end of the hall, she turns to see Case's retreating back. His hands in his pockets. She puts her shoes on and takes the stairs. At the exit, she can see three taxis outside. Hallelujah. She puts on her coat. The sleeves end below her wrists. That's strange. And it doesn't fit across her chest. And the collar has fake fur.

The sound reaches Imogene's ears before the clatter of the second-floor door. It is a metallic, piercing wail that rattles through the stairwell. Sherrie's hair and eyes are a hate storm, charging down the steps, all red velvet fury and Imogene's black coat clutched in her hand. Imogene shucks off Sherrie's coat and bolts out the door. She is almost at the first cab when her heel shims off a chunk of ice and then there is the shock of pavement and freezing wet and Sherrie's hard, pounding frame on her back. Three clouts to Imogene's head punctuated by screams and stars. "How. Could. You." And then the weight is off her and Sherrie is a yowling snarl carried backwards by Case and another guy, the drummer, both in dress shirts, they must be cold. Imogene is pulled up and her coat is passed to her and her lips taste like dirt slush. And when they let go of her to see if she can stand, she lurches into the cab. She says her address in three syllables to the driver. The cab pulls away. Outside, there are three people watching and one is Winston in a long black coat smoking a cigarette and another is Jamie with his arms shock straight in his handsome jacket and his mouth wide open.

Imogene stares at the ashtray inserted in the back of the driver's seat. Like a silver secret door. She considers it until the house appears and she opens the car door and hands him the bills. She crumples up the walk, her ankles shake in her stupid shoes, fucking goddamn keys, blood and tears in her eyes. The keys fall into a deep blue tunnel in the snow and her hand is a hero that dives in to rescue them and the pain is a million stinging points of cold that make her legs give out. Whole body in snow now. Immersed in cold and she and Jamie are never, ever going to happen. Everyone knows they will never happen and everyone knows about her and Casey and everyone knows about Cecil. She can't get up. Snow on new dress. Fucking useless garbage dress. Hoped it would get ripped off. Nope, just shoved up. Her dress is also a kind of door. A swinging door. Ha, good one.

The sting of snow on her bare legs feels like bleeding, then like hot water, then comfortable. She'll stay here, as still as possible and focus on the snowflakes filling in the painful spot on her head. Maybe Jamie is back in the room now. Maybe he's trying to calm Sherrie down. They can all talk about her and she'll be here, under the snow. Stupid naïve Imogene Jesso. Her empty head is a crevice for snow collection. And if she stays still, her head won't hurt so much. She'll look like someone who began a snow angel and changed their mind.

Now she is spinning. How embarrassing to die of hypothermia, choke on her own vomit in a snowbank. She'll be found dead on New Year's Day. Nan will slip on the stairs running out to her and break her hip. Maggie will have to deal with everything. She'll have a nervous breakdown. They cannot cope. She needs to close her eyes against their lack of coping. Their lack of coping is replaced by a white hot screen that stings her face, but then it's warm and compact and will hide her.

And then she is floating, up through heat and white screens and higher and higher still. And everything is suddenly stuffy and sugary, vanilla candles and Christmas trees. Burning bright? No, the lights, turn off the damn lights. And here is Maggie, nightie and winter boots, arms a rash of goosebumps. And Imogene is in the tub, with rubber flowers on the bottom, warm water screaming all around her. And there are other sounds. Sobs, her own misery. Maggie's voice. "Okay. Okay, sweetie. Okay."

There is a hot facecloth, wiping her face and the back of her neck. Her dress is heavy with water and chunks of snow.

"We're going to warm you up. Did you take anything?"

"Take? What did you take? Maybe you should take something."

"Imogene, did you take something?"

"Just drinks."

"What happened to your head? There was a piece of gravel. Did you fall?"

"Yeah, I fell. Three times. Do I need stitches?"

"I don't think so. There's blood, but it's just broken skin. You might have a bump."

"Oh well."

"I'll get a band-aid and some ice. We'll get some warm fluids in you. If you weren't so drunk, I'd say you should take an Advil."

Maggie moves to the cabinet. She pulls cotton swabs and a jar of Ponds from behind the mirror. Her dark hair held up with a burgundy scrunchie and her plaid robe is loosely hitched. Soft cloth Maggie. She returns and peers into Imogene's face. "If you close your eyes," she says, "do you think you can stay awake?"

"Yeah."

"You scared the shit out of me. I looked out and you were half covered in snow. I was staring at your shoes. I didn't know what I was looking at."

"I thought I was going to puke."

"I'm surprised you didn't."

"I was turning green before, but nothing green came out. Cause there weren't no green in the first place." Imogene points at her chest and then at the bathtub. "There ain't no Green in this Tubbs. Get it?" She smacks the side of the tub and laughs.

"Give me your face. I'll take off your makeup."

"It's not green, but it's greasy Cec. I *know*, you know. I know." Imogene stares forward, her eyes at the slack opening of Maggie's robe. A small red mark over her breast.

"Close your eyes."

She does and liquid coolness smoothes over her eyelids. The shock makes her gasp a little. She feels like crying again. Maggie wipes the cool white circles across the bridge of Imogene's nose and her cheeks. All the spots Jamie kissed. A gurgling sob rises up.

"Let's get you to bed."

Maggie sturdies one arm around Imogene and up she rises. The dress is left in a wet lump and she is wrapped in thick bath towels. In the bedroom, Maggie puts her in soft gym pants and a sweatshirt. She lays Imogene down and puts blanket over blanket on her. "I'm going to get you something warm to drink."

Imogene nods. Jamie might be in the hotel room now. Or dancing. His eyes on other places, other people. Like Winston. Jesus Christ. Winston and his stoned laugh, his big eyes. Winston, who can never leave them alone. How did she not see?

The kettle hisses beyond the room. Tomorrow will be New Year's dinner with Uncle Kenneth and Susan and questions about how the party went and why don't you have a boyfriend and what about that nice young man you're always with. Well, he's escaping to the mainland where he'll be doing what he's always wanted with other men. Nan's mouth wide, her spoon dropping on her saucer. Imogene closes her eyes. Sleep wants to swim in.

Maggie comes in with a steaming mug. "Tea," she says. "Sit up." Imogene leans over the side of the bed. Maggie kneels with the mug. "You still have your earrings in," Maggie says. Imogene pulls them out. "Where do they go?"

"They go in a box under my bed," Imogene says. "Pull it out and see what's inside. That's where they go." Maggie kneels in front of the bed, her hands reaching underneath. Imogene takes a long sip of tea, puts the mug down and closes her eyes.

eighteen

There is a glass of water on the nightstand with two white pills on a saucer. Her hand steals out of the comforter and cups them. How rotten will her head be? Here comes the slosh of settling hangover. Here comes the lumps Sherrie made. But it's not too bad. She stuffs the pills in her mouth and swallows hard; their bitter shapes edge their way down her esophagus. The image of Jamie's pleading face seeps into memory. She is a blind moron. Her eyes heat up and boil over. Her body needs water. Or she could just weep herself into annihilating dehydration.

A single knuckle tap at the door. Maggie brings forth a tray. Toast, tea, and a lime popsicle, like a mirage.

"How are you feeling?" She cracks the popsicle in half inside the paper. Imogene hauls herself up onto her elbows, shrugs. Is Nan up? She may be outside, waiting to pounce on her guilt. Just the idea of Nan makes her feel shameful.

"Here." Maggie offers her the popsicle. "These are my hangover cure. Great for when you're dehydrated, but too sick to drink."

"Oh God, thank you," Imogene says. The popsicle in her mouth is like desert needs the storm. She closes her eyes. When she blinks, Maggie is holding the heart-shaped pendant in her open palm.

"Where did you find this?" she says.

Imogene stares at the locket. She should feel uncomfortable. But all she feels is hungry for more toast. "I found it on a shelf in Cecil Jesso's house."

"When?"

"When I was sixteen. I wasn't there 'socially' or anything. Liam and I broke in."

"You broke into someone's house?"

"Once."

"That's...Okay, you know that's dumb."

"I'm aware."

"Okay. Anyway. Just once?'

"Yes."

Maggie frowns at the locket. "I'm surprised he still had it."

"He had it hidden. Like a trophy."

"Find anything else?"

"Some cash. Some of it is still in that box."

"I saw. Keeping money under beds like that isn't safe."

"It wasn't safe to say where I got the money either."

"And you did this with that Lundrigan boy? I don't remember this."

"He moved away after Christmas in grade eleven. He dropped out and went to work in Alberta or something."

"I see. Mom never mentioned him."

"She didn't really know about him."

"Yeah, she doesn't pay attention really. Well. That's not really fair of me to say." Maggie rubs her thumb over the pendant. "Are you seeing anyone now? I don't really know what's going on with you."

"No. I had someone in mind. But it's never going to happen."

"Why not?"

"He's gay."

"Oh, I see...Do you mean Jamie?"

"Yes, him. Why do you say him?"

"He's the only boy I've met, really. Plus something Mom said."

"What did she say?" Maybe Imogene is the only one who didn't realize he was gay. She is the twit of the universe.

"She made a comment that he seems like someone who needs a place to hide. 'That boy doesn't want to go home.' It's wrong of me to say she doesn't pay attention, I guess."

Imogene turns the popsicle stick in her hand. Nan and her hospitality. *You can stay here whenever you like, Jamie. Our house is your house.* "Yeah, he told me last night," she says. "He's gay and he's moving to Ottawa in two days and I'll never see him and it will never, ever happen." A tear plops into her tea.

Maggie gets tissues. "If there's anything worse than being hungover, it's being emotionally hungover as well."

"I've never heard that term before."

"I'm not sure it's actually a term."

Imogene blows her nose. Maggie holds the tissue box like a prayer offering. Happy New Year, everyone, may old acquaintance bawl their faces off. "Are you still sad about Robert?" she says.

"Yes and no. We tried really hard for a long time." She lays the pendant on the comforter. "And he is a very controlling man. Not in a fierce way. I mean we argued a lot and it got worse instead of better. But it took me a long time to realize that he really didn't want to see things my way at all."

"I'm sorry."

"Oh, don't be. Thanks."

They are so formal. It's like talking to one of the librarians at work. *How was your weekend? Oh fine, thanks for asking.* "I'm sorry I scared you."

"Don't worry about it." Maggie sits up straight. "Do you want to talk about this?" She holds up the necklace.

"If you want to." Imogene says. Christ. 1994, the year of awful truths.

"Your father was one of the things Robert and I argued about. He said I should be open with you and I told him you'd ask if you wanted to know."

"But I did ask."

"I know." Maggie sighs. "I guess I wasn't ready."

"Do you feel ready now?"

"No. But I want you to know."

"Okay."

Maggie produces a pack of cigarettes. "I have to quit these. New Year's resolutions start tomorrow." She moves to the window and opens it a couple of inches. Imogene wraps the blanket around herself.

"I told Robert that it was likely Tony knew about you and chose to do nothing. I said if you were going to have a father, I didn't want it to be a reluctant father. Which really is why I never moved you up to Ontario with us. Mom had concerns about Robert as a parent."

"What kind of concerns?"

"That he really didn't want to be one. It was another big issue. We would talk about you moving up and as long as it was a moment far in the future, he was on board. But when it got to a certain point, like the end of the school year, he'd bring up what a big adjustment it would be for you and us. That living in St. Felix's was a nice life for you. Like that African proverb, raised by a village. And to be honest, I was really scared too." Maggie lights a cigarette and inhales. "Christ. We managed to procrastinate being your parents your whole life."

Imogene focuses on her breath to keep her belly and mind together. Maggie keeps smoking without looking at her.

"Robert said that Tony should pay child support. And I would say even if we found Tony, he'd be resistant because of our age difference at the time. Statutory rape doesn't have a statute of limitations. And Robert said, fine, let's threaten him with a criminal sentence if he doesn't pay. And everything he said made sense, but I just didn't want to go through with it. It just felt like regurgitating the worst time of my life. After Dad died, I felt...I don't know, I think I confused grief with wisdom. I believed it made me a grown up. And now my memories of Tony and everything at that time all feel like...I don't know. Shadows now. Do I need to seek out this guy—I mean, who is he? Would it be worth dragging you through DNA tests and a court battle? And then suddenly there's this strange man in your life who could be any kind of person. I mean, that night at Cecil's, Tony might have been upset that I was younger, but it didn't stop him for one last time. I'm sorry, is this all too much?"

"No."

Imogene gets up to join her. Her head is raw, but not painful. She takes a cigarette from the pack and lights one. Maggie taps hers out the window.

"He and I went to Cecil's a bunch of times. Really, there was nowhere else to go. It was mostly guys Tony worked with. Murray Wells and Bryce Benoit sometimes.

"Mom had no idea. She was just going through the motions. The way she is now, but so much worse, for a long time. And Dad had been the one who needed to know where I was going, who I was with. No make-up, no dances, home by nine thirty.

"That summer, I'd come home and find Mom in bed, staring at the wall. She'd pile pillows along his side of the bed, under the covers like he was there. I went out as often as I could. I'd say I was walking to Kelly Abbott's house and Tony would pick me up down the road. We'd go parking or down to the beach after dark, we'd skinny dip.

"The night Tony and I broke up, I had gone to Cecil's to meet him. Cecil was always friendly, but I only talked to him when there were other people around. He made me nervous, but Tony said he was alright. Cecil gave me a glass of something, it was lemony and sweet. I asked him what it was and he asked me if I liked it and I said yes and he said drink up, my love. I finished it and he poured me some more and Murray said, be careful, my dear, that's just moonshine with a lot of Kool Aid in it.

"So I was shitfaced when Tony showed up. I remember sitting on his lap in the living room and trying to keep from sliding off. He got annoyed with me. He said we had to talk. I think what happened was that one of the guys asked Tony if he had slept with me yet. And he said yes. Because it was true, and he wanted to brag, I guess. At that point, someone told him I was fourteen.

"I remember he pulled me into the bedroom to ask me about my age. I remember him shaking his head and pushing me away as I tried to kiss him. He walked out. I sat on the bed and cried. I remember feeling so rotten, like so much had been taken away from me.

"And then there was all this noise outside the door. Men's voices, laughing, teasing sounds. 'Go on, go on.' The door opened and Tony came back in. I remember his face was flushed. He shut the door and I heard someone shout something. It sounded like, 'If you don't, I will.' I'm not one hundred percent, but that's how I remember it.

"We had sex. I don't remember passing out, but when I woke up, I was naked on the bed. Tony was gone. The lights were on. Cecil was standing beside the bed. He was holding my clothes and staring at me. I covered myself with my hands and said no. I remember that I could hardly move. I tried to pull the blanket over me. He reached out and yanked it out of my hand. He said, 'Let me look' or something.

"And then I threw up. Just like, everywhere. He dropped my clothes and left. I think getting some of it out of my system helped me move. I threw my clothes back on and ran out. I remember I grabbed my shoes at the door and he said something shitty and I threw a bottle at him. It's all a blur.

"The next day, I went down to the boats and looked for Tony. He was gone. Nobody would tell me how to get a hold of him. The rest of the summer, I cried most nights, everything was Dad and Tony and everything just feeling awful. And then I was pregnant. I didn't know for a long time. I thought I was getting fat. Aunt Bride figured it out. She asked Mom about my periods. You do her laundry, Agnes, you must know when she's on her period. And Mom came in my room, told me to haul my top up. I think when Bride pointed it out, it woke her up from her grief.

"Later on, Mom said she sent letters and she talked to enough people who knew him that he must have known. But she never heard from him directly. And who is he, anyway? He's a man who has sex with a fourteen year old and leaves her naked on a bed, in a house full of raging drunks. And if he knows, and I find it hard to believe he doesn't—he didn't do anything about it."

Maggie chucks her cigarette butt out the window. It makes a *pfft* in the snow. She watches the flakes whirl around. Imogene should hug her or touch her hand.

"Do you want another?" Imogene says. "I'm going to have one."

"Yeah."

Imogene lights another cigarette and passes it to her. Maggie inhales.

"Even now, if I'm stressed or upset, I dream of those voices outside the door. And Cecil's voice," she says. "He always says something like, 'lemme see.' He always sounds so fucking sooky. Like I was taking something away from him."

"So he didn't..."

"I wish I could say there's no chance. In my gut, no. I see Tony in you. But it's hard because no one else really knew him. So it's just my opinion."

Imogene inhales for lack of words. And of course, maybe she sees Tony because that's what she wants to see. That's what she's trying to say.

"I've never said that out loud," Maggie says. "I wish I had told someone though. After you were born, I heard things once in a while. About things happening with other girls at his place. If I had spoken up, I don't know, maybe someone else would have too. And now these women have spoken up, now that Cec is dead and no one is holding court at his house. I never imagined that would happen. Part of me wishes I'd been brave enough at the start. But I couldn't risk hurting you. I couldn't do that to you."

Through Imogene's wet eyes, Maggie is a blur, framed by the window. Imogene goes to the bed and lies down. She closes her eyes and shoves the popsicle back in her mouth like a baby with a pacifier. She hears Maggie moving and the door closes with a soft click. She finishes the popsicle. She counts her breaths until she falls asleep again.

When she awakes again, she needs the bathroom. Swollen eyes in the mirror, mattress lines mesh cheeks like tree roots.

In the kitchen, the air is pea soup pungent. Nan sits back on to her on the sofa. The year in highlights on NTV.

"Look who's up," Nan says. Voice flat as old Pepsi. "I'm not judging," she adds. "It's good to let loose sometimes."

Imogene ladles soup into a bowl. "Where's Maggie?"

"She went out. Some supper with her boss. Or they're going out for supper." Nan gestures towards the phone. "Jamie called."

Imogene cuts a dumpling with the edge of her spoon. A little broken cloud.

"You going to call him back?"

"Not right now."

"You two have a fight?"

Christ, why does she always need to know? "Good soup, Nan," she says.

"Right, well. He'll be off soon." Nan turns to look at Imogene. "You'll be finishing up in two years and a bit. Time works fast."

Perhaps it is Nan's New Year's resolution to state the obvious. Imogene concentrates on blowing ripples across the soup to cool it.

"Maggie brought up a few things to me today," Nan says. She points to the kitchen table. A white envelope sits in the middle. "She wants to change a few things with the apartment downstairs. You should have a look."

"It's her house, she can do what she wants."

"Have a look."

Maggie has sealed the envelope. Why do that? Imogene hooks her thumb into the corner and rips it open. One folded sheet of paper, Maggie's focused handwriting.

Dear Imogene,

I'm sorry. I should have talked about everything a long time ago.

Right before Robert and I broke up, he told me he had hired a private investigator to track Tony down. He didn't ask my permission. As I said, Robert thought he should pay child support. It was the cause of probably the biggest fight we ever had.

After I left your room this morning, I called Robert. He still has the information from the private investigator. Tony's address and phone number are on the back of this sheet. He's been living in the States for over ten years now.

Here's a photo of him. Check out that smile. That's what you look like when you smile.

I don't think it's fair that you're sleeping on the couch. The couple downstairs have moved out. I think you should have the basement apartment. You're an adult, you need your privacy.

Happy New Year.
Maggie

nineteen

The third Polaroid is like the one she found in Maggie's photo album, but taken seconds before or after it. Maggie smiles in her tank-top and cutoffs and Tony is laughing, head tilted back.

"That's the spit of you when you laugh," Jamie says. "It's a pretty freaky resemblance, actually."

"Don't we all look kind of alike when we laugh?"

"His mouth is the same shape as yours. Like when you laugh hard."

Three days ago, the thought of Jamie noticing the shape of her mouth would have made her all tingly. Now it leaves an embarrassed thud in her gut.

He lays the Polaroid on the table away from his wet glass. Twenty minutes until he needs to be at the gate. The airport restaurant has notoriously slow service, but they can pour a beer somewhat quickly. None of Jamie's family has come. "I told them I had a ride," Jamie says. And technically he does. His car is in the *Buy and Sell* and Imogene will deal with it. "I don't trust my brothers with any money it might get," he says. "And I'd rather have the Tubbs ladies get some use out of it until it sells."

The last-minute gift of the car gives them something to talk about. Transferring over the insurance, the way the passenger door sticks. They yammer about this for the drive to the airport, New Year's Eve unmentioned, like condensation on the windows.

"Maureen says to call her," Jamie says. "She's been on Sherrie duty the past few days."

"I will."

"She's not mad. Maureen, I mean. But this is awkward for her."

"How's Sherrie?"

"Really fucking upset."

"Oh God."

"You're some minx. I'm not judging—I mean, things happen." He takes a swig of his pint. Here they are, talking about her sleeping with someone else. He obviously knows about "things happening." Enough not to judge her. She tries not to look at his mouth. He has a whole secret life she knows nothing about.

"Maureen says Sherrie might forgive him," he says.

"Why? Jesus."

"I think he's feeding her a bunch of stuff about being drunk and not knowing what he was doing."

She laughs. It is the first time she's laughed in days. Jamie stares at her. She stops. "Yeah, that's it. He was drunk and I seduced him. What will his excuse be next time?"

"I guess it's what she wants to believe." He picks up the Polaroid again. "I'm really glad you have this," he says. "Must feel like closure."

Imogene shrugs. Believing the man in the picture is her father is a thin comfort. It feels like instead of one asshole, there are two. But maybe she is too. Maybe she's inherited his disregard and his smile. When she thinks of Sherrie, there is embarrassment, but no puddles of guilt. Sherrie will find another boyfriend. Or Casey will go on cheating on her with other people. Or he won't. Maybe they'll work it out.

"Not that it matters at all," Jamie says.

"What doesn't?"

"Closure. Knowing where your DNA comes from. Who cares? It doesn't change you or how you're loved."

"It would have though. If I had always been sure, it would have made a difference."

"Only to you. The rest of us have always been sure about you."

"Sure about what?"

"Sure that you're wonderful."

"Pack off."

"I'm going to, in about fifteen minutes."

"Proper thing."

"But you know you are, Imogene. You saved me this year."

Yeah, and now you're fucking leaving me, Imogene thinks. She wishes she had a wristwatch to check. "We should get you through security," she says.

When it's Jamie's turn for the security queue, he gives Imogene a hug, a peck on the cheek. "After I start school and learn some things, I want to come home and go on a road trip," he says. "Photograph the island. Come with me?"

"Sure."

"I really want to go out to the West Coast. We can go out to St. Felix's."

"If you come with me, I'll go," she says. "You'd make it fun."

She watches him place his bag on the conveyor belt, rifle out change and keys from his pockets. And then he's through the metal detector and gone from her sight. He joked that he would try to wave from the plane, but she just wants out of the airport, away from families and couples kissing goodbye.

On her way to the exit, she walks back towards the departures' area. There is a lone Air Canada agent set up just for ticket sales. She tells her she wants to buy a ticket to New York, for the end of April.

"That will be a nice trip," the agent says. "A treat for the end of term."

"Can I get a second one?" Imogene says. "Like, an open one? I'm going to bring a friend, but they don't know yet."

"How nice. Wish I had friends like you," the agent says.

Imogene pulls out a stack of bills. They're soft with age and five years of consideration. The agent gives her back change: $87.55. Enough for a textbook. Maybe.

The address Maggie gave her is in Flushing. Whoever comes with her, they can help her look it up on a map. She's going to need back-up. A city of distractions may not be enough. She'll need someone on her side, Maureen, Jamie, even Rita or Maggie. She can choose soon from the people on her side.

She turns down Portugal Cove Road. It's bitter out, but no more snow yet. The sky is overcast and the traffic is light. The dull ache of her disappointment is still there, but as she gets farther away from the airport, her chest is lighter. When she gets home, she can look through the flyers for sales on bookshelves. She can make a list of things she needs for the basement apartment. She'll call Maureen.

As she drives Jamie's car past the old stadium, glimmers of light break through the clouds. It reflects off the snowbanks making everything radiate with white light, warm, rich, and overdue. Just this morning, Nan said the forecast called for rain, but there it is, the prodigal St. John's sun. It doesn't show any signs of not sticking around.

acknowledgements

Some People's Children received invaluable feedback from its early readers. Much gratitude to Paul Butler, the late, great Mark Collins, Elisabeth de Mariaffi, Lisa Moore, Christa Pauwels, Michelle Porter, Tamara Reynish, Deirdre Snook, Tracey Waddleton, Grant Weir, and my writing group, The Naked Parade Writing Collective. Thanks especially to Ed Kavanagh for his guidance and mentorship.

I snagged the idea for Jamie's eyelash trimming from Jason Sellers and the mention of the miners taken by faeries from Gail Hussey Weir's *The Miners of Wabana*. Thank you both for your inspiration.

Editor Kate Kennedy's expertise made this a better book. Thank you so much, Kate.

Thanks to the team at Breakwater for their passion for Newfoundland and Labrador stories. What a bunch. I am so very lucky to live in a community that accepts, supports, and inspires me.

Thanks to my family and friends for their love and patience, and to my partner, Jon, for being friggin' awesome.

Bridget Canning's debut novel, *The Greatest Hits of Wanda Jaynes*, was selected as a finalist for the 2017 BMO Winterset Award, the Margaret and John Savage First Book Award, the NL Fiction Award, and was longlisted for the International Dublin Literary Award. She is the recipient of the 2018 ArtsNL Emerging Artist Award. She was raised on a sheep farm in Highlands, Newfoundland, and currently lives in St. John's where she writes and teaches.